ALSO BY SIMON R. GREEN

The Nightside

INTO THE NIGHTSIDE
HAUNTING THE NIGHTSIDE
THE DARK HEART OF THE NIGHTSIDE

Deathstalker Novels

DEATHSTALKER
DEATHSTALKER REBELLION
DEATHSTALKER WAR
DEATHSTALKER HONOUR
DEATHSTALKER DESTINY
DEATHSTALKER LEGACY
DEATHSTALKER RETURN
DEATHSTALKER CODA

Hawk and Fisher Novels

SWORDS OF HAVEN
GUARDS OF HAVEN

Also by Simon R. Green

BLUE MOON RISING
BEYOND THE BLUE MOON
DRINKING MIDNIGHT WINE
THE MAN WITH THE GOLDEN TORC

HAUNTING THE
NIGHTSIDE

SIMON R. GREEN

SOLARIS

Nightingale's Lament first published 2004 by Ace
Hex and the City first published 2005 by Ace

This omnibus first published 2008 by Solaris
an imprint of BL Publishing
Games Workshop Ltd
Willow Road
Nottingham
NG7 2WS
UK

www.solarisbooks.com

ISBN-13: 978 1 84416 638 1
ISBN-10: 1 84416 638 4

Copyright © Simon R. Green 2004, 2005, 2008
Cover art by Jonathan Barkat

10 9 8 7 6 5 4 3 2 1

A CIP catalogue record for this book is available from the
British Library.

NIGHTINGALE'S
LAMENT

My name is John Taylor. I've made that a name to be respected and feared, but it's also made me a target my whole life.

I operate as a private eye, in a world where gods and monsters are real. The Nightside: the sick, secret magical heart of London. A place where dreams come true, whether you want them to or not. It's not easy to find a way in, and it can be even harder to find a way out.

I can find anything, solve any mystery. Except the answers to the dark and deadly secrets of my own past.

My name is John Taylor. And if you've come looking for me, either you're in trouble, or you're about to be.

ONE

THE HANGED MAN'S BEAUTIFUL DAUGHTER

There are all kinds of Powers running loose in the Nightside, but its power sources have to be rather more reliable, as well as completely divorced from outside interference. Someone's got to pump out the electricity to keep all that hot neon burning. The Nightside, being a city within a city, draws its energies from many sources—some of them illegal, some of them unnatural. Power is generated by blood sacrifices and imprisoned godlings, gestalt minds and tiny black holes held captive inside stasis fields. And there are other sources, so vast and awful, so alien and unutterably *other*, that just to glimpse their secret workings would drive a man insane. Not that anyone cares about such things in the Nightside, not as long as the lights are bright and the trains keep running. But the only really dependable source for *electricity* used to be the futuristic power plant of Prometheus Inc. Magic may be more flashy, but there's always been as much super-science as sorcery in the Nightside.

Prometheus Inc. was a fairly recent success story. Not quite six years old, it had a reputation for dependability and savagely undercutting prices, which made it the company that supplied some twelve per cent of the Nightside's electricity. So the recent sudden outbreak of sabotage and destruction inside the closely guarded power plant could not be allowed to continue. Walker made that very clear. Walker represents the Authorities, the shadowy people who run things here, inasmuch as anyone does, or can. He sends the occasional job my way, when it suits him, because I am quiet, dependable, and entirely expendable.

I stood in the shadows at the end of the street, quietly studying the hulking edifice that was Prometheus Inc. It wasn't much to look at—just another great tower block of glass and steel. The top floors were offices, administration and the like. Middle floors were laboratories, for research and development. And the bottom floor was public relations. The power plant itself, that modern wonder of efficiency and incredible output, was supposedly somewhere underground. I say supposedly, because as far as I knew, only a handful of people had ever seen it. The whole thing was automated, run from a single control centre, and even after six years no-one had any idea of what it was or how it worked. And it's not easy, keeping secrets in the Nightside.

The whole Prometheus Inc. success story had happened while I was away, trying—and failing—to live an ordinary life in the ordinary world. Now I was back, and I was quite keen to see what was being hidden under the surface of Prometheus Inc. I like knowing things that no-one else does. It's helped me keep alive, down the years. I strolled out of the shadows and headed for the office building. There was a small army of security men and rent-a-cops surrounding the place, and those nearest the main door lifted their heads and paid attention as they spotted me approaching. An awful lot of guns zeroed in on me, and the sound of safeties clicking off was almost deafening. If I'd been anyone else, I might have been worried.

I came to a halt before the main door and smiled at the rent-a-cops arrayed before me, in their wonderfully striking uniforms of midnight blue with silver piping. I nodded to the officer in charge, a tall and somewhat overweight man with cold, careful eyes. He held his ground, and his gaze didn't waver, though behind him we could both hear his men whispering my name. Some of them crossed themselves or made ancient warding signs. I let my smile widen just a little, because I could see it upset them. Ever since I tracked down the Unholy Grail and stood off two armies of angels to do it, my reputation had been going through the roof. Mostly nonsense, of course, but I did nothing to discourage the rumours, particularly the nasty ones. Nothing like a good—or more properly speaking a bad—reputation to keep the flies off.

"I'm supposed to ask for identification," said the officer. "And shoot anyone who isn't on the approved list."

"You know who I am," I said calmly. "And I'm expected."

The officer relaxed a little. "First good news I've had all night. Hello, Taylor. I'm actually glad to see you. This whole business has my people seriously spooked."

"Has anyone been killed?" I asked, frowning. "I understood this was just a sabotage case."

"No deaths as yet, but a hell of a lot of casualties." The officer scowled. "Whoever's tearing this place apart doesn't give a damn about anyone who gets in his way. I've lost forty of my people in the last three nights, and I still haven't got a clue as to who's behind it all. No-one ever sees anything, until it's too late. I've had this place closed up tighter than a duck's arse, and still the bastard keeps getting in."

"Inside job?" I asked, to show I was paying attention.

"That was my first thought, but there hasn't been anyone in there for a week. The boss sent them all home when the problems started. He's the only one left in the building. I ran the usual security checks on the staff anyway, just in case, but nothing showed up. Most of them haven't been around long enough to work up a serious grudge."

"So what's freaking your men?" I asked quietly. "If they were any more on edge, they'd be shooting each other."

The officer snorted. "I told you. No-one ever sees *anything*. I've got saturation coverage around the building, CCTV inside, and infrared and motion sensors working. And whoever it is comes and goes without setting off any of them."

"There are a lot of things in the Nightside that come and go as they please," I pointed out.

"Don't I know it. But this is supposed to be a high-tech, low-magic area. If any heavy-duty magic-user had appeared here, he'd have set off all kinds of alarms. Whoever or whatever's trying to shut this place down, it's outside anything I've ever experienced, in science or magic."

I nodded easily, doing my best to exude casual confidence. "That's why they sent for me. Because I find the answers other people can't. See you later."

I stepped past the officer and headed for the main door, only to stop abruptly as one of the rent-a-cops moved suddenly forward to block my way. He was a big lad, with muscles on his muscles, and his huge hands made the semi-automatic in his grasp look like a toy. He scowled at me in what he obviously imagined was an intimidating way.

"Everyone gets frisked for guns," he snapped. "That's the rules. No exceptions. Even for jumped-up ambulance chasers like you, Taylor."

The officer started to say something, but I stopped him with a quick gesture. The day I couldn't deal with a constipated rent-a-cop, I'd retire. I gave him my best nasty smile.

"I don't use guns. Never have. They have too many limitations."

I slowly raised my hands, opened them, and the rent-a-cop's eyes widened as a steady stream of bullets fell from my hands to bounce and rattle on the ground at his feet.

"Your gun is empty," I said. "Now get out of my way before I decide to do something unpleasantly similar to your insides."

He pulled the trigger anyway, and made a small unhappy sound in the back of his throat when nothing happened. He swallowed hard and stepped back. I walked past him as though he didn't exist. I could hear the officer chewing him out as I passed through the heavy main door into the lobby beyond.

I strolled into the luxurious reception area as though I owned the place, but the effect was wasted, because there was no-one there. I heard electronic locks closing behind me. Someone knew I was there. I looked around the lobby and quickly spotted the security cameras tucked away in the ceiling corners. All the little red lights were on, so I just stood there and let the cameras get a good look at me. I thought I looked pretty good. My white trench coat was actually a little cleaner than usual, and I was almost sure I'd remembered to shave. Appearances can be so important. There was a brief burst of static from an unseen speaker, then a familiar voice whispered in the great empty lobby.

"John, I'm so glad you're here. Come on through to the manager's office and join me. Take the blue door at the end of the lobby, and follow the arrows. Don't go wandering. I've got booby-traps set up everywhere. And watch your back. We never know when the saboteur's going to strike next."

I passed through the blue door and followed the glowing arrows that appeared on the wall beyond.

After the luxurious reception lobby, the inner workings of Prometheus Inc. turned out to be decidedly functional. Narrow corridors with bare walls, numbered doors, and scuffed carpeting. It was all very quiet, as though the whole building was tense, waiting for something bad to happen. The arrows finally led me to a door with the Prometheus company logo on it, and there waiting to greet me was the manager-owner himself, Vincent Kraemer.

He nodded and smiled and shook my hand, but it was clear his thoughts were somewhere else. The man was seriously worried, and it showed. He ushered me into his office, looked quickly down the corridor, and shut and locked the door. He waved me to the visitor's chair and seated himself behind the magnificent mahogany desk. The office looked comfortable, lived-in. Nice prints on the walls, deep, deep carpet, and a high-tech drinks cabinet in the corner. All the usual signs of success. But the desk top was covered in papers that had overflowed and almost buried the In and Out trays, and one whole wall of the office was covered in CCTV monitor screens, showing ever-shifting views of the power plant interior. I studied them for a while, to show I was taking an interest, but it was all just machinery to me. I couldn't tell a turbine from a teapot, unless one of them had a tea cosy on it. Everything seemed to be working okay for the moment, and the walkways were deserted. I turned my attention back to the manager, and he flashed me another preoccupied smile.

I knew him vaguely, from several years back. Vincent Kraemer was one of those people who was always running around like a mad thing, trying to put far-fetched and precarious deals into motion, chasing after the one Big Score that would make him horribly wealthy. He finally made it, with Prometheus Inc. Vincent was tall, buff, immaculately dressed, with a prematurely lined face and no hair left to speak of. His suit probably cost more than I used to make in a year.

"Good to see you again, John." His voice was steady, cultivated, and artificially calm. "Been hearing interesting things about you since you got back."

"And you've done very well," I said courteously. "Is wealth and success everything you thought it would be?"

He laughed briefly. "Pretty much. What do you think of my pride and joy, John?"

"Impressive, but I'm not really equipped to appreciate it. Technology has always been a mystery to me. I have to get my secretary to work the timer on my video."

He laughed dutifully. "It's your other areas of expertise I need, John. I need you to find out who's trying to drive me out of business."

And then he stopped, because he saw I was looking at the only photo on his desk. A wedding scene, in a simple silver frame. Bride, groom, best man, and me. Six years ago, and still as fresh in my memory as though it had happened yesterday. It should have been the happiest day in the lives of two wonderful young people, but instead it became a tragedy that everyone still talked about. Mostly because no-one had ever been found to blame it on.

The bride was Melinda Dusk, also known as the Hanged Man's Beautiful Daughter. The groom was Quinn, also known as the Sunslinger. She wore a wedding gown of brilliant white, with a long creamy train. He wore his best cowboy outfit, all black leathers studded with dazzling displays of steel and silver. And standing on either side of the happy couple, doing our best to look at ease in our rented tuxedos, Vincent Kraemer as best man, and me as the bride's oldest friend. Melinda and Quinn—scions of the two oldest and most powerful families in the Nightside. Married and murdered in the same day.

There aren't many happy endings in the Nightside. Even the greatest celebrities and the most powerful people aren't immune to tragedy. Melinda was of the dark, her powers those of shadow and sorcery. Quinn was of the light, the deadly energies he controlled derived from the power of the sun itself. Their ancestors, the original Hanged Man and the original Sunslinger, had been deadly enemies hundreds of years ago, and all the generations since then had continued the feud, polishing their hatred with years of constant use. And Melinda and Quinn, the two latest avatars in this ongoing struggle, raised to hate and fight each other to the death, happened to meet during one of the rare truces. And it was love at first sight.

They continued to meet in secret for months, but finally went public. Their families went berserk and almost went to war. But Melinda and Quinn stood firm, secure in the powers they wielded, and threatened to disown their families and elope if they weren't given permission to marry. It was a magnificent wedding in the end, attended by absolutely every member of both families, partly as a show of strength and partly to make sure neither side tried to pull a fast one. There were famous faces and celebrities everywhere, and Walker himself turned up to run security. It should have been the safest place in the Nightside.

Vincent and I also worked as ushers, showing people to their seats, frisking them for weapons, keeping everyone in order, always ready to jump on anyone who even looked like doing anything funny. We were both young men then, still building our reputations. They called Vincent the Mechanic, because he could build or fix anything. Magic was good for short cuts, he was fond of saying, but technology was always going to be the more dependable in the long run. He'd built an automatic confetti-thrower, especially for the wedding, and kept dashing off to tinker with it when he wasn't needed. He and Quinn had been friends since they were kids, and he had risked his life many times to act as go-between for the two lovers. Melinda was one of the few friends I had left from childhood, one of the few powerful enough in her own right that my enemies didn't dare mess with her.

The wedding ceremony went fine, the families behaved themselves, and no-one got the words wrong or dropped the ring. And when it was all over, everyone cheered and applauded and some of us dared to think that just maybe the long war was over at last. Bride and groom left the church together, looking radiant. As though they belonged together. As though they completed each other. The automatic confetti-chucker worked first time.

Everyone posed for photographs, drinks circulated, snacks were consumed, and old enemies nodded to each other from a safe distance, even exchanging a few polite words. Bride and groom accepted the bridal cup, full to the brim with the very best champagne, and toasted their families and the bright future ahead. Ten minutes later, they were both dead. Poison in the bridal cup. It was all over so quickly that neither magic nor science could save them. Whoever had chosen the poison had known what they were doing. There wasn't even a sign of symptoms until Quinn suddenly fell dead to the ground. Melinda lived long enough to hold her dead husband in her arms, her tears dropping onto his dead face, then she collapsed across him and was gone.

If Walker and his people hadn't been there, the wedding party would have turned into a massacre. Both families went crazy, blaming each other. Somehow Walker kept the sides separated until they all left, swearing vengeance, then he organised a full investigation, using all his considerable resources. He never found anything. There was no shortage of suspects, of people in both families who'd spoken out loudly against the wedding and the truce, but there was no proof, no evidence. Meanwhile, the two families fought running battles in the streets, mercilessly slaughtering anyone foolish enough to be caught out on their own. Finally, the Authorities stepped in and shut it down, threatening to banish both families from the Nightside. A slow, sullen armed truce prevailed, but only just. That was six years ago. Melinda and Quinn were cold in their separate family graves, and still no-one had any idea of the who or why of it. There are loads of conspiracy theories, but then, there always are.

I would have done my best to find the killer, but shortly after the wedding my own life went to hell in a hurry, and I ended up running from the Nightside with Suzie Shooter's bullet in my back, vowing never to return.

"Such a terrible tragedy," said Vincent. He picked up the photo and studied it. "I still miss them. Like part of me died with them. Sometimes I think I keep this photo on my desk as a reminder of the last time I was really happy." He put the photo down and smiled briefly at me. "I wish they could have seen this place. My greatest achievement. And now someone, or something, is trying to shut it down. Which is why I asked Walker to contact you, John. Can you help me?"

"Perhaps," I said. "I'm still trying to get a feel for what's going on here. Talk me through it, from the beginning."

Vincent leaned back in his manager's chair and linked his fingers together across his expansive waistcoat. While he talked, his voice was calm and even, but his gaze kept flickering to the CCTV monitors.

"It started two weeks ago, John. Everything normal, just another day. Until one of the main turbines suddenly stopped working. My people investigated and found it had been sabotaged. Not a professional job—the whole interior had simply been... ripped apart. My people repaired it and got it back on-line in under an hour, but by then systems were breaking down all through the plant.

And that's been the pattern ever since. As fast as we fix things, something else goes wrong. It's costing us a fortune in spare parts alone. There's nothing sophisticated about the sabotage, just brutal, senseless destruction.

"No-one ever sees the saboteur. You've seen the security I've hired, but they haven't made a blind bit of difference. I've got cameras everywhere, and they never see anything either. I've had the videotapes checked by experts, but there's no trace of anything. We can't even tell how the bastard gets in or out! The destruction's getting steadily worse. Repairs and reconstruction are starting to fall behind. It's only a matter of time before it starts affecting our power output. And a whole lot of people depend on the electricity we produce here."

And if Prometheus Inc. goes down, so do you, I thought, but I was still being polite, so I didn't say it aloud.

"How about rivals?" I said. "Perhaps someone in the same line of business, looking to profit at your expense?"

"There are always competitors," said Vincent, frowning. "But there's no-one else big enough to take over if we go under. Prometheus Inc. supplies twelve point four per cent of the Nightside's electricity needs. If we crash, there'll be power outages and brownouts all across the Nightside, and no-one wants that. The other companies would have to push themselves almost to destruction to take up the slack."

"All right," I said. "How about people who just don't like you? Made any new enemies recently?"

He smiled briefly. "A month ago, I would have said I didn't have an enemy in the world. But now..." He looked at the wedding photo on his desk again. "I've been having dreams... about Melinda and Quinn, and the day they died. And I have to wonder... if the bastard who killed them is coming after me."

I hadn't seen that twist coming. "Why you? And why wait six years?"

"Maybe the killer thinks I know something, though I'm damned if I know what. And just maybe it's all started up again because you're back, John. An awful lot of old grudges and feuds have bubbled to the surface since you returned to the Nightside."

He had a point there, so I decided to change the subject. "Let's talk about the actual damage here. You said it was... unsophisticated."

"Hell yes," said Vincent. "It's clear the saboteur has no real technical knowledge. There are a dozen places he could have hit that would shut the whole plant down if they were even interfered with. But none a layman could hope to recognise. And, of course, there's the secret process at the heart of Prometheus Inc. that makes this whole operation possible. I invented it. But that's kept inside a steel vault, protected by state-of-the-art high-tech defence systems. Even the Authorities would have a hard time getting to it without the right pass codes." Vincent leaned forward across the desk and fixed me with a pleading gaze. "You've got to help me, John. It's not only my livelihood we're talking about here. If Prometheus Inc. is forced off-line, and power levels drop all across the

Nightside, people are going to start dying. Hundreds of thousands of lives could be at risk."

I should have seen what was coming. But I always was a sucker for a sob story.

Vincent took me on a tour through the plant, the underground section that outsiders never got a chance to see. It was all spotlessly clean and eerily quiet. The actual generators themselves turned out to be much smaller than I expected, and made hardly a sound. There were panels and gauges and readouts and any amount of gleaming high tech, none of which meant anything to me, though I was careful to make impressed sounds at regular intervals. Every bit of it had been designed by Vincent, back when he was the Mechanic, rather than the Manager. He kept up a running commentary throughout the tour, most of which went right over my head, while I nodded and smiled and kept an eye out for the saboteur. Eventually Vincent ran out of things to point at, and we stopped at the end of a cavernous hall, before a large, closed, solid steel door. He looked at me, clearly expecting me to say something.

"It's all... very clean," I said. "And very impressive. Though it's hard to believe you produce so much of the Nightside's electricity with... just this. I was expecting something ten times the size."

Vincent grinned. "None of the power comes from *this*. All the machinery does is convert the power produced in there into electricity. The secret lies in my own special process, behind this sealed door. A scientific marvel, if I do say so myself."

I glared suddenly at the steel door. "If you're about to tell me you've got a nuclear pile in there..."

"No, no..."

"Or a contained singularity..."

"Nothing so crude, John. My process is perfectly safe, with no noxious by-products. Though I'm afraid I can't show it to you. Some things have to remain secret."

And then he broke off, and we both looked round sharply as we heard something. A harsh juddering began in one of the machines at the far end of the hall, and black smoke billowed suddenly from a vent, before an alarm shrilled loudly and the machine shut itself down. Vincent shrank back against the steel door.

"He's here! The saboteur... he's never got this far before. He must have been following us all this time... Are you armed, John?"

"I don't use guns," I said. "I've never felt the need."

"Normally I don't, either, but ever since this shit began happening, I've felt a lot more secure knowing I've got a little something to even out the odds." Vincent produced a gleaming silver gun from inside his jacket. It looked sleek and deadly and very futuristic. Vincent hefted it proudly. "It's a laser. Amplified light to fight the forces of darkness. Another of my inventions. I always meant to do more with it, but the power plant took over my life. I can't see anyone, John. Can you see anyone?"

A machine a little further down the hall exploded suddenly. More black smoke, and the hum of the other machines rose significantly, as though they were having to work harder. A third machine blew apart like a grenade, throwing sharp-edged steel shrapnel almost the length of the hall. Some of the overhead lights flickered and went out. There were shadows everywhere now, deep and dark. Some of the other machines began making unpleasant, threatening noises. And still there was no sign of the saboteur anywhere.

Vincent's face was pale and sweaty, and his hand trembled as he swept his laser gun back and forth, searching for a target. "Come on, come on," he said hoarsely. "You're on my territory now. I'm ready for you."

Something pale flashed briefly at the corner of my eye. I snapped around, but it was already gone. It appeared again, just a glimpse of white in the shadows between two machines. It flashed back and forth, appearing and disappearing in the blink of an eye, darting up and down the length of the hall. Glimmers of shimmering white as fleeting as moonlight, but I thought I was beginning to make out an impression of a pale, haunted face. It moved in the shadows, never venturing out into the light. But it was gradually drawing nearer. Heading for us, or perhaps for the steel door behind us and the secret vulnerable heart of Prometheus Inc.

My first thought was that it had to be a ghost of some kind, maybe a poltergeist. Which would explain why the CCTV cameras hadn't been able to see anything. Ghosts could operate in science- or magic-dominated areas, provided their motivation was strong enough. In which case, Vincent needed a priest or an exorcist, not a private eye. I suggested as much to Vincent, and he shrugged angrily.

"I had my people do a full background check on this location before we began construction; and they didn't turn up anything. The whole area was supposed to be entirely free from magical or paranormal influences. That's why I built here. I'm the Mechanic, I build things. It's a talent, just like your talent for finding things, John. I don't know about ghosts. You're the expert on these matters. What do we do?"

"Depends what the ghost wants," I said.

"It wants to destroy me! I would have thought that was obvious. *What was that?*"

The white figure was flashing in and out of the shadows, on every side at once, drawing steadily closer all the time. Shimmering white, ragged round the edges, with long, reaching arms and a dark malevolent glare in an indistinct face. It gestured abruptly, and suddenly all the shrapnel scattered across the floor rose and hammered us like a metallic hailstorm. I put my arms over my head and did my best to shield Vincent with my body. The rain of objects ended as suddenly as it began, and we looked up to see something pale and dangerous squatting on one of the machines, tearing it apart with unnatural strength. Vincent howled with rage and fired his laser, but the figure was gone long before the light beam could reach it. I glared about me, my back pressed hard against the steel door. There were no other exits, no way to escape. So I did the only thing I could. I used my talent.

I don't like to use it too often, or for too long. It helps my enemies find me.

I reached inside, concentrating, and my third eye, my private eye, slowly opened. And just like that, I could see her clearly. As though my psychic gaze had focussed her, made her plain at last, she walked out of the shadows and into the light, standing openly before us. She nodded to me, then glared at Vincent with her deep dark eyes. I knew her immediately, though she looked very different from her wedding photo. Melinda Dusk, dead these six years, still wearing her wonderful white wedding dress, though it hung in tatters about her corpse-pale body. Her raven black hair fell in thick ringlets to her bare shoulders. Her lips were a pale purple. Her eyes... were black on black, like two deep holes in her face. She looked angry, haunted, vicious. The Hanged Man's Daughter, mistress of the dark forces, still beautiful in a cold, unnatural way. She raised one hand to point accusingly at Vincent, her fingernails grown long in the grave. I glanced at Vincent. He was breathing fast, his whole body trembling, but he didn't look particularly surprised.

I shut down my talent, but she was still there. I took a step forward, and the ghost turned her awful unblinking gaze upon me. I held up my hands to show they were empty.

"Melinda," I said. "It's me, John."

She looked away. I wasn't important. All her attention, all her rage, was focussed on Vincent.

"Talk to me, Vincent," I said quietly. "What's going on here? You knew who and what it was all along, didn't you? Didn't you! Why is she so angry with you, angry enough to pull her up out of her grave after six years?"

"I didn't know," he said. "I swear I didn't know!"

"He knew," said Melinda. Her voice was clear but quiet, like a whisper in my ear, as though it had to travel impossible distances to reach me. "You chose this place well, Vincent. As far as you could get from my family plot, and still be in the Nightside. And the sacrifices you made here in secret, before construction began, the innocent blood you spilled, and the promises you made... they would have kept out anyone else but me. I am an avatar of the dark, and every shadow is a doorway to me. Six years it took me, to track you down. But you could never hope to keep me out, not when the only thing that matters to me is still here. I will have my revenge, Vincent. Dear good friend Vincent. For what you did, to me and to Quinn."

And that was when I finally understood. I looked at Vincent, too shocked even to be angry, for the moment.

"You killed them," I said. "You murdered Melinda and Quinn. But you were their friend..."

"Best friends," said Vincent. He'd stopped shaking, and his voice was steady. "I would have done anything for you two, Melinda, but when the time came, you let me down. So I poisoned the bridal cup. It was necessary. And surprisingly easy. Who'd ever suspect the best man? No-one ever did, not even Walker himself." He looked at me suddenly, and he was smiling. "I was pretty sure my little problem had to be Melinda, but I needed you here to make certain. That's why I asked Walker to contact you, on my behalf. Because your talent to find things holds her in one place, one shape. All you have to do is hold her here, and my laser light will disrupt her, take her apart so thoroughly she'll never be able to put herself back together again. Do this for me, John, and I'll make you a partner in Prometheus Inc. You'll be wealthy and powerful beyond your wildest dreams."

"They were my friends, too," I said. "And there isn't enough money in the Nightside to turn me against a friend."

"Be my friend, John," said Melinda. She'd drifted very close now, and I could feel the cold of the grave radiating from her. "Be my friend and Quinn's, one last time. Find the source of Vincent's power. His secret source."

Vincent fired his laser at her. The light beam punched right through her shimmering form, but if it hurt her she didn't show it.

I called up my talent again, focussing my inner eye, my private eye from which nothing can be hidden, and immediately I knew where the secret was, and how to get to it. I turned to the steel door and punched in the correct entry codes. The heavy door swung slowly open. Vincent shouted something, but I wasn't listening. I walked through the opening, Melinda drifting after me, and there in the underground chamber Vincent had made specially for him, was the reason Vincent had been able to produce power so easily. It was Quinn, the Sunslinger.

He still looked a lot like he had in his wedding photo, but like Melinda, he had been through some changes. Quinn still wore his black leathers, though the steel and silver were dirty and corroded. His body was contained in a spirit bottle, a great glass chamber designed to contain the souls of the dead.

Electricity cables penetrated the sides of the bottle, plugging into Quinn's eye sockets, his wedged-open mouth, and holes cut in his torso. Quinn, the Sun-slinger, whose power had been to channel and direct energies from the sun, had been made into a battery. The spirit bottle trapped his soul with his dead body and made him controllable. The cables leeched his power, and Vincent's machines turned it into electricity to feed the Nightside.

Ingenious. But then, the Mechanic had never been afraid to think big.

Melinda hovered beside the spirit bottle, staring at what had been done to her dead love with yearning eyes, unable to touch him for all her ghostly power. I ran my fingertips down the glass side of the spirit bottle, testing its strength.

"Get away from that, John," said Vincent.

I looked round to see Vincent stepping through the doorway, his laser gun trained on me. He laughed, a little shakily.

"Ordinary guns are no use against you, John. I know that. I know all about that clever trick you do with bullets. But this is a laser, and it will quite definitely kill you. It's a clever little device. Draws its power directly from Quinn. So you're going to do exactly what I tell you to do. You're going to use your talent to fix and hold Melinda in one place, one shape, while I kill her. Or I'll kill you. Slowly and very nastily."

"How will you stop Melinda without me?" I said.

"Oh, I'm sure I'll be able to think of something, now I know for sure it's Melinda. Maybe I'll build another spirit bottle, just for her."

"What happened?" I said, careful to keep my voice calm and my hands still. "You three were friends for years, closer than family. So what happened, Vincent? What turned you into a murderer?"

"They let me down," he said flatly. "When I needed them most, they weren't there for me. I dreamed up this power station, you see. A way at last to provide dependable electricity for the Nightside. A licence to print money. My big score, at last. And all I needed to make it work was Quinn. I was sure studying his powers under laboratory conditions would enable me to build something that would power the plant. But when I told him, he turned me down. Said his secrets were family secrets and not for sharing. After all the things I'd done for him! I talked to Melinda, tried to get her to persuade him, but she didn't want to know either. She and Quinn were planning a new life together, and there was no room in it for me.

"But I'd already sunk all my money into this project, and a hell of a lot more I'd borrowed from some really unpleasant people. It had never occurred to me that Quinn would turn me down. The project was already under way. It had to go on. So I killed Quinn and Melinda. It was their own fault, for putting their own selfish happiness ahead of my needs, my success. I would have made them partners. Made them rich. After they were dead, my financial associates retrieved Quinn's body from his grave, leaving a duplicate behind, and brought him here. Where he ended up working for me anyway. My... silent partner, if you like."

Melinda looked at me, silently pleading. The spirit bottle was full of light, with no shadows she could use. I looked at the bottle thoughtfully. Vincent aimed the laser at my stomach.

"Don't even think it, John. If you break the bottle, that breaks the connection between Quinn and my machines, and that would shut down the whole plant. No more of my electricity for the Nightside. Power cuts everywhere. Thousands of people could die."

"Ah, well," I said. "What did they ever do for me?"

It was the easiest thing in the world for my talent to find the entry point into the spirit bottle and nudge it open just a crack. That was all Quinn needed. His dead body convulsed and suddenly blazed with light. Brilliant sunlight, too bright for mortal eyes to look upon. Vincent and I both had to turn away, shielding our eyes with our arms. The spirit bottle exploded, unable to contain the released energies of the Sunslinger. Glass fragments showered down. I made myself turn back and look through dazzled eyes as Quinn strode out of the wreckage, pulling the cables out of his face and his body. They fell to twitch restlessly on the floor, like severed limbs.

The dead man looked upon the ghost, and they smiled at each other, together again for the first time since their wedding day. And Vincent stumbled forward with his laser gun. His eyes weren't really clear yet, and I wasn't entirely sure who he was trying to point the gun at, but I didn't feel like taking any chances. So I reached down, grabbed one of the twitching cables from the floor, and lunged forward to jam one end of the cable into Vincent's eye. It plunged into his eye socket, burrowing beyond, and Vincent screamed horribly as his own machines sucked the life energies out of him. He was dead before his twitching body hit the floor.

Melinda Dusk and Quinn—the Hanged Man's Beautiful Daughter and the Sunslinger—dead but no longer separated, were already gone, too wrapped up in each other to care about lesser needs like vengeance. Quinn's body lay still and empty on the floor beside that of his old friend Vincent. I looked at Quinn's body and thought about whether I should take it back to his family, for a proper burial. But I had no proof of what had happened here, and as long as the armed truce between the two families continued, it was better not to stir things up. After all, who would Vincent have gone to first for financial backing? Who did he know who would still lend him money after all his failures, except for certain factions in the two families?

I walked out of the secret vault, leaving the dead past behind, and used my talent one last time to find the self-destruct mechanism for the power plant. I knew there had to be one. Vincent was always very jealous about guarding his secrets. I allowed myself enough time to get clear, then set the clock ticking. I told the security men outside to start running, and something in my voice and my gaze convinced them. I was three blocks away when the whole of Prometheus Inc. went up in one great controlled explosion. I kept walking and didn't look back.

Not exactly my most successful case. My client was dead, so I wasn't going to get paid. Walker was probably going to be pretty mad that the power plant was gone, and God alone knew how much damage its loss was going to cause the Nightside. But none of that mattered. Melinda Dusk and Quinn had been my friends. And no-one kills a friend of mine and gets away with it.

TWO

BETWEEN CASES

Everyone needs somewhere to go, when it all goes pear-shaped. A bolt-hole to shelter in, till the shit-storm passes. I usually end up in Strangefellows, the oldest bar in the world. A (fairly) discreet drinking establishment, tucked away in the back of beyond, at the end of an alley that isn't always there, Strangefellows is a good place to booze and brood and hide from any number of people, most of whom wouldn't be seen dead in such a dive. It was run with malice aforethought by one Alex Morrisey, who didn't allow any trouble in his bar, most especially from me.

I found a table in a corner, so I wouldn't have to watch my back, and indulged myself with a bottle of wormwood brandy. It tastes like a supermodel's tears and is so potent it can catch alight if someone at the next table strikes a match. I kept my head well down and looked about me surreptitiously. If anyone had noticed me come in, they were keeping their excitement well under control. Certainly no-one was rushing for the exit to tell on me. Perhaps word hadn't got around yet as to how royally I'd screwed up this time. There were any number of people who weren't going to be at all pleased with me for knocking out twelve per cent of the Nightside's electricity supply. Not least Walker, who'd got me the job in the first place. I faked a careless shrug. If they couldn't take a joke, they shouldn't hire me.

It was a quiet night at Strangefellows, for once. All the lights were out, and the whole place was illuminated by candles, hurricane lamps, and the occasional hand of glory. It gave the place a pleasant golden haze, like an old photo of better times. Alex explained when I got my drink that the power was down in various spots all over the Nightside, and I just nodded and grunted. Alex was severely pissed off by the inconvenience and loss of takings, but that was nothing new. Strangefellows's owner and bartender was a thin pale streak of misery who only wore black because no-one had come up with a darker colour yet. He wore a snazzy black beret to hide his bald patch and designer shades to tone down the perpetual glare with which he regarded the world.

He's a friend of mine. Sometimes.

Music was playing from a portable CD player, rising easily over the bare murmur of conversation from the few regulars nursing their drinks in the back booths. Most of the bar's usual crowd were probably out and about in the Nightside, taking advantage of the blackouts to do unto others and run off with the takings. It would be a busy time for the Nightside's fences, before the lights went on again. Alex's pet vulture was perched over the till, cackling to itself and giving the evil eye to anyone who looked like getting too close. The bar's muscular bouncers, Betty and Lucy Coltrane, were occupying themselves with a flex-off at the end of the bar, frowning seriously as muscles distended and veins popped up all over their sculpted bodies. Pale Michael was running a book as to which one would pass out first.

And my teenage secretary, Cathy Barrett, was dancing wildly on a tabletop, to the music of Voice of the Beehive's "Honey Lingers." Blonde, bubbly, and full of more energy than she knew what to do with, Cathy ran the business side of my life. I'd rescued her from a house that tried to eat her, and she adopted me. I didn't get a say in the matter. Dancing opposite her on the tabletop, in a leather outfit, cape, mask, and six-inch stiletto heels, was Ms. Fate, the Nightside's very own transvestite superhero, a man who dressed up as a superheroine to fight crime and avenge injustice. He was actually pretty good at it, in her own way. Cathy and Ms. Fate danced their hearts out, pounding their heels on the table to "Monsters and Angels," and I had to smile. They were the brightest things in the whole bar.

I topped up my glass with the murky purple liquor and drank to the memory of Melinda Dusk and Quinn. It was good to know they were finally at rest, together, their murders avenged. I don't have that many friends. Either my enemies kill them, or I do. Morality can be a shifting, treacherous thing in the Nightside, and both love and loyalty have a way of getting drowned in the bigger issues. My few longtime friends have all tended to be dangerous as hell in their own right, and more than a little crazy. People like Razor Eddie and Shotgun Suzie... both of whom have tried to kill me in the past. I don't hold it against them. Much. It's a hard life in the Nightside, and a harder death, usually. I sipped my drink and listened to the music. I wasn't in any hurry. I had the rest of the bottle to get through.

I've never found it easy to mourn, though God knows I've had enough practice.

I looked around the bar, searching for something to distract myself with. A sailor had passed out at the main bar, and the tattoos on his back were quietly arguing matters philosophical over the low rumble of his snores. A mummy at the other end of the long wooden bar was drinking gin and tonics while performing necessary running repairs on his yellowed bandages. Roughly midway between the two, an amiable drunk in a blood-stained lab coat was endeavouring to explain the principles of retro-phrenology to a frankly disinterested Alex Morrisey.

"See, phrenology is this old Victorian science, which claimed you could determine the dominant traits of a man's personality by studying the bumps on his head. The size and position of these bumps indicated different personality traits. See? Now, *retro-phrenology* says, why not change a man's personality by hitting him on the head with a hammer, till you raise just the right bumps in the right places!"

"One of us needs a lot more drinks," said Alex. "That's starting to make sense."

Cathy suddenly slammed down into the chair opposite me, breathing harshly and radiating happy sweat. She flashed me a cheerful grin. She'd picked up a fresh flute of champagne from somewhere and drank from it thirstily. Cathy always drank "champers," and nearly always found a way to stick me with the bill.

"I love to dance!" she said cheerfully. "Sometimes I think the whole world should be put to music and choreographed!"

"This being the Nightside, someone somewhere is undoubtedly working on that very thing, right now," I said. "Where's your partner, the Dancing Queen?"

"Oh, he's nipped off to the loo, to freshen her make-up. You know, John, I could see you brooding from right across the room. Who died this time?"

"What makes you think someone died?"

"You only drink that wormwood muck when you've lost someone close to you. I wouldn't use that stuff to clean combs. I thought the Prometheus gig was a straightforward deal?"

"I really don't want to talk about it, Cathy."

"No, you'd rather sulk and be miserable and pollute the atmosphere for everyone else. If you're not careful, you'll end up like Alex."

Cathy could always make me smile. "There's no danger of that. I'm not in Alex's class. That man could brood for the Olympics, and pick up a bronze in self-pity while he was at it. He's why there's never been a Happy Hour in Strangefellows."

Cathy sighed, leaned forward, and gave me her best exasperated look. "Get another case going, John. You know you're really only happy when you're working. Not that that's much healthier, given the cases you specialise in. You need to get out more and meet people, preferably people who aren't trying to kill you. You know, I found this really great new dating site for professional singles on the Net the other day..."

I shuddered. "I've seen some of those. *Hi! I'm Trixi, and I've got diseases so virulent you can even catch them down a phone line! Just give me your credit card number, and I guarantee to make your eyes water in under thirty seconds!* No, Cathy! I'm quite happy with my solitary brooding. It builds character."

Cathy pouted, then shrugged. She never could stay unhappy for long. She finished off the last of her champagne, hiccuped happily, and looked hopefully round the bar for another dancing partner. I'd never admit it to her, but she was mostly right. My work was all I had to give my life meaning. But since my last successful case earned me a quarter of a million pounds, plus bonuses, I could afford to be more particular about what work I chose to take on. (I located the Unholy Grail for the Vatican, and faced down Heaven and Hell in the process. I'd *earned* that money.) Maybe I should start looking for a new case, if only to take the taste of Prometheus Inc. out of my mouth.

"I'm bored," Cathy announced, slapping both hands on the table to prove it. "Bored of sitting around your expensive new office with nothing to do. It's all very comfortable, I'm sure, and I love all the new equipment, but a growing girl can't spend all her life surfing dodgy porn sites on the Internet. Like you, I need to be doing. Earning my keep and smiting the ungodly where it hurts. There must be something in all the messages I've taken that appeals to you. What about the case of the missing shadows? Or the guy who lost his adolescence in a rigged card game?"

"Hold everything," I said sternly. "A disturbing thought has just occurred to me. Who's looking after things in my expensive new Nightside office, while you're out cavorting and carousing in dubious drinking establishments?"

"Ah," said Cathy, grinning. "I got a really good deal on some computers from the future. They practically run the whole business on their own, these days. They can even answer the phone and talk snotty to our creditors."

"Just how far up the line did these computers come from?" I said suspiciously. "I mean, are we talking Artificial Intelligence here? Are they going to want paying?"

"Relax! They're data junkies. The Nightside fascinates them. Why don't we ask them to find something that would interest you?"

"Cathy, I only took on the Prometheus case to keep you quiet..."

"No you didn't!" Cathy said hotly. "You took that on because you wanted Walker to owe you a favour."

I scowled and addressed myself to my drink. "Yes, well, that didn't actually work out as well as I'd hoped."

"Oh, God," said Cathy. "Am I going to have to start locking the doors and windows and hiding under the desk again, when he comes around?"

"I think it would be a better idea if we both stayed away from the office completely, just for a while."

"That bad?"

"Pretty much. Let Walker argue with the computers and see how far it gets him."

There was a sudden flare of brilliant light, and a man fell out of nowhere into Strangefellows. He crashed to the floor just in front of the bar, his New Romantic silks in shreds and tatters. Static sparks discharged from every metal object in the bar, and the air was heavy with the stench of ozone—the usual accompanying signs of time travel. The newcomer groaned, sat up, and wiped at his bloody nose with the back of his hand. He'd clearly been through a hell of a fight recently, and just as clearly lost. I knew him, though if I met him in the street, I tried very hard not to. He was Tommy Oblivion, a fellow private investigator, though he specialised in cases of an existential nature. He lurched to his feet, leaned his back against the bar for support while he pulled his ragged silks around him, then saw me watching him. His battered face purpled with rage, and he stabbed a shaking finger at me.

"You! Taylor! This is all your fault! I'll have your balls for this!"

"I haven't seen you in months, Tommy," I said calmly.

"No, but you will! In the future! Only this time I'll be ready for you, and better prepared! I'll have guns! Big guns!"

He continued to spit abuse at me, but I couldn't be bothered. I looked at Alex, and he gestured at his two bouncers. Betty and Lucy hurried forward, glad of an excuse for a little action. Tommy made the mistake of threatening them, too, and the two girls briskly knocked him to the floor, kicked him somewhere painful, and then frog-marched him out of Strangefellows. Cathy gave me a hard look.

"What was that all about?"

"Beats the hell out of me," I said honestly. "Presumably I'll find out. In time."

"Excuse me," said a voice with a cultured French accent. "Have I the honour of addressing Mr. John Taylor?"

Cathy and I both looked round sharply. Standing right before us was a short, comfortably padded, middle-aged man in an expertly cut suit. He looked supremely elegant, not a hair out of place, and his smile was sophisticated charm itself. There was no way he could have entered the bar and approached my corner table without being seen, but there he was, large as life and twice as French. He nodded courteously to me, smiled at Cathy, and kissed her proffered hand. She gave him a dazzling smile in return. I decided not to like him, on general principles. I really don't like being sneaked up on. It's bad for my health. I gestured for the Frenchman to pull up a chair. He studied the empty chair solemnly for a moment, then produced a blindingly white handkerchief from an inner pocket and flicked the seat of the chair a few times before deigning to sit on it. I gave him my best intimidating glare, to remind him who was boss around here.

"I'm John Taylor," I growled. "You're a long way from home, *m'sieu*. What can I do for you?"

He nodded easily, entirely unimpressed. "I am Charles Chabron, for many years one of the most respected bankers in Paris. And I have come a very long way to meet with you, Mr. Taylor, and inquire whether I might hire your professional services."

"Who recommended me to you?" I said carefully.

He flashed his charming smile again. "An old friend of yours who does not wish to be identified."

He had me there. "I get a lot of that," I admitted. "What is it you want, Mr. Chabron?"

"Please, call me Charles. I am here because of my daughter. You may have heard of her. She is currently the new singing sensation of the Nightside. She calls herself Rossignol, though that is of course not her real name. Rossignol is merely French for nightingale. She first came to London, then the Nightside, some five years ago, determined to make for herself a career as a singer. And this last year she has been singing very successfully to packed houses in nightclubs all over the Nightside. I understand there's even talk of a recording contract with one of the major companies. Which is all well and good.

"However, since she took up with her new management, a Mr. and Mrs. Cavendish, she only sings at one nightclub, Caliban's Cavern, and she has... changed. She has broken off all contact with her old friends and family. She does not answer phone calls or letters, and her new management won't let anyone get near her. They say they do this at her explicit request and justify it in the name of protecting her from over-zealous fans of her new fame. But I am not so sure. Her mother is frantic with worry, convinced that the Cavendishes have poisoned our daughter's mind against her family, and that they are, perhaps, taking advantage of her. And so I have come here, to you, Mr. Taylor, in the hope that you can establish the truth of the matter."

I looked at Cathy. The music scene was her speciality. There wasn't a club in the Nightside she hadn't drunk, danced, and debauched in at one time or another. She was already nodding.

"Yeah, I know Rossignol. And the Caliban club, and the Cavendishes. They run Cavendish Properties. They have a collective finger in practically every big deal in the Nightside. They were big in real estate, until the market crashed just recently, after the angel war. Lot of people lost a lot of money in that disaster. Mr. and Mrs. Cavendish moved sideways into entertainment, representing clubs, groups, people... nothing really mega yet, but they've quickly made themselves a power to be reckoned with. Other agents cross themselves when they see the Cavendishes coming."

"What sort of people are they?" I asked.

Cathy frowned. "If the Cavendishes have first names, no-one knows or uses them. They don't get out much, preferring to work through intermediaries. Not at all averse to playing hardball during negotiations, but then, nice people don't tend to last long in show business. There are rumours they're brother and sister, as well as husband and wife... Cavendish Properties is based on *old* money, going back centuries, but there's a lot of gossip going round that says the current owners are hungry for money and not too fussy about how they acquire it. There's also supposed to be a scandal about their last attempt at building Sylvia Sin into a singing sensation. But they spent a lot of money to cover it up. But there's always gossip in the Nightside. They could be on the level with Rossignol. I just hope her agent checked the small print in their contract carefully."

"She has no agent," said Chabron. "Cavendish Properties represents Rossignol. You can understand why I am so concerned."

I looked at him thoughtfully. There were things he wasn't telling me. I could tell.

"What brought your daughter all the way to London, and the Nightside?" I said. "Paris has its own music scene, doesn't it?"

"Of course. But London is where you have to go to be a star. Everyone knows that." Chabron sighed. "Her mother and I never took her singing seriously. We wanted her to take up a more respectable occupation, something with a future and a pension plan. But all she ever cared about was singing. Perhaps we pressured her too much. I arranged an interview for her, with my bank. An entry-level position, but with good prospects. Instead, she ran away to London. And when I sent people to track her down, she disappeared into the Nightside. Now... she is in trouble, I am sure of it. One hears such things... I wish for you to find my daughter, Mr. Taylor, and satisfy yourself on my behalf that she is well and happy, and not being cheated out of anything that is rightfully hers. I am not asking you to drag her back home. Just to assure yourself that everything is as it should be. Tell her that her friends and her family are concerned for her. Tell her... that she doesn't have to talk to us if she doesn't want to, but we would be grateful for some form of communication, now and then. She is my only child, Mr. Taylor. I need to be sure she is happy and safe. You understand?"

"Of course," I said. "But I really don't see why you want me. Any number of people could handle this. I can put you onto a man called Walker, in the Authorities..."

"No," Chabron said sharply. "I want you."

"It doesn't seem like my kind of case."

"People are dying, Mr. Taylor! Dying, because of my daughter!" He took a moment to calm himself, before continuing. "It seems that my Rossignol sings only sad songs these days. And that she sings these sad songs so powerfully that members of her audience have been known to go home and commit suicide. Already there are so many dead that not even her management can keep it quiet. I want to know what has happened to my daughter, here in your Nightside, that such a thing is possible."

"All right," I said. "Perhaps it is my kind of case after all. But I have to warn you, I don't come cheap."

Chabron smiled, back on familiar ground. "Money is no problem to me, Mr. Taylor."

I smiled back at him. "The very best kind of client. My whole day just brightened up." I turned to Cathy. "Go back to the office and get your marvelous new computers working on some background research. I want to know everything there is to know about the Cavendishes, their company, and their current financial state. Who they own, and who they owe money to. Then see what you can find out about Rossignol, before she went to work for the Cavendishes. Where she sang, what kind of following she had, the usual. Mr. Chabron..."

I looked around, and he was gone. There was no sign of him anywhere, even though there was no way he could have made it to any of the exits in such a short time.

"Damn, that's creepy," said Cathy. "How does he *do* that?"

"There's more to our Mr. Chabron than meets the eye," I said. "But then, that's par for the course in the Nightside. See what you can find out about him, too, while you're at it, Cathy."

She nodded quickly, blew me a kiss, and hurried away. I got up and wandered over to the bar. I shoved the cork back into the bottle of wormwood brandy and handed it over to Alex. I didn't need it any more. He made it disappear under the bar and gave me a smug smile.

"I used to know Rossignol. Bit skinny for my tastes, but a hell of a set of pipes on her. I hired her a few years back to provide cabaret, to add some class to the place. It didn't work, but then this bar is a lost cause anyway. You couldn't drive it upmarket with a chair and a whip."

"Were you eavesdropping again, Alex?"

"Of course. I hear everything. It's my bar. Anyway, this Rossignol was pretty enough, with a good if untrained voice, and more importantly, she worked cheap. In those days she'd sing anywhere, for peanuts, for the experience. She had this need, this hunger, to sing. You could see it in her face, hear it in her voice. And it wasn't just your usual singer's ego. It was more like a mission with her. I wouldn't say she was anything special back then, but I always knew she'd go far. Talent isn't worth shit if you haven't got the determination to back it up, and she had that in spades."

"What kind of songs did she sing, back then?" I asked.

Alex frowned. "I'm pretty sure she only sang her own material. Happy, upbeat stuff, you know the sort of thing, sweet but forgettable. There were definitely no suicides when she sang here, though admittedly this is a tougher audience than most."

"So she was nothing like the deadly diva her father described?"

"Not in the least. But then, the Nightside can change anyone, and usually not for the better." Alex paused and gave the bar top a polish it didn't need, so he wouldn't have to look me in the eye as he spoke. "Word is, Walker's looking for you, John. And he is not a happy bunny."

"Walker never is," I said, carefully casual. "But just in case he shows up here, looking for me, you haven't seen me, right?"

"Some things never change," said Alex. "Go on, get out of here, you're lowering the tone of the place."

I left Strangefellows and walked out into the night. One by one the neon signs were flickering on again, like road signs in Hell. I decided to take that as a good omen and kept walking.

THREE

DOWNTIME IN UPTOWN

If you're looking for the real nightlife in the Nightside, you have to go Uptown. That's where you'll find the very best establishments, the sharpest pleasures, the most seductive damnations. Every taste catered for, satisfaction guaranteed or your soul back. They play for keeps in Uptown, which is, of course, part of the attraction. It was a long way from Strangefellows, so I took my courage in both hands, stepped right up to the very edge of the passing traffic, and hailed a sedan chair.

The sedan chair was part of a chain I recognised, or I wouldn't have got in it. The traffic that runs endlessly through the rain-slick streets of the Nightside can be a peril to both body and soul. I settled myself comfortably on the crimson padded leather seat, and the sedan chair moved confidently out into the flow. The tall wooden walls of the box were satisfyingly solid, and the narrow windows were filled with bulletproof glass. They were proof against a lot of other things, too. There was no-one carrying the chair, front or back. This particular firm was owned and run by a family of amiable poltergeists. They could move a lot faster than human bearers, and even better, they didn't bother the paying customers with unwanted conversation. Poltergeist muscle was also handy when it came to protecting their chairs from the other traffic on the roads. The Nightside is a strange attractor for all kinds of traffic, from past, present, and future, and a lot of it tend towards the predatory. There are taxis that run on deconsecrated altar wine, shining silver bullets that run on demons' tears and angels' urine, and things that only look like cars but are always hungry.

A pack of headless bikers tried to crowd the sedan chair with their choppers, but the operating poltergeist flipped them away like poker chips. The roaring traffic gave us a bit more room after that, and it wasn't long at all before we were cruising through Uptown. You could almost smell the excitement, above the blood, sweat, and tears. Nowhere does the neon blaze more brightly, neon noir and Technicolor temptation, the sleazy signs pulsing like an aroused heartbeat. You can bet the lights here never even dimmed during the recent power outages. Uptown would always have first call on whatever power was available. But even so, it's always that little bit darker here, in the world of three o'clock in the morning, where the pleasures of the night need never end, as long as your money holds out.

You can find the very best restaurants in Uptown, featuring dishes from cultures that haven't existed for centuries, using recipes that would be banned in saner places. There are even specialised restaurants, offering meals made entirely from the meats of extinct or imaginary animals. You haven't lived till you've tasted dodo drumsticks, roc egg omelettes, Kentucky-fried dragon, kraken sushi surprise, chimera of the day, or basilisk eyes (that last entirely at your own risk). You can find food to die for, in Uptown.

Bookshops contain works written in secret by famous authors, never intended to be published. Ghostwritten books, by authors who died too soon. Volumes on spiritual pornography, and the art of tantric murder. Forbidden knowledge and forgotten lore, and guide-books for the hereafter. One shop window boasted a new edition of that infamous book *The King in Yellow*, whose perusal drove men mad, together with a special pair of rose-tinted spectacles to read it through.

People bustled through the streets, following the lure of the rainbow neon. Scents of delicious cooking pulled at the nose, and snatches of beguiling music spilled from briefly opened doors. Long lines waited patiently outside theatres and cabaret clubs, and crowded round newsstands selling the latest edition of the *Night Times*. More furtive faces disappeared into weapons shops, or brothels, where for the right price you could sleep with famous women from fiction. (It wasn't the real thing, of course, but then it never is, in such places.) Uptown held every form of entertainment the mind could conceive, some of which would eat you alive if you weren't sharp enough.

And nightclubs, of every form and persuasion. Music and booze and company, all just a little hotter than the consumer could comfortably stand. Some of the clubs go way back. Whigs and Tories argue politics over cups of coffee, then sit down to wager on demon-baiting matches. Romans recline on couches, pigging out on twenty-course meals, in between trips to the vomitorium. Other clubs are as fresh as today and twice as tasty. You'd be surprised how many big stars started out singing for their supper in Uptown.

The streets became even more thickly crowded as the sedan chair carried me deep into the dark heart of Uptown. Flushed faces and bright eyes everywhere, high on life and eager to throw their money away on things they only thought they needed. In and among the fevered punters, the people who earned their living in the clubs and nightspots of Uptown rushed from one establishment to another, working the several jobs it took to pay their rent or quiet their souls. Singers and actors, conjurers and stand-up comedians, strippers and hostesses and specialist acts—all of them thriving on a regular diet of buzz, booze, and bennies. And walking their beats or standing on corners, watching it all go by, the ladies of the evening with their kohl-stained eyes and come-on mouths, the twilight daughters who never said no to anything that involved hard cash.

This still being the Nightside, there were always hidden traps for the unwary. Smoke-filled bars where lost weekends could stretch out for years, and clubs where people couldn't stop dancing, even when their feet left bloody marks on the dance floor. Markets where you could sell any part of your body, mind, or soul. Or someone else's. Magic shops that offered wonderful items and objects of power, with absolutely no guarantee they'd perform as advertised, or even that the shop would still be there when you went back to complain.

There were homeless people, too, in shadowed doorways and the entrances of alleyways, wrapped in shabby coats or tattered blankets, with their grubby hands held out for spare change. Tramps and vagabonds, teenage runaways and people just down on their luck. Most passersby have the good sense to drop them the odd coin or a kind word. Karma isn't just a concept in the Nightside, and a surprising number of street people used to be Somebody once. It's always been easy to lose everything, in the Nightside. So it was wise to never piss these people off, because they might still have a spark of power left in them. And because it might just be you there, one day. The wheel turns, we all rise and fall, and nowhere does the wheel turn faster than in Uptown.

The sedan chair finally dropped me off right outside Caliban's Cavern. I checked the meter, added a generous tip, and dropped the money into the box provided. No-one ever cheats the poltergeists. They tend to take it personally and reduce your home to its original components while you're still in it. The chair moved off into the traffic again, and I studied the nightclub before me, taking my time. People flowed impatiently around me, but I ignored them, concentrating on the feel of the place. It was big, expensive, and clearly exclusive, the kind of place where you couldn't get in, never mind get a good table, unless your name was on someone's list. Caliban's Cavern wasn't for just anybody, and that, of course, was part of the attraction. Rossignol's name blazed above the door in Gothic neon script, giving the times of her three shows a night. A sign on the closed front door made it clear the club was currently in between shows and not open for business. Even the most upmarket clubs have to take time out to freshen the place up in between sets. A good time for someone like me to do a little sneaking around. But first, I wanted to make sure this wasn't a setup of some kind.

I have enemies who want me dead. I don't know who or why, but they've been sending agents to try and kill me ever since I was a child. It has something to do with my absent mother, who turned out not to be human. She disappeared shortly after my father discovered that, and he spent what little was left of his life drinking himself to death. I like to think I'm made of harder stuff. Sometimes I don't think about my missing mother for days on end.

I studied the crowd bustling around and past me, but didn't spot any familiar faces. And the sedan chair would have let me know if someone had tried to follow us. But the case could be nothing more than a way of bringing me here, so that I could be ambushed. It's happened before. The only way to be sure there were no hidden traps was to

use my Sight, my special gift that lets me find anything, or anyone. And that was dangerous in itself.
When I open up my third eye, my private eye, my
mind burns very brightly in the endless night, and
all kinds of people can see me and where I am. My
enemies are always watching. But I needed to
know, so I opened up my mind and Saw the larger
world.

Even in the Nightside there are secret depths,
hidden layers, above and below. I could See ghosts
all around me, running through their routines like
shimmering video loops, moments trapped in
Time. Ley lines blazed so brightly even I couldn't
look at them directly, criss-crossing in brilliant
designs, plunging through people and buildings as
though they weren't really there. In the passing
crowds, dark and twisted things rode on people's
backs—obsessions, hungers, and addictions. Some
of them recognised me and bared needle teeth in
defiant snarls to warn me off. Giants walked in
giant steps, towering high above the tallest buildings. And flitting here and there, the Light People,
forever bound on their unknowable missions,
occasionally drawn to this person or that for no
obvious reason, but never interfering.

But what really caught my third eye were the layers of magical defences surrounding Caliban's
Cavern. Intersecting strands of hexes, curses, and
anti-personnel runes covered every possible way in
and out of the club, all of them positively radiating
maleficent energies. This was heavy-duty, hard-
core protection, way out of the range of even the
most talented amateurs. Which meant someone
had paid a pro a small fortune, just to protect an

up-and-coming singing sensation. However, none of those defences were targeted specifically at me, which argued against this being a trap. I shut down my Sight and looked thoughtfully at the closed door before me. As long as I didn't use magic, the defences couldn't see me, so... I'd just have to think my way past them.

Luckily, most magical defences aren't very bright. They don't have to be. I grinned, stepped forward, and knocked firmly on the door. A staggeringly ugly face rose before me, forming itself out of the wood of the door. The varnish cracked loudly as the face scowled at me. Wooden lips parted, revealing large jagged wooden teeth.

"Forget it. Go away. Push off. The club is closed between acts. No personal appearances from the artistes, no autographs, and no, you don't get to hang around the stage door. If you want tickets, the booking office will be open in an hour. Come back then, or not at all. See if I care."

Its message over, the face began to subside back into the door again. I knocked again on the broad forehead, and the face blinked at me, surprised.

"You have to let me in," I said. "I'm John Taylor."

"Really? Congratulations. Now piss off and play with the traffic. We are very definitely closed, not open, and why are you still standing there?"

There's nothing easier to outmanoeuvre than a pushy simulacrum with a sense of its own self-importance. I gave the face my best condescending smile. "I'm John Taylor, here to speak with Rossignol. Open the door, or I'll do all kinds of horrible things to you. On purpose."

"Well, pardon me for existing, Mr. *I'm going to be Somebody someday.* I've got my orders. No-one gets in unless they're on the list, or they know the password, and it's more than my job's worth to make exceptions. Even if I felt like it. Which I don't."

"Walker sent me." That one was always worth a try. People were even more scared of Walker than they were of me. With very good reason.

The face in the door sniffed loudly. "You got any proof of that?"

"Don't be silly. Since when have the Authorities ever bothered with warrants?"

"No proof, no entry. Off you go now. Hop like a bunny."

"And if I don't?"

Two large gnarled hands burst out of the wood, reaching for me. There was no way of dodging them, so I didn't try. Instead, I stepped forward inside their reach and jabbed one hand into the wooden face, firmly pressing one of my thumbs into one of its eyes. The face howled in outrage. I kept up the pressure, and the hands hesitated.

"Play nice," I said. "Lose the arms."

They snapped back into the wood and were gone. I took my thumb out of the eye, and the face pouted at me sullenly.

"Big bully! I'm going to tell on you! See if I don't!"

"Let me in," I said. "Or there will be... unpleasantness."

"You can't come in without saying the password!"

"Fine," I said. "What's the password?"

"You have to tell me."

"I just did."

"No you didn't!"

"Yes I did. Weren't you listening, door? What did I just say to you?"

"What?" said the face. "What?"

"What's the password?" I said sternly.

"Swordfish!"

"Correct! You can let me in now."

The door unlocked itself and swung open. The face had developed a distinct twitch and was muttering querulously to itself as the door closed behind me. The club lobby looked very plush, or at least, what little of it I could see beyond the great hulking ogre that was blocking my way. Eight feet tall and almost as wide, he wore an oversized dinner jacket and a bow tie. The ogre flexed his muscled arms menacingly and cracked his knuckles loudly. One look at the low forehead and lack of chin convinced me there was absolutely no point in trying to talk my way past this guardian. So I stepped smartly forward, holding his eyes with mine, and kicked him viciously in the unmentionables. The ogre whimpered once, his eyes rolled right back in their sockets, and he fell over sideways. He hit the lobby floor with a crash and stayed there, curled into a ball. The bigger they are, the easier some targets are to hit. I walked unchallenged past the ogre and all the way across the lobby to the swinging doors that led into the nightclub proper.

Most of the lights were turned down here, and the Cavern was all gloom and shadows. Bare stone walls under a threateningly low stone ceiling, a waxed and polished floor, high-class tables and chairs, and a raised stage at the far end. The chairs were stacked on top of the tables at the moment, and there were multi-coloured streamers curled around them and scattered across the floor. The only oasis of light in the club was the bar, way over to the right, open now just for the club staff and the artistes. A dozen or so night-time souls clustered together at the bar, like bedraggled moths drawn to the light.

I stepped out across the open floor towards them. Nobody challenged me. They just assumed that if I'd got in, I was supposed to be there. I nodded politely to the cleaning staff, busy getting the place ready for the next shift—half a dozen monkeys in bellhop uniforms, hooting mournfully as they pushed their mops around, passing a single hand-rolled back and forth between them. Lots of monkeys doing menial work in the Nightside these days. Some still even have their wings.

At the bar, the ladies in their faded dressing gowns and wraps didn't even look up as I joined them. The smell of gin and world-weariness was heavy on the air. Come showtime, these women would be all dolled up in sparkly costumes, with fishnet tights and high heels and tall feathers bobbing over their heads, hair artificially teased, faces bright with gaudy make-up... but that was then, and this was now. In the artificial twilight of the empty club, the chorus line and backup singers and hostesses wore no make-up, had their hair up in curlers, and as often as not a ciggie protruding grimly from the corner of a hardened mouth. They looked like soldiers resting from an endless war.

The bartender was some kind of elf. I can never tell them apart. He looked at me suspiciously.

"Relax," I said. "I'm not from Immigration. Just a special investigator, hoping to spread a little bribe money around where it'll do the most good for everyone concerned."

The ladies gave me their full attention. Cold eyes, hard mouths, ready to give away absolutely nothing without seeing cold cash up front. I sighed inwardly, pulled a wad of folding money out of an inner pocket, and snapped it down on the bar top. I kept my hand on top of it and raised an eyebrow. A short-haired platinum blonde leaned forward so that the front of her wrap fell open, allowing me a good look at her impressive cleavage, but I wasn't that easily distracted. Though it really *was* impressive...

"I'm here to see Rossignol," I said loudly, keeping my eyes well away from the platinum blonde. "Where can I find her?"

A redhead with her hair up in cheap plastic curlers snorted loudly. "Best of luck, darling. She won't even speak to me, and I'm her main backing vocalist. Snotty little madam, she is."

"Right," said the platinum blonde. "Too good to mix with the likes of us. Little Miss Superstar. Speak to Ian, that's him up there on the stage. He's her roadie."

She nodded towards the shadowy stage, where I could just make out a short sturdy man wrestling a drum kit into position. I nodded my thanks, took my hand off the wad of cash, and walked away from the bar, letting the ladies sort out the remuneration for themselves. There was the sound of scuffling and really bad language by the time I got to the stage. I knocked on the wood with one knuckle, to get the roadie's attention. He came out from the drum kit and nodded to me. He seemed quite cheerful, for a hunchback. He swayed slightly from side to side as he came forward to join me, and I pulled myself up onto the stage. Up close, he was only slightly stooped on his bowed legs, with massive arms. He wore a T-shirt bearing the legend *Do Lemmings Sing the Blues?*

"How do, mate. I'm Ian Auger, roadie to the stars, travelling musician, and good luck charm. My grandfather once smelled Queen Victoria. What can I do for you, squire?"

"I'm looking to speak with Rossignol," I said. "I'm..."

"Oh, I know who you are, sunshine. John bloody Taylor, his own bad and highly impressive self. Private eye and king-in-waiting, if you believe the gossip, which I mostly don't. You're here about the suicides, I suppose? Thought so. Word was bound to get out eventually. I warned them, I said they couldn't hope to keep a lid on it for long, but does anyone here ever listen to me? What do you think?" He grinned cheerfully and lit up a deadly little black cigar with a battered gold lighter. "So, John Taylor. You here to make trouble for my little girl?"

"No," I said carefully. Behind the cheerful conversation, Ian's blue eyes were as cold as ice, and he had the look of someone who had very straight forward ideas on how to deal with problems. And the ideas probably involved blunt instruments. "I'm just interested in what's happening here. Maybe I can find a solution. It's what I do."

"Yeah, I've heard of some of the things you do." He considered the matter for a long moment, then shrugged. "Look, mate, I've been with Ross a long time. I'm her roadie, I set up the equipment and do the sound checks, I play her music, I take care of all the shit work so she doesn't have to. I look after her, right? I do the work of three men, and I don't begrudge a moment of it, because she's worth it. I've roadied for all sorts in my time, but she's the real thing. She's going to be big, really big. I was her manager, originally. The first one to see what she had and what she could be. I took her here and there in the Nightside, got her started, but I always knew she'd leave me behind. It doesn't matter. A voice like hers comes along once in a lifetime. I just wanted to be part of her legend."

"I thought Rossignol was managed by the Cavendishes," I said.

He shrugged. "I always knew she'd move on. I couldn't open the doors for her that the Cavendishes could. They're big, they're *connected*. But..."

"Go on," I prompted him, when he paused a little too long. He scowled and took his cigar out of his mouth and looked at it so he wouldn't have to look at me.

"This should have been Ross's big break. Caliban's Cavern; biggest, tastiest nightspot in the whole of Uptown. Just the right place to be seen, to be heard, to be *noticed*. But it's all gone wrong. She's changed since she came here. All she ever sings now are sad songs, and she sings them so powerfully that people in the audience go home and kill themselves. Sometimes they don't make it all the way home. God knows how many there've been... The Cavendishes are doing their best to cover it up, at least until the recording contract's signed, but word's getting out. They do so love to gossip in the music biz."

"Doesn't it put people off coming to see her?" I said.

Ian almost laughed. "Nah... that's all part of the thrill, innit? Makes her even more glamorous, to a certain type of fan. This is the Nightside, after all, always looking for the next new sensation. And Russian roulette is so last week..."

"What are the Cavendishes doing to investigate the phenomenon?"

"Them? Naff all! They never even show their faces down here. Just send the bullyboys around, to keep an eye on things, and put the wind up any investigative journalists that might come sniffing around." He smiled briefly. "They don't much care for private eyes either, mate. You watch yourself."

I nodded, carefully unimpressed. "Where can I find Rossignol?"

"She's still my girl," said Ian. "Even if she doesn't have much time for me these days. Are you here to help her, or are you just interested in the bloody *phenomenon*?"

"I'm here to help," I said. "Stopping innocent people dying has got to be in everyone's best interests, hasn't it?"

"She's in her dressing room, round the back." He gave me directions, then looked away from me, his gaze brooding and strangely sad. "I wish we'd never come here, her and me. This wasn't what I wanted for her. If it was up to me, I'd say stuff the money and stuff the contract, something's *wrong* here. But she doesn't listen to me any more. Hardly ever leaves her dressing room. I only get to see her when I'm onstage playing for her to sing to."

"Where does she go when she isn't here?"

"She's always here," Ian said flatly. "Cavendishes arranged a room for her, upstairs. Very comfortable, all the luxuries, but it's still just a bloody room. I don't think Ross has left the club once since she got here. Doesn't have a private life, doesn't care about anything but the next show, the next performance. Not healthy, not for a growing girl like her, but then, there's nothing healthy about Ross's career, since she took up with the bloody Cavendishes."

I started to turn away, but Ian called me back.

"She's a good kid, but... don't expect too much from her, okay? She's not herself any more. I don't know who she is, these days."

I found Rossignol's dressing room easily enough. The two immaculate gentlemen guarding her door weren't everyday bodyguards. The Cavendishes had clearly spent some serious money on internal security. These bodyguards wore Armani suits, and each bore a tattooed ideogram above his left eyebrow that indicated they were the property of the Raging Dragon Clan. Which meant they were magicians, martial artists, and masters of murder. The kind of heavy-duty muscle who usually guarded emperors and messiahs-in-waiting. A sensible man would have turned smartly about and disappeared, at speed, but I just kept going. If I let myself get intimidated by anyone, I'd never get anything done. I came to a halt before them and smiled amiably.

"Hi. I'm John Taylor. I do hope there's not going to be any unpleasantness."

"We know who you are," said the one on the left.

"Private eye, con man, boaster, and braggart," said the one on the right.

"King-in-waiting, some say."

"A man of little magic and much bluff, say others."

"We are combat magicians, mystic warriors."

"And you are just a man, full of talk and tricks."

I stood my ground and said nothing, still smiling my friendly smile.

The bodyguard on the left looked at the one on the right. "I think it's time for our coffee break."

The one on the right looked at me. "Half an hour be enough?"

"Three-quarters," I said, just to show I could play hardball.

The two combat magicians bowed slightly to me and walked unhurriedly away. They just might have been able to take me, but they'd never know now. I've always been good at bluffing, but it helps that most people in the Nightside aren't too tightly wrapped, at the best of times. I knocked on the dressing room door, and when no-one answered, I let myself in.

Rossignol was sitting on a chair, facing her dressing room mirror, studying her reflection in the mirror. She didn't even look round as I shut the door behind me. Her face was calm, and quietly sad, lost in the depths of her own gaze. I leaned back against the closed door and looked her over carefully. She was a tiny little thing, only five feet tall, slender, gamine, dressed in a blank white T-shirt and washed-out blue jeans.

She had long, flat, jet-black hair, framing a pale pointed face that was almost ghostly in the sharp unforgiving light of the dressing room. She had high cheekbones, a long nose, pale pink lips, and not a trace of make-up. If she was thinking anything, it didn't show in her expression. Her hands were clasped loosely together in her lap, as though she'd forgotten they were there. I said her name aloud, and she turned slowly to face me. I did wonder for a moment whether she might have been drugged, given a little something to keep her calm and manageable, but that thought disappeared the moment I met her gaze. Her eyes were large and a brown so dark they were almost black, full of fire and passion. She smiled briefly at me, just a faint twitching of her pale mouth.

"I don't get many visitors these days. I like it that way. How did you get past the two guard dogs at my door?"

"I'm John Taylor."

"Ah, that explains many things. You are perhaps the only person in the Nightside with a more disturbing reputation than mine." She spoke English perfectly, with just enough of a French accent to make her effortlessly charming. "So now, why would the infamous John Taylor be interested in a poor little nightclub singer like me?"

"I've been hired to look into your welfare. To make sure you're all right and not being taken advantage of."

"How nice. Who hired you? Not the Cavendishes, I assume."

I gave her a brief smile of my own. "My client wishes to remain confidential."

"And I do not get a say in the matter?"

"I'm afraid not."

"It is my life we are discussing, Mr. Taylor."

"Please. Call me John."

"As you wish. You may call me Ross. You still haven't answered my question, John. What makes you think I need your assistance? I assure you, I am perfectly safe and happy here."

"Then why the heavy muscle outside your door?"

Her mouth made a silent moue of distaste. "They keep the more obsessive fans at bay. The over-enthusiastic and the stalkers. Ah, my audience! They would fill every moment of my life, if they could. I need time to myself, to be myself."

"What about friends and family?"

"I have nothing to say to them." Ross folded her arms across her chest and gave me a hard, angry stare. "Where were they when I needed them? For years they didn't want to know me, never answered my letters or my pleas for but a little support, to keep me going until my career took off. But the moment I became just a little bit famous, and there was the scent of real money in the air, ah then, suddenly all my family and my so-called friends were all over me, looking for jobs and hand-outs and a chance to edge their way into the spotlight, too. To hell with them. To hell with them all. I have learned the hard way to trust no-one but myself."

"Not even your roadie, Ian?"

She smiled genuinely for the first time. "Ian, yes. Such a sweet boy. He believed in me, even during the bad times when I was no longer sure myself. There will always be a place for him with me, for as long as he wants it. But at the end of the day, I am the star, and I will decide what his place is." She shrugged briefly. "Not even the closest of friends can always climb the ladder at the same pace. Some will always be left behind."

I decided to change the subject. "I understand you live here, in the club?"

"Yes." She turned away from me and went back to looking at herself in the mirror. She was looking for something, but I didn't know what. Maybe she didn't either. "I feel safe here," she said slowly. "Protected. Sometimes it seems like the whole world wants a piece of me, and there's only so much to go round. It's not easy being a star, John. You can take lessons in music, and movement, and how to get the best out of a song, but there's no-one to teach you how to be a success, how to deal with suddenly being famous and in demand. Everybody wants something... The only ones I can trust any more are my management. Mr. and Mrs. Cavendish. They're only interested in the money I can make for them... and I can deal with that."

"There have been stories, of late," I said carefully. "About mysterious, unexplained suicides..."

She looked back at me, smiling sadly. "You of all people should know better than to believe in such gossip, John. It's all just publicity stories that got out of hand. Exaggerations, to put my name on everyone's lips. Everyone claims to have heard the story direct from a friend of a friend, but no-one can ever name anyone who actually died. The Nightside does so love to gossip, and it always prefers bad news to good. I'm just a singer who loves to sing... Talk to the Cavendishes, if you're seriously worried. I'm sure they will be able to reassure you. And now, if you will be so good as to excuse me, I need to prepare myself. I have a show to do soon."

And she went back to staring at her face in the mirror, her chin cupped in one hand, her eyes lost in her own thoughts. I let myself out, and she didn't even notice I was gone.

FOUR

CAVENDISH PROPERTIES

I made my way back to the club bar, the tune from "There's No Business Like Show Business" playing sardonically in the back of my head. My encounter with Rossignol hadn't been everything it might have been, but it had been... interesting. My first impressions of her were muddled, to say the least. She'd seemed sharp enough, particularly her tongue, but there was no denying there was something *wrong* about Rossignol. Some *missing* quality... as though some vital spark had been removed, or suppressed. All the lights were on, but the curtains were a little too tightly closed. It didn't seem to be drugs, but that still left magical controls and compulsions. Not to mention soul thieves, mindsnakes, and even possession. There's never any shortage of potential suspects in the Nightside.

Though what major players like that would want with a mere up-and-coming singer like Rossignol... Ah hell, maybe she was just plain crazy. No shortage of crazies in the Nightside either. In the end, it all came down to her singing. I'd have to come back again, watch her perform, listen to what she did with her voice. See what it did to her audience. After taking certain sensible precautions, of course. Certain defences. There are any number of magical creatures, mostly female, whose singing can bring about horror and death. Sirens, undines, banshees, Bananarama tribute bands...

Back at the bar I used their phone to call my new Nightside office and see how Cathy was getting on with her research into the Cavendishes. The elf bartender didn't raise any objections. He saw me coming and retreated quickly to the other end of the bar, where he busied himself cleaning a glass that didn't need cleaning. The chorus in their wraps and dressing gowns now had a bottle of gin each and were growing definitely raucous, like faded birds of paradise with a really bad attitude. One of them had produced a copy of the magazine *Duelling Strap-ons*, and they were all making very unkind comments about the models in the photos. I looked deliberately in the opposite direction and pressed the phone hard against my ear.

I don't use a mobile phone in the Nightside any more. It makes it far too easy for anyone to find me. Besides, signals here have a tendency to go weird on you. You can end up connected to all kinds of really wrong numbers, talking to anyone or anything, from all kinds of dimensions, in the past, present, and future. And sometimes in between calls, you can hear something whispering what sounds like really awful truths... I had my last mobile phone buried in deconsecrated ground and sowed the earth with salt, just to be sure.

My secretary answered the phone before the second ring, which suggested she'd been waiting for my call. "John, where the hell are you?"

"Oh, out and about," I said cautiously. "What's the matter? Problems?"

"You could say that. Walker's been by the office. In his own calm and quiet way he is really not happy with you, John. He started with threats, escalated to open menace, and demanded to know where you were. Jail was mentioned, along with excommunication, and something that I think involves boiling oil and a funnel. Luckily, I was honestly able to say I hadn't a clue where you were, at the moment. You don't pay me enough to lie to Walker. He once made a corpse sit up and answer his questions, you know."

"I know," I said. "I was there. Where's Walker now?"

"Also out and about, looking for you. He says he's got something with your name on it, and I'm pretty sure it's not a warrant. Did you really black out half the Nightside? Do you need backup? Do you want me to contact Suzie Shooter or Razor Eddie?"

"No, thank you, Cathy. I'm quite capable of handling Walker on my own."

"In your dreams, boss."

"Tell me what you've found out about the Cavendishes. Anything useful? Anything tasty?"

"Not much, really," Cathy admitted reluctantly. "There's very little direct information available about Mr. and Mrs. Cavendish. I couldn't even find out their first names. There's nothing at all on them in any of the usual databases. They believe very firmly in keeping themselves to themselves, and their business records are protected by firewalls that even my computers from the future couldn't crack. They're currently sulking, by the way, and comforting themselves by sending abusive e-mails to Bill Gates. I've been ringing round, tapping all my usual sources, but once I mention the Cavendishes, most of them clam up, too afraid to speak, even on a very secure line. Of course, this being the Nightside, you can always find someone willing to talk... It's up to you how much faith you want to put in people like that."

"Just give me what you've got, Cathy."

"Well... Current gossip says that given the kind of deals the Cavendishes have been making recently—sales of property, calling in debts, grabbing at every short-term deal that's going—it's entirely possible they have an urgent need for money. Liquid cash, not investment. There are suggestions that either a Big Deal went seriously wrong, and won't be paying off as hoped, or that they need the money to support a new Big Deal. Or both. There are definite indications that the Cavendishes have recently moved away from their usual conservative investments in favour of high-risk/high-yield options, but that could just be the market."

"When did they make the move into show business?"

"Ah," said Cathy. "They've spent the last couple of years establishing themselves as big-time agents, managers, and promoters of up-and-coming new talent. They've thrown around a lot of money, without much to show for it so far. And again there's gossip that something went seriously wrong with their earlier attempt to promote a new singing sensation at Caliban's Cavern. Sylvia Sin really looked like she was going places for a time. Her face was all over the covers of the music and lifestyle magazines last year, but she went missing very suddenly, and no-one's seen her since. Sylvia Sin has completely disappeared, which isn't an easy thing to do, in the Nightside."

"Give me the bottom line, Cathy."

"All right. Cavendish Properties is an important, respectable, and wide-ranging business, with most of its money still in property and shares. Their showbiz ventures are backed up by serious capital investment, but though they've got dozens of acts on their books, Rossignol is the only potential big breakout. There's a lot of money riding on her being a big success. They can't afford for her to be another Sylvia Sin."

"Interesting," I said. "Thanks, Cathy. I'll look by later, when I get a chance. If Walker should show up again..."

"I know, hide in the loo and pretend no-one's home."

"Got it in one," I said. "Now, tell me where to find the Cavendishes."

Clearly the next logical step was to go and brace the Cavendishes in their lair and ask a few impertinent questions, so I left Caliban's Cavern and went walking through the long night, heading through Uptown towards the Business Area. It wasn't a long walk, and the crowds thinned away appreciably as I left show behind and headed towards business. In the end, it was like crossing a line between tinsel and glamour, and stark reality. Bright and gaudy clubs and restaurants were replaced by sober, stern-faced buildings, and the clamour of the Nightside at play was replaced by the thoughtful quiet of the Nightside at work. The Business Area was right on the edge of Uptown, and as close to respectable as the Nightside got. All City Gents in smart suits, with briefcases and rolled umbrellas. But it still paid to be wary—in the Nightside, business people aren't always people. Beings from higher and lower dimensions were always setting up shop here, hoping to make their fortune, and the battles were no less vicious for being waged in boardrooms.

The Cavendishes' building was right where Cathy had said it would be—an old Victorian edifice, still defiantly old-fashioned in aspect, with no name or number anywhere. Either you had business there, and knew where to find it, or the Cavendishes didn't give a damn. They weren't supposed to be easy to find. The Cavendishes weren't just successful, they were exclusive, like their club. I stood some distance away from the front door and looked the place over thoughtfully. The Cavendishes had surrounded their own private little kingdom with a hell of a lot of magical protection, most of it so strong I didn't even need to raise my Sight to detect it. I could feel it, like insects crawling over my skin. There was a tension on the air, of some terrible unseen watching presence, of immediate and dreadful danger. The building was definitely protected by Something, either from Above or Below. The feelings weren't strong enough to scare off anyone who had proper business in the building, but it was more than enough to put the wind up casual visitors or even innocent passersby. And certainly enough to keep most visitors cautious, and maybe even honest.

There was nothing subtle about this building's defences. The Cavendishes wanted everyone to know they were protected.

I approached the front door confidently, as though I had every reason to be there, and pushed it open. Nothing happened. I strode into the lobby like I owned the place, trying hard to ignore the feeling that I had a target painted on my forehead. The lobby was large, plush, very comfortable. Pictures on the walls, fresh flowers in vases, business men sitting in upholstered chairs, reading the *Night Times* and waiting to be called. I headed for the reception desk, and a young man and a young woman moved immediately forward to intercept me. It seemed I was expected. The two combat magicians at the nightclub must have phoned home. I smiled at the man and the woman heading my way, started to say something clever, and stopped. There was no point. They were both Somnambulists. Dressed in basic black, their faces were pale and calm and empty, their eyes tight shut. They were both fast asleep. Somnambulists rent out their sleeping bodies for other people to use. Usually they're indentured servants, paying off debts. They have no say in what's done with their bodies, and any resulting damage is their problem. Their owners, or more properly their puppet masters, can do anything they want, indulge any appetite or fantasy, for as long as the contract lasts. Or until the body wears out. That's the deal.

The real problem, for people like me, is that Somnambulists can't be bluffed or fooled or distracted by clever words. Which meant I was in real trouble. So I just shrugged and smiled and nodded to them, and said, "Take me to your leader."

The man punched me in the head. He moved so quickly I didn't even see it coming. I fell to the floor, and the woman kicked me in the ribs. I tried to scramble away, but in a moment they were all over me, both of them kicking me so hard I could feel ribs cracking. They kept in close, leaving me no room to escape, so I curled into a ball, protecting my head as best I could. The attack had been so sudden and so brutal I couldn't get my thoughts together to try any of my usual defences. All I could do was take it, and promise myself revenge later.

The beating went on for a long, long time.

Occasionally I'd get a glimpse of the other people in the lobby, but none of them even looked my way. They knew better than to get involved. They had their deals with the Cavendishes and absolutely no intention of putting them at risk. And I knew better than to call for help. I curled up tight, my body shuddering with every blow, damned if I'd give my enemies the satisfaction of hearing me cry out. And then one boot connected solidly with my head, and everything went fuzzy for a while.

The next thing I knew I was in an elevator, going up. The Somnambulists were standing on either side of my slumped body, faces empty, eyes closed. I lay still, doing nothing that might attract their attention. I hurt everywhere I could feel, pain so bad it made me sick. My thoughts were slow and drifting. I flexed my fingers slowly, then my toes, and they all worked. Breathing hurt, which suggested cracked and maybe even broken ribs. My mouth was full of blood. I let it drool out one side and tested my teeth with my tongue. A few felt worryingly loose, but at least I hadn't lost any. I hoped I hadn't wet myself. I hate it when that happens. It had been a long time since I took a beating this bad. Probably piss blood for a week. I'd forgotten the first rule of the Nightside—it doesn't matter how bad you think you are, there's always someone nastier. Still, this visit wasn't a total loss. I'd come looking for evidence that the Cavendishes were guilty of something, and this would do just fine.

The elevator stopped with a jerk that rocked my body, and the pain almost made me cry out. The doors opened, and the Somnambulists bent down, picked me up and carried me out. I didn't try to fight them. Partly because I wasn't in any shape to, but mostly because I was pretty sure they were taking me where I wanted to go—to meet their masters, the Cavendishes. They carried me across an office and dropped me like a rubbish bag before the reception desk. The thick carpet absorbed some of the impact, but it still hurt like hell, and I went away for a few moments.

When I came back, the Somnambulists were gone. I turned my head slowly, cautiously, and saw the door to an inner office closing. I relaxed a little and slowly forced myself up onto my hands and knees. New pains flared up with every move, and I spat mouthfuls of thick and stringy blood onto the luxurious carpet. I ended up sitting awkwardly, favouring the ribs on my left side, leaning the other side carefully against the reception desk for support. Someone was going to pay for this.

I was hurt, shaken, sick, and dizzy, but I knew I had to get my wits back together before the Somnambulists returned, to drag me before the Cavendishes. They didn't want me dead, or at least, not yet. The beating had been to soften me up, before the interrogation. Well, bad luck for them. I don't do soft. I had to wonder what they thought I knew... I eased a handkerchief out of my pocket with a shaking hand and gently mopped the worst of the blood from my bruised and beaten face. One eye was already so swollen and puffy that I couldn't see out of it. The handkerchief was so much a mess when I'd finished that I just dropped it on the expensive carpet. Let someone else worry about it.

I peered up and over the reception desk, and saw one of those icily gorgeous secretaries who are de rigueur in all the better offices. The kind who would bite their own limbs off before letting you past without an appointment. She studiously ignored me. The phone rang, and she answered it in a cool and utterly business like way, as though there wasn't a half-dead private eye bleeding all over her lousy carpet. It could have been just another day in any office, anywhere.

I turned around slowly, gritting my teeth against the shooting pains, and put my back against the desk. After I'd got my breath back from the exertion, I realised there were other people in the office apart from me. In fact, there was quite a crowd of them, filling all the chairs, sitting cross-legged on the carpet, and leaning against the walls. Young, slim, fashionable and Goths to a boy and a girl, they lounged bonelessly, flipping through music and lifestyle magazines, chatting quietly and comparing tattoos, and checking out their elaborate make-up in hand mirrors. They all had the same uniform of black on black, pale faces and heavy dark eye make-up. Skin like chalk, eyes like holes—Death's clowns. Piercings and purple mouths and silver ankhs on chains. A spindly girl curled up in a chair noticed me watching and put aside her copy of *Bite Me* magazine to consider me dispassionately.

"Damn, they really put a world of hurt on you. What did you do to make them mad?"

"I was just being me," I said, trying hard to keep my voice sounding light and effortless. "I have this effect on a lot of people. What are you doing here?"

"Oh, we're all just hanging out. We run errands, sign fan photos for the stars, do a bit of everything really, just to help out. In return, we get to hang, hear all the latest gossip first. And sometimes we even get to meet the stars, when they show up here. Our favourite's Rossignol, of course."

"Of course," I said.

"Oh, she is just the best! Sings like a dark angel, love and death all wrapped up in one easy-on-the-eyes package. She sings like she's been there, and it's all going to end tomorrow... we all just adore Rossignol!"

"Yeah," said a skull-faced boy, in his best sepulchral growl. "We all love Rossignol. We'd die for her."

"What makes her so special?" I asked. "Worth dying for?"

They all looked at me like I was mad.

"She is just so *cool*, man!" a barely legal girl said finally, tossing her long black hair angrily, and I knew that was all the answer I was going to get.

"So," said one of the others. "Are you, you know, anyone?"

"I'm John Taylor," I said.

They all looked at me blankly and went back to their magazines and their conversations. If you weren't in the music biz, you weren't anyone. And none of them gave a damn about my condition or predicament. They wouldn't risk doing anything that might get them banned from the office and their chance to meet the stars. Fans. You have to love them.

The door to the inner office swung open, and the Somnambulists reappeared. They headed straight for me, and I tried not to wince. They picked me up with brutal efficiency and half carried, half dragged me into the inner office. They dumped me on the floor again, and it took me a moment to get my breath back. I heard the door close firmly shut behind me. I forced myself up onto my knees, and then two hands slapped down hard on my shoulders to keep me there. Two stern figures were standing before me, wearing matching frowns, but I deliberately looked away. The inner office was surprisingly old-fashioned, almost Victorian in its trappings—all heavy furniture and solid comforts. Hundreds of identical books lined the walls, looking as old and well used as the furniture. No flowers here. The room smelled close and heavy, like clothes that had been worn too long.

Finally, I looked at my hosts. The Cavendishes resembled long spindly scarecrows clad in undertakers' cast-offs. Even standing still, there was something awkward and ungainly about them, as though they might topple over if they lost concentration. Their clothes were City Gent, both the man and the woman—characterless, anonymous, timeless. Their faces were unhealthily pale, the skin unnaturally perfect, without flaw or blemish, with that tight, taut look that usually comes from too many face-lifts. I didn't think so, in their case. The Cavendishes' faces were unlined because they'd probably never experienced an honest emotion in their lives.

They both stepped forward suddenly, to stand right in front of me, and their movements were eerily synchronised. Mr. Cavendish had short dark hair, a pursed pale mouth, and a flat, almost emotionless glare, as though I was less an enemy than a problem that needed solving. Mrs. Cavendish had long dark hair, good bone structure, a mouth so thin there were hardly any lips to it, and exactly the same eyes.

They made me think of spiders, contemplating what their web had brought them.

"You have no business here," the man said suddenly, the words cold and clipped. "No business. Isn't that right, Mrs. Cavendish?"

"Indeed it is, Mr. Cavendish," said the woman, in a very nearly identical voice. "Up to no good, I'll be bound."

"Why do you interfere in our business, Mr. Taylor?" said the man.

"You must explain yourself," said the woman.

Their manner of speech was eerily identical, almost without inflection. Their gaze bored into mine, stern and unblinking. I tried a friendly smile, and a thin rill of blood spilled down my chin from a split lip.

"Tell me," I said. "Is it really true you're brother and sister as well as husband and wife?"

I braced myself for the beating, but it still hurt like hell. When the Somnambulists finally stopped, at some unseen signal, it was only their grip on my shoulders that kept me upright.

"We always use Somnambulists," said the man. "The very best kind of servants. Isn't that so, Mrs. Cavendish?"

"Indeed yes, Mr. Cavendish. No back talk, and no treacherous independence."

"Good help is so hard to find these days, Mrs. Cavendish. A sign of the times, I fear."

"As you have remarked before, Mr. Cavendish, and quite rightly." The woman and the man looked at me all the time they were speaking, never once even glancing at each other.

"We know of you, John Taylor," said the man. "We are not impressed, nor are we disposed to endure your famous insolence. We are the Cavendishes. We are Cavendish Properties. We are people of substance and of standing, and we will suffer no intrusions into our affairs."

"Quite right, Mr. Cavendish," said the woman. "You are nothing to us, Mr. Taylor. Normally, you would be utterly beneath our notice. You are only one little man, of dubious parentage. We are a corporation."

"The singer Rossignol is one of our Properties," said the man. "Mrs. Cavendish and I own her contract. Her career and life are ours to manage, and we always protect what's ours."

"Rossignol belongs to us," said the woman. "We own everything and everyone on our books, and we never let go of anything that's ours."

"Except to make a substantial profit, Mrs. Cavendish."

"Right you are, Mr. Cavendish, and I thank you for reminding me. We don't like anyone taking an unhealthy interest in how we manage our affairs, Mr. Taylor. It is no-one's business but ours. Many would-be heroes have tried to meddle in our concerns, down the years. We are still here, and mostly they are not. A wise man would deduce a useful lesson from these facts."

"How are you planning to stop me?" I said, not quite as distinctly as I would have liked. My lower lip was swelling painfully. "These sleeping beauties can't follow me around all the time."

"On the whole, we deplore violence," said the man. "It's so... common. So we have others perform it for us, as necessary. If you annoy us again, if you so much as approach Rossignol again, you will be crippled. And if you choose not to heed that warning, you will be killed. In a sufficiently unpleasant manner to discourage any others who might presume to interfere in our business."

"Still," said the woman, "we are reasonable people, are we not, Mr. Cavendish?"

"Business people, Mrs. Cavendish, first and foremost."

"So, let us talk business, Mr. Taylor. How much do you require to work for us, and only us?"

"To become one of our people, Mr. Taylor."

"A valued part of Cavendish Properties, and thus entitled to enjoy our goodwill, remuneration, and protection."

"Not a chance in hell," I said. "I'm for hire, not for sale. And I already have a client."

The Somnambulists stirred on either side of me, and I flinched despite myself, expecting another beating. A sensible man would have played along, but I was too angry for that. They'd taken away my pride—all I had left was my defiance. The Cavendishes sighed in unison.

"You disappoint us, Mr. Taylor," said the woman. "I think we will let the proper Authorities deal with you, this time. We have already contacted Mr. Walker, to complain about your unwanted presence, and he was most interested to learn of your present location. It seems he is most anxious to catch up with you. He is on his way here now, in person, to express his displeasure with you and take you off our hands. Whatever can you have done, Mr. Taylor, to upset him so?"

"Sorry," I said. "I never kiss and tell."

The Somnambulists started to move again, and I reached into an inside pocket of my trench coat and grabbed one of the packets I kept there for emergencies, recognising it immediately by shape and texture. I pulled the packet out as the

Somnambulists leaned over me, tore it open, and threw the pepper into their faces. The heavy dark powder hit them squarely in the nose and eyes, and they both breathed it in before they could stop themselves. And then they were both sneezing, loud, vicious sneezes that made their whole bodies convulse. Tears rolled out from under their closed eyes, and they fell back from me, sneezing so hard and so often they could hardly stay upright. And still the sneezing went on as the pepper did its unrelenting work.

Both Somnambulists bent forward from the waist, tears forcing themselves from their closed eyes, and in a moment they were both wide awake. The shock to their systems had been too much, the sheer strength of the involuntary physical reactions had been enough to overcome their enforced sleep. They were both wide awake, and hating every moment of it. They clutched at each other for support and looked around through watering eyes. I lurched to my feet and glared at them both.

"I'm John Taylor," I said, in my very best Voice of Doom. "And I am really upset with you."

The two awakened Somnambulists looked at me, looked at each other, in between sneezes, then turned and ran. They practically fought each other over who got to go through the door first. I grinned, despite my split and swollen lips. There are times when a carefully cultivated bad reputation can come in very handy. So can pepper, and salt. I always keep packets of both in my pockets. Salt is very good for dealing with zombies, for tracing protective circles and pentacles, and as a general purifier. Pepper has many practical uses, too. I carry other things in my pockets, some of them potentially quite viciously nasty, and right then I was in a mood to use every single one of them on the Cavendishes.

I'd like to say I waited till I'd learned all I could before I used the pepper. But the truth is, it had taken me until then to find the strength of will to use it.

I fixed the Cavendishes with a heavy glare. They stared back, apparently unmoved, and the man turned abruptly, picked up a silver bell from his desk, and rang it loudly.

A transport pentacle flared into life in one corner of his office, the pentacle's design shining suddenly in bright actinic lines as it activated, and in a moment there was someone else in the room with us. Someone I knew. He was dressed very formally, in a midnight blue tuxedo, a blindingly white shirt and bow tie, and a sweeping opera cloak, complete with scarlet lining. His carefully styled hair was jet-black, as was his neatly trimmed goatee. His eyes were an icy blue, and his mouth was set in a supercilious sneer. Anyone else would have been impressed, but I knew better.

"Hello, Billy," I said. "Like the outfit. How long have you been a waiter?"

"You look a mess, John," the newcomer said, stepping elegantly out of the transport pentacle, which flickered away into nothing behind him. He checked his cuffs were straight and looked me over disapprovingly. "Nasty. I always said that someday you'd run into trouble your rep couldn't get you out of. And don't call me Billy. I am Count Entropy."

"No, you're not," I said. "You're the Jonah. Count Entropy was your father, and a far greater man than you. I remember you, Billy Lathem. We grew up together, and you were a useless little tit then, too. I thought you wanted to be an accountant?"

"I decided there was no money in it. Real money is to be made working for people like the Cavendishes. They keep me on a very handsome retainer, just for such occasions as this. And since my father is dead, I have inherited his title. I am Count Entropy. And I'm afraid I'm going to have to kill you now, John."

I sniffed. "Don't try and impress me, Billy Lathem. I've sneezed scarier-looking objects than you."

Why do bad things happen to good people? Because people like Billy Lathem profit from them. Essentially, he had the power to alter and control probabilities. The Jonah could see all the intertwining links of destiny, the patterns in the chaos, and reach out to choose the one-in-a-million chance for everything to go horribly wrong, and make that single possibility the dominant one. He caused bad luck and delighted in disasters. He destroyed lives and brought down in a moment what it had taken others a lifetime to build. When he was a kid, he did it for kicks—now he did it for money. He was the Jonah, and the misfortunes of others were his meat and drink.

"You're not fit to be Count Entropy," I said angrily. "Your father was a mover and a shaker, one of the Major Powers, revered and respected in the Nightside. He redirected the great energies of the universe."

"And what did it get him, in the end?" said Billy, just as angrily. "He made an enemy of Nicholas Hob, and the Serpent's Son killed him as casually as he would a fly. Forget the good name and the pats on the back. I want money. I want to be filthy, stinking rich. The title's mine now, and the Nightside will learn to fear it."

"Your father..."

"Is dead! I don't miss him. He was always disappointed in me."

"Well, gosh," I said. "I wonder why."

"I'm Count Entropy!"

"No. You'll only ever be the Jonah, Billy. Bad luck to everyone, including yourself. You'll never be the man your father was, and you know it. Your dreams are too small. You're just the Bad Luck Kid, a small-time thug for hire."

He was breathing hard now, his face flushed, but he controlled himself with an effort and gave me his best disdainful sneer.

"You don't look like much right now, John. Those Somnambulists really did a job on you. You look like a passing breeze would blow you away. It shouldn't be too difficult to find a blood clot in your heart, or a burst blood vessel in your brain. Or maybe I'll start with your extremities and work inwards. There are so many nasty things I can do to you, John, so many bad possibilities."

I smiled back at him, showing him my bloody teeth. "Don't you mess with me, Billy Lathem. I'm in a really bad mood. How would you like me to use my gift, and find the one thing you're really afraid of? Maybe if I tried really hard... I could find what's left of your daddy..."

All the colour fell out of his face, and suddenly he looked like a child dressed up in an adult's clothes. Poor Billy. He really was very powerful, but I've been playing this game a lot longer than he has. And I have this reputation... I nodded to the Cavendishes, turned my back on them, and walked out of their office. And then I got the hell out of their building as fast as my battered body could manage.

No-one tried to stop me.

FIVE

THE SINGER, NOT THE SONG

I must be getting old. I don't take beatings as well as I used to. By the time I got out of the Cavendishes' building, my legs were barely holding me up, and a cold sweat was breaking out all over my face. Every breath hurt like someone had stabbed me, and a rolling blackness was moving in and out at the edges of my vision. There was fresh blood in my mouth. Never a good sign. I still kept moving, forcing myself on through sheer effort of will. I needed to be sure I was far enough away from the Cavendishes that they couldn't send the building's defence spells after me. And even when I was sure, I kept going, though I was having to stamp my feet down hard to feel the pavement beneath me. I might look a sight, with my swollen face and blood-stained trench coat, but I couldn't afford to appear weak and vulnerable. Not in the Nightside. There are always vultures hovering, ready to drop on anything that looks like prey. So, stare straight ahead and walk like you've got a purpose. I caught a glimpse of myself, reflected in a window, and winced. I looked almost as bad as I felt. I had to get off the streets.

I needed healing and general repairs, and time out to get my strength back. But I was a long way from home, and I couldn't go to any of my usual haunts. Walker would have his people staking them all out by now. Even the ones he wasn't supposed to know about. And if I called any of my friends or allies, you could bet Walker would have someone listening in. The man was nothing if not thorough.

Well, when you can't go to a friend, go to an enemy.

I dragged my battered, aching body down the street, glaring at everyone to keep them from bumping into me, and finally reached a public phone booth. I hauled myself inside and leaned heavily against the side wall. It felt so good to be able to rest for a moment that I briefly forgot why I'd come in there, but I made myself pick up the phone. The dial tone was loud and reassuring. There tends to be very little vandalism of public phone booths in the Nightside. The booths defend themselves, and have been known to eat people who venture inside for reasons other than making a call.

I didn't know Pew's current number. He's always on the move. But he always makes sure to leave cards in phone booths so that people can find him in an emergency. I peered blearily at the familiar card (bright white with an embossed bloodred crucifix) and stabbed out the numbers with an unsteady hand. I was pretty much blind in one eye by then, and my hands felt worryingly numb. I relaxed a little as I heard the number ringing. I studied the other cards plastered across the glass wall in front of me. The usual mixture—charms and potions and spells, love goddesses available by the hour, transformations and inversions, and how to do horrible things to a goat for fun and profit.

Someone picked up the phone at the other end and said, "This had better be important."

"Hello, Pew," I said, trying hard to sound natural through my puffed-up mouth. "It's John Taylor."

"What the hell are you doing, calling me?"

"I'm hurt. I need help."

"Things must really be bad if I'm your best bet. Why me, Taylor?"

"Because you're always saying you're God's servant. You're supposed to help people in trouble."

"People. Not abominations like you! None of us in the Nightside will be safe until you're dead and buried in unconsecrated ground. Give me one good reason why I should put myself out for you, Taylor."

"Well, if charity won't do it, Pew, how about this? In my current weakened state, I am vulnerable to all kinds of attack, including possession. You really want to face something from the Pit in my body, with my gift?"

"That's a low blow, damn you," said Pew. I could practically hear him thinking it over. "All right, I'll send you a door. If only because I'll never really be sure you're dead unless I've finished you off myself."

The phone went dead, and I put it down. There's no-one closer, outside of family and friends, than an old enemy.

I turned around, slowly and painfully, pushed the booth door open and looked outside. A door was standing right in front of me, in the middle of the pavement. Just a door, standing alone, old and battered with the paint peeling off in long strips, and a rough gap showing bare wood where the number had once been. Probably stolen. Pew lived by choice in the rougher neighbourhoods, where he felt his preaching was most needed. I left the phone booth and headed for the door with the last of my strength. Luckily everyone else was giving it plenty of room, probably because it was so obviously downmarket as to be beneath their notice. I hit the door with my shoulder, and it swung open before me, revealing only darkness. I lurched forward, and immediately I was in Pew's parlour. The door slammed shut behind me.

I headed for the bare table in front of me and leaned gratefully on it as I got my breath back. After a while, I looked around me. There was no sign of Pew, but his parlour seemed very simple and neat. One table, bare wood, unpolished. Two chairs, bare wood, straight-backed. Scuffed lino on the floor, damp-stained wallpaper, and one window smeared over with soap to stop people looking in. The window provided the only illumination. Pew took his vows of poverty and simplicity very seriously. One wall was covered with shelves, holding his various stock in trade. Just useful little items, available for a very reasonable price, to help keep you alive in a dangerous place.

The door at the far end of the parlour slammed open, and Pew stood there, his great head tilted in my general direction. Pew—rogue vicar, Christian terrorist, God's holy warrior.

"Do no harm here, abomination! This is the Lord's place! I bind you in his word, to bring no evil here!"

"Relax, Pew," I said. "I'm on my own. And I'm so weak right now, I couldn't beat up a kitten. Truce?"

Pew sniffed loudly. "Truce, hellspawn."

"Great. Now do you mind if I sit down? I'm dripping blood all over your floor."

"Sit, sit! And try to keep it off the table. I have to eat off that."

I sat down heavily and let out a loud, wounded sigh. Pew shuffled forward, his white cane probing ahead of him. He wore a simple vicar's outfit under a shabby and much-mended grey cloak. His dog collar was pristine white, and the grey blindfold covering his dead eyes was equally immaculate. He had a large head with a noble brow, a lion's mane of grey hair, a determined jaw, and a mouth that looked like it never did anything so frivolous as smile. His shoulders were broad, though he always looked like he was several meals short. He found the other chair and arranged himself comfortably at the opposite end of the table. He leaned his cane against the table leg so he could find it easily, and sniffed loudly.

"I can smell your pain, boy. How badly are you injured?"

"Feels pretty bad," I said. My voice sounded tired, even to me. "I'm hoping it's mostly superficial, but my ribs are holding out for a second opinion, and my head keeps going fuzzy round the edges. I took a real beating, Pew, and I'm not as young as I once was."

"Few of us are, boy." Pew got to his feet and moved unerringly towards the shelves that held his stock. Pew might be blind, but he didn't let it slow him down. He pottered back and forth along the wall, running his hands over the various objects, searching for something. I just hoped it wasn't a knife. Or a scalpel. I could hear him muttering under his breath.

"Wolfsbane, crows' feet, holy water, mandrake root, silver knives, silver bullets, wooden stakes... could have sworn I still had some garlic... dowsing rods, pickled penis, dowsing rod made from a pickled penis, miller medallions... Ah!"

Pew turned back to me, triumphantly holding up a small bottle of pale blue liquid. And then he stopped, his mouth twisted, and his other hand fell to the rosary of human fingerbones hanging from his belt. "How has it come to this? You, alone and helpless in my home, in my power... I should kill you, damnation's child. Bane of all the chosen..."

"I didn't get to choose my parents," I said. "And everyone said my father was a good man, in his day."

"Oh, he was," Pew said unexpectedly. "Never worked with him myself, but I've heard the stories."

"Did you ever meet my mother?"

"No," said Pew. "But I have seen the auguries taken shortly after your birth. I wasn't always blind, boy. I gave up my eyes in return for knowledge, and much good it's done me. You will be the death of us all, John. But my foolish conscience won't let me kill you in cold blood. Not when you come of your own free will, begging my help. It wouldn't be... honourable."

He shook his great head slowly, came forward, and stopped just short of the table. He placed the phial of blue liquid on the table before me. I considered it, as he shuffled back to his chair. There was no identifying label on the phial, nothing to tell whether it was a cure or a poison or something else entirely. Pew collected all kinds of things on his travels.

"Hard times are coming," he said suddenly, as he sat down again. "The Nightside is very old, but it is not forever."

"You've been saying that for years, Pew."

"And it's still true! I know things. I See more without my eyes than I ever did with them. But the further ahead I look, the more unclear things become. By saving you here today, I could be damning every other soul in the Nightside."

"No-one's that important," I said. "And especially not me. What's in the phial, Pew?"

He snorted. "Something that will taste quite appalling, but should heal all your injuries. Knock it back in one, and you can have a nice sweetie afterwards. But magic has its price, John, it always does. Drink that, and you'll sleep for twenty-four hours. And when you wake up, all your injuries will be gone, but you'll be a month older. The price you pay for such accelerated healing will be a life one month shorter than it would otherwise have been. Are you ready to give that up, just to get well in a hurry?"

"I have to," I said. "I'm in the middle of a case, and I think someone needs my help now, rather than later. And who knows, maybe I'll find a way to get the lost month back again. Stranger things have happened, in the Nightside." I paused and looked at Pew. "You didn't have to help me. Thank you."

"Having a conscience can be a real bastard sometimes," said Pew solemnly.

I unscrewed the rusted metal cap on the phial and sniffed the thick blue liquid within. It smelled of violets, a sweet smell to cover something fouler. I tossed down the oily liquid in one and just had time to react to the truly awful taste before everything went black. I woke up lying on my back on the table. My first feeling was relief. Although I'd tried hard to sound confident, there was a real chance Pew might have decided to finish me off while he had the chance. He'd tried often enough in the past. I sat up slowly. I felt stiff, but there was no pain anywhere. Pew had taken off my trench coat and folded it up to make a pillow for my head. I swung my legs down over the side of the table and stretched slowly. I felt good. I felt fine. No pain, no fever, and even the taste of blood was gone from my mouth. I put my hand to my face and was startled to encounter a beard. A month of my life had flown by while I slept... I got to my feet, went over to the wall shelves, and scrabbled among Pew's stock until I came up with a hand mirror. My reflection was a surprise, if not a shock. I had a heavy ragged beard, already showing touches of grey, and my hair was long and straggling. I looked... wild, uncivilised, intimidating. I didn't like the new look. I didn't like to think I could look like that. Like someone Pew would have a right to hunt down and kill.

"Vanity, vanity," said Pew, entering the room. "I knew that would be the first thing you'd do. Put the mirror back. They're very expensive."

I held on to it. "I look a mess!"

"You just be grateful I remembered to dust you once in a while."

"Have you got a razor, Pew? This beard has to go. It's got grey in it. It makes me look my age, and I can't have that."

Pew grinned nastily. "I have a straight razor. Want me to shave you?"

"I don't think so," I said. "I don't trust anyone that close to my throat with a sharp blade."

He chuckled and handed me a pearl-handled straight razor. One dry shave later, with the help of the hand mirror, and I looked like myself again. It wasn't a very good or even a very close shave, but I got tired of nicking myself. I handed back the razor, then did a few stretches and knee bends. I felt fit to take on the world again. Pew sat on his chair like a statue, ignoring me.

"Once you leave here," he said suddenly, "you're fair game again."

"Of course, Pew. You wouldn't want people to think you were getting soft."

"I will kill you one day, boy. The mark of the beast is upon your brow. I can See it."

"You know," I said thoughtfully, changing the subect, "I could use one last piece of help..."

"God save us all, haven't I done enough? Out, out, before you ruin my reputation completely!"

"I need a disguise," I said firmly, not moving. "I have to get back on my case, and I can't afford to be recognised. Come on, you must have something simple and temporary you can let me have..."

Pew sniffed resignedly. "Let this be a lesson to me. Never help the stranger upon his way, because he'll only take advantage, the bastard. Where is it you have to go next?"

"A nightclub called Caliban's Cavern."

"I know it. A den of iniquity, and the bar prices are an outrage. I'd better make you a Goth. There are so many of the grubby little heathens around that place, one more shouldn't be noticed. I'll put a seeming on you, a simple overlay illusion. It won't last more than a couple of hours, and it certainly won't fool anyone with the Sight..." He was pottering along the shelves again, picking things up and putting them down until finally he came up with an Australian pointing bone. He jabbed it twice in my direction, said something short and aboriginal, and put the bone back on the shelf again.

"Is that it?" I said.

Pew shrugged. "Well, you can have all the chanting and gesturing if you want, but I usually save that for the paying customers. It's really nothing more than window dressing. When you get right down to it, magic's never anything more than power and intent, no matter what the source. Look in the mirror."

I did so, and again someone else looked back at me. My face was entirely hidden under a series of swirling black tattoos, thick interlocking lines that made up a series of designs of ancient Maori origin. Along with the shaggy hair, the new look made me completely unrecognisable.

"You'll need another coat, too," said Pew. "Your trench coat's a mess." He held up a battered black leather jacket with *God Give Me Strength* spelled out on the back with steel studs. "You can have this instead."

I tried on the jacket. It was a bit on the large side, but where I was going they wouldn't care. I made my good-byes to Pew, and the parlour door opened before me, revealing a familiar blackness. I walked into the dark, and immediately I was back in Uptown again, only a few minutes' walk from Caliban's Cavern. I heard the door close firmly behind me and knew it would be gone before I could turn to look. I smiled. Pew probably thought he'd put one over on me, by keeping my trench coat. A personal possession like that, liberally stained with my own blood, would make a marvellous targeting device for all kinds of magic. Certainly Pew could use it to send all kinds of nastiness my way. Which was why I'd taken out a little insurance long ago, in the form of a built-in destructive spell for the trench coat. Once I was more than an agreed distance away, the coat would automatically go up in flames. As Pew should be finding out, right about now.

Of course, I'd been careful to transfer all my useful items from the coat to my nice new jacket before I left.

Pew was good, but I was better.

By the time I got back to Caliban's Cavern, the queue was already forming for Rossignol's next set. I'd never seen so many Goths in one place. All dark clothes and brooding faces, like a gathering of small thunderclouds. They were all talking nineteen to the dozen, filling the night with a clamour of anticipation and impatience. Every now and again someone would start chanting Rossignol's name, and a dozen others would take it up until it died away naturally.

Ticket touts swaggered up and down beside the queue, fighting each other to be the first to target latecomers, offering scalped tickets at outrageous prices. There was no shortage of takers. The growing crowd wasn't just Goths. There were a number of celebrities, complete with their own entourages and hangers-on. You could always recognise celebrities from the way their heads swivelled restlessly back and forth, on the lookout for photographers. After all, what was the point of being somewhere fashionable if you weren't seen being there?

The queue stretched all the way down the block, but I didn't let that bother me. I just walked to the very front and took up a position there like I had every right to be there. Nobody bothered me. You'd be amazed what you can get away with if you just exude confidence and glare ferociously at anyone who even looks like questioning your presence. One of the ticket touts was rude enough to make sneering comments about my tattoos, though, so I deliberately bumped into him and pickpocketed one of his best tickets. I like to think of myself sometimes as a karma mechanic.

Caliban's Cavern finally opened its doors, and the queue surged forward. The Cavendishes had hired a major security franchise, Hell's Neanderthals, to man the door and police the crowd, but even they were having trouble handling the pressure of so many determined Rossignol fans. They pressed constantly forward, shouting and jostling, and the security Neanderthals quickly realised that this was the kind of crowd that could turn into an angry mob if its progress was thwarted. They were there to see Rossignol, and no-one was going to get in their way. So, the Hell's Neanderthals settled for grabbing tickets and waving people through. I would have given them strict orders to frisk everyone for weapons and the like, but it was clear any attempt to slow the fans down now would have risked provoking a riot. The fans were close to their goal, their heroine, and they were hungry.

Inside the club, all the tables and chairs had been taken out to make one great open space before the raised stage at the far end of the room. The crowd poured into it, gabbling excitedly, and quickly filled all the space available, packing the club from wall to wall. I was swept along and finally ended up right in front of the stage, with elbows digging into my sides, and someone's hot breath panting excitedly on the back of my neck. The club was already overpoweringly hot and sweaty, and I looked longingly across at the bar, with its extra staff, but it would have taken me ages to fight my way through the tightly packed crowd. No-one else seemed interested in the bar. All the crowd cared about was Rossignol. Their diva of the dark.

There were far too many people in the club, packed in like cattle in their stalls. It didn't surprise me. The Cavendishes hadn't struck me as the type to care about things like safety regulations and keeping fire exits clear. Not when there was serious money to be made.

Set off by a single bright spotlight, a huge stylised black bird (presumably someone's idea of a nightingale) covered most of the wall behind the stage. It looked threatening, wild, ominous. Looking around, I could see the design everywhere on the fans, on T-shirts, jackets, tattoos, and silver totems hanging on silver chains. I could also see the celebrities jammed in the crowd like everyone else, their hangers-on struggling to form protective circles around them. There were no real movers or shakers, but I could see famous faces here and there. Sebastian Stargrave, the Fractured Protagonist; Deliverance Wilde, fashion consultant to the Faerie; and Sandra Chance, the Consulting Necromancer. Also very much in evidence were the supergroup Nazgul, currently on a comeback tour of the Nightside with their new vocalist. They looked just as freaked and excited as everyone else.

And yet, for all the excitement and passion in the air, the overall mood felt decidedly unhealthy. It was the wrong kind of anticipation, like the hunger of animals waiting for feeding time. The hot and sweaty air had the unwholesome feel of a crowd gathered at a car wreck, waiting for the injured to be brought out. These people weren't just here to hear someone sing—this was a gathering throbbing with erotic Thanatos. The mood was magic. Dark, reverent magic, from all the wrong places of the heart.

The crowd was actually quietening down, the chanting dying out, as the anticipation mounted. Even I wasn't immune to it. Something was going to happen, and we could all feel it. Something big, something far out of the ordinary, and we all wanted it. We needed it. And whether what was coming would be good or bad didn't matter a damn. We were a congregation, celebrating our goddess. The crowd fell utterly silent, all our eyes fixed on the stage, empty save for the waiting instruments and microphone stands. Waiting, waiting, and now we were all breathing in unison, like one great hungry creature, like lemmings drawn to a cliff edge by something they couldn't name.

Rossignol's band came running onto the stage, smiling and waving, and the crowd went wild, waving and cheering and stamping their feet. The band took up the instruments waiting for them and started playing. No introductions, no warm-up, just straight in. Ian Auger, the cheerful hunchbacked roadie, played the drums. And the bass and the piano. There were three of him. I felt he might have mentioned it earlier. Next a quartet of backing singers came bounding onstage, wearing old-fashioned can-can outfits, with teased high hairstyles, beautiful and glamorous, with bright red lips and flashing eyes. They joined right in, belting out perfect harmonies to complement the music, stamping their feet and flashing their frills, singing up a storm. And then Rossignol came on, and the massed baying of the crowd briefly drowned out the music. She wore a chic little black number, with long black evening gloves that made her pale skin look even more funereal. Her mouth was dark, and so were her eyes, so that she seemed like some old black-and-white photograph. Her feet were bare, the toenails painted midnight black.

She grabbed hold of the mike stand at the front of the stage with both hands and clung to it like it was the only thing holding her up. As the show progressed, she rarely let go of it, except to light a new cigarette. She stood where she was, her mouth pressed close to the mike like a lover, swaying from side to side. She had a cigarette in one corner of her dark mouth when she came on, and she chain-smoked in between and sometimes during her songs.

The songs she sang were all her own material; "Blessed Losers," "All the Pretty People," and "Black Roses." They had good strong tunes, played well and sung with professional class, but none of that mattered. It was her voice, her glorious suffering voice that cut at the audience like a knife. She sang of lost loves and last chances, of small lives in small rooms, of dreams betrayed and corrupted, and she sang it all with utter conviction, singing like she'd been there, like she'd known all the pain there ever was, all the darknesses of the human heart, of hope valued all the more because she knew it wasn't real, that it wouldn't help; and all the loss and heartbreak there ever was filled her voice and gave it dominion over all who heard it.

There were tears on many faces, including my own. Rossignol had got to me, too. I'd never heard, never felt, anything like her songs, her voice. In the Nightside it's always three o'clock in the morning, the long dark hour of the soul—but only Rossignol could put it into words.

And yet, despite all I was feeling, or was being made to feel, I never entirely lost control. Perhaps because I'm more used than most to the dark, or simply because I had a job to do. I tore my eyes away from Rossignol, reached inside my jacket pocket, and pulled out a miller medallion. It was designed to glow brightly in the presence of magical influence, but when I held it up to face Rossignol, there wasn't even a glimmer of a glow. So Rossignol hadn't been enchanted or possessed or even magically enhanced. Whatever she was doing, it came straight from her, and from her voice.

The audience was utterly engrossed, still and rapt and silent, drinking their diva in with eyes and ears, immersing themselves in emotions so sharp and melancholy and compelling that they were helpless to do anything but stand there and soak it up. It was all they could do to come out of it to applaud her in between songs. The three Ian Augers and the quartet of backing singers were looking tired and drawn, faces wet with sweat as they struggled to keep up with Rossignol, but the crowd only had eyes for her. She hung on to her microphone stand as though it was a lifeline, smoking one cigarette after another, blasting out one song after another, as though it was all she lived to do.

And then, as she paused at the end of one song to light up another cigarette, a man not far from me pressed right up against the edge of the stage, a man who'd been staring adoringly at Rossignol from the moment she first appeared, smiled at her with tears still wet on his cheeks and drew a gun. I could see it happening, but I was too far away to stop it. All I could do was watch as the man put the gun to his head and blew his brains out. All over Rossignol's bare feet.

At the sound of the gun, the Ian Augers looked up sharply from their instruments. The backing singers huddled together, eyes and mouths stretched wide. Rossignol stared blankly down at the dead man. He was still standing there, because the press of the crowd wouldn't allow him to fall, even though half his head was missing. And in the echoing silence, the crowd slowly came back to themselves. As though they'd been shocked awake from a deep dark dream where they'd all been drifting towards... something. I knew, because I'd been feeling it too. Part of me recognised it.

Then the crowd went crazy. Screaming and shouting and roaring in what might have been shock or outrage, they all surged determinedly *forward*. They wanted, they needed, to get to the stage, get to *her*. They fought each other with hands and elbows, snapping like animals. People were crushed, dragged down and trampled underfoot. Those nearest the dead man at the front tore him apart, literally limb from limb, scattering the bloody body parts among them like sacrificial offerings. There was an awful feeling of... celebration in the crowd. As though this was what they'd all been waiting for, even if they didn't know themselves.

I'd already vaulted up onto the stage and out of the way. Rossignol snapped out of her horrified daze, turned, and ran from the stage. The crowd saw her disappear and howled their rage and disapproval. They started to scramble up onto the stage. The backing singers ran forward to the edge of the stage and kicked viciously at people trying to pull themselves up. The three Ian Augers came forward and reinforced the singers with large, bony fists. But they were so few, and the crowd was so large, and so determined. Hell's Neanderthals waded into the crowd from the rear, slapping people down and throwing them in the direction of the exit, whether they wanted to go or not. I started after Rossignol. One of the Ian Augers reached out to grab me, but I've had a lot of practice at dodging unfriendly hands. I headed backstage, just as the first wave of the crowd boiled up over the edge.

Backstage, no-one tried to stop me. Everyone there had their own problems, and once again as long as I moved confidently and like I had a purpose and a right to be there, no-one even looked at me. I saw the two combat magicians coming and ducked through a side door for a moment. They hurried past, dark sparks already sputtering around their fists as they prepared themselves for some magical mayhem. They should be able to hold off the crowd, assuming Stargrave and Chance didn't get involved. If they did, there could be some serious unpleasantness. I waited until I was sure the combat magicians were gone, then headed for Rossignol's dressing room.

She was sitting there alone, again, with her back to the mirror this time. Her eyes were wild, unfocussed, as she struggled to cope with what had just happened. She was trying to scrub the blood and gore off her bare feet with a hand towel. And yet, for all her obvious distress, it seemed to me that this was the most alive I'd ever seen her. She looked up sharply as I came in and shut the door behind me.

"Get out! Get out of here!"

"It's all right, Ross," I said quickly. "I'm not a fan." I concentrated and shrugged off the seeming Pew had placed on me. It was only a small magic, after all. Rossignol recognised me as the tattoos disappeared from my face, and she slumped tiredly.

"Thank God. I could use a friendly face."

She suddenly started to tremble, her whole body shuddering, as the shock caught up with her. I took off my leather jacket and wrapped it gently around her shoulders. She grabbed my hands, squeezing them hard as though to draw some of my strength and warmth into her, then suddenly she was in my arms, holding me like a drowning woman, her tear-stained face pressed against my chest. I held her and comforted her as best I could. We all need a little simple human comfort, now and again. Finally, she let go, and I did, too. I knelt, picked up the hand towel, and cleaned the last of the blood off her feet to give her a moment to compose herself. By the time I'd finished and was looking around for somewhere to dump the towel, she seemed to have calmed down a little.

I straightened up, sat on the dressing room table, and dropped the towel beside me. "Has anything like this ever happened to you before, Ross?"

"No. Never. I mean, there have been rumours, but... no. Never right in front of me."

"Did you recognise the guy?"

"No! Never saw him before in my life! I don't mix with my... audience. The Cavendishes insist on that. Part of building the image, the mystique, they said. I never really believed the rumours... I thought it was just publicity, stories the Cavendishes put about to work up some excitement. I never dreamed..."

"As if we would ever do such a thing, dear Rossignol," said a cold, familiar voice behind me. I got to my feet and looked round, and there in the dressing room doorway were Mr. and Mrs. Cavendish. Tall and aristocratic, and twice as arrogant. They glided in like two dark birds of ill omen, ignoring their property Rossignol to consider me with a cold, thoughtful gaze.

"You do seem in very rude health, Mr. Taylor," said the man. "Does he not, Mrs. Cavendish?"

"Indeed he does, Mr. Cavendish. Quite the picture of good health."

"Perhaps some of the stories about you are true after all, Mr. Taylor."

I just smiled and said nothing. Let them wonder. It all added to the reputation.

"We did think you'd learned your lesson, Mr. Taylor," said the woman.

"Afraid not," I said. "I'm a very slow learner."

"Then we shall just have to try harder," said the man. "Won't we, Mrs. Cavendish?"

Rossignol was looking back and forth, confused. "You know each other?"

"Of course," said the man. "Everyone in the Nightside comes to us, eventually. Do not concern yourself, my dear. And most of all, do not worry yourself about the unfortunate incident during the show. Mrs. Cavendish and I will take care of everything. You must allow us to worry for you. That is what you pay us our forty per cent for."

"*How much?*" I said, honestly outraged.

"Our hard-won expertise does not come cheaply, Mr. Taylor," said the woman. "Not that it is any of your business. Isn't that correct, dear Rossignol?"

She seemed to shrink under their gaze, and she looked down at the floor like a scolded child. "Yes," she said, in a small voice. "That's right."

"What's happening out in the club?" I said.

"The club is being cleared," said the man. "It is a shame that the show had to be cut short, but we did make it clear on the tickets that there would be no refunds, under any circumstances."

"I am sure they will be back again, for the next show," said the woman. "Everyone is so desperate to hear dear Rossignol sing."

"You expect her to go on again, after what just happened?" I said.

"Of course," said the man. "The show must go on. And our dear Rossignol only lives to sing. Isn't that right, dear child?"

"Yes," said Rossignol, still staring at the floor. "I live to sing."

"People are dying!" I said loudly, trying to get a reaction from her. "Not just here, not just right now. This is only the most recent suicide, and the most public. People are taking their own lives because of what they hear when Rossignol sings!"

"Rumour," said the woman. "Speculation. Nothing more than tittle-tattle."

"And there will always be fanatics," said the man. "Poor deranged souls who fly too close to the flame that attracts them. You are not to concern yourself, dear Rossignol. The club will be cleared soon, and all will be made ready for your next performance. We will have extra security in place and take all the proper precautions to ensure your safety. Leave everything to us."

"Yes," said Rossignol. Her voice was heavy now, almost half-asleep. Just the presence of the Cavendishes had reduced her to the same dull state in which I'd first found her. There was no point in talking to her any more. So I shrugged mentally and took my jacket back from around her shoulders. She didn't react. I put it on, and the Cavendishes stepped back to make room for me to leave. I headed for the door like it was my decision, and the Cavendishes glided smoothly aside to let me pass. I was almost out of the room when Rossignol's voice stopped me. I looked back. She had her head up again, and her voice was quiet but determined.

"John, find out what's happening. I need to know the truth. Do this for me. Please."

"Sure," I said. "Saving damsels in distress is what I do."

SIX

ALL THE NEWS, DAMMIT

Every good guest knows better than to outstay his welcome. Especially if he's an uninvited guest, and his hosts want his head on a platter. So I slipped quietly away, passing unnoticed in the general chaos and hysteria backstage, and finally made my exit by a sinfully unguarded back door. The back alley was surprisingly clean and tidy, not to mention well lit, though I did surprise half a dozen of the cleaning monkeys caught up in a red-hot dice game. I murmured my apologies and hurried past them. Monkeys can get really nasty if you interrupt their winning streak.

I moved quietly round the corner of the club and peered down the side alley that led back to the main street. It was empty, for the moment, but there were clear sounds of trouble and associated mayhem out on the street. I padded cautiously forward, sneaking the occasional quick look over my shoulder, and eventually eased up to the front corner of Caliban's Cavern. Someone had already smashed the street-light there, so I stood and watched from the shadows as a riot swiftly put itself together outside the nightclub.

Out in front of Caliban's Cavern, a loud and very angry crowd was busily escalating a commotion into an open brawl. The recently ejected audience was feeling distinctly put upon and out of sorts at being cheated out of their show, and even more upset at the management's firm *no refunds* policy. A few of the crowd, most definitely including the various celebrities, were not at all used to being manhandled in such a peremptory manner, and many had taken it upon themselves to express their displeasure by tearing apart the whole front edifice of the club. Windows were smashed, facia torn away, and anything at all fragile ended up in small pieces all over the pavement. The outnumbered security staff retreated back inside the club and locked the front doors. The increasingly angry crowd took that as a challenge and set about kicking the doors in. Some even levered up bits of the pavement to use as missiles or battering rams.

An even larger crowd gathered, to watch the first crowd. Free entertainment was always highly valued in the Nightside, especially when it involved violence and the chance of open mayhem. On learning the reason for the riot, some of the new arrivals expressed their solidarity by joining in, and soon an army of angry faces were attacking the front of Caliban's Cavern with anything that came to hand. And it's surprising how many really destructive things can just come to hand, in the Nightside.

A roar of rabid motorcycles announced the arrival of security reinforcements. The outer edges of the huge seething mob looked round to see a pack of almost a hundred Hell's Neanderthals slamming to a halt on their stripped-down chopper bikes. They quickly dismounted and surged forward, howling their pre-verbal war cries and brandishing all sorts of simple weaponry. The mob turned to face them, happy and eager for a chance to have living targets to take out their fury on. The two sides joined battle with equal fervour, and soon half the street was a war zone, with bodies flying this way and that, and blood flowing thickly in the gutters. The watching crowd retreated to a safe distance and booed the newly arrived security for the spoil-sports they were.

It seemed to me that this was a good time to make myself scarce, while the Cavendishes' attention would be focussed on more immediate problems. I skirted round the edges of the boiling violence, firmly resisting all invitations to become involved, and walked briskly back towards the business area of Uptown. I'd thought of someone else to go to in search of answers. When in doubt, go to the people who know everything, even if they can't prove any of it. Namely journalists, gossip columnists, and all the other nosey parkers employed by the *Night Times*, the Nightside's very own newspaper.

It didn't take long to reach Victoria House, the large and comfortably run-down building that housed the *Night Times*. It was a big and bulky building because it had to be. Within its heavy grey stone walls the paper was written, edited, published, printed, and distributed every twenty-four hours, all under the guardianship of its remarkable owner and editor, Julien Advent. The legendary Victorian Adventurer himself. Advent had to keep everything under one roof because that was the only way he could ensure the paper's safety and independence. I paused outside the front door to look up at the gargoyles sneering down from the roof. One of them was scratching itself listlessly, but otherwise they showed no interest in me. I took that as a good sign. The gargoyles were always the first to make it clear when you were out of favour with the paper, and some of them had uncanny aim and absolutely no inhibitions when it came to bodily functions.

The *Night Times* has prided itself throughout its long history in telling the truth, the whole truth, and as much gossip as it could get away with it. This had not endeared it to the Nightside's many powerful movers and shakers, and they had all made attempts, down the years, to shut the paper down by magic, muscle, political and business pressure. But the *Night Times* was still going strong, over two centuries old now, and as determined as ever to tell the general populace where the bodies were buried. Sometimes literally. It helped that the paper had almost as many friends and admirers as enemies. The last time some foolish soul tried to interfere with the *Night Times*'s distribution, by sending out a small army of thugs to intimidate the news vendors, the Little Sisters of the Immaculate Chain Saw had made one of their rare public appearances to deal with the matter and made such a mess of the thugs it was three days before the gutters ran freely again.

I stepped up to the front door very carefully, ready to duck and run at a moment's notice. I was usually welcome at the *Night Times* offices, but it paid to be cautious. Victoria House had really heavy-duty magical defences, of a thorough and downright vicious nature that would have put the Cavendishes' defences to shame. They'd been built up in layers over two hundred years, like a malevolent onion. A subsonic avoidance spell ensured that most people couldn't even get close to the building unless they were on the approved list, or had legitimate business there. I'm not saying I couldn't get in if I really had to, but nothing short of a gun at the back of my head would convince me to try. The last time some idiot tried to smuggle a bomb into Victoria House, the defences turned him into something. No-one was quite sure what, because you couldn't look at him for more than a moment or two without projectile vomiting everything you'd ever eaten, including in previous lives. I'm told he, or more properly it, works in the sewer systems these days, and the rat population is way, way down.

I pushed the front door open, tensed, then relaxed as nothing awful happened to me. I counted my fingers anyway, just in case, and then strode into the lobby, smiling like I didn't have a care or guilty secret in the world. It's important to keep up appearances, especially in front of journalists. It was a wide-open lobby, to allow for a clean line of fire from as many directions as possible, and the receptionist sat inside a cubicle of bulletproof glass, surrounded by a pentacle of softly glowing blue lines. It was said by many, and believed by most, that you could nuke the whole building and the receptionist would still be okay.

The old dear put down her knitting as she saw me coming, studied me over the top of her granny glasses, and smiled sweetly. Most people thought of her as a nice old thing, but I happened to know that her knitting needles had been carved from human thigh-bones, and if she smiled widely enough, you could see that all her teeth had been filed to points.

"Ah, hello there, Mr. Taylor. So nice to see you back again. You're looking very yourself. Would I be right in thinking you're here to have a wee word with the man himself?"

"That's right, Janet. Could you ring up and ask Julien if he'll see me?"

"Oh, there's no need for that, you wee scamp. News of your latest exploits has already reached Mr. Advent, and he is most anxious to get all the details from you while they're still fresh in your mind." She shook her grey head and tut-tutted sadly. "Such a naughty boy you are, Mr. Taylor, always getting into trouble."

I just smiled and nodded, though I wasn't all that sure what she was talking about. Surely Julien couldn't know about my part in the destruction of Prometheus Inc. already? Janet hit the concealed switch that opened the elevator doors at the back of the lobby. She was the only one who could open the doors from this side, and she took her responsibility very seriously. There were those who said she never left her cubicle. Certainly no-one else had ever been seen in her place. I walked across the lobby, carefully not hurrying in case it made me look too anxious, and stepped into the waiting elevator. The steel doors closed silently, and I hit the button for the top floor.

Top floor was Editorial. I'd been there often enough before that my unexpected appearance shouldn't ring too many alarm bells. I used to do occasional legwork for the editor, in my younger days, before I had to leave the Nightside in a hurry. My gift for finding things came in very handy when Julien Advent needed to track down witnesses or people in hiding. I hadn't done anything for him recently, but he did still owe me a couple of favours... Not that I'd press the point. In the past, I'd always been careful to keep our relationship strictly business, because the great Victorian Adventurer had always been a man of unimpeachable and righteous morality, and such people have always made me very nervous. They tend not to approve of people like me, once they get to know me.

I'd never been sure how much Julien knew about my various dubious enterprises. And I've never liked to ask.

The elevator doors opened with a bright and cheerful chiming sound, and I stepped out into the plain, largely empty corridor that led to Editorial. The only decoration consisted of famous front pages from the *Night Times*'s long history, carefully preserved behind glass. Most were from way before my time, but I glanced at some of the more recent examples as I headed for the Editorial bullpen. *Angel War Ends in Draw, Beltane Blood Bonanza, New Chastity Scare, Who Watches the Authorities?* And, from its brief tabloid incarnation, *Sandra Chance Ate My Haploids!* (Julien Advent had been on vacation that month.) I stopped outside the bullpen to consider the *Night Times*'s famous motto, proudly emblazoned over the door.

ALL THE NEWS, DAMMIT.

The solid steel door had a wild mixture of protective runes and sigils engraved into its surface. It was sealed on all kinds of levels, but it recognised me immediately and opened politely. The general bedlam from within hit my ears like a thunderclap, and I braced myself before walking in like I had every right to be there. The long room was full of people, working at desks and shouting at each other. A few people ran back and forth between the desks, carrying important memos and updates, and the even more important hot coffee that kept everybody going. The bullpen ran at full blast, non-stop, in three eight-hour shifts, to be sure of covering everything as it happened. The computers were never turned off, and the seats were always warm. A few people looked round as I entered, smiled or grimaced, and went straight back to work. This wasn't a place for hanging around watercoolers—everyone here took their work very seriously.

The place hadn't changed at all in the five years I'd been away. It was still a mess. Desks groaned under the weight of computer equipment, tottering stacks of books, and assorted magical and high-tech paraphernalia. Piles of paper over-flowed the In and Out trays, and the phones never stopped ringing. Ever-changing displays on the far wall showed the current times and dates within all the Timeslips operating within the Nightside, while a large map showed the constantly con-tracting and expanding boundaries of the Nightside itself. Occasional details within the map flickered on and off like blinking eyes, as reality rewrote itself. Slow-moving ceiling fans did their best to move the cigarette smoke around. No-one had ever tried to ban smoking here—journalism in the Nightside was a high-stress occupation.

I breezed down the central aisle, nodding and smiling to familiar faces, most of whom ignored me. Junior reporters brushed past me as they scur-ried back and forth, trying to outshout each other. A zone of magical silence surrounded the commu-nications section, cut off from the rest of the room as they chased up the very latest stories on tele-phones, crystal balls, and wax effigies. I stopped as the copyboy came whirling towards me. Otto was an amiable young poltergeist who manifested as a tightly controlled whirlwind. He bobbed up and down before me like a miniature tornado, tossing the papers he carried inside himself towards In trays and waiting hands with uncanny accuracy.

"Hello, hello, Mr. Taylor! So nice to have you back among us. Love the jacket. You here to see the gaffer, are you?"

"Got it in one, Otto. Is he in?"

"Well, that's the question, isn't it? He's in his office, but whether he's in to you... Hang on here while I nip in and check."

He shot off towards the soundproofed glass cubicle at the end of the bullpen, singing snatches of show tunes as he went. I could just make out Julien Advent sitting behind his editor's desk, making hurried last-minute corrections to a story, while his sub-editor hovered frantically before him. Julien finally finished, and the sub snatched the pages from the desk and ran for the presses. Julien looked up as Otto swirled into his office, then looked round at me.

I looked around the bullpen. Hardly anyone looked back. Despite all my previous hard work for the *Night Times*, they didn't consider me one of them. I didn't share their holy quest for pursuing news. And as far as newsies were concerned, it was always going to be them versus everyone else. You couldn't afford to get close to someone you might have to do a story on someday.

Not all of the staff were human. The editor operated a strictly equal opportunity employment programme. A semi-transparent ghost was talking to the spirit world on the memory of an old-fashioned telephone. Two ravens called Truth and Memory fluttered back and forth across the room. They were moonlighting from their usual job, working as fact-checkers. A goblin drag queen was working out the next day's horoscopes. His fluffy blonde wig clashed with his horns. It probably helped in his job that he was a manic depressive with a nasty sense of humour. His column might be occasionally distressing, but it was never boring. He nodded casually to me, and I wandered over to join him. He adjusted the fall of his bright green cocktail dress and smiled widely.

"See you, John! Who's been a naughty boy, then? That creep Walker was here looking for you earlier, and he was not a happy bunny."

"When is he ever?" I said calmly. "I'm sure it's all a misunderstanding. Any idea why the editor wants to see me?"

"He hasn't said, but then he never does. What have you been up to?"

"Oh, this and that. Anything in the future I should know about?"

"You tell me, pet. I just work here."

We shared a laugh, and he went back to scowling over his next column, putting together something really upsetting for tomorrow's Virgos. I strolled down the central aisle towards the editor's cubicle, as slowly as I thought I could get away with. There was no telling what Julien knew, or thought he knew, but I had no intention of telling him anything I didn't have to. Knowledge was power here, just as in the rest of the Nightside. A lot of the staff were affecting not to notice my presence, but I'm used to that. The haunted typewriter clacked busily away to my left, operated by a journalist who was murdered several years ago, but hadn't let a little thing like being dead interfere with his work. One of the *Night Times*'s few real ghost writers.

I'd almost reached the editor's cubicle, when the paper's gossip columnist pushed his chair back to block my way. Argus of the Thousand Eyes was a shapeshifter. He could be anyone or anything, and as a result was able to infiltrate even the most closely guarded parties. He saw everything, overheard all, and told most of it. He had an endless curiosity and absolutely no sense of shame. The number of death threats he got every week outnumbered those of all the rest of the staff put together. Which was probably why Argus had never been known to reveal his true shape or identity to anyone. Rumours of his complicated sex life were scandalous. For the moment he was impersonating that famous reporter Clark Kent, as played by Christopher Reeve in the *Superman* movies.

"So, tell me," he said. "Is it true, about Suzie Shooter?"

"Probably," I said. "Who's she supposed to have killed now?"

"Oh, it's something much more juicy than that. According to a very reliable source, dear Suzie has been hiding some really delicious secrets about her family..."

"Don't go there," I said flatly. "Or if Suzie doesn't kill you, I will."

He sneered at me and changed abruptly into an exact copy of me. "Maybe I should go and ask her yourself."

I gripped him firmly by the throat and lifted him out of his chair, so I could stick my face right into his. Or, rather, mine. "Don't," I said. "It isn't healthy to be me at the best of times, and I don't need you muddying my waters."

"Put him down, John," said Julien Advent. I looked round, and he was standing in the open door of his cubicle. "You know you can't kill him with anything less than a flamethrower. Now get in here. I want a word with you."

I dropped Argus back into his chair. He stuck out my tongue at me and changed into an exact copy of Walker. I made a mental note to purchase a flamethrower and went over to join Julien in his office. He shut the door firmly behind me, then waved me to the visitor's chair. We both sat down and considered each other thoughtfully.

"Love the jacket, John," he said finally. "It's so not you."

"This from a man who hasn't changed his look since the Nineteenth Century."

Julien Advent smiled, and I smiled back. We might never be friends, or really approve of each other, but somehow we always got along okay. It probably helped that we had a lot of enemies in common.

Julien Advent was the Victorian Adventurer, the greatest hero of his age. Valiant and daring, he'd fought all the evils of Queen Victoria's time and never once looked like losing. He was tall and lithely muscular, impossibly graceful in an utterly masculine way, with jet-black hair and eyes, and an unfashionably pale face. Handsome as any movie star, the effect was somewhat spoiled by his unwaveringly serious gaze and grim smile. Julien always looked like he didn't believe in frivolous things like fun or movie stars. He still wore the stark black-and-white formal dress of his time, the only splash of colour a purple cravat at his throat, held in place by a silver pin presented to him by Queen Victoria herself. And it had to be said, Julien looked a damn sight more elegant than the Jonah. Julien had style.

There were any number of books and movies and even a television series about the great Victorian Adventurer, most of them conspiracy theories as to why he'd disappeared so suddenly, at the height of his fame, in 1888. And then he astonished everyone by reappearing out of a Timeslip into the Nightside in 1966. It turned out he'd been betrayed by the only woman he ever loved, who lured him into a trap set by his greatest enemies, the evil husband-and-wife team known as the Murder Masques. The three of them tricked him into a pre-prepared Timeslip, and the next thing he knew he'd been catapulted into the future.

Being the great man that he was, Julien Advent soon found his feet again. He went to work as a journalist for the *Night Times* and made a great investigative reporter—partly because he wasn't afraid of or impressed by anyone and partly because he had an even scarier reputation than the villains he pursued so relentlessly. Julien still fought evil and punished the guilty—he just did it in a new way. He was helped in adjusting to his new time by his newfound wealth. He'd left money in a secret bank account, when he disappeared from 1888, and the wonders of compound interest meant he'd never have to worry about money ever again. Eventually Julien became the editor, then the owner, of the *Night Times*, and that great crusading newspaper had become the official conscience of the Nightside and a pain in the arse to all those who liked things just fine the way they were.

Still, everybody read the *Night Times*, if only to be sure they weren't in it.

Julien Advent was in every way a self-made man. He hadn't started out as a hero and adventurer. He was just a minor research chemist, pottering away in a small laboratory on a modest stipend. But somehow he created a transformational potion like no other, a mysterious new compound that could unlock the secret extremes of the human mind. A potion that could make a man absolute good or utter evil. He could have become a monster, a creature that lived only to indulge itself with all manner of violence and vice, but being the good and moral man that he was, Julien Advent took the potion and became a hero. Tall and strong, fast-moving and quick-thinking, courageous and magnificent and unwaveringly gallant, he became the foremost adventurer of his time.

A man so perfect, he'd be unbearable if he wasn't so charming. He had tried to re-create his formula over the years, but to no success. Some unknown ingredient escaped him, some unknown impurity in one of the original salts... and Julien Advent remained the only one of his kind.

He never did discover what happened to the Murder Masques. That terrible husband-and-wife team, who ran all the organised crime in the Victorian Nightside, their faces hidden behind red leather masks, were long gone... no more now than a footnote in history. Only really remembered at all as the main adversaries of the legendary Victorian Adventurer. Some said progress changed London and the Nightside so quickly that they couldn't keep up, or they were brought down by others of their vicious kind. And some said they just got old and tired and slow, and younger wolves dragged them down. Julien had tried to determine their fate, using all the considerable resources of the *Night Times*, but the Murder

Masques were lost in the mists of history and legend.

The woman who betrayed Julien to his mortal enemies hadn't even made it into the legends, her very name forgotten. Julien had been known to say that that was the best possible punishment he could have wished for her. Otherwise, he never spoke of her at all.

And now he sat behind his editor's desk, studying me intently with his dark eyes and sardonic smile. Julien was still a man who saw the world strictly in black and white, and despite all his experience of life in the current-day Nightside, he still would have no truck with shades of grey. As a result, he was often not at all sure what to make of me.

"I'm putting together a piece on the recent unexpected power cuts," he said abruptly. "You wouldn't know anything about them, of course."

"Of course."

"And Walker's appearance here looking for you with fire and brimstone in his eyes was nothing but a coincidence."

"Couldn't have put it better myself, Julien. I'm all tied up with a new case at the moment, investigating the Cavendishes."

Julien frowned briefly. "Ah yes, the reclusive Mr. and Mrs. Cavendish. A bad pair, though always somehow just on the right side of the law. For all their undoubted influence in the Nightside, all I have on them are rumours and unsubstantiated gossip. Probably time I did another piece on them, just to see what nastiness they're involved with these days. They haven't sued me in ages. But don't change the subject, John. Why is Walker after you?"

"Don't ask me," I said, radiating sincerity. "Walker's always after me for something, you know that. Are you going to tell him I was here?"

Julien laughed. "Hardly, dear boy. I disapprove of him even more than I do of you. The man has far too much power and far too little judgement in the exercising of it. I honestly believe he has no moral compass at all. One of these days I'll get the goods on him, then I'll put out a special edition all about him. I did ask him if he knew what was behind the blackouts, but he wouldn't say anything. He knows more than he's telling... but then, he always does."

"How bad were the blackouts?" I asked cautiously.

"Bad. Almost half the Nightside had interruptions in their power supply, some of them disastrously so. Millions of pounds' worth of damage and lost business, and thousands of injuries. No actual deaths have been confirmed yet, but new reports are coming in all the time. Whoever was responsible for this hit the Nightside where it hurt. We weren't affected, of course. Victoria House has its own generator. All part of being independent. You were seen at Prometheus Inc., John, just before it all went bang."

I shrugged easily. "There'd been some talk of sabotage, and I was called in as a security consultant. But they left it far too late. I was lucky to get out alive."

"And the saboteur?"

I shrugged again. "We'll probably never know now."

Julien sighed tiredly. "You never could lie to me worth a damn, John."

"I know," I said. "But that is my official line as to what happened, and I'm sticking to it."

He fixed me with his steady thoughtful gaze. "I could put all kinds of pressure on you, John."

I grinned. "You could try."

We both laughed quietly together, then the door banged open suddenly as Otto came whirling in, his bobbing windy self crackling with energy. An eight-by-ten shot out of somewhere within him and slapped down on the table in front of Julien. "Sorry to interrupt, sir, but the pictures sub wants to know whether this photo of Walker will do for the next edition."

Julien barely glanced at the photo. "No. He doesn't look nearly shifty enough. Tell the sub to dig through the photo archives and come up with something that will make Walker look actually dishonest. Shouldn't be too difficult."

"No problem, chief."

Otto snatched the photo back into himself and shot out of the office, slamming the door behind him.

I decided Julien could use distracting from thoughts about Prometheus Inc., so I told him I'd been present at Caliban's Cavern when one of Rossignol's fans had shot himself right in front of her. Julien's face brightened immediately.

"You were there? Did you see the riot as well?"

"Right there on the spot, Julien. I saw it all."

And then, of course, nothing would do but I sit down with one of his reporters immediately and tell them everything while the details were still fresh in my mind. I went along with it, partly because I needed to keep Julien distracted, and partly because I was going to have to ask him a favour before I left, and I wanted him feeling obligated towards me. Julien's always been very big on obligation and paying off debts. I tend not to be. Julien used his intercom to summon a reporter to his office, a young up-and-comer called Annabella Peters. I tried to hide my unease. I knew Annabella, and she knew far too much about me. She'd already published several pieces on my return to the Nightside, after five years away, and she had speculated extensively about the reasons for my return, and all the possible consequences for the Nightside. Some of her guesses had been disturbingly accurate. She came barging into Julien's office with a mini tape recorder at the ready, a bright young thing dressed in variously coloured woollens, with a long face, a horsey smile and a sharp, remorseless gaze. She took my offered hand and pumped it briskly.

"John Taylor! Good to see, good to see! Always happy to have a little sit down and chat with you."

"Really?" I said. "In your last piece, you said I was a menace to the stability of the whole Nightside."

"Well, you are," she said reasonably. "What were you doing at Prometheus Inc., John?"

"We've moved on from that," I said firmly. "This is about the riot at Caliban's Cavern."

"Oh, the Rossignol suicide! Yes! Marvellous stuff, marvellous stuff! Did she really get his brains all over her feet?"

"Bad news travels fast," I observed. Annabella sat down opposite me and turned her recorder on. I told her the story, while downplaying my own involvement as much as possible. I suggested, as strongly as I could without being too obvious about it, that I was only there as part of my investigation of the Cavendishes, and not because of Rossignol at all. I never discuss my cases with journalists. Besides, putting the Cavendishes in the frame as the villains of the piece would make it easier for me when I had to ask Julien for that favour. The two of us had worked together in the past, on a few cases where our interests merged, but it never came easily. I finished my story of the riot by telling how I'd been swept outside along with the rest of the ejected audience and only saw the resulting mayhem from a safe distance. Julien nodded, as though he'd expected nothing else from me. Annabella turned off her mini recorder and smiled brightly.

"Thanks awfully, John. This will make a super piece, once I've chopped it down to a reasonable length. Pity you weren't more personally involved with the violence, though."

"Sorry," I said. "I'll try harder next time."

"One last question…" She surreptitiously turned her recorder back on again, and I pretended I hadn't noticed. "There are rumours circulating, suggesting the Nightside was originally created for a specific purpose, and that this is somehow connected with your missing mother's true nature and identity. Could you add anything to these rumours?"

"Sorry," I said. "I never listen to gossip. If you do find out the truth, let me know."

Annabella sighed, turned off her recorder, and Julien held the door open for her as she left. She trotted off to write her piece, and Julien shut the door and came back to join me.

"You're not usually this cooperative with the press, John. Would I be right in assuming you're about to beg a favour from me?"

"Nothing that should trouble your conscience too much, Julien. It wouldn't break your heart if I was to bring the Cavendishes down, would it?"

"No. They're scum. Parasites. Their very presence corrupts the Nightside. Just like the Murder Masques in my day, only without the sense of style. But they're very big and very rich, and extremely well connected. What makes you think you can hurt them?"

"I may be onto something," I said carefully. "It concerns their new singer, Rossignol. What can you tell me about her?"

Julien considered for a moment, then used his intercom to summon the gossip columnist Argus. The shapeshifter breezed in, looking like Kylie Minogue. Dressed as a nun. She sat down beside me, adjusting her habit to show off a perfect bare leg. Julien glared at Argus, and she sat up straight and paid attention.

"Sorry, boss."

"Rossignol," said Julien, and that was all the prompting Argus needed.

"Well, I heard about the suicides, of course, everybody has, all of them supposedly linked to Rossignol's singing, but nobody's come forward with any real proof yet. For a long time we all thought it was just a publicity stunt. And, since no-one famous, or anyone who really matters, has died yet, the Authorities don't give a damn. They never do, until they're forced to. But... the word is that the Cavendishes have a lot riding on Rossignol's success. They need her to make it big. Really big. Their actual financial state is a lot dodgier than most people realise. A lot of their money was invested in property in the Nightside, most of which was thoroughly trashed during the recent Angel War. And of course insurance doesn't cover Acts of God. Or the Adversary. Or their angels. It was in the small print; the Cavendishes should have looked.

"Anyway, Rossignol is all set to be their new cash cow, and they can't afford to have anything go wrong with her big launch onto the music scene. Especially with what happened to their last attempt at creating a new singing sensation, Sylvia Sin. You wouldn't remember her, John. This was while you were still away. Sylvia Sin was going to be the new Big Thing. A marvellous voice, a face like an angel, and breasts to die for. She could whip up a crowd like no-one I ever saw. But she vanished, very mysteriously, just before her big opening night. Her current whereabouts are unknown. Lots of rumours, of course, but no-one's seen anything of her in over a year."

"She could have had it all," said Julien. "Fame, money, success. But something made her run away and dig a hole so deep no-one can find it. Which isn't easy, in the Nightside."

And that was when all hell broke loose out in the bullpen. All the supernatural-threat alarms went off at once, but it was already too late. Julien and I were immediately on our feet, staring out through the office's glass walls as a dark figure roared through the bullpen, throwing desks and tables aside, casually overturning and smashing computer equipment. Journalists and other staff dived for cover. Truth and Memory flew round the room, screeching loudly. Argus peered past my shoulder, her Kylie eyes wide. The dark figure paused for a moment, looking around for new targets, and it was only then that I realised it was Rossignol. She looked small and compact in her little black dress, and extremely dangerous. The expression on her face was utterly inhuman. She saw Julien and me watching, picked up a heavy wooden desk, and threw it the length of the bullpen. We scattered out of the way as the desk smashed through the cubicle's glass wall and flew on to slam against the opposite wall, before finally dropping to the floor with a crash.

Julien and I were quickly back at the shattered glass wall. Argus hid under the editor's desk.

"How the hell did she get in here, past all our defences?" Argus yelled.

"Language, please," Julien murmured, not looking round. "Only one answer—someone must have followed you here from the club, John. You brought her in with you."

"Oh, come on, Julien. I think I would have noticed."

"That isn't Rossignol," Julien said firmly. "No-one human is that strong. That is a sending, probably from the Cavendishes, guided by something they planted on your person."

"No-one planted anything on me!" I said angrily. "No-one's that good!"

I searched my pockets anyway, paying special attention to the jacket Pew had given me, but there was nothing anywhere on me that shouldn't have been there. The fake Rossignol advanced menacingly on a group of journalists trying to build a barricade between themselves and her, and Julien decided he'd had enough. He strode out of his office and into the bullpen, heading straight for Rossignol. He might be an editor these days, but he was still every inch a hero. I hesitated, then went after him. I couldn't see how I might have brought that creature here, but Julien had made me feel responsible. He's good at that. Argus stayed in her hiding place.

Rossignol raged back and forth across the bullpen, smashing computer monitors with flashing blows of her tiny fists. The staff scattered back and forth, trying to keep out of her way. The ones that didn't got hurt. Her strength was enormous, impossible, as though she moved through a world made of paper. Her smile never wavered, and her eyes didn't blink. One journalist didn't move fast enough, and she grabbed him by the shoulder with one hand and slammed him against a wall so hard I heard his bones break. Julien was almost upon her. She dropped the limp body and turned suddenly to face him. She lashed out, and Julien only just dodged a blow that would have taken his head clean off his shoulders. Julien darted forward and hit her right on the point of the chin, and her head hardly moved with the blow.

Otto the poltergeist came bobbing over to join me, as I moved cautiously forward. "You've got to stop her, Mr. Taylor, before she destroys everything!"

"I'm open to suggestions," I said, wincing as another vicious blow only just missed Julien's head. "I'm a bit concerned that if we hurt or damage whatever the hell that thing is, we might hurt or damage the real thing."

"Oh, you don't have to worry about that," said Otto. "She's not real. Well, she is, in the sense that she's very definitely kicking the crap out of our revered editor right now, but that thing isn't in any way human. It's a tulpa, a thought form raised up in the shape of whatever person it's derived from. You must have brought something with you that came from the real Rossignol, something so small you didn't even notice."

I thought hard. I was sure Rossignol hadn't actually given me anything, which meant whatever it was must have been planted on me after all. I checked all my pockets again, and again came up with nothing. Julien was bobbing and weaving, snapping out punches that rocked the fake Rossignol back on her heels without actually hurting her. The goblin drag queen suddenly tackled Rossignol from behind and pinned her arms to her sides. Julien picked up a desk with an effort and broke it over her head. Rossignol didn't even flinch. She freed herself from the goblin's grasp with a vicious back elbow that left him gasping, and went after Julien again. She wasn't even breathing hard from her exertions. I decided, very reluctantly, that I was going to have to get involved.

I circled behind Rossignol, picked up a heavy paperweight, and bounced it off the back of her head. She spun round to face her new enemy, and Julien kicked her neatly behind her left knee. She staggered, caught off-balance, and Julien and I hit her together, putting all our strength into our blows. She just shrugged us off. We both backed away and circled her. She turned smoothly to keep us both in view. I looked around for something else to use and spotted a large bulky object with satisfyingly sharp points. Perfect. I reached for it, then hesitated as Annabella hissed angrily at me from behind an overturned table.

"Don't you dare, you bastard! That's my journalist of the year award!"

"Perfect," I said. I grabbed the ugly thing and threw it with all my strength. Rossignol snatched it out of mid air and threw it straight back, and it only just missed my head as I dived for cover. Julien yelled back at his office.

"Argus! Get your cowardly self out here! I've got an idea!"

"I don't care if you've got a bazooka, I'm not budging! You don't pay me enough to fight demons!"

"Get your miserable self out here, or I'll cut off your expenses!"

"Bully," said Argus, but not too loudly. He came slouching out of the editor's office, trying to look as anonymous as possible. His face was so bland as to be practically generic. He edged towards the ongoing battle, while Julien glared at him.

"Look like Rossignol! Do it now!"

Argus shapeshifted and became an exact copy of Rossignol. The tulpa looked at the new fake Rossignol and paused, bewildered. Julien caught my attention and gestured at an overturned table. I quickly saw what he had in mind, and we picked it up between us. The tulpa Rossignol had just started to come out of her trance when we hit her from behind like a charging train. Caught off-balance, she fell forward, and we threw our combined weight onto the table, pinning the tulpa to the ground. She struggled underneath us, trying to find the leverage to free herself. And I used my gift and found just what it was that the tulpa was using as its link. On the shoulder of my jacket was a single black hair from Rossignol's head, almost invisible against the black leather. It must have happened when I held her in my arms to comfort her. No good deed goes unpunished, especially in the Nightside. I held up the hair to show it to Julien, while the table bucked beneath us. He produced a monogrammed gold lighter and set fire to the hair. It burned up in a moment, then the table beneath us slammed flat against the floor. There was no longer anything underneath it.

Julien and I helped each other to our feet. We were both breathing hard. He looked about his devastated bullpen, as journalists and other staff slowly emerged from the wreckage. Somebody found a phone that still worked and called paramedics for the injured. Julien looked at me, and his dark eyes were very cold.

"This has to be the Cavendishes' work. And that makes this personal. No-one attacks the *Night Times* and gets away with it. I think I'll send the arrogant swine a bill for damages and repairs. Meanwhile, I'm starting a full-scale investigation into what they're up to, using all my best people. And John, I suggest you go and see Dead Boy. If anyone knows where Sylvia Sin is hiding, it will be he."

I nodded. That was the favour I'd been hoping for.

Julien Advent looked back at his wrecked bullpen. "No-one attacks my people and gets away with it."

SEVEN

DEATH AND LIFE, SORT OF

I left the *Night Times* riding in Julien Advent's very own Silver Ghost Rolls-Royce. He wanted to make sure I got where I was going and didn't die anywhere near him or the *Night Times*'s offices. I considered this a thoughtful gesture and left him and the rest of the staff to clean up the extensive mess and damage caused by Rossignol's tulpa. My chauffeuse was a slender delicate little flower in a full white leather outfit, right down to the peaked chauffeur's hat pulled firmly down over her mop of frizzy golden hair. She asked me where she was to take me, then refused to say another word. I have that effect on women sometimes. Either that, or Julien had warned her about me. I sprawled happily on the polished red leather seat and indulged myself with a very good brandy from the built-in bar. It does the heart and soul good to travel first-class once in a while. The Rolls purred along, sliding smoothly through the packed and snarling traffic of the Nightside, where the only rule of the road is survival. Most of the other vehicles had enough sense to give the Rolls plenty of room—they knew that a vehicle that expensive had to have state-of-the-art defences and weaponry.

But there's always one, isn't there? I was peering vaguely out the side window, not really thinking about anything much, except trying to remember whether Dead Boy and I had parted on good terms the last time we'd met, when I gradually became aware of a battered dark saloon car of unfamiliar make easing in beside us. It didn't take me long to realise it wasn't a proper car. I sat up straight and paid attention. All the details were wrong, and when I looked closely, I could see that the car's wheels weren't turning at all. I looked at the chauffeuse. She was staring straight ahead, apparently not at all concerned. I looked at the black car again. The outlines of the doors were just marks on the chassis, with no depth to them, and though the back windows were opaque, I could see the driver through the front side window. He wasn't moving at all. I was pretty sure he was a corpse, just put there to add verisimilitude and fool the casual eye.

The Rolls was moving pretty fast, and so was the thing that wasn't a car. It really was getting very close. A split appeared in the side facing me, stretching slowly to reach from one end to the other. It opened like a mouth, revealing rows of bloodred cilia within, thrashing hungrily. They sprouted vicious barbs and lashed out at the Rolls's windows. I retreated to the opposite side of the seat, as the cilia scratched futilely at the bullet-proof glass. The chauffeuse reached for the weapons console on the dashboard.

And then the fake car lurched suddenly, as huge feet slammed down from above, burying long claws in the fake roof. Blood spurted thickly from the wounds the claws made. The thing surged back and forth across the road, trying to break the claws' hold, and couldn't. Its wide mouth screamed shrilly as it was lifted suddenly up and off the road. There was the sound of very large leathery wings flapping, and the thing that only looked like a car was gone, snatched up into the night skies. It had made a very foolish mistake—in becoming so fascinated by its prey it forgot the first rule of the Nightside. No matter how good a predator you are, there's always something bigger and stronger and hungrier than you, and if you let yourself get distracted, it'll creep right up behind you.

The Rolls-Royce purred on its way, the traffic continued as though nothing had happened, and I drank more brandy.

It took about half an hour to reach the Nightside Necropolis, site of Dead Boy's current assignment. The Necropolis takes care of all funerals for those who die in the Nightside and is situated right out on the boundary, because no-one wanted to be too close to it. Partly because even the Nightside has some taboos, but mostly because on the few occasions when things go wrong at the Necropolis, they go *really* wrong.

It is the management's proud claim that they can provide every kind of service, ritual, or interment you can think of, including a few best not thought of at all if you like sleeping at night. Their motto: It's *Your* Funeral. In the Nightside, you can't always be sure that the dear departed will rest in peace, unless the proper precautions are taken, so it pays to have professionals who specialise in such matters. They charge an arm and a leg, but they can work wonders, even when there isn't an actual body for them to work with.

So when things do go wrong, as they will in even the best regulated firms, they tend to go spectacularly wrong, and that's when the Necropolis management swallows its considerable pride and calls in the Nightside's very own expert in all forms of death—the infamous Dead Boy.

The chauffeuse brought the Rolls to a halt a respectful distance away from the Necropolis. In fact, I could only just make out the building at the end of the street. I'd barely got out of the car and slammed the door shut behind me before the Rolls was backing away at speed, heading back to the more familiar dangers of Uptown. Which if nothing else solved the nagging problem of whether I was supposed to tip the chauffeuse. I've never been very good at working out things like that. I set off down the street, which was very quiet and utterly deserted. All the doors and windows were shut, and there were no lights on anywhere. My footsteps sounded loud and carrying, letting everyone know I was coming.

By the time I got to the Necropolis building itself, my nerves were absolutely ragged, and I was ready to jump right out of my skin at the first unexpected movement. The huge towering edifice before me was built of old brick and stone, with no windows anywhere, and a long sharp-edged gabled roof. It had been added to and extended in all directions, down the long years, and now it sprawled over a large area, the various contrasting styles not even trying to get along with each other. It was a dark, lowering, depressing structure with only one entrance. The massive front door was solid steel, rimmed with silver, covered with deeply etched runes, sigils, and other dead languages. I pitied the poor sod who had to polish that every morning. Two huge chimneys peered over the arching roof, serving the crematorium at the back, but for once there was no black smoke pumping up into the night sky. There was also supposed to be a hell of a graveyard in the rear, but I'd never seen it. Never wanted to. I don't go to funerals. They only depress me. Even when my dad died, I only went to the service. I know too much about pain and loss to take any false comfort from planting people in the ground. Or maybe I've just seen too many people die, and you can't keep saying good-bye.

Dead Boy's car was parked right outside the front entrance, and I strolled over to it. Gravel crunched loudly under my feet as I approached Dead Boy's one known indulgence—his brightly gleaming silver car of the future. It was long and sleek and streamlined to within an inch of its life, and it had no wheels. It hovered a few inches above the ground and looked like it ran on liquid starlight. Probably had warp drive, deflector shields, and, if pushed, could transform itself into a bloody great robot. The long curving windows were polarised so you couldn't see in, but the right-hand front door was open. There was one leg protruding. It didn't move as I drew near, so I had to bend over and peer into the driving seat. Dead Boy smiled pleasantly back at me.

"John Taylor. So good to see you again. Welcome to the most popular location in the Nightside."

"Is it really?"

"Must be. People are dying to get into it."

He laughed and took a long drink from his whiskey bottle. Dead Boy was seventeen. He'd been seventeen for over thirty years, ever since he was murdered. I knew his story. Everybody did. He was killed in a random mugging, because such things do happen, even here in the Nightside. Clubbed to death in the street, for his credit cards and the spare change in his pockets. He bled to death on the pavement, while people stepped over and around him, not wanting to get involved. And that should have been it. But he came back from the dead, filled with fury and unnatural energies, to track down and kill the street trash who murdered him. They died, one by one, and did not rise again. Perhaps after all the awful things Dead Boy had done to them, Hell seemed like a relief. But though they were all dead and gone long ago, Dead Boy went on, still walking the Nightside, trapped by the deal he made.

Who did you make your deal with? he was often asked. *Who do you think?* he always replied.

He got his revenge, but nothing had ever been said in the deal he made about being able to lie down again afterwards. He really should have read the small print. And so he goes on, a soul trapped in a dead body. Essentially, he's possessing himself. He does good deeds because he has to. It's the only chance he has of breaking the compact he made. He's a useful sort to have on your side—he doesn't feel pain, he can take a hell of a lot of damage, and he isn't afraid of anything in this world.

He's spent a lot of time researching his condition. He knows more about death in all its forms than anyone else in the Nightside. Supposedly.

He got up out of his car to greet me, all long gangling legs and arms, then leaned languidly against the side of the car. He was tall and adolescent thin, wearing a long, deep purple greatcoat over black leather trousers and shining calfskin boots. He wore a black rose in one lapel. The coat hung open, revealing his bare scarred torso. Being the revived dead, his body doesn't decay, but neither does it heal, so when he gets damaged on a case, as he often does, having no sense of self-preservation, Dead Boy stitches, staples, and superglues his corpse-pale flesh back together again. Occasionally, he has to resort to duct tape. It's not a pretty sight. There were recent bullet holes in his greatcoat, but neither of us mentioned them.

His long pale face had a weary, debauched, pre-Raphaelite look, with burning fever-bright eyes and a sulky pouting mouth with no colour to it. He wore a large floppy black hat over long dark curly hair. He drank whiskey straight from the bottle and munched chocolate biscuits. He offered me both, but I declined.

"I don't need to eat or drink," Dead Boy said casually. "I don't feel hunger or thirst, or even drunkenness any more. I just do it for the sensations. And since it's hard for me to feel much of anything, only the most extreme sensations will do." He produced a silver pill-box from inside his coat, spilled half a dozen assorted pills out onto his palm, and knocked them back with more whiskey. "Marvellous stuff. Little old Obeah woman makes them for me. It's not easy getting drugs strong enough to affect the dead. Please don't look at me like that, John. You always were an overly sensitive soul. What brings you to this charmless spot?"

"Julien Advent said you were working a case here. If I help you out, would you be willing to work with me on something?"

He considered the matter, eating another biscuit and absently brushing the crumbs off his lapels. "Maybe. Does your case involve danger, gratuitous violence, and kicking the crap out of the ungodly?"

"Almost certainly."

Dead Boy smiled. "Then consider us partners. Assuming we survive my current assignment, of course."

I nodded at the silent, brooding Necropolis. "What's happened here?"

"A good question. It seems the Necropolis suffered an unexpected power cut, and all hell broke loose. I've been telling them for years they should get their own generator and hang the expense, but... Anyway, the cryonics section was very badly hit. I warned them about setting that up, too, but oh no, they had to be up to date, up to the moment, ready to meet any demand their customers might come up with." He paused. "I did try it out myself, once, wondering whether I could sleep it out in the ice until someone found an answer to my predicament, but it didn't work. I didn't even feel the cold. Just lay there, bored... Took me ages to get the icicles out of my hair afterwards, as well."

I nodded like I was listening, but inside I was cursing silently. Another consequence of my actions at Prometheus Inc. No good deed goes unpunished...

If the cryonics section was the problem here, we were in for a really rough ride. Bodies have to be dead before they can be frozen and preserved, which means the soul has already departed. However, since some people have a firm suspicion of where their souls might be headed, they see cryonics as their last hope. Get a necromancer in after the body dies, and have him perform the necessary rituals to tie the soul to the body. Then freeze it, and there they are, all safe and sound till Judgement Day. Or until the power cuts out. There were supposed to be all kinds of safe-guards, but... Once the power failed, all the frozen bodies would start defrosting, and the spell holding the souls to them would be short-circuited. So you'd end up with a whole bunch of untenanted thawing bodies, every one of them a ripe target for possession by outside forces.

"So," I said, trying hard to sound calm and casual and not all worried. "Do we know what's got into them?"

"Afraid not. Facts are a bit spotty. About two hours ago, everyone who worked here came running out screaming and refused to go back. Most just kept running. And given the appalling things they deal with here every day as a matter of course, I think we can safely assume the *oh shit* factor is way off the scale. According to the one member of the Necropolis management I talked to who wasn't entirely hysterical, we have five newly thawed bodies to deal with, all of them taken over by *Something From Outside*. Doesn't exactly narrow the field down, does it? The only good news is that the magical wards surrounding the Necropolis are still intact and holding. So whatever's in there is still in there."

"Can't we just turn the power back on?" I said hopefully.

Dead Boy gave me a pitying smile. "Try and keep up with the rest of us, John. Power was reconnected some time back, but the damage had been done. The corpsicles' new tenants have made themselves at home, and their influence now extends over the whole building. The Necropolis's own tame spellslingers have tried all the usual techniques for putting down unwanted visitors from Beyond, from a safe distance, of course, but it seems the possessors are no ordinary imps or demons. We're talking extra-dimensional creatures, elder gods, many-angled ones—the right bastards of the Outer Dark. Not the sort to be bothered by your everyday expulsions or exorcisms. No, something really nasty has taken advantage of the situation to wedge open a door into our reality, and if we don't figure out a way to slam it shut soon, there's no telling what might come howling through. So we get to go in there and serve the extradition papers in person. Aren't we the lucky ones?"

"Luck isn't quite the word I was going to use," I said, and he laughed, entirely unconcerned.

I looked down at the ground before me. A narrow white line crossed the gravel, marking the boundary of the protective wards surrounding the Necropolis. It had been laid down in salt and silver and semen centuries before, to keep things in and keep things out. It remained unbroken, which was a good sign. Those old-time necromancers knew their business. I crouched down and touched the white line with a tentative fingertip. Immediately I could feel the presence of the force wall, like an endless roll of thunder shaking the air. I could also feel a great pressure, pushing constantly from the other side. Something wanted out bad. It was raging at the wall that held it imprisoned, and it was getting stronger all the time. I snatched my hand back and straightened up again.

"Oh, yes," said Dead Boy, draining the last of his whiskey and throwing the bottle aside. "Nasty, isn't it?" The bottle smashed on the gravel, but the sound seemed very small. Dead Boy fixed the front door of the Necropolis with a speculative look. "Any ward will go down, if you hit it hard enough and long enough. So it's up to thee and me to go in there and clean their extra-dimensional clocks, while there's still time. Ah me, I do so love a challenge! Stop looking at me like that, it's going to be fun! Stick close to me, John. The charm the management gave me will get us past the wards, but it won't let you out again if we get separated."

"Don't worry," I said. "I'll be right behind you. Hiding."

Dead Boy laughed, and we crossed the barrier together.

It hit us both at the same time, a psychic assault so powerful and so vile we both staggered and almost fell. Something was watching us, from behind the blind, windowless walls of the Necropolis. A presence permeated the atmosphere, hanging on the air like an almost palpable fog, something dark and awful and utterly alien to human ways of thinking. It felt like crying and vomiting and the smell of your own blood, and it throbbed with hate. Approaching the Necropolis was like wading through an ocean of shit while someone you loved thrust knives into your face. Dead Boy just straightened his shoulders and took it in his stride, heading directly for the front door. I suppose there's nothing like having already died to put everything else in perspective. I gritted my teeth, hugged myself tightly to keep from falling apart, and stumbled forward into the teeth of the psychic assault.

We got to the door without anything nasty actually turning up to rip chunks off us, and Dead Boy rattled the door handle. From his expression, I gathered it wasn't supposed to be locked. He pushed at it with one hand, and it didn't budge. Dead Boy pulled back his hand and looked at it thoughtfully. I put my hand against the solid steel door, and it gave spongily, as though the substance, the reality of it, was being slowly leached out of it. My skin crawled at the contact, and I snatched my hand back and rubbed it thoroughly against my jacket. Dead Boy raised one booted foot and kicked the door in. The great slab of steel and silver flew inwards as though it were weightless, torn away from its hinges. It fell forward and slapped against the floor inside, making a soft, flat sound. Dead Boy strode over it into the entrance hall beyond. I hurried in after him as he struck a defiant pose, hands on hips, and glared into the gloom ahead of him.

"Hello there! I am Dead Boy! Come out here so I can kick your sorry arse! Go on, give me your best shot! I can take it!"

"You see?" I said. "This is why other people don't want to work with you."

"Bunch of wimps," he said, indifferently.

The smell was really bad. Blood and rot and the scent of things that really belonged inside the body. The only light in the great open hall came from a thin, shifting mist that curled slowly on the air, glowing blue-silver like phosphorescence. My eyes slowly adjusted to the dim light, then I wished they hadn't as for the first time I saw the walls, and what was on them. All around us, the walls were covered with a layer of human remains. Corpses had been stretched and flattened and plastered over the walls from floor to ceiling, layering the hall with an insulating barrier of human skin and guts and fractured bones. There were hundreds, thousands of distorted faces, from bodies presumably torn from the graveyard out back. The human remains had been given a kind of life. They stirred slowly as they became aware of us. Eyes rolled in tightly spread faces, tracking the two of us as we advanced slowly across the great open hall. Hands and arms stretched out from the walls as though to grab us, or appeal for help. I could see hearts and lungs, pulsing and swelling in a mockery of life. I was just glad I didn't recognise any of the faces.

At least the floor was clear. Dead Boy strode forward, not even glancing at the walls, and I went with him. I felt somebody sane should be present when push inevitably came to shove. The sound of our feet on the bare floor was strangely muffled, and the shadows around us were very dark and very deep. It felt like walking down a tunnel, away from our world and its rules into... somewhere else.

We were almost half-way across the hall before we got our first glimpse of what was waiting for us. At the far end, in the darkest of the shadows, barely illuminated by the light of the swirling mists, were five huge figures. The corpsicles. Thawed from unimaginable cold, revived from the dead, reanimated by abhuman spirits from Outside, they didn't look human any more. The forces that possessed the vacant bodies were too strong, too furious, too *other* for merely human frames to contain. They had all grown and expanded, forced into unnatural shapes and configurations by the pressures within, and now they were changed and mutated in hideous ways. It hurt to look at them. Their outlines seethed and fluctuated, trying to contain more than three dimensions at once. Mere flesh and blood and bone should have broken down and fallen apart, but the five abominations were held together by the implacable will of the creatures possessing them. They needed these bodies, these vacant hosts. The corpsicles were their only means of access to the material world. I kept wanting to look away. The shapes the bodies were trying to take were just too complex, too intricate for simple human minds to deal with.

We were getting too close. I grabbed Dead Boy by the arm and made him stop. He glared at me.

"We need information," I murmured. "Talk to them."

"You talk to them. Find me something useful I can hit."

One of the shapes leaned forward. It was twice as tall as a man, and almost as wide, its pale, sweating skin stretched painfully tight. A head craned forward on the end of a long, extended neck. Bloody tears fell constantly, to hiss and steam on the hall floor. Bone horns and antlers thrust out of the distorted face, and, when it spoke, its voice was like a choir of children whispering obscenities.

"We are The Primal. Purely conceptual beings, products of the earliest days of creation, before the glory of ideas was trapped and diminished in the narrow confines of matter. Kept out of the material world, to protect its fragile creatures of meat and mortality. Ever since Time was, we were. Waiting and watching at the Edge of things, searching eternally for a way in, to finally show our contempt and hatred for all the lesser creations, that dare to dream of being more than they are. We are The Primal. We were here first. And we will be here when all the meat that dares to think has been stamped back into the mud it came from."

"Typical bloody demons," said Dead Boy. "Created millennia ago, and still sulking because they didn't get better parts in the story. Let's get this over with. Come on, let's see what you can do!"

"Can you at least try for a more rational attitude?" I said sharply. And then I broke off, as the head turned suddenly to look at me.

"We know you, little prince," said the choir of whispering voices. "John Taylor. Yes. We know your mother, too."

"What do you know about her?" My mouth was painfully dry, but I fought to keep my voice steady.

"She who was first, and will be first again, in this worst of all possible worlds. She's coming back. Yes. Soon, she will come back."

"But who is she? What is she?"

"Ask the ones who called her up. Ask the ones who called her back. She is coming home, and she will not be denied."

"You're scared of her," I said, almost wonderingly. *And you're scared of me, too,* I thought.

"We are The Primal. There is still time to play in the world, before she comes back to take it for her own. Time to play with you, little prince."

"This is all terribly interesting," said Dead Boy. "But enough of the chit-chat. Back me up, John. I have a plan."

And he ran forward and threw himself at the nearest shape.

"That's your idea of a plan?" I shrieked, and plunged after him, because there was nothing else to do. It's times like this I wish I carried a gun. A really big gun. With nuclear bullets.

Dead Boy reached out to grab the extended head of the speaking Primal, and its whole body surged suddenly forward to engulf and envelop him, holding him firm like an insect in amber. It wanted to possess him, but Dead Boy was already possessing his body, and his curse didn't allow room for anyone else. The Primal convulsed and spat him out, repulsed by his very nature. Dead Boy hit the floor hard, but was back on his feet in a moment, looking around for something he could hit. The Primal raised their voices in a terrible harmony, chanting something in a language full of higher things than words. And the reanimated dead plastered across the walls heard them. They slipped slowly down the walls and slid across the floor towards Dead Boy and me, a sea of body parts oozing and undulating towards us from all directions, spitting and seething and sprouting distorted limbs like weapons. Stomach acids burned the wooden floor. Eyeballs rose up on wavering stalks. Hands flexed fingers with nails long as knives, sharp as scalpels.

I grabbed two handfuls of salt from my jacket pocket and scattered it in a wide circle around Dead Boy and myself, yelling to him to stay inside it. I wasn't sure even his legendary invulnerability would stand up to being torn apart and digested in a hundred undead stomachs. The oozing biomass hesitated at the salt, then formed itself into high, living arches to cross over it. I glared about me, while Dead Boy slapped and punched at the nearest extensions of the biomass. He was shouting all kinds of spells, from elvish to corrupt Coptic, but none of them had any obvious effect. The reanimated tissues were charged with the energies of The Primal, forces old when the world was new, and even Dead Boy had never come across anything like this before.

I looked at The Primal. They were watching me, rather than Dead Boy, and I remembered my original insight, that they'd seemed almost afraid of me. Why me? What could I do to hurt them? I didn't even have the few battle magics Dead Boy had. There was my gift of finding, but I didn't see it being much use just then. *Think, think!* I looked hard at the five distorted bodies possessed by The Primal. They looked horrible, yes, but also... strained, stretched thin, unstable. Human bodies weren't meant to hold Primal essences. Maybe all the pressure within needed was a little extra nudge...

I was off and running even while the thought was still forming in my mind, my feet slapping and sliding on the slippery rotting organs beneath me. I headed straight for the nearest shape, the speaking Primal, shouting, "YOU THINK YOU'RE SO HARD, POSSESS ME, YOU BASTARDS!" while at the same time thinking, *I really hope I'm right about this.* I hit the first Primal even as it tried to draw back, and I slammed right into the heart of it. The body sucked me in like a mud pool, and I clapped a hand over my mouth and nose to keep it out. I felt cold, impossibly cold, like the dark void between the stars, but even worse than that, I could feel a vast and unknowable mind in there with me, in the cold and the dark, pressing upon me from all sides. And then suddenly there was screaming, an awful sound of outrage and betrayal, as the possessed body exploded.

I'd been too much for The Primal to manage. My body was still tenanted, soul intact, and The Primal couldn't cope. Something had to give, and it turned out to be the possessed body. It blew apart in a wet, sticky explosion, like a grenade inside a small furry creature, and the violence of the explosion ruptured the integrity of the four other bodies, setting them off like a row of firecrackers. It was all over in a moment, and Dead Boy and I stood looking around us, drenched in blood and gore, surrounded by a sea of unmoving body parts, already rotting and falling apart. Dead Boy looked at me.

"And people say I'm impulsive and hard to get along with. What did you just do to them?"

"I think I gave them indigestion. And, possibly, I am a bit special, after all."

Dead Boy sniffed. "God, I'm a mess. So are you. I really hope they've got some showers here somewhere. And a really good laundry."

Two long and very thorough showers later, Dead Boy and I climbed back into our very thoroughly laundered clothes. The Necropolis staff returned in dribs and drabs once it was clear the danger was over, and, with many a sigh and muttered oath, they began cleaning up the mess. A slow process that involved body bags, strong stomachs, not a little use of buckets and mops, and a *really* big bottle of Lysol. The Necropolis management made a brief appearance, to shake our hands and assure Dead Boy the cheque was in the post. They meant it. Absolutely no-one wanted Dead Boy mad at them. He tended to come round to where you lived and pull it down around you. As Dead Boy and I were leaving the Necropolis, two young men were staggering in, carrying a very large crate with the words *Air Fresheners* stencilled on the side.

We headed for Dead Boy's car of the future, and the doors swung open without being asked. Dead Boy slipped in behind the wheel, and I sank carefully into the luxurious front seat. The doors closed by themselves. The dashboard had more controls and displays than the space shuttle. Dead Boy produced an extra-large Mars bar from somewhere and ate it in quick, hungry mouthfuls. When he'd finished, he crumpled up the wrapper and dropped it on the floor, where it joined the rest of the junk. He stared moodily out the windscreen. He looked like he wanted to scowl, but couldn't work up the energy.

"I'm tired," he said abruptly. "I'm always tired. And I am so bloody tired of being tired. Everything's such an effort, whether it's fighting elder gods or just getting through another day. You have no idea what it's like, being dead. I can't feel the subtle things any more, like a breeze or a scent, or even hot and cold. I have no appetites or needs, and I never sleep. I can't even remember what it was like, to be able to put aside the cares of the day and escape into oblivion, and dreams. Even my emotions are only shadows of what I remember them being like. It's hard to care about anything, when the worst thing that can happen to you has already happened. I just go on, doing my good deeds because I have no choice, throwing myself into danger over and over again for the chance to feel *something*... You sure you still want me to partner you, John?"

"I could use your help," I said. "And your insights. It's not much of a case, but it is... interesting."

"Ah well," said Dead Boy. "I can make do with interesting. Where are we going?"

"That's rather up to you. I'm looking for an ex-singer called Sylvia Sin. Used to be managed by the Cavendishes. Julien Advent thought you might know where she's hidden herself."

Dead Boy gave me a look I didn't immediately recognise. "I'm surprised you're interested in someone like her, John. Not really your scene, I would have thought. Still, far be it for me to pass judgement..."

"She's part of the case I'm working," I said. "Do you know where she is?"

"Yes. And I know what she's doing these days. You're wasting your time there, John. Sylvia Sin doesn't care about anyone or anything except what she does."

"I still have to talk to her," I said patiently. "Will you take me to her?"

He shrugged. "Why not? If nothing else, it should be interesting to see your face when we get there."

Dead Boy's car of the future slid smoothly through the Nightside traffic, all of which gave it plenty of room. Probably afraid of phasers and photon torpedos. If the engine made a noise, I couldn't hear it, and the car handled like a dream. I couldn't feel the acceleration, even though we were moving faster than anything else on the road. All too soon we'd left the main flow of traffic behind and were cruising through the quiet back streets of a mostly residential area. We glided past rows of typically suburban houses and finally stopped in front of one that looked no different from any of the others. Even the Nightside has its quiet backwaters, and this was one of the quietest.

Dead Boy and I got out of the car, which locked itself behind us. I hunched inside my jacket against a slow sullen drizzle. The night had turned gloomy and overcast, with heavy clouds hiding the stars and the oversized moon. The yellow street-lights gave the scene a sick, sleazy look. There was no-one else around, and most of the houses had no lights showing. Dead Boy led the way through an overgrown garden and up to the front door, then stood aside and indicated for me to knock. Again, his expression was hard to read. There being no bell, I knocked, and the door opened immediately. As though someone had been watching, or waiting.

The man who opened the door might as well have had a neon sign hanging over his head saying *Pimp*. The way he looked, the way he stood, the way he smiled, all combined to make you feel welcome and dirty at the same time. He wore an oriental black silk wraparound, with a bright red Chinese dragon motif. He was short and slender, almost androgynous. There were heavy silver rings on all his fingers, and a silver ring pierced his left nostril. His jet-black hair was slicked back, and there was something subtly *wrong* about his face. Something in the angles, or perhaps in the way he held his head. He never stopped smiling, but the smile didn't touch his dark, knowing eyes.

"Always happy to see new faces," he said, in a light breathy voice. "All are welcome here. And such famous faces. The legendary Dead Boy, and the newly returned John Taylor. Honoured to make your acquaintance, sirs. My name is Grey, entirely at your service."

"We need to see Sylvia," said Dead Boy. "Or at least, John does."

"But of course," said Grey. "No-one ever comes here to see me." He turned his constant smile in my direction. "What's your pleasure, sir? Whatever you want, whoever you want, I can promise you'll find it here. Nothing is forbidden, and everything is encouraged. Dear Sylvia is always very accommodating."

"Don't I need an appointment?" I said. I shot Dead Boy a quick glare. He should have warned me.

"Oh, Sylvia always knows when someone is coming," said Grey. "As it happens, she's just finished with her last client. You can go straight up, once we've agreed on a suitable fee, of course. In an ideal world such vulgarity would be unnecessary, but alas..."

"I'm not interested in buying her services," I said. "I just need to talk to her."

Grey shrugged. "Whatever you choose to do with her, it all costs the same. Cash only, of course."

"Go on up, John," said Dead Boy. "I'll have a nice little chat with Grey."

He moved forward, and Grey fell back, because people do when Dead Boy comes walking right at them. Grey quickly recovered himself and put out a hand to stop Dead Boy. Magic sparkled briefly on the air between them, then sputtered and went out. Grey backed up against a wall, his eyes very large.

"Who... *what* are you?"

"I'm Dead Boy. And that's all you need to know. Get a move on, John. I don't want to be here all night."

I pulled the door shut behind me, strode past Dead Boy and Grey, and started up the narrow stairs. Sylvia was on the next floor. I could feel it. The house was cold and grim, and the shadows were very dark and very deep. The stairs were bare wood, without carpeting, but still my feet made hardly any sound as I climbed. It was like moving through one of those houses we find in nightmares. Familiar and yet horribly alien, where every door and every window is a threat, every sight heavy with terrible significance. Distances seemed to stretch and contract, and it took forever to get to the top of the stairs.

There was a door right in front of me. A terrible door, holding awful secrets behind it. I stood there, breathing hard, but whether from fear or anticipation I couldn't tell. It was Sylvia's door. I didn't need to be told that. I could feel her presence, like the pressure of a coming storm on the evening air. I pushed the door with the fingertips of one hand, and it swung smoothly open before me, inviting me in. I smelled something that made my nostrils flare, and I walked in.

In the room, in the red room, in the room of rose-petal light and shifting shadows, it was like walking into a woman's body. It was warm and humid, and the still air was heavy with sweat and musk and perfumed hair. There was no obvious source for the light, but there were shadows everywhere, as though the delights the room offered were too subtle to be exposed by bright light. I felt welcomed and desired, and I never wanted to leave.

It was like walking into an antechamber of Hell. And I loved it.

The woman lying at her ease on the oversized bed, naked and smiling and unashamed, was entirely horrible and horribly attractive, like a taste for rotting meat or Russian roulette. She squirmed slowly on the crimson covers like a single maggot in a pool of blood. The details of her face and shape were always moving, changing, shifting subtly from one moment to the next, and even her height and weight were never constant. She could have been one woman or a hundred, or a hundred women in one. Her movements were slow and languorous, and her skin was as white as the white of an eye. Her face was a hundred kinds of beautiful, even when it was unbearably ugly. Her bone structures rose and fell like the turning of the tide, her mouth pursed and widened and changed colour, and her dark, dark eyes promised the kind of pleasures that would make a man cry out in self-disgust as much as passion. I wanted her like I'd never wanted anyone. Her presence filled the room, overpoweringly sexual, awfully female.

And I wanted her the way you always want things you know are bad for you.

"John Taylor," said the woman on the bed. Her voice was soft and caressing, every woman's voice in one. "They thought you might come here. The Cavendishes. I've been so looking forward to having you. They're the ones who made me what I am, even if the result wasn't exactly what they intended. I was just a singer in those days, and a good singer, too, but that wasn't enough for the Cavendishes. They wanted a star who would appeal to absolutely everyone. And this is what they got, this is what their money bought. A woman transformed, a chimera of sex, everything anyone ever desired, and a joy forever."

She laughed, but there was little humour and less humanity in the sound. Her flesh pulsed and shifted in slow rolling movements, never the same twice. My skin crawled, and I couldn't look away to save my life. I had an erection so hard it hurt. Only sheer willpower held me where I was, just inside the doorway. I couldn't go any closer. I didn't dare. I wanted to do things to her, and I wanted her to do things to me.

And then she lazily brought one hand up to her ever-changing mouth. There was something red and sticky on her fingers, and she put it to her mouth and ate it, chewing slowly, savouring the taste. For the first time, as my eyes grew accustomed to the rose-petal light, I realised there was someone else in the room, lying on the floor beside the bed. A man, lying very still, mostly hidden in shadows. A dead man, with his skull caved in. There was a gaping hole in the side of his head, and, as I watched, Sylvia lowered her hand to the hole, dug around in it with her fingers, and pulled out some more brains.

Sylvia's just finished with her last client, Grey had said.

She saw the expression on my face and laughed again. "A girl has to live. There's a price that comes with being what I am, but luckily I'm not the one who has to pay it. They come to me, all the men and the women, drawn to me by desires they didn't even know they had, and I let them sink themselves in my flesh. And while they're busying themselves, I take my toll. I drain them of their desires, their enthusiasms, their faiths and their certainties, and eventually their lives. Though by that stage they usually don't care. And afterwards, I eat them all up. Their vitalities keep me alive, and their flesh helps me maintain my shape. A balance must be struck, between stability and chaos. You wouldn't like what I look like, when I can't get what I need. Oh, don't look so shocked, John! The Cavendishes' magic made me all the women you could ever desire, and I love it. Those who come to me know the risks, and *they* love it. This is sex the way it should be, free from all restraints and conscience. Total indulgence, in this best of all possible worlds." She glanced down at the dead body on the floor. "Don't mourn him. He was all used up. No good to himself, or anyone else, except me. And he did die with a smile on his face. See?"

I couldn't speak, couldn't answer her.

She stretched slowly, voluptuous beyond reason. "Don't you want me, John? I can be anyone you ever wanted, and you can do things with me you wouldn't dare do with them. I live for pleasure, and my flesh is very accommodating."

"No." I made myself say it, even though the effort brought beads of sweat out on my face. I learned self-discipline early, just to stay alive. And I was used to not getting what I wanted. But it still took everything I had to stay where I was. "I need... to talk to you, Sylvia. About the Cavendishes."

"Oh, I don't think about them any more. I don't care about the outside world. I have made my own little world here, and it is perfect. I never leave it. I glory in it. Have you come here to tell me of the Nightside? Is it still full of sin? How long has it been, since I came here?"

"Just over a year," I said, taking a step forward.

"Is that all? It feels like centuries to me. But then time passes so slowly, in Heaven and Hell."

I took another step forward. Her body called to my body, in a voice as old as the world. I knew it would cost me my life and my soul, and I didn't care. Except some small part of me, screaming deep within me, still *did* care. So I did the only thing I could do, to save myself. I called up my gift, my power, and looked at Sylvia Sin with my third eye, my private eye. I used my gift to find the woman she used to be, before the Cavendishes changed her, and brought her back.

Sylvia screamed, convulsing on the bed, her white flesh boiling and seething, then one shape snapped into focus, one body rising suddenly out of all the others, and the changes stopped. Sylvia lay on the bed, curled up into a ball, breathing hard. One woman, with flesh-coloured flesh and a pretty, ordinary face. I was breathing hard, too, like a man who'd just stepped back from the very brink of a cliff. The overpowering sexual pressure was gone from the room, though faint vestiges of its presence still lingered on the air. Sylvia sat up slowly on the bed, naked and normal, and looked at me with merely human eyes.

"What did you do? *What have you done to me?*"

"I've given you back yourself," I said. "You're free now. Entirely normal."

"I didn't ask to be normal! I liked who I was! What I was! The pleasures and the hungers and the feeding... I was a goddess, you bastard! Give it back! Give it back to me!"

She threw herself at me, launching herself off the bed like a wildcat, going for my eyes with her hands, my throat with her teeth. I jumped to one side, and she missed me, betrayed by her unfamiliar, limited body. She crashed against the wall by the door, started to move away and found she couldn't. The wall wouldn't let her go. Her skin was stuck to the rose-petal surface. And that was when I realised at last where the rosy light came from, and why there was still that faint trace of a presence on the air. You do magical crazy things in a room long enough, and you get a magical crazy room. I'd brought Sylvia back, but the room still remained. She cried out and hit the wall with her fist, and the fist stuck to the wall. Already she was sinking into it, as though into a rosy pool, her body being absorbed the same way she'd engulfed so many others. She didn't even have time to work up a proper scream before she was gone, and the sexual presence was suddenly that much stronger, like the eyes of a hungry predator suddenly turning in my direction.

I ran out of the room, and all the way back down the stairs.

I stopped at the foot of the stairs and concentrated on slowing my breathing. My heart was pounding like a hammer in my chest. There's always temptation in the Nightside, and one of the first lessons you learn is that when you've got away, you don't ever look back. Sylvia Sin was gone, and the room should starve to death soon enough. As long as some poor damned fool didn't start feeding it... I looked around for Grey. He was crouching huddled in a corner, shaking and shuddering and crying his eyes out. I looked at Dead Boy, leaning casually against the front door.

"What happened to him?" I said.

"He wanted to know what it was like, being dead," said Dead Boy. "So I told him."

I looked at Grey and shuddered. His eyes were very wide and utterly empty.

"So," said Dead Boy. "All finished with Sylvia, are you?"

"She's finished," I said. "The Cavendishes did something to her. Made her a monster. Maybe they've done something to Rossignol, too. I have to go see her again."

"Mind if I tag along?" said Dead Boy. "At least around you death's never boring."

"Sure," I said. "Just let me do all the talking, okay?"

EIGHT

DIVAS!

Like most cities, there's never anywhere to park in the Nightside when you need it. There are high- and low-rise tesseract car parks and protected areas, but they're never anywhere useful. And cars left unattended on Nightside streets tend to be suddenly stolen, or eaten, or even evolve into something else entirely while your back's turned. But Dead Boy pulled his car of the future in to the kerb, just down the street from Caliban's Cavern, got out, and walked away without even a backward glance. I went with him, but couldn't help looking back uncertainly. The shining silver car looked distinctly out of place in the steaming sleazy streets of Uptown. Already certain eyes were studying it with thoughtful intent.

"It will take more than automatic locks to protect your car here," I pointed out.

"My car can take care of itself," Dead Boy said easily. "The onboard computers have access to all kinds of defensive weaponry, together with an exceedingly nasty sense of humour and no conscience at all."

We strolled up the rain-slick street, and the crowds parted in front of us to let us pass. The blazing neon was as sharp and sleazy as ever, and hot saxophone music and heavy bass beats drifted out of the clubs we passed. A small group were sacrificing a street mime to some lesser god, while tourists clustered round with camcorders. A teddy bear with his eyes and mouth sewn shut was handing out flyers protesting animal experimentation. Cooking smells from a dozen different cultures wafted across the still night air. And more than one person saw Dead Boy coming and chose to walk in another direction entirely.

We finally stopped and studied Caliban's Cavern from a discreet distance. The exterior of the nightclub had been thoroughly trashed during the riot, and a team of specialist restorers were on the scene, clearing up the mess and making good with style and speed and uncanny precision. The Nightside has always had a tendency to mayhem and mass destruction, so there's never any shortage of firms ready and willing to undertake quick repairs and restoration, for the usual exorbitant prices. Most of the big concerns were still busy dealing with the chaos and devastation left behind after the recent Angel War, but it seemed the Cavendishes had been able to raise enough cash-in-hand to get some firm on the job straight away. Three builder magicians were using unification spells to put the facia back together. It was quite fun watching the broken and shattered pieces leaping up from the pavement to fit themselves neatly together again like a complex jigsaw. Some other poor sod had the unenviable task of putting the front door back on its hinges, while the simulacrum in the wood cursed him steadily as an unfeeling incompetent, in between lengthy crying jags.

A crowd had gathered to watch, Nightsiders always being interested in free entertainment, and other people had arrived to sell the crowd things it didn't need, like T-shirts, free passes to clubs no-one in their right mind would visit anyway, and various forms of hot food. This usually consisted of something nasty and overpriced in a bun, that only the most newly arrived tourists would be dumb enough actually to eat.

Dead Boy sniffed loudly as some fool in a grubby dressing gown handed over good money in return for something allegedly meat-based in a tortilla. "Proof, if proof were needed," he said loudly, "that tourists will eat absolutely anything. Truth in advertising, that's what's needed here. See how well that stuff would sell if the vendors were obliged to shout the truth. *Something wriggling on a stick! Pies containing creatures whose name you couldn't even spell! Food so fast it will be out your backside before you know it!*"

"Buyer beware," I said easily. "That should be the Nightside's motto. Nothing's ever what it seems..."

We watched interestedly as one of the builder magicians used a temporal reverse spell to restore some damaged woodwork, then joined in the general jeering as he let the spell get away from him, and time sped back too far, so that the wood started sprouting branches and leaves again. Dead Boy looked the nightclub over with his professionally deceased eyes.

"There are new and really nasty magical wards all over the place," he said quietly. "They're well disguised, but there's not much you can hide from the dead. It's mostly shaped curses and proximity hexes, an awful lot of them keyed specifically to your presence, John. We're only just out of range here. The Cavendishes really don't want you any- where near their club again."

"How nasty are we talking?" I said.

"Put it this way—if you were to trigger even one of these quite appalling little bear-traps, they'll be scraping your remains off the surroundings with a palette knife."

"Ouch," I said. "I still have to get in to see Rossignol. Any ideas?"

Dead Boy considered the matter. People saw him frowning and moved even further away, just in case. "I could walk in," he said finally. "Those defences are only dangerous to the living."

"No," I said. "First, Rossignol wouldn't talk to you, only me. And second, you'd be bound to set off all kinds of alarms. I really don't want to attract the Cavendishes' attention if I can help it. They've got a Power on their side. The Jonah."

"Ah yes, young Billy. Nasty piece of work. If he ever grew a pair, he could be really dangerous."

"The odds are, Rossignol is still in her room over the club, guarded by a couple of heavy-duty combat magicians. I bluffed them once, but twice would definitely be pushing it. And who knows what other surprises they've got set up in there..."

"So what do you want to do, John?" said Dead Boy, just a little impatiently. "We can't just stand around out there. Word will get around. How are we going to get to your deadly little songbird? Come on, think devious. It's what you do best."

"If we can't get in to her," I said slowly, "she'll have to come out to us. We'll send her a message. Most of the club's staff will be kicking their heels somewhere close at hand, keeping out of the way and waiting for the repairs to be finished. All we have to do is track them down and find someone we can bribe, convince, or intimidate into passing Rossignol our message."

"They could be anywhere," Dead Boy said doubtfully. "What are you going to do, use your gift to locate them?"

"No," I said. "I don't think so. I've been using my gift too much, too often, lately. And every time I open up my mind, my thoughts blaze like a beacon in the night. My enemies can use that to find me. And you know some of the things they've sent after me. No, I've pushed my luck as far as I dare. It's time to be sensible and stick to simple deduction. All we have to do is check out the local bars, cafes, and diners, and we'll find the club. Theatricals never can go for long without their creature comforts."

We found them all just a short walk further up the street, at the Honey Bee, an overly lit but very clean theme coffee bar, where all the waitresses were obliged to wear puffy black-and-yellow-striped bee outfits, together with bobbly antennae and spiked heel stilettos. They didn't look too happy about it as they tottered unsteadily between

the tables, reeling off the specials through practised smiles. The chorus girls from Caliban's
Cavern had wedged themselves into a corner, nursing their cups of distressed coffee, chattering
loudly and smoking up a storm. Also present was
one Ian Auger, roadie and musician, and the only
one who seemed at all pleased to see me as Dead
Boy and I approached their table.

"Oh, it's you again, is it?" said the platinum
blonde backing singer, flicking her ash disdainful-
ly onto the floor. "Trouble on legs and twice as
unfortunate. Everything was fine until you turned
up. Then you show your face, and we get a suicide
in the front row and a riot in the house. The
Authorities should ban you, on general principles."

"It's been tried," I said calmly. "And I'm still
here. I need someone to take a message to Rossignol." I looked around, hoping for a sympathetic
smile, but it was all glowering faces and curled
lips. I couldn't really blame them. One of the problems of having a carefully cultivated bad
reputation like mine is that I tend to get the blame
for everything that goes wrong around me.

"Who's your pale friend with no fashion sense?"
said the blonde.

"This is Dead Boy," I said, and the whole coffee-
house went suddenly quiet. Ian Auger pushed back
his chair and stood up.

"Let's talk outside," he said resignedly. "You
mustn't mind the girls. They're never keen on anything that might put their jobs at risk." We moved
over to stand in the doorway, while the other customers and staff studied us warily. Ian Auger looked

at me, frowning. "I'm worried about Ross. The Cavendishes have been all over her since the suicide, telling her what to do, what to say, what to think. All they seem to care about is what spin they can put on the suicide for the music media. Ross is practically a prisoner at the moment, under armed guard. Are you still interested in helping her?"

"Of course," I said. "Can you get a message to her?"

"Maybe," said Ian. "At least, one of me might be able to."

"Which one of them are you?" I said.

"All of them," Ian Auger said cheerfully. "I'm a temporal triplet. One soul, three bodies, no waiting. Close-part harmonies a speciality. Me mum always said Destiny stuttered when I was born. Right now my other two selves are busy inside the club, putting the stage set back together again. They're listening to you through me. What's the message?"

"Nothing good," I said. "The Cavendishes tried to make one of their singers into a superstar before. They had a young girl called Sylvia Sin magically augmented, to make her even more popular, and it turned her into a monster. Quite literally. I've seen what they did to her, what she became, and I don't want anything like that to happen to Ross. I need her to sneak out of the club and join me somewhere safe, so we can work out what to do for the best. I don't trust the Cavendishes to have her best interests at heart. It shouldn't be too difficult for Ross to get out. Bodyguards are usually more interested in watching for people trying to sneak in."

Ian scowled fiercely. "Sylvia Sin. There's a name I haven't thought of in a while. Always wondered what happened to her. All right, one of me will talk to Ross. She might listen, now the Cavendishes have left the club. She always seems brighter and more independent when they're not around."

"They do seem to have an unhealthy hold over her," I said. "Could they already have done something to her?"

"I don't know," said Ian. "No-one's allowed to get too close when the Cavendishes are in private conference with Ross. And there's no denying she's not been acting like herself since she came to live in that room over the club. You think if the Cavendishes have done something, that's what's causing the suicides?"

"Could be," I said.

"All right," said Ian. "If I can get a message to her, and if I can get her out of the club, where do you want to meet? It has to be somewhere secure, somewhere she can feel safe, and somewhere she won't be noticed. She has got a pretty famous face now, you know."

"I know the perfect place to hide a famous face," said Dead Boy. "Hide her in a whole crowd of famous faces. Tell Rossignol to meet us at Divas!"

Divas! is one of the more famous, or possibly infamous, nightclubs in Uptown, where you can go to see and hear all the most famous female singers in the history of entertainment. Of course, none of them are real. They're not even female. The famous faces are in fact transvestites, men dressed up as the women they adore. But dressed in style and made up to the nines, the illusion is more than perfect, for these trannies have taken their obsession one step further than most—they have learned to channel the talents and sometimes the personalities of the divas concerned. Dead or alive, the greatest stars of show business all come to Divas!, in proxy at least.

Dead Boy had clearly been there before. The doorman held the door to the club open and bowed very low, and no-one asked us if we were members, or even to pay the cover charge. The hatcheck girl was a 1960s Cilla Black in a black bustier, and from the wink she dropped Dead Boy it was clear he was a regular. Cilla did her best to ignore me, but I'm used to that. Dead Boy is one of the Nightside's celebrities. I'm more of an anti-celebrity. We made our way into the club itself, which was all silks and flowers and bright colours. The furniture was all art deco, and everywhere you looked was every kind of kitsch fashion you ever shuddered at in disbelief. Chandeliers and disco balls hung side by side from the ceiling.

The main floor was crowded, and the noise level was appalling. The night is always jumping at Divas! Dead Boy and I edged between the tightly packed tables, following a waitress. All the waitresses were channelling Liza Minnelli tonight, dressed in her *Cabaret* outfit. We ended up at a table tucked away in a corner and ordered over-priced drinks from the Liza. I asked for a glass of Coke, and then had to go through my usual routine of *No, I don't want a Diet Coke! I want a real Coke! A man's Coke! And I don't want a bloody straw either!* Dead Boy ordered a bottle of gin and the best cigar they had. I made a note of the prices for my expenses sheet. You have to keep track of things like that, or you can go broke on some cases.

"What if Rossignol doesn't turn up?" said Dead Boy, raising his voice to be heard over the general clamour. "What if she can't get away?"

"Then we'll think of something else," I said. "Relax. Enjoy the show. It's costing us enough."

"What do you mean *us*, white man?"

Up on the stage at the far end of the room, an Elaine and a Barbara were dueting on a pretty accurate rendition of "I Know Him So Well." The channelling must be going well tonight. Other famous faces paraded across the floor of the club, there to see and be seen, stopping at tables to chat and gossip and show themselves off. Marilyn and Dolly, Barbra and Dusty. Elaine and Barbara were replaced on stage by a Nico, who favoured us with her mournful voice and presence as she husked "It Took More Than One Man to Change My Name to Shanghai Lily" into the microphone, accompanying herself on the accordion. I just hoped she wouldn't do the Doors' "The End." There's only so much existential angst I can take before my ears start bleeding.

A few tables away, two Judys were having a vicious wig-pulling fight. Spectators cheered them on and laid bets.

And then Ian Auger came in, with Rossignol on his arm, and no-one in Divas! paid her any attention, because everyone assumed she was another trannie, perhaps a little more convincing than some. Ian escorted her over to our table, pulled out her chair for her, introduced her to Dead Boy, and politely but firmly refused to sit down himself.

"I can't hang about here. I've got to get back. There's still a lot of work to do in the club, and I don't want to be missed."

"Any trouble getting Ross here?" I asked.

"Surprisingly, no. I just told the bodyguards that John Taylor was somewhere on the loose in the building, and they all went running off to look for you. We strolled right out. Look, I really do have to go. Ross, remember you're due to go on again in just under an hour."

Rossignol let him kiss her on the cheek, and he hurried away, his hunchback giving him a weird rolling gait. The waitress Liza came back to take Rossignol's order. I looked Rossignol over as she studied the wine list. She looked different. Same pale face, dark hair, little black dress. But she seemed somehow sharper, brighter, more focussed. She looked up, caught me watching, and smiled broadly.

"Ah, John, it is so good to be out and about for a change. You know what I want? I want five whiskey sours. I want them all at once, all lined up in front of me so I can look at them while I'm drinking them. I'm never allowed to drink in Caliban's Cavern, by order of the Cavendishes, though strangely, mostly I don't want to. I stick to the healthy diet they provide, and I never complain, both of which are also very unlike me. Cake! I want cake! Bring me the biggest, gooiest chocolate gateau you have, and a big spoon! I want everything that's bad for me, and I want it right now!"

The waitress whooped with glee. "You go, girl!"

I indicated for the waitress to bring Rossignol what she wanted, and the Liza tottered away on her high heels. Rossignol beamed happily.

"The Cavendishes are always very strict about what I'm allowed to have, and do. They act more like my mother than my managers."

"I notice they didn't stop you smoking," I said.

She snorted loudly. "I'd like to see them try." She stopped smiling suddenly and gave me a hard look. "Ian tells me that you've been out and about on my behalf, speaking to people. And that you found out something concerning my predecessor with the Cavendishes. I remember her face being on all the magazine covers, then... nothing. What did happen to her, John? What did the Cavendishes do to her?"

I told her enough of the story to scare her, without dwelling on some of the nastier details. Dead Boy shot me the occasional glance as he realised what I was doing, but he kept his peace. He'd already drunk half his bottle of gin and had started eating his cigar. When I finally finished, Ross let out a long sigh.

"I had no idea. The poor thing. And the Cavendishes did that to her?"

"More likely had it done," I said. "Have they ever offered to... do anything for you?"

"No. Never." Rossignol's voice was firm and sharp. "I'd have told them where they could stick their magic. I don't need any of that shit to be a success. I'm a singer, and all I've ever needed are my songs and my voice." And then she stopped and frowned suddenly. "And yet, having said that... things have changed since I came to live in my little room over the club. My songs are always sad songs now. And there are some odd gaps in my memory. I feel cold, and tired, all of the time. And the way I act when the Cavendishes are around... doesn't feel like me at all. Could they have worked a magic on me, without my knowing?"

"It's possible," I said carefully. "They could have done something, then made you forget it. The Cavendishes don't strike me as being particularly burdened with professional ethics."

The waitress arrived with the five whiskey sours on a tray. Rossignol cooed happily as they were lined up in front of her, then knocked back the first two, one after the other. She breathed heavily for a moment, then giggled happily, like a small child who's just done something naughty and doesn't give a damn. "Yes! Oh yes! That hit the spot!" She smiled charmingly at me, then at Dead Boy. "So, what's it like, being dead?"

"Don't tell her!" I said sharply, then looked apologetically at the startled singer. "Sorry about that, but some questions are best left unanswered. Especially when it concerns him."

"Like why he's eating that cigar instead of smoking it?"

"Very probably."

She smiled at me again, a warm and embracing moment quite at odds with her earlier, somewhat distanced personality. "You've been known to avoid answering questions yourself on occasion, *monsieur* mystery man." Her French accent had become slightly more pronounced after the third whiskey sour. I couldn't get over how alive she seemed. She looked at me thoughtfully. "You don't really think the Cavendishes would do anything to harm me, do you? I mean, they're relying on me to make them a great deal of money."

"Maybe they thought they were helping Sylvia," I said. "But there's the suicides, Ross. The Cavendishes have to be connected to that somehow. I don't trust them, and you shouldn't either. You say the word, and Dead Boy and I will take you away from them right now. We'll find you somewhere safe to lie low while we get some lawyers in to check out your contract, and maybe a few experts to make sure you haven't been messed about with magically. You don't have to worry. I can guarantee your safety. I know any number of people who'd be only too happy to bodyguard you. Not very nice people, perhaps, but..."

"No," said Rossignol, kindly but firmly. "It's a very generous offer, John, and I do appreciate you're only trying to help, but..."

"But?"

"But this is my big break. My chance to be a star. No-one has connections like the Cavendishes. They really can get me a contract with a major recording studio. I have to do this. I have to sing. It's all I've ever wanted, all I've ever cared about. I can't back out now. I won't back out over what could be just a case of nerves. You don't have any proof they've done anything wrong, do you?"

"No," I said. "But the suicides..."

She grimaced. "Trust me, I haven't forgotten. I'll never forget the look on that poor man's face as he pulled the trigger right in front of me. He looked right into my eyes, and he was smiling... I can't let that go on. My singing was always supposed to make people feel good! I wanted to lift their hearts and comfort them, send them back out to face the world feeling renewed... If the Cavendishes really have done something to corrupt my songs, my voice..." She shook her head sharply. "Oh, I don't know! I don't know what to do!" She picked up the fourth whiskey sour and stared at it moodily.

We all sat and considered the matter for a while. Up on the stage, a Whitney was singing "I Will Always Love You." Rossignol sniffed loudly.

"Never cared for that. Far too strident."

"I prefer the Dolly Parton version," said Dead Boy, unexpectedly. "More warmth."

I looked at him. "You're just full of surprises, aren't you?"

"You have no idea," said Dead Boy.

Rossignol put the fourth whiskey sour to one side as the chocolate gateau arrived. It really was very big, with scrapings of dark and white chocolate sprinkled on the top. Rossignol made ooh- and aah-ing noises, and her eyes went very wide. She grabbed the spoon and stuck it in, and soon there were chocolate smears all round her mouth. I considered her thoughtfully. An unpleasant idea had suggested itself. Perhaps the reason why this Rossignol seemed so different from the one I'd encountered at Caliban's Cavern, was because this was an entirely different Rossignol. Another duplicate, like the tulpa who'd wrecked the *Night Times*'s offices. It would explain a lot, including how she'd been able to get out of the club so easily.

"I think I need to go to the little boy's room," I said loudly, giving Dead Boy a meaningful look.

"Fine," he said. "Thanks for sharing that with us, John."

"This is the first time I've been to this club," I said pointedly. "Why don't you show me where the Gents is?"

"I've never had to use it," said Dead Boy. "One of the few advantages of being dead."

I glared at him and made furious eyebrow gestures while Rossignol was busy making ecstatic chocolate-eating noises, and he finally got the point. We got to our feet, excused ourselves, and headed for the nearby door marked *Stand Up*. Once inside, the shiny-tiled expanse was empty apart from a Kylie standing at the urinal with his skirt hiked up. Dead Boy and I waited until he'd finished, taking a keen interest in the vending machines, and once the Kylie was gone, Dead Boy gave me a hard look.

"This had better be important, John. Just being in here alone with you is undoubtedly doing my reputation no good at all."

"Shut up and listen. The Cavendishes have already sent one duplicate Rossignol after me—a tulpa with supernatural strength and a really bad attitude. Is there any way you can tell whether that's the real Rossignol or not? You're always saying nothing can be hidden from the dead."

"Oh, sure. I've already checked her out."

"And?"

"She is the original. And she's dead."

I looked at him for a long moment. "She's *what?*"

"She doesn't have an aura. It was the first thing I noticed about her."

"Well, why didn't you say anything?"

"It's none of my business if she's mortally challenged. You need to be more open-minded, John."

"You mean, she's dead, like you?"

"Oh, no. I'm a special case. And she's far too bright and bubbly to be a zombie. But you can't be alive without an aura. Everyone has one."

"Really?" I said, momentarily distracted. "What does mine look like?"

"Lots of purple."

"How can she be dead and not know it?" I said, almost as angry as I was exasperated. "She's out there right now giving every indication of being very much alive. Dead people don't have orgasms over chocolate gateau."

"Denial isn't just a river in Egypt. Or perhaps it's something to do with the Cavendishes and their hold over her. Do you want me to break the news to her?"

"No, I think it should come from someone who's at least heard of tact. And she did say she wanted the truth, whatever it was." I scowled at the immaculately shining white tiles. "How do you tell someone they're dead?"

"With your mouth. After all, it could be worse."

"How?"

Dead Boy gave me one of his looks. "Trust me, John. You really don't want to know."

"Oh, shut up."

By the time we got back to our table, Rossignol had demolished fully half of the gateau and drunk the other two whiskey sours. She waved happily at us the moment we reappeared and stopped to suck the chocolate smears off her fingers. Her face was flushed, and she kept lapsing into fits of the giggles. Dead Boy and I sat down facing her.

"I want more drinks!" she said cheerfully. "Everybody should have lots more drinks! Do you want some cake? I can ask them for another spoon. No? You don't know what you're missing. Some days, chocolate is better than sex! Well, some sex, anyway. What are you both looking so dour for? Did you find your phone number on a wall in there?"

I took a deep breath and told Rossignol what Dead Boy had discovered about her, and what it meant. I said it as simply and straightforwardly as I could, and then I sat there, waiting to see how she'd take it. All the bounce went out of her, but her face was set and calm. Her gaze was far away and thoughtful, as she slowly licked chocolate off the back of her spoon. She might have been considering a business proposition, or the loss of a distant relative. When she finally looked at me, her gaze was entirely steady, and when she spoke, her voice seemed more resigned than anything else.

"It would explain a lot," she said. "The gaps in my memory, why I'm always so cold, why I'm always so docile when the Cavendishes are around. They did this to me. The old me, the true me, would never have put up with the way they've been treating me. Being here, away from them, is like waking up from some dark, listless nightmare. Only I'm not going to wake up from this dream, am I? I'm dead."

I wanted to take her in my arms and comfort her, tell her everything was going to be all right, but I'd promised her I'd never lie to her. She worried her lower lip between her teeth for a while, then she looked from me to Dead Boy and back again.

"Is there anything you can do to help me? Or at least find out what these cochons did to me?"

"I can try," said Dead Boy, surprisingly gently. "I have learned to See all kinds of things that are hidden from the living. It helps that you and I are both dead. It gives me a link I can use." He took her hand in his and gestured for me to take his other hand. I did so, a little hesitantly. I still remembered what he'd done to Grey. Dead Boy smiled briefly. "Don't wet yourself, John. I'm just going to look into Rossignol's mind and call up a vision of her last moments alive. Her memory is probably blocked by the trauma of what happened. As long as both of you are linked to me, you'll be able to see what I See. But remember, it's just a vision of the past. We can't interfere or intervene. The past cannot be changed, no matter how much we might wish to."

His grip tightened on my hand, and suddenly we were somewhere else. No incantations, no objects of power—just the will of a man who'd been dead for thirty years and still wouldn't lie down. We were in the Cavendishes' inner office, the place to which I had been dragged, broken and bleeding. Mr. and Mrs. Cavendish were smiling at a preoccupied and scowling Rossignol. She was trying to tell them something, but they weren't listening. Mrs. Cavendish poured Rossignol a glass of champagne and said something soothing. Rossignol snatched the glass out of her hand, knocked it back in one, and threw the glass aside. Then she fell heavily to the floor, as her legs betrayed her.

She lay there, convulsing and frothing at the mouth, while Mr. and Mrs. Cavendish looked on, smiling. Until, finally, she lay still. Then the Cavendishes looked at someone standing in the shadows, but I couldn't make out who the third person was.

We were suddenly back at our table again. Dead Boy had let go of our hands. Rossignol was trembling, but her mouth was a firm, flat line. She made herself be still with an effort of will.

"The Cavendishes poisoned me?" said Rossignol. "Why would they want to murder their meal ticket?"

"A good question," I said. "And one I think we should ask them, in a pointed and forcible manner."

"You could also ask them what they did to her afterwards," said Dead Boy. He looked at Rossignol speculatively. "You don't act like any kind of zombie I'm familiar with. You're quite definitely deceased, but there are still traces of life about you."

"Could the Cavendishes have made a deal like yours?" I said. "Presumably on her behalf, as her management."

"No," Dead Boy said firmly. "Such compacts can only be entered into willingly. That's the point. You can't just lose your soul—you have to sell it."

"Still," I said, "any kind of magic that can raise the dead is by definition the work of a major player. There was someone else in that office, even if we couldn't make out who it was. The only Power the Cavendishes have on their side that I know of is the Jonah. And while he may become a Power and a Domination eventually, like his father, he's no necromancer."

"How does any of this tie in to the people killing themselves after they've heard me sing?" said Rossignol. Her face was still calm and controlled, but her voice was becoming increasingly brittle.

"You went into the dark," said Dead Boy. "And when you came back, you brought some of it with you. It comes out in your songs, when you sing. That's what's killing people."

"*How could they?*" said Rossignol. "How could the Cavendishes do something like that? My songs were always about life and being positive, even when I wrote about sad things. My voice was meant to raise people up, not destroy them! The Cavendishes have ruined the one thing that gave my life meaning!" Her voice threatened to crack then, but still she held on with iron self-control. Her hands were clenched into fists on top of the table. "I won't let this go on. No more people dead because of me. I want my old voice back. I want my life back!" She glared at Dead Boy, then at me. "Can you help me? Either of you?"

"I can't even help myself," Dead Boy said quietly.

"Let's not give up all hope just yet," I said quickly. "Dead Boy, you said yourself she's not like any other revenant you've ever met. Let's find out exactly what was done to her. Some magical deaths can be reversed."

"You think the Cavendishes will agree to that?" said Dead Boy.

"I don't plan to give them any choice," I said, and my voice was so cold that even Dead Boy had to look away.

And that was when a wave of quiet swept across the club. The music and the singing cut off abruptly in mid-number, and the chatter from the surrounding tables died swiftly away to nothing. We all looked around and found every diva in the place staring straight at us. Every trannie, every celebrity by proxy, was up on their feet and staring at us with dark, malignant eyes. Their painted faces were suddenly strange, twisted, shaped by new and deadly emotions. It was like being suddenly surrounded by a pack of wolves. Rossignol and Dead Boy and I rose slowly to our feet, and a frisson of anticipation moved through the menacing crowd. They all smiled at the same moment, a grimace that was all teeth and no humour. One of the Marilyns produced a knife from out of his puffed sleeve. As though that was a signal, dozens of other divas suddenly had weapons in their hands, everything from knives to razor blades to the occasional derringer. Several of them smashed bottles and glasses against tables to make jagged-edged weapons.

"They've been possessed," Dead Boy said quietly. "I know the signs. Their auras have changed. They were channelling the talents and even some of the personalities of their heroines, but that channel has been overridden by a stronger signal, imposed from outside. There's something new and a whole lot nastier in those bodies now."

"Could it be The Primal?" I said. "Back for another crack at us?"

"No," said Dead Boy. "The signs are still human."

A Dusty lurched suddenly forward to stare at Rossignol with unblinking eyes. "We are your greatest fans. We worship you. We adore you. We would die for you. You shouldn't be here. We have come to take you back where you belong."

"Bloody hell," I said. "It's that bunch of Goths and geeks the Cavendishes let hang around their outer office. The fan club from Hell. The Cavendishes must have put them in the divas' heads and sent them to bring Ross back."

"You can't stay here," the Dusty said to Rossignol, ignoring me. "These people are no good for you. You must come with us, back to the Cavendishes. They will make you the star you were born to be. Come with us, now."

"And if she doesn't?" I said.

Without any change of expression, the Dusty slashed at my throat with his knife. I jerked my head back, and he only just missed. The other divas surged forward, raising the weapons in their hands. All the Judys, Kylies, Marilyns, Nicos, and Blondies. Famous faces, marred and twisted by second-hand rage and envy. Someone was threatening to take their goddess away from them, and they would die or kill to prevent that. In their minds, they were rescuing their heroine. Dusty cut at me again. I caught his wrist, twisted it till the fingers reluctantly opened, dropping the knife, then I punched him out. Dead Boy was picking divas up and throwing them around like rag dolls. But there were always more, pressing remorselessly closer, some with improvised weapons like spiked stiletto heels, long hairpins, and clawed fingernails. A Kate Bush came at me shrieking, with a long dagger in his hand. I grabbed Dead Boy and pulled him between us, using his dead body as a shield. The knife slammed into his chest up to the hilt.

"You bastard, Taylor!" said Dead Boy, and then rather spoiled the effect by giggling. I heaved his dead body this way and that, deflecting attacks. It soaked up the punishment, and Dead Boy didn't object. I think he was getting a weird kind of kick out of it. Rossignol was beside me, fighting dirty, pulling trannies' wigs down over their eyes and kicking them in the nuts when she could get a clear target. My back slammed up against the wall behind me, and I yelled past Dead Boy's shoulder for Rossignol to overturn our table and make it a barricade. She broke away from shoulder-charging a Nico and pulled the table over, and soon all three of us were sheltering behind it.

"I'm bored with this," said Dead Boy. "I know a curse that will boil their brains in their heads."

"No!" I said quickly. "We can't kill any of them! The divas aren't responsible for this. They're the victims here."

"Oh, hell," said Dead Boy. "It's good deeds time again, is it?"

The divas, all of them eerily silent, swarmed around us, trying to reach us with their weapons and clawed hands. We were safe for the moment, but we were trapped in our corner. There was nowhere left for us to go, and soon enough the divas would work together to pull the table away; and then... I swore regretfully, and reluctantly did what I do best. I concentrated and opened up my inner eye, my third eye, and used my gift to find the channel the fans were using to drive the divas. It was like suddenly seeing a shimmering latticework of silver strings, rising up from the divas' heads and sailing off into infinity. And having seen it, it was the easiest thing in the world to locate the single thread they all connected to, the focus for the overlaying signal. It turned out to be a single diva, a Whitney, standing watching from the stage. All I had to do was point the Whitney out to Dead Boy, and he made a swift crushing motion with his fist. The Whitney crumpled unconscious to the stage, and all of the silver lines snapped off.

The spell was broken in a moment, and the attacking divas were suddenly nothing more than disoriented men in frocks and make-up. They stopped where they were, shocked and confused, some clinging to each other for mutual support and comfort. Possession is a kind of violation, of the mind and the soul. For a moment, it actually seemed the danger was over. I should have known better.

The trannies suddenly screamed and scattered as a dozen dark and dangerous figures appeared out of nowhere. Tall menacing figures, with smart suits and no faces. I had used my gift once too often, burned too brightly in the night, and now my enemies had found me again. They had sent the Harrowing for me. The trannies quickly cleared the floor and disappeared out the exits. It had all been too much for them. I would have run, too, if

I could. The Harrowing advanced slowly towards us, unstoppable figures of death and horror. They had human shapes, but they didn't move like people did, and the faces under their wide-brimmed hats were only stretches of blank skin. They had no eyes, but they could see. One of them raised its hand, showing me the hypodermic needles where its fingernails should have been. Thick green drops pulsed from the tips of the needles, and I shuddered. Rossignol was clutching my arm so hard it hurt. Dead Boy was frowning for the first time.

"Would I be right in thinking events have just taken a distinct turn for the worse?"

"Oh, yes," I said. "They're the Harrowing. The hounds my enemies send after me. You can't hurt or kill them because they're not real. Just constructs. And there's nothing you or I can do to stop them."

"How do you normally deal with them?" said Rossignol.

"I run like hell. I've spent a lot of my life running from the Harrowing." I raised my gift again, desperately trying to find a way out, but there wasn't one. There was no exit close enough to reach, and the overturned table wouldn't slow them down for a second. The dozen vicious figures moved towards us, relentless as cancer, implacable as destiny. And then a female figure came howling out of nowhere and launched itself at one of the Harrowing. The attacker had been a Kylie once, but all traces of glamour and femininity had been torn away by recent traumas. All that mattered to the Kylie now was that there was a target for his rage. He stabbed the Harrowing in the chest, and its pliant body just absorbed the blow, taking no damage and trapping both the knife and the hand inside its unnatural flesh. The Harrowing made a brief slashing gesture with one hand, and the Kylie just fell apart into a hundred pieces, blood spurting and gushing all over the floor.

"Damn," said Dead Boy. "That is seriously nasty. You know, I have to wonder... how many pieces could you cut me into, and I'd still be able to put myself back together again?"

"Well, unless you fancy life as a jigsaw, stop wondering about it and bloody well do something," I said, stridently.

"Boys," said Rossignol. "They really are getting terribly close. Please tell me one of you has something resembling a plan."

"When you get right down to it," said Dead Boy, "I'm just a walking corpse who's picked up a few unpleasant stratagems along the way. There's nothing in my bag of tricks that could even slow those bastards down. You have really powerful enemies, John."

"Okay," I said, my mouth almost painfully dry. "That's it. Dead Boy, grab Ross and run like hell. As long as you're not a threat, they might not bother with you. They're only here for me."

"What will they do to you?" said Rossignol.

"If I'm lucky, they'll kill me quickly," I said. "But I've never been that lucky. The Harrowing are horror and despair. Please, get out of here."

"I can't leave you," said Dead Boy. "Good deeds, remember? Abandoning you now would set me back years."

"And I won't leave you," said Rossignol. "If only because you're my only hope of breaking free from the Cavendishes."

"Please," I said. "You don't understand. If you stay, they'll do... horrible things to you. I've seen it happen before."

"You'll think of something, John," said Rossignol. "I know you will."

But I didn't. I'd never been able to face the Harrowing, only run from them. My very own pursuing demons. The first of the Harrowing grabbed one edge of our barricading table with a puffy corpse-pale hand and threw it aside as though it were nothing. Dead Boy braced himself, and I pushed Rossignol behind me, sheltering her with my body. And then all the Harrowing stopped and turned their featureless faces, as though listening to something only they could hear. They started to shake and shudder, and then one by one they fell apart into rot and slime, slumping shapelessly to the floor. One moment a dozen menacing figures were closing in on us, and the next there was nothing but thick puddles of reeking ooze, spreading slowly. Dead Boy and I looked at each other, and then we both glared round sharply at the sound of soft, mocking laughter. And there, standing on the stage at the end of the room was Billy Lathem, the Jonah, in his smart, smart suit. He looked very pleased with himself. Standing on either side of him in their undertakers' clothes were Mr. and Mrs. Cavendish.

"I told you, John," said the Jonah. "I am far more powerful than you ever realised. I am

entropy, the end of all things, and not even send-
ings like those ugly bastards can stand against me.
Now, you have something that doesn't belong to
you. And I have come to repossess it."

"Come along, dear Rossignol," said Mr.
Cavendish. "You'll be late for your show."

"You don't want to be late for your show, do
you?" said Mrs. Cavendish.

Rossignol was still gripping my arm tightly. "I
won't go with them. Don't let them take me, John.
I can't go back to being the half-asleep thing I was,
nodding and smiling and agreeing to everything
they said. I'd rather die."

"You don't have to go anywhere you don't want
to," I said, but it didn't sound convincing, even to
me. I was still stunned at how easily the Jonah had
destroyed the Harrowing. He *had* become a Power
and a Domination, like his late father, Count
Entropy, and I was just a man with a gift. And a
bad reputation... I raised my head and gave Billy
Lathem one of my best enigmatic looks.

"We've done this dance before, Billy. Back off, or
I'll use my gift..."

"You don't dare," said the Jonah, grinning nastily. "Not now your enemies know where you are.
What do you think they'll send next, if you're
dumb enough to open up your mind again? Something so appalling even I might not be able to deal
with it. No, your only option now is to hand over
the girl and skulk off out of here, before your enemies track you down anyway." He laughed
suddenly. "You'll never be able to bluff anyone
ever again, John. Not after I tell everyone how I
saw you cringing and helpless, and hiding behind

a table. And all from things I turned to rot and slime with just a wave of my hand. Now, you back off, John. Or I'll use my power to find the one piece of bad luck that will break you forever."

NINE

SEEING THE
LIGHT, AT LAST

And so, one of the messiest and most messed-up cases of my career came to this—showdown at the Divas! saloon. The only trouble was, in the Jonah the Cavendishes had by far the biggest gun. His reducing of the Harrowing to so much multi-coloured mush had been truly impressive. Never thought the boy had it in him. Perhaps staring him down and humiliating him in front of his employers hadn't been such a great idea after all. Certainly something had put a rocket up his arse. You could practically see his power crackling on the air around him, writhing and coiling, bad luck waiting to be born and cursed on the living.

We stood there in our two groups, at opposite ends of the ballroom, separated by a sea of over-turned tables and chairs, and the suppurating remains of the Harrowing. Mr. and Mrs. Cavendish in their shabby undertakers' outfits, and the Jonah in his smart, smart suit, standing by the entrance doors. And me, Dead Boy, and Rossignol, standing by our abandoned barricade. The good guys and the bad guys, face to face for the inevitable confrontation.

I was looking unobtrusively around for an exit. I've never been much of a one for this kind of confrontation if there's an exit handy.

"Kill them," said Mr. Cavendish, in his cold, clipped voice.

"Kill them all," said Mrs. Cavendish, in her sharp clear voice.

"No," said the Jonah, and both the Cavendishes looked at him, surprised. He smiled, unmoved. "I want to see them suffer first."

The Cavendishes looked at each other. Both of them started to say something, then stopped. They considered the Jonah thoughtfully. Something had just changed in their relationship with their hired gun, and they weren't sure what.

"Come up onstage, all of you," said Billy Lathem, the Jonah, son of Count Entropy. "I want you to know exactly how badly you've failed, John. I want to explain it all to you, so you can see you never really stood a chance."

"Why should I do anything you say, Billy?" I said, genuinely interested in what his answer would be.

"Because I'll tell you the truth about what we did to poor dear Rossignol," said the Jonah.

Just like that he had me where he wanted me, and we both knew it. So I shrugged casually and headed for the stage, with all my hackles stirring. Something bad was coming, I could feel it, and it was aimed right at me. Dead Boy and Rossignol came with me. The Jonah said a few low words to the Cavendishes, and they followed him up onto the opposite side of the stage. We all stopped a cautious distance apart, then we all looked at the Jonah, to see how he wanted to play this. He was smiling a happy cruel smile, a predator about to play with his prey, for a while.

"We allowed Rossignol to escape from Caliban's Cavern," the Jonah said easily, "in order that we could follow her, to you. We were waiting for someone to make contact with her, and it wasn't really any surprise when the go-between turned out to be the besotted and predictable and stupidly loyal Ian Auger. The Cavendishes wanted me to trail Rossignol, then... take care of things, but I persuaded them to come along. I wanted them to see me take you down, John, to watch and appreciate as I destroy you, inch by inch. They don't get out much these days. Well, you can tell that from their awful pallor, can't you? I've seen things crawl out from under rocks sporting better tans. And they really don't like to be out and about in public, but I wanted them to be here, so here they are. Isn't it marvellous how things can work out, if you just put your mind to it?"

"So the servant becomes the master," I observed to the Cavendishes. "Or the monster turns on his creator, if you prefer. Not for the first time, of course. You do remember Sylvia Sin, don't you?"

"Charming girl," said Mr. Cavendish. "Always said she'd go far, didn't I, Mrs. Cavendish?"

"Indeed you did, Mr. Cavendish." The woman looked at me thoughtfully. "Have you seen the dear girl recently?"

"Yes," I said. "She was a monster. So I put her out of the misery you put her into."

"Oh, good," said the woman. "We do so detest loose ends. And as for the Jonah—why, he is our dear friend and ally, and we are very proud of him. We predict great things for him, in the future."

"Couldn't have put it better," said the man. "A person to be watched, and studied."

"What happened to Ian?" Rossignol said suddenly. "What did you do to him?"

"Ah, yes," said the Jonah. "Never cared much for the shifty little runt. Let's just say that the trio... has now become a duet." He sniggered loudly at his own wit, while Rossignol turned her head away. The Jonah looked at the Cavendishes. "Tell them. Tell them everything. I want them to know it all, to know how badly they've failed, before I do terrible things to them. You can start by telling them who you really are."

"Why not?" said the man. "It's not as if they will be around to tell anyone else."

"You tell it, Mr. Cavendish," said the woman. "You have always had a way with words."

"But you have always been the better story-teller, Mrs. Cavendish, and I won't have you putting yourself down."

"And I thank you kindly for saying that, my dear, but..."

"Get on with it!" said the Jonah.

"We are older than we look," said the man. "We have assumed many names and identities, down the years, but we are perhaps still best known for our original nom de guerre, in the nineteenth century—the Murder Masques."

"Yes," said the woman, smiling for the first time as she took in our expressions. "That was us. Uncontested crime lords of old London, the greatest villains of the Victorian Age. No sin was ever practised there, but we took our commission. We laughed at police and politicans. We even brought down the great Julien Advent himself."

"Or rather, you did," said the man. "Credit where credit is due, my very dear."

"But I couldn't have done it without you, dearest. Now, where was I? Ah, yes. We became involved with corruption in business, along with everyone else, and discovered to our surprise that there was far more money to be made in business than in crime, if business was approached with the right attitude. So we put aside our famous masques, cut off our old contacts, and made new names for ourselves in Trade. We prospered, mostly at the expense of our more timid competitors, and soon enough we became a Corporation. And as corporations are immortal, so we became immortal. Such things happen, in the Nightside. As our business thrives, so do we. As long as it exists, so shall we. Money is power, power is magic. And, of course, when the well-being of Cavendish Properties is threatened, so are we."

"So we take all such threats very seriously," said the man. "And we take all necessary steps to defend ourselves."

"You're just vultures," said Dead Boy. "Profiting from the weaknesses of others, feeding on the carcasses of those you bring down."

"The very best kind of business," said Mrs. Cavendish. "Born of the Age of Capitalism, we now embody it."

"That's why you call yourself Mr. and Mrs. all the time," I said, just to feel I was contributing something. "Because you've had so many identities, you have to keep reminding yourselves who you are these days."

"True," said Mr. Cavendish. "But irrelevant."

"Julien Advent will track you down," I said. "He's never forgotten you."

The Cavendishes shared a warm smile. "And we have never forgotten him," said the woman. "Because there's one part of the story, that oft-told legend, which dear Julien has never got around to telling. The great love of his life, the one who betrayed him to the Murder Masques and their waiting Timeslip, was me. I shall never forget the look of shock and horror on his face when I took off my Masque. I thought I'd never be able to stop laughing."

"He cried," said the man. "Indeed he did. Real tears. But then Julien always was a sentimental sort."

"He really had no-one but himself to blame," said the woman. "I was working as a dancer in the chorus line when he met me. Just another pretty face with an average voice and a good pair of legs, but he took a fancy to me. Gentlemen often did, in those days. He introduced me to a better life, to all sorts of expensive tastes and appetites. Some of which he proved unwilling to provide. He thought he was saving me. He should have asked me whether I wanted to be saved.

"Since he wouldn't give me what I wanted, I went looking for someone who would, and at one of Julien's soirees, I made the acquaintance of the generous gentleman at my side. The Murder Masque himself. He showed me a whole new world of monies and pleasures, and I took to it as to the manner born. And so I took up a Masque, too, and I found far more thrills as a lord of crime than I ever did in poor Julien's arms. In the end, when I pushed him into the Timeslip to be rid of him, I didn't feel anything at all."

"Tell them," the Jonah said impatiently. "Tell John what we did to Rossignol. I want to see his face, once he realises there's nothing he can do to save her."

"Our Rossignol grew just a little too independent as she became more popular," said Mr. Cavendish. He sounded stiff and even bored, as though he was only saying this to satisfy the Jonah's wishes. "She started taking meetings on her own, without consulting us first. Executives at the record companies professed to be concerned by the terms of our deal, though Rossignol had been glad enough to sign it at the time, when no-one else would touch her. Those executives assured Rossignol she could do much better with them. They promised their lawyers would easily break the contract, if she would only transfer her allegiance to them. So she came to us and demanded a better deal, or she would leave."

"The impudence of the girl!" said Mrs. Cavendish. "Of course, we couldn't allow her to do any such thing. Not after all the money we'd already invested in her. And all the money we stood to make. We found her, we made her, we groomed her. We made Rossignol into a viable product. We had a right to protect our investment. Don't think you're fighting the good fight here, Mr. Taylor. This damsel in distress doesn't need rescuing. From what, after all? Fame and fortune? We promised we would make her a star, and so we shall. But she is our property, and no-one else's."

"What about freedom of choice?" I said.

"What about it?" said Mr. Cavendish. "This is business we're talking about. Rossignol signed away all such nonsense when she put her fate in our hands. Rossignol belongs to Cavendish Properties."

"Is that why you murdered her?" said Dead Boy. "Because she wanted to leave and run her own life?"

The Cavendishes didn't seem at all surprised by the accusation. If anything, they preened a little.

"We didn't actually kill her," said the woman.

"Not quite," said the man.

"She isn't entirely dead," said the woman. "The poison we gave her took her to the very edge of death, then the Jonah found and imposed the one chance in a million that held her there, at death's very door, in an extended Near-Death Experience. And when she came back from the edge, and we revived her, the profound shock had reduced her will and vitality to such a malleable state that she imprinted on us and accepted us as surrogate parents and authority figures. We had to keep her isolated, of course, to preserve this useful emotional connection. But even so, she persisted in displaying annoying signs of independence... perhaps we need to poison her again and repeat the process, to put her back in the right frame of mind."

"You bastards," said Rossignol.

"Oh, hush, child," said the man. "Artistes never know what's best for them."

"But the best bit," said the Jonah, beaming happily, "the best bit is that only my will holds her where she is, on the very edge of death. My magic, my power. Her life is irrevocably linked to mine now. If you attack me, John, if you kill me, she goes all the way into the dark. Forever and ever. You don't dare threaten me."

"That's as may be," Dead Boy said mildly. "But what can you threaten me with? I only just met this girl, and her life and death are a small thing to me. You, on the other hand, have dared to meddle in my province, and I won't have that. I think I'll kill you anyway, Billy boy."

"Don't call me that! That's not my name any more! I'm..."

"The same irritating little tit you've always been, Billy."

"I'll..."

"You'll what? Kill me dead? Been there, done that, stole the T-shirt. And you're nowhere near powerful enough to break the compact I made."

"Perhaps not," said the Jonah, and suddenly he was smiling again. I stirred uneasily. I really didn't like that smile. The Jonah stepped forward to lock glares with Dead Boy. "You've done a really good job of stitching and stapling yourself together, down the years. All the wounds and damage you took, and never thought twice. Holding your battered and broken body together with superglue and duct tape. But... what if none of it had ever held? What if all your repairs just... failed?"

He made a short chopping gesture with one hand, and it was as though Dead Boy's body exploded. His back arched as black duct tape suddenly unwrapped and sailed away like streamers. Stitches and staples shot out, pattering softly to the stage, and his clothes were only tatters. No blood flowed, or any other liquid, but all at once there were gaping wounds opening everywhere in Dead Boy's death-white flesh. He collapsed as his legs failed him, pale pink organs and guts falling out of him, and he hit the stage hard. One hand fell away entirely, the fingers still twitching. Dead Boy lay still, wounds opening slowly like flowers. I'd never realised how much damage he'd taken. Rossignol gripped my arm so hard it hurt, but didn't make a sound. And I just stood where I was, because I couldn't think of a single damned thing I could do to help my friend.

"Entropy," the Jonah said smugly, "means *everything* falls apart. Look at you now, Dead Boy. Not so big now, are you? Can you still feel pain? I do hope so. You must have made a hell of a deal, to be able to survive so much punishment... Not that it's done you any good, in the end. Tell you what, Mr. and Mrs. Cavendish, why don't you come over here and do the honours. Send him on his way. I wouldn't want to be accused of hogging all the fun."

The Cavendishes looked at each other, sighed quietly, then moved forward to indulge the Jonah. They stood over Dead Boy and studied his stubbornly existing body with thoughtful frowns.

"We could always feed him into a furnace," said Mr. Cavendish.

"Indeed we could," said Mrs. Cavendish. "I always enjoy it so much more when they're still alive to appreciate what's happening."

"But I think a more immediate end is called for here," said the man. "Major players like Dead Boy have a habit of escaping their fates, if given the slightest chance."

"And we haven't existed this long by taking unnecessary chances with our enemies, Mr. Cavendish."

"Quite right, my dear."

They both drew handguns from hidden holsters and shot Dead Boy in the heart and in the forehead. He jerked convulsively, pink-and-grey brains spraying out the back of his head. And then he lay back and was perfectly still, and his eyes looked at nothing at all. The Cavendishes turned to face me, and I gave them my best sneer.

"Your guns don't have bullets in them any more, you bastards."

The Cavendishes pulled the triggers anyway a few times, but nothing happened. They shrugged pretty much in unison and went back to stand behind their Jonah.

"We've always believed in delegation," said the man.

"You wanted him, dear Billy," said the woman. "He's all yours."

The Jonah stepped forward, smiling his cocky smile like he had all the time in the world and wouldn't have rushed this for anything. "Still got a few tricks left up your sleeve, eh, John? But then, tricks are all you ever really had. Your precious gift for finding things was never a real power, not like mine. There's nothing you can do to stop me killing you and taking Rossignol back where she belongs. How shall I kill you, John? Let me count the ways... The cancers that lie in wait, needing only a nudge to swell and prosper. The arthritis that lurks in every joint, the bacteria and viruses to boil in your blood... Perhaps all of them at once might be amusing. You might even explode like Dead Boy! Or maybe... I'll find that one-in-a-million chance where you were born horribly deformed and helpless, and leave you like that. So everyone can see what happens to anyone foolish enough to cross the Jonah."

He could do it. He had the power. And all I had was a gift I didn't dare use again. Now my enemies knew exactly where I was, if I opened my mind to use my gift, they'd attack my mind directly. They'd take control of my mind and my soul in a second, then... there are worse things than death, in the Nightside. But without my gift, I didn't have anything strong enough to stop the Jonah and save Rossignol. All I had... was myself. I smiled suddenly, and the Jonah's grin faltered.

"Billy, Billy," I said, calm and easy and utterly condescending, "you never did understand the true nature of magic. It's not based in the power we wield or the gifts we inherit. In the end, it all comes down to will and intent. And the mind and soul behind them."

I locked eyes with the Jonah, and he stood very still. The whole world narrowed down to just the two of us, eye to eye, will to will. All we were, brought out onto the brightly lit mental stage, peeling back the layers to show who and what we were at the core. And for all his power, and despite everything he'd done, Billy Lathem looked away first. He actually staggered back a few steps, breathing hard, his face pale and sweaty.

"Who the hell are you?" he whispered. "What are you? You're not human..."

"More human than you, you little prick," said Rossignol. She stepped past me, and when the Jonah looked at her, she sang right into his face. Her voice was strong and true and potent, and she aimed it like a weapon right at him. I fell quickly backwards, clapping my hands to my ears. Beyond the Jonah, the Cavendishes were retreating, too, and protecting their ears. Rossignol sang, face to face with the Jonah—a sad, sad song of love lost and lovers gone, and all the secret betrayals of the heart. She sang directly at him, and he couldn't look away, couldn't back away, like a mouse hypnotised by a snake, like a fish on a hook. She held him where he was, with a merciless song of violation and isolation and the corruption of talent. Everything that had been done to her, she threw back at him. And the more she sang, the more it was the story of his life, too. Of poor little Billy Lathem, who might have been a Power and a Domination like his father, but had never been anything more than a hired thug.

The Cavendishes huddled together for comfort, as far away as they could get. I had my hands pressed so tightly to my ears I thought my skull would collapse under the pressure, and still the edges of the song ripped and tore at me, till my heart felt it would tear loose in my chest. Tears were running down my face. And Billy Lathem, forced to face the truth at last, whispered, *Daddy, I only wanted you to be proud of me...* and disappeared. Air rushed in to fill the space his body had occupied, as Billy turned his power on himself and selected the one chance where he was never born.

Rossignol stopped singing, though the power of her voice still seemed to reverberate on the air. She swayed suddenly on her feet, then collapsed. I grabbed her before she hit the floor, but caught off-balance, her weight carried both of us down. I sat on the stage, holding her in my arms, and only then realised she was dying. Her breathing was slowing, and I could feel her heart counting down to zero. Only the Jonah's will had kept her from death's door, and with him gone her long-delayed destiny was finally catching up with her. Vitality drained out of her, as though someone had opened a tap. I held her to me fiercely, as though I could stop it going through sheer force of will, but that trick never works twice.

"I promised I'd save you," I said numbly.

"You promised me the truth," said Rossignol, with pale lips that hardly moved. "I'll have to settle for that. Not even the great and mighty John Taylor can keep all his promises."

And just like that, she was gone. She stopped talking, she stopped breathing, and all the life went out of her. I still held her in my arms, rocking her quietly, still trying to comfort her.

"Oh dear," said Mr. Cavendish. "What a pity. Now we'll have to start all over again, with someone else."

"Never mind, Mr. Cavendish," said the woman. "Third time lucky."

I looked up at them, and there was murder in my eyes. They started pushing bullets into their guns, but their hands were trembling. And then we all looked round, startled, as Dead Boy spoke. It was just a whisper, with most of his lungs gone, but it was still and quite clear in the quiet.

"It's not over yet," he said, staring blindly up at the ceiling. "Rossignol is dead, but not actually departed. Not yet. There's still time, John. Still time to save her, if you've got the will and the courage."

"How is it you're still with us?" I said, too numb to be properly surprised. "Half of your insides are scattered across the stage. They blew your brains out, for God's sake!"

He chuckled briefly. An eerie, ghostly sound. "My body's been dead for years. It doesn't really need its internal organs any more. They don't serve any purpose. This body is just a shape I inhabit. A habit of living. Like eating and drinking and all the other things I do to help me pretend I'm still alive. You can still rescue Rossignol, John. I can use your life force to power a magic, to send both of us after her. Into the dark lands, the borderlands we pass through between this life and the next. When I died and came back, the door was left open a crack for me. I can go after her, but only a living soul can bring her back again. I won't lie to you, John. You could die, doing this. We could all go through that final door and never return. But if you're willing to try, if you're willing to give up all your remaining years in one last gamble, I promise you, we have a chance."

"You can really do this?" I said.

"I told you," said Dead Boy. "I know all there is to know about death."

"Ah, hell," I said. "I never let a client down yet."

"An attitude like that will get you killed," said Dead Boy.

"What if the Cavendishes attack us while we're gone? Destroy our bodies, so there's nothing left to come back to?"

"We'll be back the same moment we left. Or we won't be back at all."

"Do it," I said.

Dead Boy did it, and we both died.

Powered by all the remaining years of my life, Dead Boy and I went into the dark together, and for the first time I discovered there is a darkness even darker than the Nightside. A night that never ends, that never knew stars or a moon. The coldest cell, the longest fall. It was the absence of everything, except for me and Dead Boy. I was just a presence, without form or shape, a scream without a mouth to limit it, but I calmed somewhat as I sensed Dead Boy's presence. We spoke without voices, heard though there was no sound.

There's nothing here. Nothing...

Actually there is, John, but you're still too close to life to be able to appreciate it. Think yourself lucky.

Where's Ross?

Think of the darkness as a tunnel, leading us to a light. A way out. This way...

Yes... How can there be a direction when there's nothing...

Stop asking questions, John. You really wouldn't like the answers. Now follow me.

You've been this way before.

Part of me is always here.

Is that supposed to make me feel better? You're a real spooky person, you know that?

You have no idea, John. This way...

And we were falling in a whole new direction. It did help to think of the darkness as a tunnel, leading somewhere. We were definitely approaching something, though with no landmarks it was impossible to judge our speed or progress. I should have been scared, terrified, but already my emotions were fading away, as though they didn't belong there. Even my thoughts were growing fuzzy round the edges. But then I began to feel there was something ahead of me, something special, calling me. A speck of light appeared, beautiful and brilliant, all the colours of the rainbow in a single sharp moment of light. It grew unhurriedly, a great and glorious incandescence, yet still warm and comforting, like the golden beam from a lighthouse, bringing ships safely home through the long lonely nights. And then there was another presence with us, and it was Rossignol.

Are you angels?

Hardly, Ross. I don't think they're talking to me any more. This is John, with Dead Boy. We've come to take you home.

But I can hear music. Wonderful music. All the songs I ever wanted to sing.

For her it was music, for me it was light. Like the warm glow from a window, the friendly light of home after a long hard journey. Or pehaps the last light of the day, when all work is over, all responsibilities put aside, and we can all rest at last. Day is done. Welcome home, at last.

Oh, John, I don't think I want to go back.

I know, Ross. I feel it, too. It's like... we've been playing a game, and now the game's over, and it's time to go back where we belong...

There was a sense of taking her hand in mine, and we moved towards the light and the music. But Dead Boy had been there before. Kindly, remorselessly, he took us both by the hand and pulled us away, back to life and bodies and all the worries of the world.

I sat up sharply, dragging air deep into my lungs as though I'd been underwater for ages. The lesser light of the world crashed in around me. I'd never felt so clearly, starkly *alive*. My skin tingled with a hundred sensations, the world was full of sound, and Ross was right there beside me. She threw herself into my arms, and for a long moment we hugged each other like we'd never let go. But eventually we did and got to our feet again. We were back in the real world, with all its own demands and priorities. Dead Boy was standing before us, complete and intact again, resplendent in his undamaged finery. The only difference was the neat bullet hole in his forehead.

"Told you I know all there is to know about death," he said smugly. "Oh, I used some of your life energy to repair the damage the Jonah did to my body, John. Knew you wouldn't mind. Trust me, you won't miss it."

I glared at him. "Next time, ask."

Dead Boy raised an eyebrow. "I hope very much there isn't going to be a next time."

"Just how much of my life force did we use up on this stunt anyway?"

"Surprisingly little. It seems there is more to you than meets the eye, John. Mind you, there would have to be."

"You were dead!" said Mr. Cavendish, just a little shrilly. He sounded like he might be going to cry. "You were all dead, and now you're alive again! It just isn't fair!"

"That's the trouble with the Nightside," Mrs. Cavendish said sulkily. "You can't rely on people staying dead. Next time, do remember to bring some thermite bombs with us."

"Quite right, Mrs. Cavendish. Still, they all look decidedly weakened by whatever unnatural thing it was they just did, so I think it's back to the old reliable bullet in the head. Lots of them, this time."

"Exactly, Mr. Cavendish. If we can't have Rossignol, no-one can."

They aimed their reloaded guns at her. I moved to put myself between her and the guns, but that was all I could do. My time in the dark had taken everything else out of me, for the moment. I looked at Dead Boy, who shrugged.

"Sorry, I'm running on empty, too. Rossignol, any chance of a song?"

"Darling, right now I couldn't even squeak out a note. There must be something we can do!"

"Oh, shut up and die," said Mrs. Cavendish.

The two of them approached us, guns extended, taking their time, enjoying seeing their enemies helpless before them. They were going to shoot us all, and I had no magics left to stop them. But I've never relied on magic to get me through the many and varied dangers of the Nightside. I've always found using my wits and being downright sneaky much more reliable. So I waited till the Cavendishes were right in front of me, then I dug a good handful of pepper out of my hidden stash and threw it right into their smug, smiling faces. They both screamed pitifully as the pepper ground into their eyes, and I slapped the guns out of their flailing hands and gave the two of them a good smack round the back of the head, just on general principles. Dead Boy kicked their feet out from under them, and they ended up sitting on the stage, huddled together and clawing frantically at their streaming eyes.

"Condiments," I said easily. "Never leave home without them. And once the Authorities get here, I'll rub salt into your wounds as well."

At which point, an unconscious combat magician came flying onto the stage from the wings, upside down and bleeding heavily. He'd barely hit the stage with a resounding thud before two more combat magicians were backing quickly onto the stage, retreating from an unseen foe. Zen magics spat and shimmered on the air before them, as their rapidly moving hands wove cat's cradles of defensive magics. But Julien Advent, the great Victorian Adventurer himself, was more than a match for them. He bounded onstage with marvellous energy, dodging the thrown spells with practised skill, and proceeded to run rings around the bewildered combat magicians with breathtaking acrobatics and vicious fisticuffs. He moved almost too quickly to be seen, impossibly graceful, smiling all the time, smiting down the ungodly with magnificent ease.

Being an editor for thirty years didn't seem to have slowed him down at all.

He finally stood over three unconscious combat magicians, not even breathing hard, the bastard. Dead Boy and Ross and I applauded him because, you had to, really. Julien Advent actually was all the things they said he was. He shot me a quick grin as he took in the defeated Cavendishes.

"I see the cavalry probably wasn't needed after all. Good work, John. We were afraid we might be a little overdue."

I'd only just started to process the word *we* and get the beginnings of a really bad feeling, when Walker strolled on from the wings, and all I could think was *Oh shit. I'm really in trouble now.*

Walker strode over to consider the weeping, red-eyed Cavendishes, his face as always completely calm and utterly unreadable. Walker, in his neat city suit and bowler hat, representative of the Authorities, and quite possibly the most dangerous man in the Nightside. He had been given power over everyone and everything in the Nightside, and if you were wise, you didn't ask by whom. I would have run like hell, if I'd had any strength left.

The Cavendishes became aware of Julien's presence. They forced themselves up onto their feet and faced him defiantly. He studied their faces for a long moment, his smile gone, his eyes cold.

"I've always known who you were," he said finally. "The infamous Murder Masques, still villains, still unpunished. But I could never prove it, until now." He looked at me. "I knew if anyone could bring them down, it would be you, John. If only because you were too dumb to know it was impossible. So after you came to me, I contacted Walker, and we've been following you ever since. At a discreet distance, of course. We even stood in the wings and listened as the Cavendishes incriminated themselves with their gloating. It was all so very interesting I almost didn't hear the combat magicians until it was too late. I should have known the Cavendishes would bring backup."

"I speak for the Authorities," Walker said to the Cavendishes. "And I say you're history."

"It all began with them," said Julien. "They Timeslipped me because they wanted to seize my transformational potion, as their first big business venture. Typical, really. They couldn't just earn their money. They had to cheat. Little good it did them, because it was only after I was gone, slammed eighty years into the future in a moment, that they discovered there was no formula anywhere among my notes. I'd kept all the details in my head."

He stopped then and looked directly at Mrs. Cavendish. She stood a little straighter, still knuckling tears from one eye. The legendary Victorian Adventurer and his legendary lost love, the betrayed and the betrayer, face to face for the first time in over a century.

"Irene..."

"Julien."

"You haven't changed at all."

"Oh, don't look at me. I look awful."

"I've always known it was you. Hidden behind your new names and identities."

"Then why did you never come for me?"

"Because even the greatest love will die, if you stick a sharp enough knife through its heart. I knew it was you, but I couldn't prove it. You and your husband were very well protected. And in the end, I just didn't care any more. It was all such a long time ago, and I never did believe in living in the past."

She gaped at him, almost horrified. "All those years we spent waiting for you to come after us. Spinning webs and layers of protections around us, always hiding... all those years of being afraid of you, and you didn't give a damn."

"I had a new life to build, Irene. And there were far worse things than you in the Nightside that needed fighting."

She looked away. "I thought, sometimes, that you might have held back... because of me."

"My love died a long time ago. I don't know you now, Irene."

"You never did, Julien."

Mr. Cavendish moved in possessively beside his wife. "Enough talk! We all know why you're here! Have your precious revenge and be done with it! Kill us, for everything we did to you!"

"You never did understand me," said Julien. He looked at Walker. "Take them away. Destroy their business, dismantle it, and you destroy their power. Bring them to trial and send them down. Make them into little people, like all the ones they hurt. What better punishment, for such as these?"

"I'd be delighted," said Walker, tipping his bowler hat to Julien. "My people are already on their way."

Julien gave Walker a hard, thoughtful look. "These two probably know all sorts of top people and secrets. Don't let them wriggle out."

"Not going to happen," Walker said easily. "I've been looking for an excuse to bring the Cavendishes down. Trouble-makers, always rocking the boat, never playing well with others. They might even have become a threat to the Authorities, in time. And we can't have that, can we?"

He turned unhurriedly to look at me, and I braced myself. "Well, John," said Walker. "You've led me quite a chase. Who's been a bad boy, then? But... not to worry. Helping me put away two big fish like these goes a long way to making up for all the trouble you've caused the Nightside tonight. Only just, mind..."

Julien looked at me sharply, suddenly scenting a story. "John, what is he talking about?"

"Haven't a clue," I lied, cheerfully.

TEN

CODA, WITH A DYING FALL

A week later, I caught Rossignol's new set at Caliban's Cavern. It was a sell-out, she was singing up a storm, and the audience loved it.

A lot had changed in the past week. The Cavendishes had had to sell Caliban's Cavern, for quick cash, to help them pay their mounting legal bills. The charges against them were building all the time, with more and more people coming out of the woodwork to kick the Cavendishes while they were safely down. It was fast becoming the Nightside's favourite sport.

Rossignol was under new management. Some group of show business lawyers who knew a good thing when they heard it and were wise enough to present Rossignol with a reasonably fair contract. They were putting a lot of money behind her, and the word was she was going to break big. She was already recording her first album, with a respected big-name producer.

The club that night was really swinging. The audience packed the place from wall to wall and danced in the aisles. It was a more usual mix this time, with hardly any of the old Goth element. Rossignol was moving upmarket with her new material. I was there on my own. Dead Boy was off working on another case, and Julien Advent had a paper to put out. I could have asked my secretary Cathy, but she'd lost interest in Rossignol once she'd gone mainstream. Cathy was strictly cutting-edge only.

Backed by two Ian Augers, a new drummer, and all new backing singers, Rossignol sang of love and light and rebirth in her clear glorious voice, touching the hearts of all who heard her. She was strong and vibrant and magnificently alive. She still hung off the microphone stand and smoked like a chimney, though. The crowd loved her. She took three encores, to rapturous applause, and nobody even looked like they were thinking of killing themselves. It's nice when a case has a happy ending.

After the show, I went round the back to her dressing room. To my surprise, the door was being guarded by Dead Boy. He had the grace to look just a little embarrassed.

"So, this is your new case," I said. "No wonder you didn't want to talk about it. Bodyguarding is a bit of a step down for you, isn't it?"

"It's only temporary," he said with great dignity. "Until she and her new management can agree on someone they trust."

"She could have asked me," I said.

"Ah," said Dead Boy. "John, she's trying to forget what happened. You can't blame her, really."

"What happened to the bullet hole in your forehead?" I said, deliberately changing the subject.

"Filled it in with builder's putty," he said briskly. "Once I've grown my hair out a bit, you'll never notice it."

"And the hole in the back?"

"Don't ask."

I knocked on the dressing room door and went in. The room was full of flowers. I would have brought some, but I never think of these things. Rossignol was taking off her make-up in front of the mirror. She didn't seem particularly pleased to see me. She gave me a quick hug, kissed the air near my cheek, and we sat down facing each other. Her face was flushed, and she was still a little breathless from the set.

"Thank you for all your help, John. I do appreciate it, really. I would have phoned, but I've been very busy putting the new set together."

"I was out there," I said. "It went over great."

"It did, didn't it? John... don't take this wrong, but, I don't want to see you again."

"There doesn't seem any good way to take it," I said, after a moment. "What brought this on, Ross?"

"You remind me too much of bad times," she said bluntly. "I need to move on, leave it all behind. Now I'm alive again, I see things differently. I live only to sing. It's all I've ever wanted or needed. There's no room for anyone else in my life, right now. And especially not for you, John. I am grateful for everything you've done, but... as near as possible, I want to live a normal life now. I'm not staying in the Nightside. It was only ever somewhere to make a start. I'm going places, John."

"Yes," I said.

"I'll write a song about you, someday."

"That would be nice."

She turned away and started removing her make-up again, pulling faces at herself in the mirror. "You never did say—who hired you to look after me?"

"It was your father."

She looked at me sharply. "John, my father's been dead for two years now."

She dug into her bag and found an old photo. It was unmistakably the man who'd come into Strangefellows to hire me. So—a ghost. Not all that unusual, for the Nightside. Rossignol was touched.

"He always was very protective."

"Well," I said, "I guess I don't get paid for this case, either."

I gave Rossignol a good-bye kiss, wished her all the luck in the world, and left her dressing room. Humming the blues.

HEX AND THE
CITY

ONE

THE
PSYCHENAUTS

You can find anything in the Nightside, from the sacred to the profane and back again, but I don't recommend attending the auctions there unless you've got a strong stomach and nerves of steel. I don't normally go to auctions any more, even though most people are afraid to bid against me. I always end up saddled with a crateful of junk, just to get the one thing I do want. One time I accidentally acquired a Pookah, and for a few months I was followed around the Nightside by a Playboy Bunny Girl invisible to everyone except me. Fun, but distracting.

However, when you work as a private investigator in the Nightside, that hidden magical heart of London, where gods and monsters walk side by side, and sometimes attend the same self-help groups, some cases almost inevitably lead you to the most unpleasant places. The head auctioneer of the Nightside's Great Auction Hall hired me to stand watch over one particularly contentious auction, to keep the bidders in line. It sounded straight forward enough, which should have been a warning. Nothing's ever straight forward in my life.

I turned up nice and early, so I could look the place over. It had been several years since I was last there, and in between I'd left the Nightside on the run, with a bullet in my back, and reluctantly returned to stage a semi-triumphant comeback. The doorman at the Hall took one look at me and didn't want to let me in, but I gave him my name, and he turned satisfyingly pale and stepped back to wave me in. A good, or rather bad, reputation will get you into places that a battalion of troops wouldn't.

The head auctioneer stopped pacing nervously up and down and came striding across the great empty Hall to greet me. She grudged me a brief smile and crushed my hand in an over-firm handshake. Lucretia Grave was a short, sturdy woman in an old-fashioned tweedy outfit, surmounted by a monocle screwed firmly into one dark, beady eye. She appeared to be in her early fifties, with a brutal bulldog face and grey hair scraped back into a really severe bun on the back of her head. She looked like she could punch her weight. She glared at me like it was all my fault, and got stuck right in.

"About time you got here, Taylor, old thing. I haven't felt safe in me own Hall since the damned thing arrived. I've had piles that gave me less problems. I know we say we'll auction anything you can find, capture, or manhandle through the doors, but some things are just more trouble than they're worth. I wouldn't have anything to do with the bloody thing, if I wasn't on commission. I've been playing the doggies again, you know how it is. Rotten animals only have to hear I've put good money on them and they immediately develop back problems and heart conditions. Still, you mark my words, old thing; this particular item is going to go for serious money." She scowled unhappily and sniffed loudly. "It's days like this I wish I was back at me old job, at Christie's. I'd go back in a second if only I could be sure the police weren't still looking for me."

I was about to ask, politely but very firmly, what the hell we were talking about, when we were interrupted by a whole bunch of six-foot-tall teddy bears, carrying in the various items up for auction that session. The bears swept straight past us, carrying the items carefully in their soft, padded arms, talking in low, growly voices. The bears all looked like they'd seen a lot of rough handling, and as they passed Lucretia Grave a few muttered loudly about the need to get unionised. They set out each object in its own glass display case, treating every item with great care and respect.

"I'd better check everything's where it's supposed to be," Grave said heavily. "They all mean well, but they're bears of very little brain. Typical bloody management, trying to save money again. You have a look around, old thing, get the feel of the place, *don't touch anything.*"

And off she strode, like a tug-boat under full steam, to hector the bears. I let her go. It was either that or throw her to the floor, tie her up, and sit on her till I got some useful answers out of her; and I couldn't be bothered. I looked around. The Great Auction Hall had started out life as a thirteenth-century tithe barn, and had changed remarkably little down the years. The walls were a creamy grey stone, in large close-fitting blocks held together by artistry and tradition rather than mortar, rising up to soaring wooden rafters that came together in a complex latticework half-hidden in shadows. There were only slit windows in the walls, and the floor was unpolished wood, covered in sawdust. Fluorescent rods provided almost painfully bright light. There were no comforts or luxuries, but then, people didn't come here to admire the scenery. The Great Auction Hall was a place of serious business.

I walked past the rows of cheap wooden folding seats, set up to face the no-frills auctioneer's stand, and looked over the various items in their display cases. It was the usual mixture, the famous and the infamous, of dubious value and debatable provenance. You could buy anything in the Nightside, whatever your interests or pleasure, but no-one guaranteed it was necessarily what it seemed to be. You could get lucky, or you could get dead, with precious little room in between. And just because you owned a thing, it didn't mean you could always hang on to it...

The first item was a heavy thigh-bone, identified as the weapon with which Cain slew Abel. There was a letter of confirmation from the ancient city of Enoch, but you took such things with a pinch of salt in the Nightside. Next in line were three different Maltese Falcons (buyer beware), a cast-brass head of JFK that supposedly spoke prophecy, Nostradamus's quill pen, one of Baron Frankenstein's scalpels, a small lacquered wooden box that claimed it held the ashes of Joan of Arc, and a Yeti's-foot umbrella stand. The rest was just junk and tat, stuff only a collector could love. Certainly nothing I'd give house-room.

I've never believed in acquiring objects of power. They always let you down. Either the batteries run out at the worst possible moment, or you go blank on the activating word; and you can never find the instruction manual when you need it. More trouble than they're worth. And far too many of them turn out to be just bits and pieces that have hung around long enough to acquire a reputation. Not unlike me, I suppose.

I paused to study myself in a tall standing mirror in an ornate silver frame. (It was labelled The Mirror of Dorian Gray; make of that what you will.) The reflection didn't look anything special; though I supposed I did at least look like a private eye. Tall, dark, and interesting-looking, wrapped in a long white trench coat that hadn't seen a laundry anywhen recent. A bit tired and battered round the edges, maybe, but that's life in the Nightside for you. I tend to get the cases no-one else wants, the kind other investigators have the good sense to turn down, and I like it that way. I have a gift for finding things, whether they want to be found or not, a hunger for the truth, and a stubborn streak that keeps me in the game long after anyone with any sense would have legged it for the horizon.

My father drank himself to death, after finding out my mother wasn't human. No-one knows who or what my mother really was, but everyone in the Nightside's got an opinion. There are those who treat me like the Antichrist, and others who see me as a king-in-waiting. And, an unknown group of enemies have been sending agents to kill me ever since I was a small child.

I try not to let it go to my head.

Lucretia Grave came stomping back to join me. She was wearing the monocle in the other eye now. I wondered whether I was supposed to say something, but decided not to. Some conversations you just know aren't going to go anywhere useful. Grave started in on me again as though we'd never stopped talking.

"We get all kinds of stuff coming through here on a regular basis, old sport, things you wouldn't believe, even for the Nightside. Some silly sod put his soul up for auction just the other week, but it didn't make the reserve. Ah yes, I've seen it all come and go, and known more than my fair share of tears and curses. Property is the curse of the thinking classes. Now, Taylor, old boy; the Hall is of course surrounded by heavy-duty wards and protections at all times, protecting us from fire, theft, substitution, and any and all outside influences, and the whole place is guaranteed neutral ground by the Authorities themselves, and respected as such even by really hard cases like the Collector. As I understand it, the Hall was the cause of so many disputes by so many high rollers that the Authorities just stepped in and took over the business themselves, to make sure all deeds were kept and honoured... So we should be safe enough..."

"But?" I said.

"But, today we're auctioning something rather special, even for us. That's why you're here, old thing. If everything does all go to Hell in a hand-cart, and I for one wouldn't be at all surprised if it did, you get to stick your hand up and say, *Stop thief*. What you do after that is your problem. Only don't look to me for help, because I shall have headed for the nearest exit. And don't look to the bears, either. They mean well, but they've only got sawdust where their balls should be. If all else fails, I suppose you can always use your famous gift to track down wherever the thief's taken it..."

"Why did you hire me?" I asked, genuinely interested.

Grave sniffed loudly. "Our insurance people insisted we hire someone, and you were the best... our budget could stretch to."

I was still looking for a response to that when we were approached by a familiar figure. It was Deliverance Wilde, fashion consultant and style guru to the Faerie of the Unseeli Court. Tall, loudly Jamaican, sharp and bitter and a defiant chain-smoker. If anyone ever found the nerve to object, she blew the smoke into their faces. She was currently wearing an elegantly tailored suit of a vivid lavender shade, which contrasted interestingly with her blue-black skin, topped by a very feathery hat. I raised an eyebrow at the new look, but as always Wilde got her retaliation in first.

"Don't show your ignorance, darling. Lavender is this season's colour, whether it likes it or not."

She struck a studiedly casual pose before me, head tilted back to better show off her high cheekbones and sensual mouth. Deliverance Wilde treated the whole world like a catwalk. Yet her eyes had trouble meeting mine, and the hand holding her cigarette wasn't as steady as it might have been. Wilde was nervous about something. Now, it might just have been the strain of meeting me. I do tend to make people nervous; it's part of my carefully crafted reputation. But Wilde wasn't really focussed on me, or even Grave. Instead, she glared about the Auction Hall, shooting quick puffs of smoke in every direction.

"I always hate coming back to the Nightside," she said abruptly. "Vulgar, darlings, utterly vulgar. I prefer to spend my time with the Faerie. They're so... delightfully shallow and superficial."

Lot you know, I thought, but had the sense not to say it aloud. Wilde had been known to stub her cigarette out on people who annoyed her.

"I only come back here to attend the fashion shows and stock up on ciggies," she continued remorselessly. "And to carry out the odd spot of business, of course." She looked at me directly for the first time. "I'm glad you're here, John. It means the Auction Hall is taking this event seriously. As they should. I have got my hands on... something rather special."

Lucretia Grave snorted loudly. "I should say so, old dear. Unique, priceless, and bloody dangerous with it. Some things should be left alone, or at the very least prodded with a stick from a safe distance."

"Would somebody please tell me what it is we're talking about?" I said, and something in my voice made them both sit up and take notice. Wilde took a last drag on her cigarette, dropped it on the floor, and ground it out under her boot. Grave glared at her. Wilde immediately lit up another, on principle, and fixed me with a thoughtful gaze.

"I have hit the big time at last, darling. I found my little prize accidentally, while looking for something else, but then, isn't that always the way? I was off on my travels, looking for Something Different with which to pique the interest of those notoriously fickle and demanding Faerie, and I ended up in Tokyo, investigating reports of this marvellous new firm that specialised in creating these utterly amazing bonsai volcanoes, complete with regular eruptions and lava flows. But by the time I got there, the firm was gone, and their shop was just this big smoking hole in the ground. I could have told them MORE BANG FOR YOUR BUCK was a really bad idea for a slogan... Anyway, I got side-tracked to China, where I found... that."

And she indicated one of the smaller display cases with a dramatic gesture and a sprinkling of ash because she'd forgotten the cigarette in her hand. She muttered a series of baby swear words and brushed the ash off the top of the case, while I leaned forward for a closer look. Behind the glass was a single butterfly, not particularly big or small, or especially pretty. In fact, it looked distinctly ordinary. It hung in mid air, in mid-flight, wings extended, surrounded by the faint shimmer of a stasis field. The butterfly had been frozen in a moment of Space and Time, like an insect preserved in amber. I looked back at Wilde, but again she got in first while I was still raising an eye-brow.

"Yes, it's rare, but not in the way you think. The explanation's a bit complex, but try and keep up. Chaos theory says that if a butterfly flaps its wings over China, we end up with a storm over America. Since everything in the world is connected, or at least on speaking terms. So, if you could identify and track down that particular butterfly... Well, I have, and there it is. The little troublemaker. A wonderfully unique item, which I intend to let go for an equally unique price. Oh, the Collector is going to be *so* jealous!"

(Wilde and the Collector had a thing going once. It didn't work out. No-one ever thought it would, but you just can't tell some people.)

"The butterfly theory is nothing new, really," said Grave, in her most academic and tweedy voice. Auctioneers always sound like failed schol-ars. Probably because most of them are. "The ancient Romans had people called Augurs who could predict the future by studying the flight of birds."

Wilde gave her a withering look. "They also had a tendency to cut open goats, then accuse people of treason over which way the goat's liver was point-ing. And give themselves lead poisoning with their choice of plumbing materials."

"Let us all make a valiant effort to stick to the point, please," I said. "Isn't the whole butterfly thing just a metaphor? There isn't a real butterfly, as such."

Wilde hit me with her most withering smile. "Metaphors can be as real as anything else in the

Nightside, darling. Symbols can have their own identity here. So, whatever lucky person takes possession of this butterfly at auction will possess the power to identify all such *butterflies*; the first domino in the line that will produce future events. The owner should then be able to predict and possibly even control the way the future turns out. The possibilities are endless! In theory, anyway. Trust me on this, John darling; I am going to be rich, rich, rich!"

"If it's so potentially powerful, why are you so ready to give it up?" I asked.

Wilde struck her best *Why am I beset by fools of no vision* pose. "John. Darling. I am not stupid enough to try and keep anything this earth-shattering for myself. I'd have to spend all my time fighting off major players who wanted to take it away from me. And you can bet the Faerie wouldn't deign to get involved, the ungrateful little shits. No, an auction, on famously neutral ground, is the best way to make a substantial profit on this little beauty." She blew a kiss at the butterfly in its case. "And then I shall take all the money and run, all the way back to the Unseeli Court, and not show my head again until the last of the shooting's died down."

"Given the clear potential for things to get really nasty really quickly, I'm surprised the Authorities haven't stepped in to confiscate the butterfly," I said, frowning. "Walker doesn't normally approve of anything that threatens to upset his precious status quo."

"Walker might like to think he's in charge of things round here," Wilde said dismissively, "but the Authorities have always understood that free enterprise has to come first."

"Philistines," said Grave, polishing her monocle furiously.

"Or," I said, "perhaps the Authorities don't believe this butterfly is the real thing, either."

Wilde smiled widely and blew a perfect smoke ring. "Don't care was made to care, darling."

By now the bidders had started filing in and were already squabbling over who had rights to seats in the front row. I politely excused myself to Wilde and Grave, and took a stroll round the perimeter of the Hall while I watched the crowd assemble noisily. Most were just anonymous faces, there to represent people or interests who didn't care to be publicly identified, or just the usual hopeful souls in search of a bargain. Some were clearly celebrity spotters, there to see history being made by the butterfly's sale. It ended up as quite a large crowd, filling all the seats and leaning against the walls. The teddy bears had to bring in more chairs, grumbling audibly under their breath as they did so. (There were human staff on hand to pass out the glossy sale brochures; apparently the bears considered doing so beneath their dignity.) The crowd buzzed with talk, of a more or less friendly kind, and there was much craning of necks to look at the butterfly, or spot rival bidders. Lucretia Grave stepped up behind her auctioneer's podium and gestured for silence with her gavel as Wilde stood proudly behind her butterfly's display case. I lurked at the back of the Hall, watching the crowd.

And then everything stopped as a huge shaggy Yeti stomped into the Hall. It was a good eight feet tall, with vast, rolling muscles under its grubby white pelt. Everyone shrank back as the great creature lumbered down the aisle, grabbed the Yeti's-foot umbrella stand, glared menacingly at one and all, then stomped out again. No-one felt like trying to stop it. After a discreet pause, to be sure the Yeti was gone and wouldn't be coming back, the auction finally got under way.

Grave started with the lesser items, and they all went fairly quickly under the hammer. Everyone was impatient to get to the star item. I concentrated on studying the more famous faces in the crowd. I wasn't surprised at Jackie Schadenfreud's presence, right in the middle of the crowd. Jackie was an emotion junkie, and I could see him savouring and sucking up the various moods of the crowd as they washed around him. Jackie had insisted on making himself known to me when he arrived, shaking me by the hand and hanging on to it just that little bit too long. He was fat and sweaty, with a twitchy smile and watery eyes. He wore a Gestapo uniform, all black leather and silver insignia, along with a Star of David on a chain round his neck. Just so he could soak up the emotions those conflicting symbols evoked. To protect him from the many who might feel outraged, Jackie was always accompanied by an oversized Dobermann that he'd had dyed pink.

Sandra Chance, the consulting necromancer, had stalked into the Hall like she owned the place, but then she always did. Chance had raised arrogance to an art form. She commandeered a seat in the front row, right before the podium, as hers by right, and no-one challenged her. Few ever did.

Chance was tall and slender, unhealthily pale under a mop of curly red hair, and wore nothing but crimson swirls of liquid latex, splashed all over her long body apparently at random. (Supposedly the liquid latex was mixed with holy water and other things, for protection.) She also had enough steel piercings in her face and body to make her a danger during thunderstorms. A simple leather belt covered in Druidic symbols hung loosely around her waist, carrying a series of tanned pouches that held the tools of her trade; grave dirt, powdered blood, eye of newt and toe of frog. The usual. I watched her very carefully. She ignored the lesser items as they went under the hammer. She was just there for the butterfly, and everyone knew it. Her face was all sharp angles, with cold intelligent eyes and a grim smile, and I knew her of old.

Chance specialised in cases where someone had died, usually suddenly and violently and very unexpectedly. She could get you answers from beyond the grave, if you weren't too fussy about the methods involved. I worked a few cases with her, back in the day, but we didn't get along. She only cared about getting results, and bad luck to anyone who got in her way. I used to be like that, but I like to think I've moved on. To me, Chance was a reminder of bad times—and two people I wasn't very fond of. She looked round suddenly, and caught my gaze. She'd always had good instincts. She nodded frostily, and I nodded back, then we both looked away again.

Chance currently had a relationship with one of the Nightside's more disturbing major players; that terrible old monster called the Lamentation.

Sometimes known as the God of Suicides or the Saint of Suffering. Just saying its name aloud had been known to push people over the edge. No-one knew exactly what kind of relationship Chance had with the Lamentation, and most people with an imagination were afraid even to guess. Some things just aren't healthy, even for the Nightside. Chance had never shown any interest in auctions before, to my knowledge; so, could she be bidding on behalf of the Lamentation? Perhaps. But what would the God of Suicides want with the chaos butterfly? Nothing anyone else would want or approve of, certainly. I wondered if perhaps I ought to do something. After all, who'd be crazy enough to bid against an agent of the Lamentation? And then I looked around me and relaxed a little. There were more than enough major players here to stand against Chance, especially if they got caught up in bidding fever.

And if by some malign chance she did end up winning, I could always do the public-spirited thing—steal the butterfly and run like hell.

Sitting not far away were the Lord of the Dance and the Dancing Queen, ostentatiously not talking to each other, on principle. Odds were neither of them actually wanted the butterfly; they just didn't want the other to have it. Once handfasted, now divorced, they each led very separate dance religions. The Lord of the Dance was currently boasting an ethnic Celtic look, complete with woad and ritual scarring, while the Dancing Queen stuck to her beloved disco diva look. It was always a joy to watch them enter a room, their every movement graceful and poised and significant, as though they were moving to music only they could hear.

Among the last to arrive had been the Painted Ghoul, openly there to bid on behalf of the Collector. (Who was too proud to appear in person, having been caught trying to steal things on three separate occasions.) The Painted Ghoul was the nastiest, most evil-looking clown you'd ever not want to meet in a back alley. His baggy costume was composed of fiercely clashing colours, and his leering, made-up face suggested unnameable depravities. He swaggered into the Hall like a pimp in a schoolyard, flashing a crimson grin full of teeth filed down to points.

"Hiya, hiya, hiya, boys and girls! Great to be here. I just flew in from Sodom and it ain't my arms that's tired! Anyone want to play Find the Lady? I'm almost sure I can remember where I buried her..."

He was the proverbial Clown at Midnight, the smile on the killer's face, the laugh that ends in a bubble of blood. But he was still really just a glorified errand boy, for all the airs he gave himself.

I looked round sharply as the bidding finally got to the butterfly. Suddenly it seemed like everyone was trying to bid at once. Grave did her best to keep order, but even her experienced auctioneer's eye had trouble following every raised hand or nodding head. Harsh words and even blows broke out here and there as people became convinced they were being deliberately overlooked. I strode quickly up and down the aisles, glaring people into better behaviour, but trouble broke out faster than I could put it down. Sandra Chance kept pushing the price up, but no-one looked like dropping out. The Paint-ed Ghoul leaned back in his seat, smiling nastily as he topped Chance's bid. Others clamoured to be heard, and open brawling broke out as Grave looked desperately this way and that. The chaos butterfly was a great enough prize to fuel anyone's ambitions. I considered the situation and didn't like what I saw. The mood of the crowd was angry and frustrated, and on the verge of getting really nasty. The Hall's built-in wards would prevent any magi-cal attacks but couldn't do anything to stop a gun or a knife. And whoever ended up winning, it prom-ised to be trouble. It looked like I was actually going to have to do something. Usually I could get away with a quiet word and a harsh look, and rely on my reputation to calm things down, but we were already well beyond that.

And that was when I noticed something... odd. Despite all the tension and chaos, and the threat of imminent violence on all sides, I was humming the tune of an old song from the Seventies. It was "Bridget the Midget the Queen of the Blues"; one of those comedy novelty singles by Ray Stevens. Hadn't thought of it in years. Even stranger, most of the people nearest me were humming the same tune. Some had even broken off bidding to sing along, though their expressions suggested they didn't know why. I got chills up my back, as I realised the song was spreading through the crowd. In the Nightside, coincidence and compul-sion often meant something. And what it usually indicated was interference from Outside.

And then even Grave stopped taking bids and rubbed hard at her forehead, as though bothered by some intrusive thought. Sandra Chance and the Painted Ghoul were both on their feet, looking confusedly about them. A growing murmur of unease ran through the crowd. The song's moment had passed, but we could all feel something—a growing sense of pressure from a direction none of us could name. More people rose to their feet, looking round wildly. No-one new had come into the Hall, but we all knew we weren't alone any more.

"Something's coming," said Sandra Chance. "Something bad."

A few people protested at the interruption of the bidding, but were quickly shouted down. Pretty much everyone was on their feet now, looking around for threats but seeing nothing. Various weapons appeared in nervous hands. The teddy bears huddled together, hints of claws appearing on their padded paws. The Hall grew silent and tense. There was a growing pressure on the air, like a gathering storm, like the moment before lightning strikes. And suddenly, all around the Great Auction Hall, wards and protections that had stood for centuries broke and blew apart in coruscations of vivid energies, shattered by a growing presence they were never meant to contain or keep out—a living presence, vast and inhuman, seeping into our reality like poison into a clear spring.

I knew what it was, what it had to be. I recognised the signs. A psychenaut; a traveller from some higher or lower dimension. An intruder that could not be stopped or turned aside because it was either too real or not real enough to be affected by human powers. I'd had some experience with psychenauts, back when I apprenticed with old Carnacki, the Ghost Finder. It didn't seem fair that I should have to face something so awful twice in one lifetime. I would have run, but I knew I'd never make it.

The crowd was already beginning to panic when the first protrusions from a lower dimension began to manifest. Unfocussed energies sleeted through the Hall, sparking black rainbows and shimmering auras around people who weren't actually there, before sinking into physical objects and lending them a horrible animation. Ugly, distorted faces formed themselves out of the materials of the walls, floor, and ceiling. Thick lips curled back to reveal jagged teeth, while dark eyes rolled grinding in their sockets, and abhuman voices shuddered through our heads, saying *We are coming, we are coming*. The wooden fingertips of a huge hand thrust slowly up from among the rows of seats, and the crowd scattered, shrieking and screaming, and shouting Words of Power that had no influence on what was forcing its way into our world from the underpinnings of reality.

The cheap wooden seats suddenly exploded into lashing wooden tentacles, springing out to wrap themselves around the fleeing crowd, holding them tightly. More screams rose as arms and legs broke under the inhuman pressure of the wooden bonds. Great faces in the floor drank up the spilled blood, making noises thick with meaning that predated language. The walls were swelling in and out, as though in rhythm to some great thing breathing, and the whole Hall shook, the floor rising and falling like a ship at sea.

Poltergeist activity stormed all around us. Events were happening so fast now no-one could react quick enough to keep up with them. Any object left unsecured flew violently back and forth, or spontaneously combusted. Clothes grew too large, or ripped and tore as they shrank. Fires burned unsupported on the air, and beads of sweat rolled sluggishly up the walls. There were hails of stones and rains of fish, and people spoke in unknown tongues.

I fought my way through the chaos to grab hold of Lucretia Grave, who was on her knees and clinging numbly to her rocking podium. I hauled her back onto her feet, and she clung to me like a child. I had hoped she'd have some emergency backup magics she could call on, but it didn't look like it. The teddy bears were staggering back and forth among the panicking crowd, trying to help, but there was little they could do except try and shield people with their padded bodies.

A genius loci invaded the Hall, overpowering and supplanting the old Barn's actual ambience, and, immediately, powerful emotions stormed our minds, slapping aside our defences with contemptuous ease. People began laughing, crying, and howling with an hysteria that shook them the way a dog shakes a rat. I was laughing so hard I hurt, but I couldn't stop. And then the horrors swept through us all, the same basic fears; of the dark, of falling, of people not being who we thought they were. People struck out at each other because they had to strike out at something. Men and women fell down and did not rise again, forced into catatonia by terrors and emotions they couldn't face.

There was a new genius loci in residence, and the Great Auction Hall had become an alien, unbearable place. A few people staggered towards the exits, only to find that the doors had disappeared. There was no way out any more.

Jackie Schadenfreud had swollen up like a blowfish, blowing off all the silver buttons on his Nazi greatcoat. He giggled painfully, soaking up the emotions around him, force-fed on feelings beyond his appetite or capacity. Thick bloody tears ran down his pink cheeks as his eyes bulged in their sockets. His dog had already torn its own guts out. The Painted Ghoul ran up a swelling wall, scuttling like an oversized insect, trying to get away from emotions he usually inflicted only on others. Sweat was making his makeup run, and he wasn't smiling any more.

Sandra Chance's magics were mostly useless, being concerned primarily with the dead, not elementals, but she was still fighting back. She stood proudly in a shimmering circle of protection, magnificently angry, forcing back the psychenaut intrusions by sheer force of will. She had an aboriginal pointing bone, and in whichever direction she trained it the animating forces were thrust out of the material world. But only for a while. They always came back.

The Lord of the Dance and the Dancing Queen, united again by the threat of a common enemy, beat out powerful harmonies on the heaving floor with their dancing feet. They danced their fury and their outrage out into the world, forcing back the invading presences. Their feet slammed down, hammering out marvellous rhythms, their every movement wonderfully graceful, their bodies radiating defiant humanity in the face of the inhuman. They had always danced their best when they danced together.

Deliverance Wilde stood inside a faerie ring, protected by her compact with the Unseeli Court, but helpless to do anything. She wrung her hands together, looking piteously about her.

And I stood alone, only marginally affected by the horrors around me, and reluctantly decided I'd have to do something.

I don't like actually having to do things. I like to keep what I can and can't do a mystery; it helps build my reputation. You can do more with a bad reputation than you can with any magic. Usually. But while the psychenauts were holding back from me for the moment, perhaps confused by my nature, there was no guaranteeing how long that would last. I knew what the problem was, and I thought I knew how to solve it, so once again it was up to me to haul everyone back from the gates of Hell. If I was wrong, the odds were I was going to die, in any number of really unpleasant ways; but I was used to that.

Back when I worked with Carnacki the Ghost Finder, he'd used a charm of Banishing on a psychenaut, driving it out of a haunted funfair, and afterwards I pocketed the charm when he wasn't looking. He had loads of the things, and I had a feeling it might come in handy someday. I dug through the various mystical junk that accumulates in my pockets and finally hauled out a golden coin that came originally from the land of Nod. It had writing on it no-one could understand, and a face that was mostly worn away, but still subtly disturbing. I've never liked relying on such things, but needs must when the Outside is kicking down your door. If it didn't work, I could hardly go back to Carnacki and complain. Objects of power rarely come with warranties.

I held up the coin and spoke the activating Word of Power, and a terrible light radiated from the coin, too bright and piercing for merely human eyes. I had to turn my head away, and my hand holding the coin felt like it was on fire. The Banishing leapt out into the Hall, eager to be about its implacable business. It roared through the Hall, speaking words in a tongue older than Humanity, tearing the animating spirits out of the physical creation and forcing them back, down through the bottom of the world, back into the underpinnings of reality. The psychenauts were gone, and with them the overpowering emotions and debilitating fears. The walls and the floor and the ceiling grew still and solid again, and the wooden arms holding men and women fell apart into splinters. People looked slowly about them, daring to believe the worst might be over.

And Sandra Chance said, in a heartbreakingly matter-of-fact voice, "Something else is coming."

It was another psychenaut. A traveller from a higher dimension this time. We could all feel it coming, could feel Something unbearably vast descending into our reality. Something so impossibly big it had to compress itself to fit into our narrow Space/Time continuum. Everyone's first impulse, including mine, was to run, but the sheer force of the approaching Presence held us helpless where we were, like mice in the gaze of the serpent, or insects caught in the heat focussed through a magnifying glass. Something finally materialised in the Great Auction Hall with us, so huge and powerful it hurt our minds even to think about it, drawing everything towards it like a massive gravity well. It was too Real for our limited reality; so Real it sucked everything else into it.

The Presence settled heavily into our world, spreading out in directions we couldn't even name; something Huge and Vast downloaded from a higher dimension. Its thoughts smashed into everyone's minds, as harsh and merciless as a spotlight, searching for the single significant thing that had brought it to this petty, limited place. It didn't take a genius to realise it must be looking for the chaos butterfly. The only truly unique thing at the auction. The psychenaut couldn't seem to locate it exactly for the moment, presumably because of the stasis field holding the butterfly temporarily outside of Time and Space. And so the Presence sank deeper into people's minds, forcing their very selves away in its search for knowledge. All around me people were crying out in pain and shock and horror, shrieking *Get it out of me!* Even the major players were on their knees, sobbing and shaking. The only one left mostly unaffected in the Hall was me, and I didn't want to think why.

The psychenaut wasn't used to thinking in only three dimensions, but eventually it would locate the chaos butterfly, if only through a process of elimination. The pull of the gravity well was growing steadily stronger. Details of this world's reality were being stripped away and sucked in, absorbed by the Presence. Not because it chose to, but just because of what it was. The teddy bears lumbered towards it, drawn by some inexorable summons, only to fall one by one to the floor, reduced to just toy bears again. Terrible changes swept through those people closest to the Presence. Suddenly, some could only be seen from the back, no matter which way you looked at them. Faces lost their individuality, becoming blank and generic. Details of clothing disappeared as though smoothed away by an unseen hand, then lost their colour. People became black-and-white two-dimensional photographs, and finally just chalk drawings, until all they were was sucked into the gravity well. Stripped of everything that made them real.

I made myself ignore the screams and howls of the damned around me, thinking hard. The charm of Banishing wouldn't work on anything as powerful as this. Hell, nothing I had would even touch it. Powers as significant as this hardly ever gave a damn about lower dimensions like ours. This one was only here because of the chaos butterfly. Presumably because whoever finally took charge of it, the ability to predict and maybe control the future would have repercussions up and down the dimensions. So the psychenauts would just keep coming, from up and down the line, until one of them finally found the butterfly. And none of them would care how much damage they did to this world and the people in it. So there was only one thing left to do.

I lurched over to the glass display cases, forcing myself against the terrible pull of the gravity well, until finally I stood before the case holding the chaos butterfly. It hung there in its stasis field, such a small thing to hold such potential power. I reached out for the case, and Wilde cried out, afraid I was going to kill the butterfly, even after all its presence had brought about. I used my gift to find things, opening the third eye deep in my mind, my private eye, to locate the necessary Word of Power that would collapse the stasis field.

I said the Word, the field collapsed, and the butterfly disappeared, free at last to return to the moment in Space and Time from which it had been snatched. And as it moved on, it became just a butterfly again, no longer significant, no longer the first domino in any line of destiny. And so became ordinary again, of no importance to anyone at all.

The Presence snapped out of reality in a moment, no longer interested, and the gravity well was gone. All across the Hall people collapsed, mostly in gratitude that their ordeal was over. I sat down with my back to a reliably strong and solid wall and let myself shake for a while.

Of course, not everyone was pleased with the way things turned out. Deliverance Wilde, for example, wandered miserably around the Hall saying *I could have been rich, rich, rich...* She could have been dead, in any number of unpleasant ways, but I was too much of a gentleman to point that out. And many of the people who'd come to bid for the butterfly came up to ask pointedly whether I couldn't have found some better way to deal with the problem. I gave them my best hard look, and they went away again. An awful lot of people were dead, or much diminished, so I helped the Auction Hall staff pile the bodies up in one corner, for the Authorities to deal with, when they finally showed up. No-one else wanted to help. Most people couldn't get out of the Hall fast enough. I decided it might be best if I was long gone, too, before Walker and his people turned up, asking awkward questions. I said as much to Wilde, and she nodded slowly.

"I suppose I could always try and track down another chaos butterfly..."

I silently indicated the wreckage and the piled-up dead, and she shuddered.

"Or perhaps not."

"Stick to fashion," I said, not unkindly. "It's a lot less dangerous."

She managed a small smile. "Lot you know," she said, and drifted away.

I went back to Grave, looking mournfully round her devastated Hall, and told her where she could send the cheque for my services. She glared at me.

"You don't seriously expect to get paid, after this debacle?"

I gave her my very best hard look. "I always get paid."

She thought about that for a moment, then said she quite understood my point. I smiled, said good-bye, and went back out into the Nightside.

TWO

WHEN LADY LUCK COMES CALLING... RUN

I eat out, mostly. Partly because the Nightside has some of the best restaurants in this and many other universes, but mostly because I have neither the gift, the time, nor the interest to cook for myself. Though of course in an emergency I am quite capable of sticking something frozen in a microwave and nuking it till it screams. I also much prefer to eat on my own, so that I can give my full attention to the excellent food I've just paid a small fortune for. But on this occasion I was lunching with my young secretary, Cathy Barrett. I was doing so because she'd made a point of phoning me from my office, just to tell me so, and as in so many other things where Cathy was concerned, I didn't get a say in the matter. I have learned to accept such defeats gracefully.

Not least because whenever Cathy insists that it's important we meet for a little chat over a meal, it nearly always means bad news is heading in my direction at warp speed. And not just your ordinary, everyday bad news, of which there is never any lack in the Nightside, but the kind of really vicious, unpleasant, and desperately unfair bad news that comes howling in from a totally unexpected direction. I considered the various awful possibilities as I headed into Uptown, and set my course for the restaurant area. Uptown is what passes for class in the Nightside, where mostly we're too busy screwing each other over to care about such things.

Hot neon blazed all around me, reflecting blurred colours on the rain-slick roads. Smoky saxophones and heavy bass lines drifted out the doorways of clubs that never close. Dawn never comes in the Nightside, so the drinking and dancing and sinning never has to end, as long as you've still got money in your pocket or a soul to barter.

As far as I knew, I had no outstanding problems. All my cases were closed, with no loose ends left hanging to come back and haunt me. I doubted there was any problem with my office, as Cathy ran it with frightening efficiency. Unless the answerphone had been possessed by Kandarian demons again. Damn, those technoexorcists are expensive. Maybe the tax people were challenging my expenses again. Oh yes; we all pay taxes in the Nightside. Though I'm not always entirely sure to whom...

Rain pooled on the pavements from the recent brief storm, but the night sky was as clear as ever. Thousands of stars shone more brightly than they ever did in the world outside, and the moon was a dozen times larger than it should be. No-one knows why; or if they do, they aren't talking. The Nightside runs on secrets and mysteries. As always, the streets teemed with men and women and things that were both and neither, all carefully minding their own business as they concentrated on the private missions and hidden passions that had led or dragged them into the Nightside. You can buy or sell anything here, especially if it's something you're not supposed to want in a supposedly civilised world. The price is often your soul, or someone else's, but then you know that going in. All kinds of pleasures and services beckoned from every window and doorway, and for those of a more traditional bent there were always the gaudy charms of the twilight daughters; love for sale, or at least for rent. The road roared with traffic that rarely stopped, or even slowed. People kept well away from the kerbs. Just because something looked like a car, it didn't mean it was.

I reached the arranged meeting place, and for a wonder Cathy had actually got there ahead of me for once. She bounced up and down on her toes, waving wildly, as though there was any chance I might have missed her. Cathy always stood out—a bright spark in a dark place. Seventeen years old, tall and blonde and fashionably slender through an iron will, she looked particularly sharp in a Go-Go checked blouse and miniskirt, with white plastic thigh boots and matching white plastic beret perched precariously on the back of her head. She'd never been the same since my occasional partner in crime Shotgun Suzie introduced her to the old *Avengers* TV show. Cathy pecked me briefly on the cheek, slipped her arm through mine, and gave me what she thinks is her winning smile.

"Where do you want to eat?" I said, smiling resignedly. "Somewhere fashionably expensive, no doubt. How about Alice's Restaurant, where you can get anything you want? Or maybe Wonka's Wondrous Warren; Chocolate With Everything? No? You have changed. There's a new place just opened up round the corner; Elizabethan Splendour..."

Cathy pulled a face. "Sounds old-fashioned."

"They specialise in the more outre items of fare from the reign of Queen Elizabeth I. Puffins, for example, which they classified as fish, so they could eat them on Fasting Days in their religion."

"But... puffins aren't fish! They've got beaks! And wings!"

"If the EEC can classify a carrot as a fruit because the Spanish make jam out of it, then a puffin can be a fish. The Elizabethans also ate hedgehogs, when they weren't using them as hairbrushes; and coneys, which were infant rabbits, torn from the breast."

"Crunchy," said Cathy. "No thank you. I've already decided where we're going."

"Now there's a surprise."

"I want to go to Rick's Café Imaginaire; you know, the place where they make meals exclusively from extinct or imaginary animals. They got this totally groovy review in the *Night Times's* lifestyle section just the other week. I know it's a bit exclusive, but you can get us in. You can get in anywhere."

"If only that were true," I said. "This way, you dolly little epicure."

I led her down the street while she clung to my arm, chattering cheerfully about nothing in particular. Apparently the bad news she was nursing was so bad it could only be discussed after a really good meal, to soften the blow. I sighed inwardly, and checked the sliver of unicorn's horn I carry like a pin in the lapel of my trench coat. Unicorn's horn is very good at detecting hidden poisons.

The entrance to Rick's Café Imaginaire was a simple, almost anonymous green door, tucked away in an alcove under a discreet hand-painted sign. They don't need to advertise. Everyone comes to Rick's. The door was spelled to admit only people with confirmed bookings, or celebrities, or those in good standing with Rick, and Cathy was visibly impressed when the door swung open immediately at my touch. We stepped through the door and found ourselves in a jungle clearing. An open area of sandy ground, surrounded by tall rain forest trees, hanging vines and lianas, for as far as the eye could see. Not that you could see all that far; the heavy jungle canopy kept out most of the light, and the shadows between the trees were very dark indeed. Animal sounds came from every direction, hoots and howls and sudden yelps, occasionally interrupted by a loud growl or scream. The air in the clearing was hot and dry and very still. It was just like being in a real jungle clearing, and perhaps we were. This was the Nightside, after all.

(No animal has ever been known to venture out of the jungle and into the clearing. They're probably quite rightly afraid of being eaten.)

The head waiter glared venomously at me as I led Cathy nonchalantly past the long line of people waiting for a table. A few of them muttered angrily as we passed, only to be hushed quickly by those who recognised me. My name moved quickly up and down the queue, murmured under the breath like a warning or a curse. I came to a halt before the head waiter, and gave him my best Don't Even Think of Starting Something look. He was a short and stocky man, stuffed inside a splendid tuxedo that was far too good for him, his sharp-edged features screwed up in what appeared to be an expression of terminal constipation. He would clearly have loved to tell me to go to Hell by the express route and call for his bouncers to start us on our way; but unfortunately for him, his boss was standing right beside him. Some of the people waiting in the queue actually hissed in disgust over such preferential treatment, without even a hint of a bribe. Rick ignored them and exchanged nods with me. He didn't believe in shaking hands. He managed a smile for Cathy, but then, everyone did. He wore a smart elegant white tuxedo, which contrasted strongly with his craggy, lived-in face. There was always a cigarette in one corner of his mouth, and his Café had never even considered having a No Smoking section.

"How is it you always know when I'm coming here?" I asked him, honestly curious.

He smiled briefly. "All part of the service. And besides, you can't afford to be surprised, in the Nightside. It can be very bad for business."

"This is my secretary, Cathy."

"If you say so, John."

"No, really; this is my secretary."

"You always were a cradle snatcher."

"Look, just get us a table for two, before I decide to rumple your nice suit."

"Of course, John. There will always be a table here for you, no matter how crowded we get."

"Why?" Cathy said immediately, scenting a story, or better yet, gossip. She likes to think her lack of tact is charming, and I don't have the heart to disillusion her.

"John once did a favour for me," said Rick. "A snack had gone missing, under questionable circumstances, and John helped me locate it. As it turned out, the snack was a snark. It had turned into a boojum, and was masquerading as a customer. Every time you think you've seen everything the Nightside has to offer, it finds a totally new way to appal you."

"What brought you to the Nightside in the first place?" said Cathy.

He smiled. "I came for the glorious sunsets."

"But it's always night here!"

"I was misinformed."

Cathy looked suspiciously at Rick, then at me, sensing she was missing out on some private joke, but had the good sense to say nothing as Rick led us to the only remaining empty table, on the furthest edge of the clearing. People sitting at the tables we passed kept their heads down and their eyes averted. Rick pulled out Cathy's chair, while leaving me to fend for myself. Good-looking youth has its privileges. The tablecloth was pristine white, the silverware immaculate, and the salt and pepper pots were practically works of art. The handwritten menu was so big you needed both hands to control it. Rick hovered just long enough to make sure we were comfortable, then decided he was urgently needed elsewhere, and strolled away. Rick didn't mix with the customers, as a rule. In fact, you could eat at his place for months and never even catch a glimpse of him, and that was the way he liked it. Cathy looked impishly at me over the top of her oversized menu.

"A table on demand, at *Rick's*! I am officially impressed."

"Don't be. I'm still expected to pay the bill before we leave. Rick wasn't that grateful."

There was a coat stand beside every table, a tall mahogany rococo effort, because none of the customers liked the idea of their coats and belongings being out of sight, where they might be tampered with by enemies. Paranoia is a way of life in the Nightside, and for many good reasons. I hung up my trench coat, after surreptitiously removing the sliver of unicorn horn from my lapel. I like to keep my little secrets to myself. It all helps build the reputation. Cathy tossed her beret casually onto the top of the coat stand. I looked at her enviously. I've never been able to do things like that. I sat down again opposite her, and we studied our menus solemnly. People at surrounding tables watched me when they thought I wasn't looking. Some crossed themselves, or made the sign of the evil eye against me. I considered how much fun could be had, just by jumping up suddenly and shouting *Boo!*, but rose above it. Cathy whistled quietly and looked at me over the top of her menu again.

"This is a seriously extreme list, John. Where does he get all this stuff?"

"Rick's place is unique, even for the Nightside," I admitted. "As far as I know, he's the only restaurateur ever to make meals out of creatures that don't usually exist. I have asked where his supplies come from, but all he'll ever say is that he has his sources. I understand he employs professional wild game hunters for the rarer specimens; no questions asked, and whatever you do don't bring them back alive. Apparently the real problem is finding and keeping first-class chefs who can deal with the problems involved in preparing some of the meals. Like being blindfolded when preparing gorgon's-eye soup. You don't want someone who'll go into hysterics when faced with moebius mice, which stuff themselves."

A waiter turned up to look down its nose at us. It was a giant penguin, complete with pencil moustache and a supercilious eye. It looked meaningfully at our menus, then recited the day's specials in a bored monotone.

"The octopus is off, but we hope to recapture it soon. And don't ask for the chameleon, because we can't find it. Today's special is long pig, because one of yesterday's customers couldn't pay his bill."

Cathy looked at me. "Is it joking?"

"I doubt it. Penguins aren't known for their sense of humour."

"Speciesist!" hissed the waiter.

We made a point of ignoring it. "Where are the kitchens in this place?" said Cathy, looking around the jungle clearing.

"Only Rick knows," I said. "And he isn't talking. I have a horrible feeling that if we ever saw the state of the kitchens, we wouldn't eat anything that came out of them."

"Did you get anything nice for me at the auction?" said Cathy, changing the subject with the artless speed of which only teenagers are capable.

"I'm afraid not. It wasn't really that kind of auction. Maybe next time." And just to show that I could do it, too; "How's your mother?"

"Fine," said Cathy, carefully studying her menu so she wouldn't have to look at me. "Rich and successful as ever. Offered me a nice little position in her firm, if I ever feel like going home, which I don't. Actually, the further away we are, the better we get on. We can be quite civil to each other, as long as we're not in the same time zone. Have you had any luck in tracking down news of your mother?"

"No." It was my turn to study the menu. "The few people who might know something refuse even to discuss the matter. It's hard to find anyone who knew her in person, who's still alive. There's Shock-Headed Peter, of course, but he's insane. My dad didn't even leave me any photos of her. Apparently he burned a whole lot of stuff when she left... when he found out what she was."

"Do you remember anything of what she looked like?"

"No. Nothing. Not even her voice. I must have been about four when she left, so I ought to remember something of her; but I don't. I have to wonder if she... did something to me, before she left. Or perhaps my father did, afterwards. There's no-one I can ask." We both considered that in silence for a while. "So," I said finally. "are you still going out with that musician guy, Leo Morn?"

"Hell no," said Cathy, with something like a shudder. "That beast? I dumped him ages ago. He thought he was the big I Am, and I should be grateful for his attention, when he bothered to show up. No-one treats me like that. And his band sucked, big-time. Gothic Punk, I ask you! Mind you; he could be a real animal between the sheets..."

"Far too much information," I said firmly. "Are you ready to go home yet, Cathy? I mean, back to the real world, and a real life?"

"No. Why? Do you want to get rid of me?"

"You know I don't. But you weren't born here, you have nothing to tie you to the Nightside. Unlike most of us, you could leave this spiritual cesspool anytime you wanted. You could make a life in the sane part of London, where people aren't always trying to kill you."

"I'm never going back." Cathy put down her menu so she could meet my gaze squarely. "I love it here. I spent most of my life trying to run away from the sane, normal, boring world where I never fit in. The Nightside is so... alive! There's always something happening! It's like a party that never ends—with the best music, the most jumping clubs, and the weirdest people... I feel at home here, John. I was looking for something like the Nightside my whole life. I belong here." She grinned. "I guess I'm just a night person."

I smiled back at her. "It's just... I worry about you, Cathy."

"I worry about you! And I've got much better reasons!"

"Are you ready yet to tell me why we're having this very expensive dinner together?"

She took a deep breath, let it out slowly, and looked me straight in the eyes, her whole manner very serious. "I want to accompany you on a case. A proper case. As your partner. I keep asking, and you keep putting me off..."

"Because you're not ready yet." I was careful to keep my voice calm and level and very reasonable. "Cathy; you've adjusted very well to living in the Nightside, ever since I rescued you from the house that tried to eat you, but you still don't take the Nightside seriously enough. You haven't developed the resources you'd need to deal with the kind of hazards you'd encounter on a real case. There are things here that would eat you up, body and soul. You get left alone most of the time because you're with me. My reputation protects you. But out in the field, the bad guys wouldn't hesitate to threaten you to get at me, or at the very least distract me."

"I can look after myself!" Cathy said indignantly.

"It's true, you go clubbing in dives I wouldn't enter without armed backup, but you don't have the experience yet to spot when you're being played, or led on."

"I spotted Leo Morn!"

"Cathy, everyone knows about Leo Morn. I'm talking about the major players, the Powers and

Dominations. They do so love to play their little mind games. More importantly, you've never had to kill anyone. Working with me, the time would come when you'd have to, to save your life or mine. Do you think you could do that? Honestly?"

"I don't know," said Cathy.

"Of course you don't. No-one ever does, until they have to. It's something that changes you forever. It's like killing something in yourself, too. I'd spare you that knowledge, for as long as possible. Until then, it's just too dangerous for you to join me on a case. A real case. Because you can never tell when they're going to turn dirty."

At which point we were interrupted by a whole bunch of lemmings escaping from the unseen kitchens. They'd launched a mass breakout, and came swarming across the floor of the clearing like a furry tide, while diners squealed and shouted and pulled up their feet. The lemmings climbed up onto chairs and tables and even lower tree branches, and threw themselves through the air, in fine old lemming fashion. Cathy and I cheered them on.

"Look; that one's got a parachute! That one's hang-gliding! Go, little fellow, go!"

It was all over in a few moments. The lemmings scattered into the surrounding jungle, singing high-pitched victory songs (something about Rick only having one ball), and everyone settled down again. No-one emerged from the unseen kitchens in pursuit. Lemmings were always on the menu (very nice, stuffed with locusts' legs, in a tart lemon sauce) and there were always more on the way. Lemmings breed like there's no tomorrow, and indeed for a whole lot of them, there isn't.

Cathy and I went back to contemplating our menus, watched over by the foot-tapping giant penguin, who'd developed a bit of a twitch in one eye.

"Don't touch the dodo steaks," I advised Cathy. "They're strictly for the tourists. They taste awful, no matter what kind of sauce they're trying to disguise them with this week. How about... the roc egg omelette? Feeds four. No? Well, there's always the jabberwocky giblets. They come with borogroves, but they're always a bit mimsy... Chimera of the day? Roast mammoth; always big helpings. Or how about Hydra?"

"No," said Cathy. "Greek food doesn't agree with me."

After a certain amount of toing and froing, we finally settled on dragonburgers (flame-grilled, of course), with a nice healthy salad on the side. For dessert, Cheshire Cat ice cream. (Because it vanishes, it's not fattening.) We'd no sooner given the waiter our order than the food arrived, hot and steaming on a hostess trolley pushed by another giant penguin, wearing a name badge that said HI! MY NAME IS... PISS OFF TOURIST. I'm convinced Rick has a precog in his kitchen. The penguins left us to our meals with a simultaneous dismissive sniff. I palmed my sliver of unicorn's horn, and surreptitiously tested both my food and Cathy's.

No trace of poison, said a snotty voice in my head. *But the calories are off the scale, and it's far too salty. I thought we'd agreed you were going on a diet?*

I put the sliver away. I hate chatty simulacra. Give them a steady job, and they think they're your mother.

Cathy and I ate in silence for a while. The dragon meat was delicious. Very smoky taste. Quiet conversation went on around us. It was all very civilised. When the dragonburgers and some of the salad were just a pleasant memory, we sat back and waited contentedly for dessert. It arrived immediately, of course, and the penguin waiter quickly cleared away the dirty plates and slapped the bill on the table. (Service not included. They wouldn't dare.) When the waiter was gone, I leaned forward to talk confidentially with Cathy.

"One thing you have always been better at than me, Cathy, and that's knowing everything about the latest trends. See the gentleman in the navy blue suit and old-school tie, two tables down? What the hell is *that* all about?"

The man in question had a hole drilled neatly through his forehead, on through his brain, and out the back of his skull, leaving a narrow tunnel all the way through his head. You could see right down it, though I tried very hard not to.

Cathy looked, and sniffed loudly. "Ultimate trepanation. The idea was, drilling a hole through your forehead would allow the bony plates of the skull to break apart and expand, allowing the brain room to expand as well, and thus make you more intelligent. This new fad just takes the idea to its logical conclusion. Personally, I would have stuck with the smart drinks. They didn't work either, but they had to be a lot less painful."

"I would have thought deciding not to drill a hole in your head was a pretty good indication of intelligence," I said, trying not to stare, or wince. "I wonder if the hole plays music when the wind blows through it? Or maybe... you could pull a cord through the hole—mental floss! Helps remove those hard-to-digest ideas!"

Cathy got the giggles, and almost choked on her dessert. She washed the ice cream down with a large glass of the complimentary house blue. The bottle Rick had provided was already almost empty, without any help from me. Cathy regarded alcohol as just another food group. I'd ordered a Coke. And insisted on the real thing, not one of those diet monstrosities. The waiter got back at me by putting a curly-wurly straw in it, the bastard.

And then all the conversation in the clearing stopped abruptly, and all the animal noises from the jungle died away. It was like the world was holding its breath. There was a soft gentle sound, like wind chimes caressed by a breeze, and Lady Luck came striding out of the jungle and into the clearing. She was slender and elegant, her every movement almost painfully graceful, wearing a long, shimmering, silver evening gown that matched her eyes. She had delicate Oriental features, with long, flat black hair, and a small mouth with very red lips. She looked right at me, and her mouth stretched suddenly into a smile to die for. She came out of the jungle darkness like a dream walking and headed right for my table. As she left the trees behind, the branches burst spontaneously into flower, or withered and cracked apart. Sometimes both. As she walked between the tables all the cutlery turned to solid gold. A blind man could suddenly see, and another man slumped forward, dead of a heart attack. And suddenly everyone in Rick's Café had an apple in their hand.

Everyone smiled at Lady Luck and reached out to touch her, but she avoided them. Some looked away. Some brandished magical charms at her. She ignored it all with aristocratic calm. People craned their heads, trying to work out whom she'd come to see. Lady Luck only ever appeared in person to the very fortunate, or the soon to be damned. Often called on, but rarely made welcome when she deigned to show up. And then she stopped at my table, and everyone else started breathing easily again.

Lady Luck sat down opposite me without waiting to be asked, on a chair that appeared out of nowhere just in time. She smiled once at Cathy, who grinned back foolishly, dazzled, then Lady Luck gave me her full attention. By now I was almost supernaturally alert, checking for any sudden changes in myself or Cathy, or our immediate surroundings, but it seemed Lady Luck had grown tired of showing off. I didn't relax. The most beautiful ones are always the most dangerous. I knew my fair share of magics and tricks, including a few I wasn't supposed to know even existed, but I had nothing that could hope to stand off a Being as powerful as Lady Luck. So, when in doubt, bluff. I gave her my best confident smile, met her silver gaze calmly, and hoped like hell I could talk my way out of this. It didn't help when Cathy suddenly threw off the glamour that had dazzled her and looked like she was about to dive under the table or try and hide in my pockets. She knew a real threat when she saw one. Attracting the attention of the gods is rarely a good idea.

I gave Cathy a reassuring look and concentrated on Lady Luck.

"I didn't call you," I said carefully, just to get the ball rolling.

"No," she said, in a soft, thrilling voice. It felt like being scratched where you itched. By a very sharp claw. "I came to you, John Taylor. I wish to hire your services, to represent me in a delicate matter. I want you to investigate for me the true nature and origins of the Nightside. I want you to discover how and where it all began, and, most especially, why and for what purpose."

I swear I just sat there for a few moments with my mouth open, utterly taken aback. I had always hoped that someday somebody would back me on what could be the greatest case of my career, but I hadn't expected it just to come out of nowhere like this. There had to be a catch. There was always a catch. Like, for example, why did a Power and Domination like Lady Luck need help from a mere mortal like me? I said as much, only much more politely, and Lady Luck hit me with her dazzling smile again. Her canines gleamed gold. It was like drowning in sunshine.

"I wish to know why probabilities are always so out of my control, in the Nightside. Why so many long shots, good and bad, come true here. Is there perhaps a hex on the Nightside, and if so, who put it there, and for what reason? I want to know these things. If I knew and understood the origins of the Nightside, I might be better able to manipulate chance here, as my role requires."

I looked at her thoughtfully, taking my time. Lady Luck was one of the Transient Beings, a physical incarnation of an abstract concept, or ideal. Appallingly powerful, but limited to the role she embodied. She normally appeared in person only once in a Blue Moon, but this was the Nightside, after all. And like every other Power and Domination, she always had her own agenda, as well as being notoriously fickle.

"I'm not the first one you've approached about this, am I?" I said finally.

"Of course not. Many others have had the honour to serve me in this matter, down the centuries. All of them failed. Or at least, none of them ever came back, to tell me how close they'd got. But it's not in my nature to give up. I am always on the lookout for a likely..."

"Sucker?" I suggested.

She favoured me with her glorious smile again. "But you are different, John Taylor. I have high hopes for your success. After all, you can find anything, can't you?"

I considered the matter, letting her wait while I examined all the angles. When something seems too good to be true, it nearly always is too good to be true. Especially in the Nightside. Lady Luck sat patiently, as relaxed as a cat in the sun. Cathy had pushed her chair back as far as it would go without her actually joining another table, and it was clear from her unhappy face that she didn't want me having anything to do with this case, or this client. But if I were afraid of taking chances, I'd never have come back to the Nightside. I nodded slowly to Lady Luck, and did my best to sound as though I knew more than I actually did.

"The few who profess to know the Nightside's true beginnings have a vested interest in keeping them secret. Knowledge is power. And these people... we're talking major players, Powers and Dominations... Beings like yourself—and greater. They won't take kindly to my barging in and treading on their toes."

"That's never stopped you before," Lady Luck said sweetly.

"True," I said. "But still, I have to ask: why haven't you gone looking for the answer yourself if you want to know so badly?"

Lady Luck nodded briefly, acknowledging the point. "I don't interfere directly in the world nearly as much as people think I do. Statistics just have a way of working themselves out. My role requires that I remain... mysterious. Enigmatic. I prefer to work at a distance, through... deniable agents."

"Expendable agents."

"That, too!"

I scowled. "I get enough of this doing jobs for Walker. Why did you choose me, particularly?"

"Because you let the chaos butterfly go free, instead of destroying it. Or trying to control it yourself."

"No good deed goes unpunished," I said.

"What will it take to hire you?" said Lady Luck. "To take this case? How much do you want?"

"How much have you got?"

Her smile was suddenly that of a cat spotting a cornered mouse. "I will give you something far more valuable than gold or silver, John Taylor. I know who and what your mother was. I will tell you, in return for you finding out what I wish to know."

I leaned forward across the table, and I could feel my face and voice going cold and ugly. "Tell me. Tell me now."

"Sorry," said Lady Luck, entirely unmoved. "You must earn your reward."

"I could make you tell me," I said.

People began getting up out of the chairs and backing away. Cathy looked as though she wanted to, but loyalty held her in place. And Lady Luck laughed softly in my face.

"No, you won't, John Taylor. Because you're as trapped in your role as I am in mine."

I sat back in my chair, suddenly very tired. Cathy scowled at me.

"You're going to do it, aren't you?"

"I have to. I want to know the origins of the Nightside as much as she does."

Cathy glared at Lady Luck. "Are you at least going to make John lucky, while he's working for you? You owe him that much."

"If I were to ally myself openly with John Taylor," said Lady Luck, "others of my kind might come out against him. You wouldn't want that, would you, John?"

"No, I bloody well wouldn't," I said. "Your kind are too powerful and too weird, even for the Nightside. But... could I perhaps say that I am working on your behalf? That would give me some authority, and might even get me into some of the more difficult places."

"If you like," said Lady Luck, "but I cannot, and will not, intervene directly in your investigation."

I grinned. "The people I'll be questioning won't know that."

"Then the mission is yours," said Lady Luck. She rose gracefully to her feet and bowed briefly. "Try not to get killed."

She vanished abruptly, in a crackle of possibilities. A spring of clear water bubbled up from the ground where she'd been standing. I didn't think Rick would be too bothered. Knowing him, he'd probably make a feature out of it. Everyone watching began to relax, and sat down again. A number of serious hushed conversations started up, combined with lots of glancing in my direction. A few began pocketing the transmuted gold cutlery, until the penguin waiters made them put it back. Rick didn't miss a trick.

"I've decided... to sit this case out," said Cathy. "I'm almost sure I have some urgent filing that needs doing, back at the office. Behind a securely locked and bolted door."

"Understandable," I said.

"You're not thinking of doing this on your own, though, are you? You are definitely going to need backup on this one. Serious backup, with hard-core firepower. What about Suzie Shooter? Dead Boy? Razor Eddie?"

I shook my head. "All good choices. Unfortunately, Shotgun Suzie is still on the trail of Big Butcher Hog, and likely to be for some time. Dead Boy is very involved with his new girl-friend, a Valkyrie. And the Punk God of the Straight Razor is currently occupied doing something very unpleasant on the Street of the Gods. It must be something especially upsetting, because some of the gods have come running out crying. No, I've got someone else in mind, for a case like this. I thought I'd approach Madman, and just maybe, the man called Sinner."

"Why don't you just shoot yourself in the head now and get it over with?" said Cathy.

THREE

DEALING WITH
REASONABLE MEN

And so I walked out into the Nightside, looking for an honest oracle. There's never any shortage of people who don't want to be found, especially in the Nightside, and I don't like to use my special gift unless I absolutely have to. My enemies still want me dead, and I shine so very brightly in the dark when I open my third eye, my private eye. Fortunately, there's also no shortage of people (and things that never were and never will be people) who specialise in Knowing Things that other people don't want known. There are those who claim to know the secrets of the past, the present, and the future; but most are only in it for the money, most of the rest can't be trusted, and they all have their own agendas. Sucker bait will never go out of fashion in the Nightside. But luckily I was once offered, as payment for a successfully completed case, the location of one of the few honest oracles left in this spiritual cesspool. The long centuries had left the creature eccentric, garrulous, prone to gossip, and not too tightly wrapped, but I suppose that goes with the territory.

I left Uptown behind me and headed back into the old main drag, where business puts on its best bib and tucker, and tarts itself up for the travelling trade. All the gaudiest establishments and tourist traps, where sin is mass-produced, and temptation comes in six-packs. In short, I was heading for the Nightside's one and only shopping mall. Mass brands and franchises from the outside world tended to roll over and die here, where people's appetites run more to the unusual and outré, but there's always the exception. The Mammon Emporium offers brand-name concessions and fast-food chains from alternative universes and divergent timetracks. There may be nothing new under the sun, but the sun never shines in the Nightside.

I strolled between the huge M and E that marked the entrance to the mall, and for once nobody crossed themselves, or headed for the nearest exit. The Mammon Emporium was one of the few places where I could hope to be just another face in the crowd. Shoppers from all kinds of Londons came here in search of the fancy and the forbidden, and, of course, that chance for a once-in-a-lifetime bargain. People dressed in a hundred different outrageous styles called out to each other in as many different languages and argots, crowding the thoroughfares and window-shopping sights they'd never find anywhere else.

Brightly coloured come-ons blazed from every store, their windows full of wonders, and countless businesses crammed in side by side in a mall that somehow managed to be bigger on the inside than it was on the outside. Apparently space expands to encompass the trade involved.

To every side of me blazed signs and logos from far and distant places. MCCAMPBELL'S DOLPHIN BURGERS. STARDOCK'S SNUFF. WILL DIZZY'S MORTIMER MOUSE. BAPTISMS R US. PERV PARLOUR. SOUL MARKET; new, used and refurbished. And of course the NOSFERATU BLOOD BANK. (Come in and make a deposit. Give generously. Don't make us come looking for you.) A dark-haired Goth girl in a crimson basque gave me the eye from the shadowy doorway. I smiled politely and continued on my way.

Right in the middle of the mall stood an old-fashioned wishing well, largely ignored by the crowds that bustled unseeingly past it. The well didn't look like much. Just a traditional stone-walled well with a circle of stunted grass around it, a red slate roof above, and a bucket on a rusty steel chain. A sign in really twee writing invited you to toss a coin in the well and make a wish. Just a little bit of harmless fun for the kiddies. Except this was the Nightside, which has never gone in for harmless fun. Most oracles are a joke. The concept of alternate timetracks (as seen every day in the Nightside's spontaneously generating Timeslips) makes prophecy largely unprofitable and knocks the idea of Fate very firmly on the head. But this particular oracle had a really good track record in predicting the present; in knowing what was going on everywhere, right now. I suppose specialisation is everything, these days. I leaned against the well's stone wall and looked casually about me. No-one seemed to be paying me or the well any special attention.

"Hello, oracle," I said. "What's happening?"

"More than you can possibly imagine," said a deep, bubbling voice from a long way below. "Bless me with coin of silver, oh passing traveller, and I shall bless thee with three answers to any question. The first answer shall be explicit but unhelpful, the second allusive but accurate, and the third a wild stab in the dark. The more you spend, the more you learn."

"Don't give me that crap," I said. "I'm not a tourist. This is John Taylor."

"Oh bloody hell; you're back again, are you?" The oracle sounded distinctly sulky. "You know very well your whole existence makes my head ache."

"You haven't got a head."

"Exactly! It's people like you that give oracles a bad reputation. What do you want? I'm busy."

"What with?" I asked, honestly curious.

"Trust me, you really don't want to know. You think it's easy being the fount of all wisdom, when your walls are covered with algae? And I hate Timeslips! They're like haemorrhoids for an oracle. And speaking of pains in the arse; what do you want, Taylor?"

"I'm looking for the man called Madman."

"Oh, God; he's even worse than you. He'd turn my stomach, if I had one. What do you want with him?"

"Don't you know?"

The oracle sniffed haughtily. "That's right, make fun of a cripple. At least I can see where he is, unlike you. But this answer will cost you. No information for free; that's the rule. Don't blame me, I just work here. Until the curse finally wears off; then I will be out of here so fast it'll make your head spin."

"All right," I said. "How many drops of blood for a straight answer?"

"Just the one, for you, sweet prince," the oracle said, its voice suddenly ingratiating. "And remember me, when you come into your kingdom."

I looked down into the shadows of the well. "You've heard something."

"Maybe I have, maybe I haven't," the oracle said smugly. "Take advantage of my sweet nature, before the price goes up."

I jabbed my thumb with a pin and let a single fat drop of blood fall into the well, which made a soft, ugly, satisfied noise.

"You'll find Madman at the Hotel Clappe," it said briskly. "In the short-time district. Watch your back there, and don't talk to any of the strange women, unless you're collecting infections. Now get the hell out of here; my head is splitting. And *carpe* that old *diem*, John Taylor. It's later than anyone thinks."

The Hotel Clappe, spelled that way to give it that extra bit of class, looked just like it sounded; the kind of dirty, disgusting dump where you rented rooms by the hour, and a fresh pair of sheets was a luxury. Good-time girls and others stalked their prey in the underlit streets, and the crabs were so big they leapt out of dark alleyways to mug passersby. Appearance was everything, and buyer beware. But there will always be those for whom sex is no fun unless it's seedy, dirty, and just a bit dangerous, so... I walked down the street of red lamps looking determinedly straight ahead and keeping my hands very firmly to myself. In areas like this, the twilight daughters could be scarier and more dangerous than most of the more obvious monsters in the Nightside. Depressingly enough, an awful lot of them seemed to know my name.

The Hotel Clappe was just another flaky-painted establishment in the middle of a long, terraced row, and no-one had bothered to repaint the sign over the door in years. I pushed the door open with one hand, wishing I'd thought to bring some gloves with me, and strode into the lobby, trying to look like a building inspector or someone else with a legitimate reason to be there. The lobby was just as foul and unclean as I expected, and the carpet crunched under my feet. A few individuals of debatable sexuality looked up from their gossip magazines as I entered, but looked quickly away again as they recognised me.

I wasn't entirely sure what Madman was doing in a place like this. I didn't think he cared any more about sane and everyday things like sex or pleasure. But then, I suppose to him one place was as good as any other. And it was a good area to hide out. It wasn't the kind of place you came to unless you had definite business here.

A couple of elfin hookers made way for me as I approached the hotel clerk, protected from his world by a heavy steel grille. The elves looked me over with bold mascaraed eyes, and gave me their best professional smiles. Their wings looked a bit crumpled, but they still had a certain gaudy glamour. I smiled and shook my head, and they actually looked a bit relieved. God alone knew what my reputation had transmuted into, down here. Certainly the clerk behind his grille didn't look at all pleased to see me. He was a short sturdy type, in grubby trousers and a string vest, a sour face, and eyes that had seen everything. Behind him a sign said simply YOU TOUCH IT, YOU PAY FOR IT. The clerk spat juicily into a cuspidor, and regarded me with a flat, indifferent face.

"I don't do questions," he said, in a grey toneless voice. "Not even for the infamous John Taylor. See nothing, know nothing; all part of the job. You don't scare me. We get worse than you coming in here every day. And the grille's charmed, cursed, and electrified, so don't get any ideas."

"And here I am, come to do you a favour," I said cheerfully, carefully unimpressed by his manner. "I've come to take Madman away with me."

"Oh, thank God," said the clerk, his manner changing in a moment. He leaned forward, his face suddenly pleading, almost pathetic. "Please get him out of here. You don't know what it's like, having him around. The screams and the howls and the rains of blood. The rooms that change position and the doors that suddenly don't go anywhere. He scares the johns. He even scares the girls, and I didn't think there was anything left that could do that. My nerves will never be the same again. He's giving the hotel a really bad reputation."

"I would have thought that was an advantage, in an area like this," I said.

"Just get Madman out of here. Please."

"We'd be ever so grateful," said one of the elfin hookers, pushing her bosoms out at me.

I declined her offer with all the politeness at my command, and the clerk gave me a room number on the second floor. The elevator wasn't working, of course, so I trudged up the stairs. Bare stone steps and no railing, the walls painted industrial grey. I could feel Madman's room long before I got anywhere near it. Like a wild beast, lying in wait around a corner. The feeling grew stronger as I moved warily out onto the second floor. Madman's room lay ahead of me, like a visit to the dentist, like a doctor bearing bad news. The air was bitter cold, my breath steaming thickly before me. I could feel my heart pounding fast in my chest. I walked slowly down the empty corridor, leaning forward slightly, as though forcing my way against an unseen pressure. All my instincts were screaming at me to get out while I still could.

I stopped outside the door. The number matched the one the clerk had given me, but I would have recognised it anyway. The room felt like the pain that wakes you in the middle of the night and makes you think awful words like *tumour* and *poison*. It felt like the death of a loved one, or the tone in your lover's voice as she tells you she's leaving you for someone else. The room felt like horror and tragedy, and the slow unravelling of everything you ever held true. Except it wasn't the room. It was Madman.

I didn't know his name. His true, original name. I don't suppose even he did, any more. Names imply an identity and a history, and Madman had torn those up long ago. Now he was a sad, perilous, confused gentleman who had only a nodding relationship with reality. Anyone's reality. What drove him mad in the first place, insane beyond any help or hope of rescue, is a well-known story in the Nightside, and one of the most disturbing. Back in the Sixties, Madman was an acid sorcerer, a guru to Timothy Leary, and one of NASA's leading scientists. A genius, with many patents to his name, and an insatiable appetite for knowledge. By the end of the Sixties, he'd moved from outer space to inner space, to mysticism and mathematical description theory. He studied and researched for many years, exploring the more esoteric areas of arcane information, trying to discover a way to view Reality as it actually is, rather than the way we all perceive it, through our limited human minds and senses.

Somehow, he found a way to See past the comfortable collective illusion we all live in, and look directly at what lies beneath or beyond the world we know. Whatever it was he Saw in that endless moment, it destroyed his sanity, then and forever. Either because baseline Reality was so much worse, or so much better, than what we believe reality to be. Unbelievable horror or beauty, I suppose both are equally upsetting ideas. These days Madman lives in illusions, and doesn't care. The difference between him and us is that he can sometimes choose his illusions. Though sometimes, they choose him.

Madman can be extremely dangerous to be around. He doesn't believe what he sees is real, so for him it isn't. Around him, the world follows his whims and wishes, his fears and his doubts, reality reordering itself to follow his drifting thoughts. Which can be helpful, or confusing, or scary, because he doesn't necessarily believe in you, either. He can change your personality or your history without your even noticing. And people who annoy or threaten him sufficiently tend to get turned into things. Very unpleasant things. So mostly people just let him wander wherever he wants to go and do whatever he feels like doing. It's safer that way. It helps that Madman doesn't want to do much. People who try to use him tend to come to bad ends.

And here I was standing outside his door, breathing hard, sweating, clenching my hands into fists as I tried to summon up the courage to knock. I was taking a hell of a risk in talking to him, and I knew it. I hadn't been this scared since I faced up to Jessica Sorrow the Unbeliever; and I'd had a sort of weapon to use against her. All I had to set against Madman were my wits and my quick thinking. And even I wouldn't have bet on me. Still, at least Madman came with his own warning signals. For reasons probably not even known to himself, Madman came complete with his own personal sound track; music from nowhere that echoed his moods and intentions. If you paid attention to the changes in style, you could learn things.

I stood before his door, one hand raised to knock. It was like standing before the door to a raging furnace, or maybe a plague ward. Open at your own risk. I took a deep breath, knocked smartly, announced my name in a loud but very polite voice, then opened the door and walked into Madman's room. From somewhere I could hear Nilsson's "Everybody's Talking at Me."

The room was far bigger than it should have been, though its shape was strangely uncertain. Instead of the pokey little crib I'd expected, it was more like a suite, with a huge bed, antique furniture, and all kinds of luxurious trappings. And all of it covered in glitter and shimmering lights. Everywhere I looked the details were all just that little bit off, subtly *wrong*. The angles between walls and floor didn't add up, the ceiling seemed to recede in uncomfortable directions, and there was no obvious source for the painfully bright light. Objects seemed to change, slumping and transmuting when I wasn't looking at them directly. The floor was solid beneath my feet, but it felt like I was standing over a precipice. Every sound in the room was dull and distant, as though I was underwater. I stood very still, concentrating on why I was there, because it felt as though I might alter and drift away if I lost my grip on who and what I was, even for a moment.

This was why people didn't like being around Madman.

He was lying on top of the covers on his oversized bed, looking small and lost. He was a squat and blocky man, with a heavy grey beard. His eyes as he suddenly sat up and looked at me didn't track properly, and there was something wild and desperate in his gaze. He looked tired and sad, like a dog that's been punished and doesn't know why. He was wearing what he always wore; a black T-shirt over grubby jeans. He always wore the same because he couldn't be bothered with inconsequential things like clothes. Or washing, by the smell of him.

All the walls in the room were covered in lines and lines of scrawled mathematical equations. They manifested wherever he stayed, apparently without Madman's noticing or caring, and they disappeared shortly after he left. No-one had ever been able to make any sense out of them, though many had tried. Just as well, probably. Madman looked at something just behind my shoulder. I didn't turn to look. Whatever he was Seeing, I was pretty sure I didn't want to see it. After a moment, Madman's gaze drifted away, and I relaxed slightly. All around us, the room was changing in subtle ways, moving with his mood as he adjusted to my presence. Shadows were gathering in the room's corners. Deep, dark shadows, with things moving in them. Things that had the simple awful threat of the monsters we see in childhood nightmares.

"Hello, Madman," I said, in a calm and neutral tone. "It's John Taylor. Remember? We've met at Strangefellows a few times, and at the Tourniquet Club. We have a mutual friend in Razor Eddie. Remember?"

"No," Madman said sadly, in his low breathy voice. "But then, I rarely remember anyone. It's safer that way. I know you, though. I know you, John Taylor. Oh yes. Very dangerous. Bad blood. I think if I really remembered you... I'd be frightened."

The thought that someone like Madman could be frightened of me was distinctly worrying, on all sorts of levels, but I pushed the thought aside to concentrate on more immediate problems. Like getting through the conversation without being changed or killed, and, somehow, persuading Madman to work with me.

"I'm going in search of the origins of the Nightside," I said. "I could use your help. And maybe along the way, we might find someone, or something, who could help you."

"No-one can help me," said Madman. "I can't even help myself." He cocked his head on one side to regard me, like a bird. "Why would you want my help, John Taylor?" He sounded almost rational, and I pressed the advantage while it lasted.

"Even I'm not strong enough to take on or bluff some of the Beings I'm going to have to talk to," I said. "So I thought I'd take you along to confuse the issue. And maybe to hide behind."

"That makes sense," said Madman, nodding in an almost normal manner. "All right, I'll go with you. I think I've been lying here for months, thinking about things, and I'm almost sure I'm bored. Yes, I'll go with you. I'm always looking for something to distract me. To keep my mind occupied, so it won't go wandering off in... unfortunate directions. I'm more scared of me than you'll ever be. Let's go."

He swung down off the bed, his movements strangely unconnected. Standing up, he was almost as tall as I, but he seemed much heavier, as though he weighed more heavily on the world. The shadows in the corners had retreated, for the moment.

Madman headed for the door, and I followed him out of the room, carefully not looking back. His sound track was playing something jazzy, heavy on the saxophone. As I closed the door, I glanced back into the room, just for a moment. It was a small, pokey room, dark and dirty and thick with dust and cobwebs. Clearly it hadn't been used in years. Something was lying on the bed. It started to sit up, and I shut the door firmly and stepped back. Madman was looking at me patiently, so I led the way to the stairs and down into the lobby. People saw us step out into the lobby and scurried to get out of our way. And so together, Madman and I went out into the Nightside in search of the man called Sinner.

Sinner was another man whose story was well-known in the Nightside, which collects legends and tragedies the way a dog has fleas. Nothing is known about Sinner's early life, but at some point the man who would be known as Sinner made the decision to sell his soul to the Devil. So he studied the subject carefully, made all the correct preparations, and called Satan up out of the Pit. Not one of his demons, or even a fallen angel, but the Ancient Enemy himself. History and literature are full of stories showing why this is always a really bad idea, but Sinner apparently believed he knew what he was doing. He called up the Devil, bound it to a pleasant form, then said he wanted to sell his soul. And when the Devil asked Sinner what he wanted in return, the man said, *True love.* The Devil was somewhat taken aback by this, and apparently remarked that True love wasn't really his line of business. But the man insisted, and a deal is a deal, so... The contract was signed in blood, and in return for his immortal soul, the man was promised ten years with the woman of his dreams.

The Devil said, Go to this bar, at this time, and she will be waiting for you. Then he laughed, and disappeared. The man went to the bar at the appointed time and did indeed meet the woman of his dreams. He fell in love with her, and she with him, and soon they were married. They enjoyed ten very happy years together, then, when the ten years were up, the Devil rose up on the last stroke of midnight, to claim the man's soul, and drag it down to Hell. The man nodded, and said; *It was worth it, to know True love.* And the Devil said, *It was all a lie. The woman was just a demon, one of mine, a succubus who only pretended to care for you, as she has cared for so many men before you.* The man said, *It doesn't matter. I loved her, and always will.* The Devil shrugged, and took the man away.

And so the man became the only soul in Hell who still loved. Despite what he knew, despite everything that was done to him; defiantly and stubbornly, he still loved. The Devil couldn't have that; it was corrupting the atmosphere. So in the end he had no choice but to throw the man out of Hell and back into the land of the living. And Heaven wouldn't take the man, because, after all, he'd made a deal with the Devil. So the man came to the Nightside, to walk its neon streets forever, neither properly living nor dead, denied by Heaven and by Hell. The man called Sinner.

He was an amiable enough sort, but most people kept well clear of him. Because he wasn't really alive, he cast no shadow, and because he couldn't die again, he was pretty much impervious to attack. He could do anything without fear of punishment, so he imposed a strict moral code upon himself. Which meant he only did really appalling things when he felt he absolutely had to. Good and Evil were beyond him, or perhaps beneath him. Mostly he kept himself to himself, and Bad Things happened to people who pestered him. A popular urban legend said that if he did enough good deeds, or bad deeds, he would be able to work his way back into Heaven or Hell. Opinion remained divided as to which direction he favoured.

I headed for Sinner's favourite haunt, the Prospero and Michael Scott Memorial Library. Madman trailed along behind me, humming along to his sound track and frightening the passersby. Sinner was often to be found at the Library, researching various projects that he always declined to discuss. People had driven themselves half-crazy just from trying to make sense of the list of books he'd read. I think he just liked to keep his mind occupied. Madman brooded, Sinner studied. It all came down to the same thing; not thinking about the one thing they couldn't stop thinking about.

I'd already phoned ahead, to make sure Sinner was there. The librarian had said, *Oh, yes, he's here.* And, *If you're coming in, Mr. Taylor, could you please return our one and only copy of Baron Frankenstein's* I Did It My Way? *It's long overdue.* I made soothing noises, signed off, and tried to remember where I'd last seen the bloody book. I was back using a mobile phone again, with misgivings. There are all kinds of dangers to using a cell phone in the Nightside, from strange voices in the aether, pop-up voice mail offering services you really didn't want, and the occasional leaking infodump from another dimension. And, of course, the phone made it far too easy for people to pinpoint your exact location. But the damn things are just so bloody useful... Cathy had promised me this new version came with all kinds of built-in protection charms and defences, so I just mentally crossed my fingers every time I had to use it and hoped for the best.

I kept Madman close at hand as we descended into the depths of the Library, and found Sinner at his usual place in the Research Section, sitting alone and poring over an old leather-bound volume. Tall stacks of books led off in every direction, like a literary maze, and the air was heavy with that distinctive old-book smell. The lighting was clear and distinct but never overpowering, and there were signs everywhere admonishing SILENCE! Discreet signs also pointed you in the direction of books on every subject under the night, some of them adding pointedly AT YOUR OWN RISK. Scholars sat at study at their separate desks, ignoring each other, immersed in their work, as devoted in their attention as old-time monks in their cells. I headed straight for Sinner, down the narrow book-lined aisles, Madman ambling along behind me. Sinner looked up as I loomed over him, and nodded thoughtfully. He was a short, compact, and very neat man in his mid forties, looking very much like a civil servant doomed always to be passed over for promotion. Middle-aged, middle weight, almost anonymous. But as his eyes met mine, his gaze was unnervingly bright, and his smile was actually disturbing. Sinner had been around, and it showed. When he finally spoke, his voice was soft and polite.

"Well, well, John Taylor. I had a feeling I'd be seeing you today, so I just sat here, reading an old favourite, and waited for you."

I looked at the book open on the table before him. It was a Bible, the old King James edition. I raised an eyebrow.

Sinner smiled. "As a wise man once said, Looking for loopholes."

All around us, people were getting up, gathering up their books and papers, and heading for the exit. It could have been Madman's presence, or mine, or perhaps the two of us and Sinner were just too worrying to bear. I couldn't honestly say I blamed any of them. A handful of really hard-core scholars held their ground, hunched protectively over their learned tomes, determined not to be driven off. You have to be pretty tough-minded, to be a scholar in the Nightside. Madman strolled off through the stacks, and the spines of the books on the shelves rippled, changing shape and texture as he passed, affected by his proximity. I had to wonder what new information those transformed books held now; and if I were to take them down and open them, would I find nonsense and gibberish, or perhaps awful wisdom and terrible secrets? I decided I didn't want to know, either way.

And then I was distracted as a lovely young thing came tripping out of the stacks, hugging a tall pile of books in her arms. She was a tall blonde teenager in an English public school uniform, complete with starched white blouse, black miniskirt and stockings, sensible shoes, and a straw boater perched on the back of her perfect head. She was bright and cheerful, heart-stoppingly pretty, far too shapely for her own good, or anyone else's, and moved with all the unrealised elegance of youth. She had a pink rosebud mouth, and eyes so dark they seemed to fall away forever. I stood up straighter and pulled my stomach in, but she flashed me only the briefest of smiles before swaying past me to put the books down on Sinner's desk. I suddenly realised Madman's sound track was playing "Tubular Bells."

"Allow me to introduce you," said Sinner, in his soft patient voice. "This is my girl-fiend. The demon succubus I fell in love with, all those years ago. I have no idea what you see when you look at her, because it is her nature to appear to everyone as the image of what they secretly most desire."

I wasn't sure if I liked what that said about me. Too many St. Trinians films in my impressionable youth, I suppose. I nodded and smiled politely to the succubus, who pouted her lips briefly as she sat on the corner of Sinner's desk, crossing her long legs to show them off. I had to wrench my gaze away. The pheromones were so thick on the air you could practically see them. It occurred to me that Sinner hadn't said what she looked like to him. Madman wandered back, gave the girl a hard look, shook his head, and wandered off again. I really didn't feel like asking what he might have Seen.

"These are the books you wanted, Sidney," said the succubus, in a rich smoky voice. "Anything else you want, just ask." She arched her back prettily, so that her breasts thrust out against the starched blouse. My mouth was very dry, and I could feel my heart heading for overdrive.

"Her name translates from the original Aramaic as Pretty Poison," Sinner observed calmly. "There are some quite specific verses about her in the Dead Sea Scrolls, none of them complimentary. In the War against Heaven, she killed more than her fair share of angels, and even she doesn't remember how many men she destroyed as a succubus, in her war against Humanity. Watch your manners around her, and never turn your back on her. I love her dearly, but she's still a demon. And by the way—she's the only one who gets to call me Sidney."

I nodded respectfully to the succubus. "How is it that thou art out of Hell?"

Pretty Poison shrugged charmingly. "I couldn't believe that any mortal could truly love me, knowing what I am. Want me, yes, that is my function, to tempt the sinner into damnation, to throw away his immortal soul for the transitory delights of the flesh. But actually to love me, as Sidney did, even knowing the truth, even in the depths of the Inferno; that was a new thing, even in my long existence. So I came back up, out of the Pit, to be with him. Ostensibly I am here as an agent of Evil, to tempt and corrupt him again, so that the Devil can rightly reclaim his soul. But actually, I came back to be with Sidney, to try and understand this thing called... true love."

"So you say," I said. "But then, to paraphrase another great thinker, you would say that, wouldn't you?"

She looked at me, still smiling, but her eyes were cold, cold. "Did you ever let your lover see the stranger in your soul? All the dark, petty, hidden things you never admit, even to yourself? Did you ever bind yourself utterly to another person, even in the hottest fires of the Inferno? My Sidney did. I have never known such a thing before. There is no love, in Hell. That's why it's Hell. I need to know why he feels the way he feels about me. I need to understand, even if I don't know why."

"But you've known so many men," I said.

"Oh yes," said Pretty Poison. "You have no idea how many, and none of them ever meant a damned thing to me. They said they loved me, here on Earth, but down in the sunless lands they all sang a different tune. They would have betrayed me a hundred times over, for just one more moment of life and light. I never mattered a damn to any of them. Sidney... is different."

"Pretty Poison was the only one of her kind not to take part in the recent Angel War over the Nightside," Sinner said mildly. "Because I asked her not to. Make of that what you will. Now, word travels quickly in the Nightside. And the word is, you've been hired to investigate the true beginnings of the Nightside. By no less a Being than the mercurial Lady Luck herself. You do mix with the most interesting people, John. I have to say, the true nature and purpose of the Nightside is a mystery that has long fascinated me. Do I take it you wish me to accompany you on this most dangerous of quests?"

"Got it in one," I said. "With you and Madman as human shields, I might get through this case alive after all. If I can drag you away from your vital researches, of course..."

Sinner closed the Bible and drummed his fingers on the cover. "My only hope of ever getting into Heaven lies in doing good deeds," he said flatly. "And I mean really impressive, major good deeds. I think keeping you alive in the face of all the really nasty Powers and Dominations who will undoubtedly try to kill you should qualify as good deeds above and beyond the call of duty."

"But what about me, Sidney?" said Pretty Poison. "You wouldn't leave me behind, would you? You know we can only be together forever in Hell."

Sinner smiled, and patted her hand fondly. "I wouldn't go to Heaven without you. Because if you weren't there, it wouldn't be Heaven."

"Dear Sidney." She leaned over, kissed him on the forehead, and tousled his hair with a lazy finger.

Sinner fixed me with a firm stare. "If I go with you on your quest, Pretty Poison comes with me. I will not be parted from her."

"Hell, I'm bringing Madman," I said. "The more firepower, the better."

"I heard that," said Madman, from deep in the stacks. "I am not firepower. I am a deterrent."

"The truth concerning the origins of the Nightside is long buried," Sinner said thoughtfully. "Probably with good cause. It stands to reason that an appalling place like this would have a truly awful beginning. The roots of the Nightside are almost certainly soaked in blood and suffering. You must understand, John—should the secrets we discover pose a threat to the safety and stability of the people of the Nightside, I could not allow them to be made public. Above all, I always strive to do no harm. Is this an acceptable condition to you?"

"Of course," I said. "I only report to my client, in this case Lady Luck. What she might do with the information afterwards is something you and she would have to sort out between you. Is that acceptable to you?"

He nodded, and we all smiled at each other in a very civilised way. Behind the smiles, I was quietly seething. Having Pretty Poison along struck me as a really bad idea. Things were going to be complicated enough without having a demon succubus from Hell peering over my shoulder. (Assuming I ever was stupid enough to turn my back on her.) But it was clear her presence was a deal-breaker for Sinner, so I had no choice but to agree, for now. Maybe we could use her for defusing booby-traps.

"Oh, dear," Sinner said abruptly, rising to his feet. "I do believe something bad is about to happen."

I looked quickly about me. "What makes you say that?"

"Because Madman's music has just got all tense and dramatic."

He was right. It had. And thirteen men in smart city suits were strolling arrogantly through the Library stacks towards us. A Devil's Dozen of proud, purposeful-looking men, all of them heading straight for me. The few remaining scholars were gathering up their papers and fading away into the surrounding stacks with remarkable speed and dexterity. Even the Library staff were making themselves scarce. They didn't want anything to do with what was about to happen, and I didn't blame them. I knew who these thirteen men were. These were Walker's famous, or more properly infamous, *I Mean Business* people—the legendary Reasonable Men. So called because Walker sent them out to reason with people who were causing the Authorities particular concern.

Every one of the Reasonable Men was a refined gentleman, in an immaculate suit set off by the old-school tie, moving with that calm, arrogant grace that only comes from centuries of breeding and lording it over the peasants. Some of them looked around the Library and sniffed superciliously, as though they were slumming just by being there; and perhaps they were. I didn't underestimate them just because they didn't have a chin among them and looked like a bunch of upper-class twits. The Reasonable Men were all trained combat magicians. Their leader crashed to a halt right in front of me and tilted his head back the better to look down his nose at me.

Jimmy Hadleigh, the professional snob, had a lot of nose to look down, and cold blue eyes that surely only the truly unkind would point out were just that little bit too close together. Otherwise handsome, with jet-black hair, his mouth came with a built-in sneer. He wore a splendidly cut suit, and smart grey gloves, so he wouldn't get his hands dirty. We knew each other. In passing. We'd never got on, partly because he considered himself an authority figure, and mostly because I considered him an overbearing little shit. Walker must be really upset with me if he'd unleashed Jimmy Hadleigh and his dogs. He looked at Sinner, Pretty Poison, and Madman, and dismissed them all with one flick of a perfect eyebrow.

"Oh, God, Jimmy," I said. "Teach me how to do that with just one eyebrow. It's so damned impressive."

"Taylor, dear boy," said Jimmy, in his best icy drawl, ignoring my attempts at humour as he always did. "I knew Walker would send me after you one of these days. Always poking your proletarian nose into the business of your betters. But now it seems you've really upset our revered lords and masters, and Walker has decided he doesn't love you any more. You're to come with us. Right now. Be a good boy and do as you're told. Because if you don't come along quietly, I'm afraid we've been authorised to do severely unpleasant things to you and bring you along anyway. Guess which way we'd prefer."

The Reasonable Men chuckled quietly behind him, striking casual aristocratic poses and making lazy magical gestures with their long, slender fingers. No-one was ever that languid by accident, the affected little mommy's boys. I still didn't underestimate them. A sense of power only barely held in check hung about them, ready to be released at any moment. Combat magicians were trained to take on major players. They were serious, dangerous people, so of course I just leaned back against a stack, crossed my arms, and sneered back at them. The day I couldn't out-think and outwit a bunch of pompous public school punks, I'd retire. I'd run rings around Powers and Dominations in my day. I was pleased to see some of the smiles disappear from their faces as it became clear I wasn't going to come quietly and that I wasn't impressed by their reputation. I just hoped they were secretly impressed by mine.

"Good to see you again, Jimmy," I said. "You're looking very inbred today. So, the Authorities don't want the origins of the Nightside investigated? Well, tough, because I'm going to do it anyway. If only because I want to know. Pardon me if I indulge in a little name-dropping, but I was hired by Lady Luck herself, and my companions here are Sinner and Madman. Which basically means I outnumber you. So you run off back to Walker, Jimmy, like the good little errand boy you are, and tell him John Taylor declines to be bothered, bullied, intimidated, or interfered with. And be quick about it, before I think of something amusing to do to you."

Several of the Reasonable Men shifted uneasily, but Jimmy Hadleigh didn't so much as flinch. "How very tedious," he murmured. "I've never believed any of the things they say about you, Taylor. You're just a dreary little man with a good line in bluff and deceit. We, however, are the real thing. So now we get to do this the hard way, and you only have yourself to blame." He looked at Sinner. "You—stay out of this. Return to your books and your brooding. We're not here for you."

Sinner laughed softly. "Walker would have to send a lot better than you, to take me anywhere against my will. And unfortunately for you, John is under my protection. Because I've decided I want to know the secret origins of the Nightside, too."

"Stand back," said Jimmy Hadleigh, and his voice was very cold.

"I have seen much scarier things than you, in my time," said Sinner. "Run away, little man. While you still can."

Two bright red spots of pure fury appeared on Jimmy's pale cheeks at being so openly defied, and he stabbed one hand at Sinner in a mystical gesture, deadly energies sparking and spitting on the air. I decided things had gone far enough, and kicked Jimmy in the balls. His eyes bulged, and he bent sharply forward at the waist, as though bowing to me. And Pretty Poison stepped forward and ripped Jimmy's head right off his shoulders. No-one threatened her Sinner and got away with it while she was around. She kissed the head on its slack lips, then tossed it aside. The headless body sank to its knees, its hands twitching aimlessly, while blood fountained from the ragged stump of the neck. Stray magics discharged harmlessly around the body, and blood splashed against the surrounding bookshelves. Sinner looked reproachfully at Pretty Poison, who just shrugged prettily.

The Reasonable Men were crying out in shock and horror and anger, only to fall silent as Sinner and I turned to look at them. Their faces froze with angry determination, and their hands snapped through mystical designs, throwing magic at us. The first spells discharged harmlessly around Sinner, and backfired horribly on a few of the spellcasters, turning them inside out. Red and purple horrors collapsed to the Library floor, squirting blood and inner liquids onto the dusty air. Other magics homed in on Pretty Poison, who snatched them out of mid air and ate them up, grinning like a naughty schoolgirl. She was a fallen angel and older than the world, and the minor magics of men were nothing to her.

I pulled a pair of chaos dice from my coat's inner pocket and tossed them into the midst of the Reasonable Men; and suddenly everything that could go wrong for them did. Spells misfired, muscles spasmed, and they fell over each other like clowns. One of them drew a heavy handgun, its gleaming steel acid-etched with potent runes and sigils. He fired it at Sinner. The bullet punched a neat hole in Sinner's chest, but no blood flowed. He stood looking down at the hole for a moment, almost sadly, then he looked at the shocked Reasonable Man.

"Magic guns? I have known the torments of Hell, boy. But still, you really shouldn't have done that. It wasn't respectful. Pretty Poison?"

"Of course, darling Sidney."

And Pretty Poison surged forward, moving almost too quickly for human eyes to follow. She raged among the Reasonable Men, tearing them, literally, limb from limb with awful, impossible strength, laughing breathily all the while. Some tried to run, but she was quicker. While they were distracted, I put my back up against a towering bookshelf, slammed my weight against it, and overturned the whole damn thing onto two of the Reasonable Men. The great weight crushed them mercilessly to the floor, and they didn't move again. And almost as quickly as that, it was over. It was quiet again in the Library, the loudest sound the slow dripping of blood from various surfaces. The Reasonable Men were all dead. It wasn't what I wanted; but this was the kind of thing that happened when you allied yourself with people like Sinner and Pretty Poison. She was looking around at all the terrible things she'd done and smiling brightly. I looked around for Madman and found that even he'd got involved, in the end. Somewhere along the way he'd decided he was in a Samurai film. He was wearing a kimono and standing over a dead Reasonable Man with a bloody katana in his hands. He'd chopped the poor bastard into bits. He looked down at the scattered bloody pieces before him and scowled balefully.

"Well? Have you had enough? Answer me!"

It would have been funny, if the man hadn't been so very dead.

Pretty Poison came tripping daintily between the corpses to embrace her Sinner and make sure he was okay. He looked sadly at her, and at all the things she'd done, but said nothing. Pretty Poison snuggled up against him, not even breathing hard. She noticed there was blood on her hands, and sucked the blood off her fingers one by one, savouring it. She saw the disappointment in Sinner's face and pouted like a child.

"I'm sorry, Sidney, but no-one gets to hurt you while I'm around. And after all, a girl has to follow her impulses."

Sinner sighed and looked out over the scattered bodies. "We should have left one alive, to take a message back to Walker."

"Oh, I think he'll get the message," I said. "Thirteen dead combat magicians makes for one hell of a powerful statement. Walker... is not going to be pleased about this."

"Good," said Madman, back in his old clothes again. "Never liked the man. He tried to have me locked up once. Well, several times, actually."

"Still," I said, thinking it through, "Perhaps I'd better go and have a word with him, smooth things over. Or he and his various bullyboys will be haunting us every step of the way. Yes, I'll go and talk with the man. I know how to handle Walker."

"Should we come with you?" said Sinner.

"I think I'll do better alone," I said. "This calls for diplomacy, fast-talking, and an outrageous amount of bluffing. Not blood and guts all over the carpet. And I can't have him thinking I need other people to back me up when I talk with him. Walker notices things like that. So keep Madman here with you and try to keep him out of trouble till I get back."

Sinner winced. "Please. Don't be long."

I made my way out of the Library, smiling apologetically at the various members of staff I passed, and called Cathy at my office, to see if she knew where Walker might be found, just at the moment.

"Oh, sure," she said almost immediately. "No problem. I'll just check the computers. We subscribe to a service that keeps constant track on all the real movers and shakers in the Nightside, and lets us know where they are at any given moment, through constant updating."

"We do?" I said.

"I knew you weren't paying attention at my last briefing! Honestly, John, you never listen to a thing I say... Now, Walker, Walker... Ah yes. He's currently dining at his Club. Alone. Anything else I can do for you? How are you getting on with Sinner and Madman?"

"It's been... interesting," I said, and hung up. I didn't want to worry her.

FOUR

WARNING SHOTS

Going to see Walker is a lot like visiting the dentist; it may be necessary, but it's never going to be much fun. Walker, that quiet and refined gentleman in his neat city suit, is the public face of the Authorities, those shadowy background forces who run things in the Nightside, inasmuch as anybody does, or can. Walker always seems to know everything that's going on in the Nightside; but if that were really true, he'd have had me arrested, suppressed, or killed long ago. Still, sending the Reasonable Men to haul me away by main force was certainly a new step in our complicated relationship. He'd never hesitated to threaten or even blackmail me in the past, when he wanted me to do something dangerous and expendable for him, or just as often, stop me doing whatever it was I was already up to. But sending the Reasonable Men—that was just downright nasty.

There are many private and even secretive Clubs in the Nightside, and nearly all of them are clustered together in a very discreet and select area called, not surprisingly, Clubland. A quiet little square in a quiet little neighbourhood, regularly patrolled and even better guarded. These Clubs exist to provide secure meeting places for the kind of groups whose beliefs or practices are so extreme that the outside world wouldn't tolerate their existence for one moment. The Clubs provide a haven for those of like tastes to band together, protect their interests, and pool their information. And do the things they need to do, behind securely locked doors. These Clubs aren't about religion; you find that on the Street of the Gods. And they're not about sex; you can find that anywhere in the Nightside. No, these Clubs are strictly for the distinct and the damned. For example: The Tribes of the Night, a Club whose membership consists solely of vampires, werewolves, and ghouls. (No half-breeds.) Then there's Club Dead, exclusively for the many creations of Baron von Frankenstein and his descendants, who have been very busy bunnies since the nineteenth century, with varying degrees of skill and success. (Club motto: We belong Dead.) And, of course, Club Life, for all the various forms of immortal. (Club dues are paid thanks to the miracle of compound interest.) Club motto: Live forever, or die trying. The old jokes are always the best.

Walker belonged to the oldest, proudest, and most select Gentleman's Club in the history of the Nightside: the Londinium Club. Where everything that matters is discussed by everyone who matters, and decisions that affect everyone's lives are made over dinner. I've never been sure the Londinium Club is really as ancient as the old Roman name implies, but I wouldn't rule it out either. The front entrance is old, old stone, and the designs surrounding the huge oaken door certainly date from the Roman period. The bas-reliefs feature activities that would have made Caligula blush, and a few that might have made him vomit. The Londinium Club represents power, and that has to include the power to do anything.

Only very old money or very real power can get you membership at the Londinium. Pop stars, actors, and celebrities are never, ever admitted. No matter how famous. Fame is fleeting; wealth and power can survive for generations.

There were guards practically everywhere as I strolled into Clubland, but none of them tried to stop me. I'm powerful, too, in my own way. I approached the short, stout, and stocky man standing grandly before the Londinium Club's only door and entrance, and he moved a few inches to the left to block my way more solidly. He stood proudly erect, nose in the air, eyes colder than the night. He looked like he was born wearing a formal suit. One eyebrow twitched briefly as I came to a halt before him, expressing his utter astonishment that such as I should dare to approach the august portals he guarded. The Doorman was magically linked to his door, and only he could open it from the outside. And like the door, he was old and strong and impervious to all harm. You'd have a better chance of sneaking past St. Peter at Heaven's gates in a false moustache. The Doorman cannot be bribed or threatened, and no-one's been able to find any branch of magic or science that can even affect him. Pretty much everything about him is a mystery, except his snobbery and glacial arrogance to all those he considers below him. Which is pretty much everyone who isn't a Member of the Londinium Club. No-one can remember a time when he wasn't the Club's Doorman, and some of the people who remember him are *very* old. I smiled at him casually, as though I met him every day.

"Hi," I said. "I'm..."

"I know who you are," said the Doorman, in a voice as harsh and implacable as an onrushing avalanche. "You are John Taylor. You are not a Member, nor ever likely to be. Kindly remove yourself from the premises."

That didn't leave a lot of room for negotiation. "Are you sure I'll never be a Member?" I said, giving him my best hard look. "There are those who say I'm a king-in-waiting."

His mouth condescended to a momentary sneer. "There have never been any shortage of titles in the Nightside, sir."

He had a point there. I hit him with my one and only trump card. "I'm here to see Walker. He's expecting me."

The Doorman sighed heavily and stood to one side. The great door swung slowly inwards, spilling heavenly light out into the night. I almost expected to hear a choir of angels. I breezed past the Doorman with my head held high and entered the Club lobby as though I was thinking of buying it. Walker's name could get you into more places than a skeleton key and half a ton of semtex. I'd barely managed half a dozen steps into the lobby before a footman appeared out of nowhere to confront me. He wore an old-fashioned frock coat and powdered wig, and had shoulders so broad he could have made two of me. Under the elegant coat he probably had muscles on his muscles. He gave me a brief smile that meant nothing at all.

"Please wait here, sir. I will inform Mr. Walker that his... guest has arrived."

He snapped his fingers, and a whole bunch of steel chains shot out of nowhere to clamp on to me. They whipped around me faster than I could react, and heavy steel manacles fastened themselves around my ankles, wrists, and throat, shackling me to a heavy steel ring that had just appeared in the heavy carpet before me. The chains snapped tight, not even leaving me room to twitch. I kept my back straight and my head up, even as the weight of the chains tried to drag me down. I glared at the footman, but he'd already headed off to ascertain that Walker really was expecting me. If he said he wasn't, the bum's rush would be the least I could expect. But I was pretty sure he'd want to see me, if only to find out why I hadn't arrived surrounded by the Reasonable Men.

In a way, the chains were a compliment. It showed that the Club's security was taking my presence seriously. They didn't want me wandering around on my own, getting into mischief and bothering the Members. And presumably they were afraid I might out-talk or outwit any human guards. It's hard to argue with a dozen lengths of steel chain. I tried hard to feel complimented, but it's not easy when you don't dare lean in any direction for fear you might topple over; and your nose itches but you can't scratch it. To distract myself, I studied my surroundings. I'd never got this far before.

The lobby of the Londinium Club was a vast expanse of blue-veined marble pillars and shiny-tiled walls, suggesting the Club might have started out as a Roman bath, back in the day. I thought it looked like the world's biggest, poshest toilet. I'd hate to be the poor slobs that had to polish all those tiles each and every day. The floor was covered by a really deep pile carpet of a rich cream hue, presumably to give the impression of walking on clouds. The entire ceiling was covered by a single great painting of magnificent design and staggering beauty. I'd heard of it, but never seen it. Not many had. No reproductions were allowed outside the Club. It was an unknown (by the outside world) Michelangelo, representing the clash of two great armies of angels in the War against Heaven. It was simply breathtaking, in its scope and splendour. Far too good to be wasted on the kind of people who belonged to the Londinium Club, but that's life for you. It seemed to me that every single angel in the painting had his or her own individual features, as though the artist had painted them from the original models; and perhaps he had.

There were also sculptures, standing here and there like grace notes, by Moore and Dali and Picasso. Strange, twisting designs that made my eyes hurt. I'd heard you were supposed to run your hands over them, experience them through your sense of touch, rather than just look at them, but I don't think I'd have been tempted, even without the chains. They were... disturbing. Besides, I was pretty sure that if any non-Member such as I even tried, whole armies of footmen would appear out of nowhere to chop off my hands. The pleasures of the Club were only for the Club.

People came and went in the lobby, important people on important missions, moving quietly, speaking softly. I smiled and nodded politely to them, just as though I wasn't wrapped in chains, and they did their very best to ignore me. Either because they didn't know me, or because they did. The age of the Club, of its building and traditions, was oppressive. Custom can be stronger than magic sometimes, in the things that are Just Not Done. Like admitting the presence of someone who was Not A Member. I wrinkled my nose, trying to relieve the itch. The footman was taking his time. I amused myself while waiting by scuffing rude words into the thick pile carpet with the toe of my shoe. Little victories...

The footman finally reappeared, his downcast face telling me that Walker had vouched for me, after all. The footman snapped his fingers sadly, and the chains disappeared back to wherever they'd come from. I stretched slowly, taking my time. When I was finished, I smiled upon the footman, and he bowed very slightly in my general direction.

"Mr. Walker is waiting for you in the Dining Room, sir. May I take your coat?"

"Not without a gun," I said.

The Dining Room was, of course, large and rich and fabulous, with dozens of tables adorned with tablecloths of dazzling whiteness. The odours of all kinds of marvellous cuisines hung heavily on the air, succulent aromas to make the mouth water uncontrollably. It was all I could do to keep from grabbing things off tables as I passed. The diners all ignored me. I recognised some famous Business faces, rich beyond the nightmares of avarice, and a sprinkling of demigods, elfin lords, magicians, and aliens. The Londinium Club was quite cosmopolitan, in its own way. Julien Advent, the legendary Victorian Adventurer, gave me a friendly nod and a smile. Walker was sitting alone at a table in the far corner, with his back set firmly to the wall, as always. A cold grey man with a cold grey face. He looked up at me, and nodded, but didn't smile.

"You were expecting me," I said.

"Of course," said Walker, in his calm dry voice. "It was inevitable, one way or another."

I sat down opposite him without waiting to be asked, and the hovering footman reluctantly asked if he could bring me a menu.

"That won't be necessary," said Walker. "He isn't staying."

"You could invite me to join you," I said.

"I could still have you killed," said Walker.

He gestured at the footman, who bowed low to Walker, then hurried away. I looked at what Walker was having for dinner and sniffed loudly. It was all very stolid and British; roast beef, Yorkshire pudding, lumpy gravy, and limp vegetables. With probably a steamed pudding for afters.

"That is so you, Walker," I said. "Dull, worthy, and supposedly good for you. Indigestion on a plate, and not a spot of imagination anywhere."

"This is good solid food," said Walker, cutting up his meat with military precision. "Sticks to the ribs and keeps the cold out."

"Public school dinners ruin the palate for real cuisine," I said.

Walker raised an eyebrow. "What would you know about public school life?"

"Not a damned thing, and proud of it," I said. "Now, Walker, we have things to discuss, you and I. You cast a long shadow over the Nightside..."

"Yes," said Walker, chewing his food thoroughly. "I do. I have many shadows; my operatives are my eyes and ears, and they are everywhere. I knew the details of your current case almost as soon as you did."

"Is that why you sent the Reasonable Men after me?"

"Yes. They may be vicious animals, but they're my vicious animals. And they do put people in the right frame of mind for talking to me, and telling me what I want to know. I knew they wouldn't be enough to stop you, but I was pretty sure they'd get your attention. May I ask why they're not here with you?"

"Because they're all dead," I said.

Walker raised an eyebrow. "Well, well. How very... impressive. You're not usually so final in your dealings with my agents."

I said nothing. Apparently he hadn't been told yet that I'd hooked up with Madman, Sinner, and Pretty Poison. So let him think I'd killed the

Reasonable Men. It all helped maintain my reputation.

"Never did take to Hadleigh," Walker admitted, spearing a piece of meat with his fork. "Dreadful fellow. Far too full of himself; downright cocky, in fact."

"Not quite the word I had in mind for him, but close," I said. "Will there be repercussions?"

"For killing thirteen bright young men with prospects, all from good families? Oh, almost certainly. I don't give a damn, but you can be sure the families, some of them very old and very connected, will be most upset with you. This time tomorrow there won't be a bounty hunter in the Nightside without paper on you. The price on your head is about to go through the roof. And don't look to me to protect you. They were my boys, after all."

"Let them all come," I said. "I've never depended on you for protection."

He nodded slightly, admitting the point. "This new case of yours, Taylor..."

"Yes."

"Drop it."

I leaned back in my chair, studying him thoughtfully. Walker isn't usually that direct. "Why?"

"Because the Authorities don't take kindly to anyone investigating the Nightside's history and beginnings."

"Why not?"

Walker sighed, as though faced with a very dim pupil. "Because it is possible that you might discover things better left lost and forgotten, things that might threaten or even upset the status quo. If only because an awful lot of people, and I use the term loosely, would be very interested in obtaining such information. And would almost certainly make every effort to buy, steal, or torture it from you. We are talking about the kind of people even you would have trouble saying no to. They might even go to war with each other over its possession, and we can't have that. We're still recovering and rebuilding after the recent Angel War—a war you helped to bring about. The Authorities would quite certainly order me to have you eliminated, rather than risk another war in the Nightside."

"And you'd hate to have to do that," I said.

"Of course," said Walker. "There's still a lot of use I was hoping to get out of you, before your inevitable early death."

"You'd really have me killed, after all the jobs I've done for you? After all the messes I've cleaned up for you? After I saved the whole Nightside by bringing the Angel War to a close?"

"Only after you started it."

"Details, details."

Walker looked at me narrowly. "There is a line you can't be allowed to cross, Taylor. A line no-one can be allowed to cross. For the good of all. So; who hired you?"

It was my turn to raise an eyebrow. "I thought you knew everything, Walker?"

"Normally, I do. Whoever hired you must be incredibly powerful, to hide their identity from my people, and that in itself is worrying."

"I never reveal the identity of a client, Walker. You know that. I will say... I was offered as payment the identity of my mother."

Walker put down his knife and fork and looked at me for a long moment. He looked suddenly older, tireder. "Trust me, John," he said finally. "You don't want to know."

When Walker starts calling me by my first name, it usually means I'm in real trouble, but this time there was something in his voice, and in his face...

"You know! All this time, you've known who my mother is and kept it from me!"

"Yes," said Walker, unmoved by the clear anger and accusation in my voice. "I never told you because I wanted to protect you. Your father and I were... close, once."

"So where were you when he was drinking himself to death?"

My voice must have been cold as ice, but Walker didn't flinch. He met my gaze squarely, and his voice was calm. "There was nothing I could have done for him. He'd stopped listening to me a long time before. And we all have the right to go to Hell in our own way. Sometimes I think that's what the Nightside is all about."

"Tell me," I said, and it wasn't a request. "Tell me the name of my mother."

"I can't," said Walker. "There are... reasons. I'm one of only two people who know, and God willing we'll take the knowledge to our graves with us."

"The other being the Collector."

"Yes. Poor Mark. And he won't tell you either. So let it go, John. Knowing who your mother was won't make you happy or wise. It killed your father."

"What if she comes back?" I said.

"She won't. She can't."

"You're sure of that?"

"I have to be." Walker leaned back in his chair. He looked smaller, diminished. "Give up this case, John. No good will come of it. The origins of the Nightside are best left lost and forgotten."

"Even to the Authorities?"

"Quite possibly. There are things they don't tell me. For my own protection. Let the past stay in the past. Where it can't hurt anyone."

I did consider it, for a moment. I'd never known Walker to be this open, this concerned, about anything before. But in the end, I shook my head.

"I can't, Walker. I have to do this. I have to *know*... About the Nightside, about my mother. My whole life has been a search for the truth, for others and myself."

Walker sat up straight, his old commanding arrogance suddenly back in place. He fixed me with a cold gaze, and said, *Drop the case, John.* His voice sounded in my head like thunder, a voice like God speaking to one of his prophets; the Voice of the Authorities, speaking through their servant Walker. They gave him the Voice that commands, that cannot be disregarded, so that he might enforce their wishes in all things. There are those who claim Walker once used his Voice to make a corpse in a mortuary sit up and answer his questions. His words reverberated in my head, filling my thoughts, pinning me in my seat like a butterfly transfixed on a pin.

And then everything on the table between us began to tremble and clatter. The cutlery and the plates jumped and bounced on the immaculate tablecloth. The table rocked back and forth, its legs slamming up and down with increasing force. The floor lurched, and the whole Dining Room shook and shuddered. People cried out and clung to their juddering tables. And then it all died slowly away, and the reverberations in my head disappeared with it. I rose easily to my feet and smiled down at the openly astonished Walker.

"How about that?" I said. "So much for His Master's Voice. Perhaps I am my mother's son after all."

I walked away, and no-one wanted to look at me. I carefully chose my path to take me past Julien Advent's table, and when I was sure there was a wide marble pillar between me and Walker's table, I dropped suddenly into a chair beside Julien, and sank down, so that his body helped to hide me. I put a finger to my lips to hush him, and he nodded agreeably. By leaning back just right, I could see Walker at his table in the corner. He was so taken up with his own thoughts it was clear he hadn't noticed I never actually left the room. I'd thought that last parting shot would distract him. I wanted to see what he would do, who he would talk to, now he knew he didn't have his Reasonable Men to hold over me.

In the end, he called for a footman to clear away the mess on his table, then looked sharply to one side and nodded. A beautiful woman appeared suddenly from behind a concealing glamour, right beside the table. I cursed quietly. I'd been so focussed on Walker, and what he was saying, that I hadn't even sensed someone else was listening, unobserved. I must be getting old. I didn't used to

make mistakes like that. And it didn't help at all
that I recognised the stunning woman smiling at
Walker.

Bad Penny was a freelance operative for hire,
always turning up when least expected. Vicious,
deadly, seductive, and entirely treacherous. An
agent *extremely* provocateur. She smiled around
the crowded Dining Room, and struck an elegant
pose, the better for everyone to admire her. Most
did, unobtrusively, though there were those who
deliberately looked away rather than admit recognising her. Bad Penny was drop-dead gorgeous,
with a voluptuous figure like a Bill Ward cartoon,
somehow stuffed into a classic little black dress,
complete with elbow-length white silk gloves,
black mesh stockings, and a cigarette in a long
black holder. She wore her night-dark hair piled up
on top of her head, above a sharp, fierce face with
strong bone structure and an openly insolent
mouth. Her eyes were dark and deep enough to
drown in. And it wasn't just her thrusting bosom
that gave Bad Penny her air of sexual intimidation;
she was a predator, in every way there was. She
radiated sex appeal on an almost brutal level, like
a weapon. She also carried two guns and any number of throwing knives about her person, though
no-one was quite sure where.

We knew each other. A bit. Ships that passed in
the night and kept on going. We didn't approve of
each other, but we had been known to work
together, occasionally. When no-one else would
do.

Walker invited her to sit down at his table, and
immediately the footman was there to pull her

chair out for her, then push it back in again. Bad Penny accepted the attention as her due, but did deign to favour him with a flashing smile; and the footman did everything but wriggle like a puppy.

"You needn't bother with a menu," Walker said calmly to the footman. "The lady isn't stopping."

Bad Penny pouted. "Wouldn't eat here if you paid me, darling. I do have my standards."

Walker waved the footman away, and he disappeared reluctantly. I leaned out a little way from Julien's table, to hear them more clearly. Bad Penny worried me; but then, she always did, even when she was supposedly on my side. Julien watched me, amused, but continued with his dinner. As editor of the Nightside's only daily newspaper, the *Night Times*, he knew he'd get a good story out of me eventually.

I was just a bit surprised that Bad Penny was working for Walker. He was usually more subtle than that. Bad Penny, on the other hand, would work for anyone with enough money, on anything from espionage to assassination. Whether she was working on the side of Good or Evil had honestly never mattered to her; as she was only too happy to point out, gold has no provenance. She had no personal preference either way, nor any ethics worth the mentioning. She was utterly amoral and quite cheerful about it. I knew she'd occasionally done the Authorities' dirty work in the past, when they felt the need for a little distance or deniability. (Strictly pro bono, in return for which they agreed to turn a blind eye to some of her more notorious activities. Business as usual, in the Nightside.)

"I do hope this isn't about a honey trap, darling, because I don't do those any more," she said flatly to Walker. "They're just too easy, my dear; there's no challenge in it. Been there, done that, starred in the video. These days I prefer to specialise in cunning thefts, daring exploits, and just a touch of the good old-fashioned ultraviolence now and again, to keep the blood flowing."

"And a little discreet blackmail," said Walker. "To keep your coffers full."

Bad Penny batted her long eyelashes at him. "A girl has to live. And I never was very good at investments. All I have to do is mention that I'm thinking of finally writing my memoirs, and you'd be surprised how fast the cheques come flooding in. Now, what is it you want me to do, Walker? Something frightfully nasty, no doubt."

"You were listening to my little chat with John Taylor."

"Well yes, but I can't honestly say it made much sense to me."

"I want you to take care of Taylor."

Bad Penny looked at him sharply. "Now you're going to have to be just a little more specific than that, darling."

"I want you to do whatever it takes to prevent him from completing his mission. I want him off his present case, and I don't care how you do it."

"So... dear John is no longer under your protection?"

"No," said Walker. "Can you take him?"

"Of course, darling! He's just a man."

"Distract him. Divert him. Do whatever you think necessary. But, if all else fails, you are authorised to eliminate him."

"I get to kill John Taylor?" said Bad Penny. "Oh, *result*, darling! This will absolutely make my reputation!"

"*If* all else fails," Walker said sternly, but Bad Penny wasn't listening.

"How shall I kill thee, let me count the ways... That Shotgun Suzie thinks she's so hot. I'll show her!"

I decided it was time to leave. Hell hath no fury like a woman you really shouldn't have slept with.

FIVE

ALL ANSWERS BECOME CLEAR, IN TIME

I'd only just sneaked out of that august establishment and snobs' central, the Londinium Club, when my cell phone rang. (It plays the theme from the *Twilight Zone* TV show. What else?) I hauled the phone out of my coat pocket and looked at it suspiciously. It very rarely rang, partly because only a very few people have my number, but mostly because they all knew better than to use it for anything less than a real run for the hills emergency. The line is not secure. Not only is there never any shortage of people potentially listening in, sometimes they actually join in the conversation. There's also the problem of pop-in advertising, intrusions from other dimensions, and the occasional possession of the phone by pervert demons with a thing about technology. I have to admit I'm not even sure how cell phones work in the Nightside, well out of reach of the everyday world's satellites and relay stations. (Though at least that means my enemies can't use Global Positioning to find me.) I've always assumed the cell phone system is supported by heavy-duty sorcery, but I have absolutely no idea who might be providing it, or why. Or when they're going to get around to charging for it. All things that would worry me, if I were the worrying sort.

I always screen my calls (after an unfortunate incident with a dead ex-girl-friend), and I relaxed slightly as I discovered the caller was Alex Morrisey. The owner and bartender of the oldest bar in the world, Strangefellows, Alex was one of the few people in the Nightside entitled to call me at any time. We were friends, sort of, which got him points for courage if nothing else. And since he'd never called me before in his life, I decided I'd better take the call. At first there was only silence at the other end, then a faint whispering of sound that might have been a wind blowing, far away. I said Alex's name twice, and when he finally spoke his voice sounded harsh, strained, under pressure.

"John. You have to come to Strangefellows. You have to come right now. It's urgent."

"Alex? What's the matter? You sound really rough. Are you okay?"

"I can't keep him out! The whole bar is reverting! The Past is breaking in everywhere! It feels like dying..."

The phone went dead, buzzing uselessly in my ear. I shut it down and put it away. I hate being interrupted in the middle of a case, but Alex sounded like he was in real trouble, and the bar itself was under threat. I had to do something. I'm very fond of that bar. Of course, the odds favoured it being some kind of trap, with Alex as the bait. All my best interests were screaming at me, and you don't tend to survive long in the Nightside without developing instincts you can trust. Walker might have had Bad Penny transported to the bar, to lie in wait for me. It was the kind of thing he'd do. So, when in doubt, depend on the element of surprise. Getting all the way across the Nightside to Strangefellows would take quite some time, whatever method I chose, more than enough time for my putative enemy to set up all kinds of booby-traps and nasty surprises. But with a little lateral thinking I could be there in moments, and maybe catch my enemy with their pants down.

A certain image of Bad Penny filled my mind, but I pushed it firmly aside.

I reached into another coat pocket and took out my special Club Membership Card. It was very special; Alex only had five made, to my knowledge. I tapped it thoughtfully against my chin, considering. They might be expecting me to use the Card... or relying on me thinking that, so as to avoid me using it... but that way madness lies. Concentrate on the matter at hand. The Card was simple embossed pasteboard, a rich cream in colour, bearing the name of the bar in dark Gothic script, and beneath that the words YOU ARE HERE, in bloodred lettering. All I had to do was press my thumbprint against the scarlet lettering, and the magic stored in the Card would immediately transport me right into the bar. Zero travelling time, and the added advantage of bypassing the watched front door. (They couldn't know about the Card. Hardly anybody knew about the Card.) In the end, all that mattered was that Alex needed my help. So I pressed my thumb down firmly, and the Card activated.

It leapt out of my hand, so fast it practically burned my fingertips, and hung on the air in front of me, shimmering with unearthly light and throbbing with stored energies. Alex always believed in putting out for the full package. The Card suddenly grew to the size of a door, and I pushed it open and walked through. And as quickly as that I was standing in Strangefellows bar. The door slammed shut behind me, and the Card was just a card in my hand again.

I glanced quickly about me, braced for any kind of trouble or attack, ready for anything except what I saw. The bar was deserted, and transformed. The low fog of early mornings covered the floor from wall to wall, grey as a shroud, swirling slowly. The air was bitterly cold, and my breath steamed before me. I could barely feel the floor beneath my feet, as though it was far away in some other distance or dimension. A wind was blowing heavily outside the bar, beating against the walls. It surged and roared, and there were voices in it. Not human voices. I'd heard this kind of wind before, announcing the breakthrough of a Timeslip, one of those brief glimpses of past or future. When the Time Winds blew, even the greatest Powers shuddered and looked to their defences. Their arrival was always a bad sign. A sign that Time was currently out of joint.

The bar was utterly empty. Not a customer anywhere. The bar only closes when Alex is off duty, and if he had been off duty, the Card wouldn't have admitted me. But here I was, alone in a room I barely recognised. The bar itself, that long slab of polished mahogany at the rear of the room, was gone, along with all the booze and accumulated trophies that were usually piled up behind it. In its place was a huge screaming face, made out of wicker. It looked big enough to burn people alive in. The expression on the green wicker face was one of horror. I shuddered suddenly, and it had nothing to do with the cold. On the phone, Alex had said the bar was *reverting*... Could this be an earlier version of the oldest bar and drinking house in the world?

I moved slowly forward, the ground fog tugging at my legs. Everywhere I looked there were overturned tables and chairs, sticking up like dark islands in the grey mists. Whatever customers were present when all this started must have left in a hurry. I had a pretty good idea why. The biggest clue to what was going on stood in the middle of the bar, dominating the room, and I stopped to study it from a cautious distance. A huge oak tree stood tall and firm, its trunk wide and gnarled, looking as though it had always been there, though I had never seen it before. Thick roots plunged down into the floor, and presumably on down into the cellars. Heavy branches thrust up through the high ceiling. There were no leaves, but the bar's two bouncers, Lucy and Betty Coltrane, had been strung up on the tree trunk, held in place by thick strands of ivy and mistletoe. They'd been battered unconscious, the blood still drying on their bruised faces. They were large, muscular women, with warriors' hearts; they would have gone down fighting. I reached out to tug at the ivy, to try and free them, and the thick strands stirred threateningly. I withdrew my hand, and they grew still again. I swore dispassionately. I knew what had happened here. Who had to be behind this.

"All right, Merlin," I said. "Show yourself."

A pentacle flared into life on the floor, right in front of the screaming wicker face, forming line by line, glowing with the blue-white glare you sometimes see in lightning strikes over graveyards. There was a growing tension on the air, as that old enchanter Merlin, Architect of Camelot, the Devil's only begotten Son, Merlin Satanspawn himself, rose unhurriedly up through the pentacle to stand before me, with his familiar cold and arrogant smile. Merlin had been dead for centuries, his body buried in the cellars under the bar not long after the fall of Logres; but being dead didn't necessarily stop you from being a major player in the Nightside. Merlin was dead, but very definitely not departed.

An awful lot of what Alex had said on the phone made sense now. All the changes in the bar were artifacts of Merlin's time, and the man himself could only manifest by possessing, or rather pushing aside, Alex Morrisey, latest in a very long line of owner/bartenders bound to Strangefellows by a geas almost as old as the bar itself. Merlin rarely appeared in person these days, to everyone's relief, and when he did, it meant bad news for everyone.

Merlin ran one hand caressingly over the screaming wicker face, perhaps savouring old memories, then he turned the full force of his attention on me. He was tall and wiry and utterly naked, his corpse-pale skin decorated from throat to toe with unpleasant Celtic and Druidic tattoos. Beneath the curling signs of power, his dead flesh was blotchy and discoloured with rot and the various stages of decay. Even Merlin's awful will couldn't fully hold back the ravages of Time. His long grey hair fell down past his bony shoulders in thick convoluted knots, packed and stuffed with clay. His heavy brow supported a crown of mistletoe, unhealthily green and white with poisonous berries. His face was long and heavy-boned, ugly with character, and two flickering fires burned in his empty eye-sockets. (*They say he has his father's eyes.*) And in the middle of his chest the old, old wound that had never healed, still showing broken bone and ruptured muscle, where the heart had been torn right out of him.

Merlin Satanspawn, perhaps the most powerful sorcerer of all time, still continuing through his own implacable will. Old and bad and dangerous to know.

"We're seeing far too much of each other," I said. "People will start to talk."

"Insolent as ever, John Taylor," said Merlin, in a voice like grinding iron, thick with an accent noone had used in over fifteen hundred years.

"You made Alex call me, before you took him over."

"Of course. It was necessary that you come here. There are things that must be said, words that must be spoken. You have set a thing in motion, and even I cannot See where it will lead."

My first impulse on hearing that was to turn and run like hell. When Merlin started plotting, even the other Powers and Dominations remembered urgent appointments elsewhere. But I couldn't abandon Alex, and I was curious as to what Merlin had to say. Besides, I was pretty sure that even if I did leg it, Merlin would just drag me back again.

"All right," I said, doing my best to sound calm and casual. "Let's talk. What's brought you back this time? Been having bad dreams?"

"The dead don't dream," said Merlin. "For which I am on occasion grateful."

I looked significantly around at the changed bar. "Why the redecorating?"

"This bar is old, older even than I. There are those who say it's very nearly as old as the Nightside itself. I used to come here, now and again, as an escape from the overwhelming *goodness* of Camelot. You'd be surprised at some of the great names who've drunk here, down the ages. Heroes and villains and all creatures great and small. This... is one of the very few places that ever felt like home to me. That's why I had my body buried here." He looked around him, taking in the changes, smiling unpleasantly as the flames in his eye-sockets danced. "Ah, memories..."

"Can we please get on with this?" I said. "So I can have Alex back?"

"He is of no importance. He only exists that he might serve me. I bound his family and his line to this bar, long and long ago, just so that I could be sure of having someone of my blood here, that I could manifest through when necessary."

"Hold everything," I said. "Your blood? I thought Alex was supposed to be descended from Uther Pendragon, and Arthur?"

Merlin laughed. "From the Pendragon? No, boy; there's nothing of kings in Alex Morrisey. He is mine, of my line, descended from my dear betrayer, the witch Nimue. He belongs to me."

I bit down hard on an angry retort. I couldn't afford to get him mad at me. Better just to get this over with as quickly as possible.

"Why did you call me here, Merlin? What do you want from me?"

A huge iron throne materialised behind Merlin, a memory made real by the power of his awful will. It was a roughly fashioned thing, all strength and power and no grace, the black metal scored with runes and sigils that seemed to move when I wasn't looking at them directly. What little of them I could read made me glad I couldn't make out the rest. Merlin sat down without looking back and settled onto his sombre throne like a dragon curling up on a mound of skulls. His pale flesh showed starkly against the dark metal. He smiled on me like a favoured son, showing aged brown teeth. I didn't smile back.

"You have a new case, John Taylor. You have been engaged to discover the true beginnings of the Nightside, by one of the Transient Beings, no less. I knew this almost as soon as you did. I have psychic alarms set in place all across the Nightside, primed to inform me immediately if such a thing should occur. You set off the alarm in the Londini-um Club. I was a Member, long ago."

Why does that not surprise me? I thought.

"This is not just another case," said Merlin. "By agreeing to undertake it, you have set in motion a thing that cannot be stopped, caused ripples in Space and Time, alerted all kinds of Powers who have waited long and long for this to happen. Old forces are awakening, in and outside the Night-side, to aid or stop you. More than you can imagine is at stake here. There was a time I would have killed you out of hand, to prevent this thing from happening. Good and bad will die, terrible forces will clash by night, and nothing will ever be the same again. But perhaps it is time for the truth to come out, at last. Perhaps it is time for a new thing to be born, out of the death of the old..." He brooded silently for a moment. "I brought you here, John Taylor, to tell you what I know. To set you on your way. Perhaps because I do not know the origins of the Nightside, and it irks me that for all my strength and power there are still things I cannot See. I want to know."

"Do you think that knowing will release you from this bar?" I said slowly. "Free you to be fully dead and gone, at last?"

Merlin laughed, though there was precious little humour in the rough, raw sound. "No, boy. No-one holds me here but me. I wait for the return of my heart, and my full power, and then... Then, there shall be a reckoning!"

(Short version. The witch Nimue stole his heart, then lost it. Everyone knew that much. And that a whole lot of Merlin's power departed with the

heart. Absolutely no-one wanted to find the heart,
or reunite it with its owner. No-one was that stupid. Merlin was dangerous enough as he was.)

"The true nature of the Nightside's birth is tied
in with the identity of your lost mother," said Merlin, almost casually. "That's one of the few things
that everyone agrees on. Though strangely no-one
can identify a definite source for that knowledge.
Don't ask me who your mother is, or might be. She
is one of the very few beings I've never been able
to See with my mind, sleeping or awake. There
was a moment, some years before you were born,
when the whole Nightside looked up, startled, as
Something utterly unexpected flared brightly in
everyone's consciousness. Something Old and terribly powerful had been reborn into the material
world, and the balance of everything changed, forever. The moment passed almost immediately, the
new arrival shielding itself from everyone's eyes.
Which should, of course, have been impossible.
Just the first of many worrying signs and por-
tents... Your mother was, and presumably still is,
at the very least a Power and a Domination.

"My own best guess is that your mother is, or
was briefly in the past, that most powerful witch
Morgan La Fae. The only one powerful enough to
oppose me during Arthur's reign. A strange creature; powerful, yes, and undeniably beautiful, but
I cannot say I ever understood her mind. I always
suspected she was much more than she ever admitted, to me or to Arthur. And I never did believe
that sob story she spun for Arthur, about being his
half-sister. She only said that to get close to him; he
always had a weakness for those he considered

family. That's what comes of being raised as an orphan. She used Arthur to produce a son, Mordred, then used that son to bring down Camelot. I have to wonder whether your mother might have produced you to bring down the Nightside. Oh yes; I know what you experienced in that Timeslip. The terrible future you saw. Everything destroyed and everyone dead, at your hands. Quite a few Powers have seen that future in visions, down the years."

"I thought you were supposed to have killed Morgan La Fae?" I said, hoping to change the subject.

"I did my best," Merlin said dryly. "But I was never sure... She always said she'd be back. Mind you, Arthur said the same thing, and I'm still waiting."

"So you're not just hanging around here for the return of your heart," I said.

Merlin nodded slowly, acknowledging the point. "Arthur... was special. I made him possible, plotting with Uther Pendragon, back when I was still playing Kingmaker. But Arthur turned out to be so much more than anyone ever thought or intended him to be. He made himself special. He was the best of us all. The only man I ever followed. I dreamed a great dream for him, and he made it come true. A single great land, founded on Reason and Compassion, sweeping aside all the old madnesses. The holy Realm of Logres, burning so very brightly in a Dark Age."

He paused, his chin resting on one hand, remembering. "I could have been much more than I was. I was supposed to be the Antichrist, the Devil's only son born of mortal woman; but I declined the honour. I was wise, even as a child, and I determined that I would follow my own path and no other's. I killed all the members of the coven that conspired to bring me into being, and all those who came afterwards, to ensure my freedom. My mother was already dead—some nameless witch who did not survive my birthing. Apparently I tore her apart, clawing my way out of her, impatient to be born."

"What about your... father?" I said.

"We don't talk. I kept myself busy for years, amusing myself with building up kings and countries, and then destroying them. And then I met Arthur, and that changed everything. He shamed me, for the shallowness of my vision. I loved him. He was my father, my son, my light in the endless dark. I knew that Hell was real, but he made me believe that Heaven was, too. I gave him my life. I would have died for him, but... I always knew I couldn't save him without making him over into something he would have abhorred. He proved his dream worthy by dying in defence of it. He and Mordred met on the battlefield and died in each other's arms, neither ever really understanding what had brought them to that bloody place. I was elsewhere, killing Morgan La Fae. Afterwards, with Arthur and Camelot gone, I didn't much care about anything any more. It was almost a relief when dear, treacherous Nimue came along and found me. She really was magnificent, boy."

I decided it was time to change the subject again. There's nothing worse than a centuries-old corpse getting maudlin. "What do you know about the Nightside's beginnings?"

Merlin stirred on his iron throne, his face cold and considering once again. "When I was young, I learned from the Powers that came before me. They taught me that the Nightside was originally created, by forces unknown, to be the one place on earth free from the control of Heaven or Hell. The only truly free place. That's why I've been able to remain here so long, despite my... diabolical beginnings. But that's really all I know for sure. You need to speak to Powers older than I. One of my old teachers is still to be found here in the Nightside, though I understand he is no longer what he once was. Herne the Hunter, the free spirit of the wild places, leader of the Wild Hunt. The untamed savage. The force that drove the great green dream of Old England, when the forests were still huge, dark and primal places."

"Where do I find him?" I said.

"Good question. I haven't spoken with him in a thousand years. The spirit of the wild woods is apparently much diminished, these days. The encroachment of cities, and civilization, the felling of the forests, all served to reduce his powers, and I dare say he is now merely a figment of the Power I knew. But he knew many things in the old days, secrets he did not choose to share with me, and it may be that you can convince him to tell you what you need to know. Use your precious gift, boy. Find Herne the Hunter. If you dare."

"Anything else you want to say to me?" I said. "Before you go."

He grinned nastily. "You know... I could make you use your gift to find my heart for me."

"You could try. But even if you could make me find it, you must know I'd destroy the heart before I ever turned it over to you."

Merlin nodded his great head slowly. "Yes. You would, wouldn't you."

He stood up, and his throne vanished. He looked around the transformed bar wistfully, then sank slowly into his pentacle, dropping back down into his grave in the cellars. The glowing lines of the pentacle blinked out one by one, and as the last line vanished Alex Morrisey reappeared, lying curled up in a foetal ball on the floor. I looked quickly around. The bar was back to normal again, the fog and the oak and the wicker face gone, the present replacing the remembered past. The Time Winds no longer blew. I let out a long slow breath. It's not easy talking with a Power that can wipe you out with a passing impulse. But luckily, that's what I do for a living, as often as not. I helped Alex to sit up and set his back against the restored mahogany bar. He was shaking, fighting back tears, as much from anger as shock.

"You never told me, Merlin," he said bitterly. "All these years, and you never told any of us. I'm not a Pendragon after all. Not a descendant of a great and holy king. Just another of Merlin's damned spawn. I'm never going to be free of this bar..."

I sympathised, but had the good sense not to say so aloud. Alex has never been comfortable with expressions of friendship or support. They got in the way of his well-rehearsed self-pity. He finally lurched back onto his feet unassisted, a long streak of misery in basic black, even down to the beret he only wore to cover his spreading bald patch. He'd put aside shock and anger in favour of a good sulk. He knew where he was with a sulk. I could see he was about to launch into one of his rants, so I pointed out his two bouncers, regaining consciousness where the oak tree had been, and encouraged him to help me revive them, to take his mind off things. He did so, grudgingly. Good staff were hard to find.

Lucy and Betty Coltrane were basically unharmed, but mad as hell. It seemed Merlin had possessed Alex without warning, made him call me, then manifested fully and changed the whole bar without so much as a by your leave. The customers all fled. When Lucy and Betty protested, Merlin slapped them down. I think they were mostly embarrassed at how easily he'd taken them out. They were big, muscular body-building girls, used to defending themselves against all comers, and in Strangefellows that covered a lot of ground. Alex and I dusted them down, in a respectful sort of way, and set them to clearing up the overturned tables and chairs. Alex and I retired to the bar proper.

"I have a horrible feeling I'm allergic to mistletoe," said Lucy, scratching madly at one arm.

"You're always being allergic to something," said Betty. "It's all in the mind."

"I think we could do with a recuperative brandy," said Alex, moving to his usual place behind the bar.

I raised an eyebrow. "On the house?"

Alex scowled. "Just this once."

While Alex busied himself pouring out two surprisingly good brandies, I filled him in on everything that had been said in his absence. He grunted here and there, but didn't seem particularly surprised by any of it. It took a lot to surprise Alex. I considered him thoughtfully.

"How do you know you're really one of Merlin's line? Usually when you're replaced, you're completely gone."

"He made me know," said Alex. "He wanted me to know."

Yet again I decided it was time to change the subject. I used my Club Membership Card to contact my new companions, back in the Library. The card made itself into a door, and opened an aperture between the bar and the Research Section. Sinner peered curiously through the new opening.

"That's a good trick," he said mildly. "I didn't think anything could get past the Library's defences."

"This is powered by Merlin's magic," I said. "There aren't many places that can keep him out."

Sinner raised an eyebrow. "You do move in high circles, John."

Pretty Poison squeezed in beside him. "Oh look, Sidney darling; it's a bar! Do let's go through. I'm positively dying for a little drinkie."

"Probably a good idea," said Sinner. "Madman's been wandering through the Religious Studies section going *No, no, that's all wrong*, and some of the books have started disappearing. Or rewriting themselves. I have a distinct feeling the Library is not going to be pleased."

"Come on through," I said.

Sinner and Pretty Poison stepped through, then we coaxed Madman into ambling through after them. He had a dangerously preoccupied look in his eyes. I shut the door down and put the Membership Card away. Alex sniffed loudly from behind the bar.

"I never meant for my Cards to be used by free-loaders. I shall have to set up a new vetting system, preferably one involving scalpels and hacksaws and absolutely no anaesthetics." He studied my new companions, and as usual was not impressed. I was actually a little relieved. Such an open display of spleen showed that Alex was feeling better and getting back to normal again. Anytime now he'd be back to giving short measures and screwing up your change. He glared openly at Madman.

"You—I know you. Stay away from the bar, in case you change all the vintages. Or sweeten the beer. Or start my bar snacks evolving again. In fact, stay away from everything. Just stand where you are, don't move, don't even breathe. I swear, John, you lower the tone of the place every time you invite your friends to join you."

"Madman will be good," I promised. "Won't you, Madman?"

"Who knows?" said Madman. "Who can tell?"

"This is Sinner," I said quickly to Alex. "And this is his ghoul-friend, Pretty Poison."

Alex gave them his best scowl. "Oh God; it's the Nightside's very own answer to *Love Story*. The infernal Odd Couple. The ultimate sucker and fall guy, and the real girl-friend from Hell. And why does she look so much like my ex-wife?"

"Let's not go there," I said. "Listen up, people. I've just had a short but nevertheless disturbing chat with Merlin, and he says I need to talk with one of the Old Folk, Herne the Hunter. Do any of you have an idea as to where he might be found? Apparently he's dropped out of sight in recent times, and I'd really prefer not to use my gift this early in the case, unless I absolutely have to."

"Of course," said Sinner. "You don't wish to attract the attention of your infamous unidentified enemies. You see, I do keep up with things. You're almost as much a legend in the Nightside as I am, these days. I know something of Herne the Hunter. There's a lot about him in the Library, most of it contradictory. But the reports all seem to agree that he's come down in the world and is no longer the Power of old. It may be that he has gone to Shadows Fall."

"Where's that?" said Madman, passing briefly through one of his lucid phases.

"It's the elephants' graveyard of the supernatural," said Alex, always glad of a chance to show off his knowledge of trivia. "It's where legends go to die when the world stops believing in them. A bit bucolic, by all accounts, but very restful. If you're inclined that way, which personally I'm not. Why is Madman's sound track suddenly playing Dolly Parton? I know; don't ask. But I don't think Herne's left the Nightside yet. I'm almost sure I was reading something about him recently..."

He reached down beneath the bar and hauled up a pile of old magazines. He sorted quickly through them, finally producing a copy of the Nightside's very own scurrilous and scabrous gossip tabloid, the *Unnatural Inquirer*. (All the stories the *Night Times* is too uneasy to print.) Alex thumbed quickly through the glossy pages, while I studied the headlines on the front cover. MADONNA IN BED WITH RAZOR EDDIE'S LOVE CHILD! PHOTOS! WE HAVE PHOTOS! And beneath that: MADONNA TO DUET WITH NIGHTINGALE! TICKETS! WE HAVE TICKETS! And right down at the bottom, in fairly small print: END OF WORLD NIGH. AGAIN.

Alex was muttering to himself as he tried to find the right page. "The Walking Man, we pay for sightings... DNA proves Royal Family are descended from lizards... Well, we all knew that... Ah, here we are. It's in their How Are the Mighty Fallen section. Apparently Herne the Hunter has been reduced to a street person, and has been seen begging for food and small change."

"Where?" I said. I wasn't all that surprised. A lot of the homeless and street people in the Nightside used to be Someone, once upon a time. Karma has teeth here, and the wheel turns for all of us.

"Says here he moves around a lot," said Alex, dropping the tabloid onto the bar. He gave me a meaningful look, and I sighed.

I reached inside my mind, concentrating in a way I could never explain to anyone, and powered up my gift. I could find anything, or anyone, if I just looked hard enough. My third eye opened deep in my mind, my private eye, and suddenly I could See all the Nightside at once, vast and full of life and death, like a playground wrapped in poison ivy, like the best present in the world studded with rusty nails. The neon-lit streets and squares flashed by beneath my searching gaze, giving me glimpses of Beings and creatures that are normally, thankfully, hidden from most people. There are many layers and levels to the Nightside, not all of them suitable for human comprehension. I hurried on, narrowing in on my target, until finally I saw a single ragged figure, mostly hidden inside a cardboard box already sodden from the falling rain. One gnarled hand protruded from the box, mutely requesting charity. People walked by without making eye contact. A great head covered by a grubby blanket slowly emerged from the box, turning slowly to look in my direction. Great jutting antlers protruded from under the blanket. Even in his fallen state, it seemed Herne could still tell when he was being watched.

And then my Sight snapped off abruptly, and I was thrust back into the bar again. I'd fixed Herne's position, but I had no time to think about him. My enemies had found me. When I use my gift I burn so very brightly, like a beacon in the night, and they had followed the light right to me. A dozen of the Harrowing, my enemies' attack dogs, appeared out of nowhere into the bar and formed a circle around me. The terrible deathless creatures my enemies had been sending to kill me for so very long, nightmares given shape and form. My nightmares.

They were human in shape, but not in nature. They wore plain suits with slouch hats, the brims pulled low to shadow their faces so they could walk unnoticed in the world of men when they chose. But here, so close to their prey, they did not bother to hide what they were. They had no faces. There was just a blank expanse of skin on the front of their heads, featureless from chin to brow. They had no eyes, but they could see me. No ears, but they could hear. No mouth or nose, but they didn't need to breathe or speak. They were fast and strong, and they never tired. I'd known them to chase and track me for miles, for hours, tearing people limb from limb just for getting in their way.

They stood unnaturally still in their circle around me, and there was no way out. The Harrowing ignored everyone else in the bar, and one by one they lifted long slender hands to show me the vicious hypodermic needles that protruded from their fingers. Drops of a dark green liquid formed at the needle tips. It wasn't enough just to kill me any more; they wanted to drag me back to wherever they came from, so they could take their time about it.

I'd been running from them off and on all my life. And I'd never known why.

My heart was hammering painfully fast in my chest, and my hands were shaking. I was breathing hard, and there was cold sweat on my face. I couldn't fight them. Their bodies were inhumanly strong, soft and yielding. You couldn't hurt them, break them, stop them, or even slow them down. I knew. I'd tried. They just kept on coming. I'd only ever been able to outrun them. I looked wildly at Alex.

"Call Merlin! We need Merlin back!"

"I can't," said Alex. "I'm sorry, John. He only comes when he wants. And if he wanted to be here, he'd be here by now."

"Hell with him," Sinner said cheerfully. "We don't need him. You've got us, John. So, these are the dreaded Harrowing. Nasty-looking things, but I've seen worse. Pretty Poison, if you wouldn't mind..."

"Of course, Sidney. Anything for you."

The demon succubus smiled a happy, terrible smile, and suddenly she didn't look pretty any more. Her teeth all had points, and her eyes glowed bloodred. She held up her hands, and they had claws. She surged forward, inhumanly fast, and tore the two nearest Harrowing apart. They didn't even have time to turn before she'd ripped off both their heads, torn away their arms, slammed their bodies to the floor, and stamped on them. There was no blood, but the scattered body parts still trembled with something like life. Pretty Poison had already moved on, tearing her savage way through the circle of Harrowing. Their resilient, yielding flesh was no match for her demonic fury.

Others of the Harrowing were turning now, responding to the unexpected threat. One advanced on Sinner, only to stop suddenly, as though it had encountered a barrier it couldn't cross. Sinner looked at it sadly, and reached out to lay a hand on its blank brow. The Harrowing crumpled up like an old leaf, and fell shuddering at his feet. Madman lurched forward to confront another of the creatures, and it melted and ran away under his fierce gaze, collapsing into a pool of bubbling protoplasm.

They're weaker here, I thought slowly. *This bar has powerful protections. Getting past Merlin's defences weakened them. For the first time, I have a chance...*

A new confidence flared up in me. I'd never seen the Harrowing fall so fast, except when Razor Eddie hit them. But here, now, they could be stopped. They could be destroyed. I could destroy them. There were six left, hovering uncertainly. I stepped forward, and they all turned together to orient on me.

"Let's do it," I said.

"Let's," said Alex, unexpectedly. "No-one gets to come into my bar and mess with my customers. It's bad for business. Betty, Lucy, time to earn your pay."

He came out from behind the bar hefting his enchanted baseball bat, while Betty and Lucy advanced on the Harrowing, cracking their knuckles noisily. I grinned. It's good to have friends. I turned my gaze on the Harrowing, and it seemed to me that they actually hesitated.

"You're going down," I said. "All the way down."

The four of us waded into the remaining Harrowing, and together we beat the crap out of them. It wasn't easy. Even weakened by Merlin's defences, their bodies were still unnaturally soft, soaking up punishment while they struggled to stab me with their needle fingers. I punched one in the face, and my fist sank almost to the back of its skull before I tugged it free again. Alex hit one with his bat, and the enchanted wood sank down through the head and on into the chest before it stopped. But soon we learned to attack their weak spots, their joints, sweeping the legs out from under them, then battering them to a pulp as they struggled to get to their feet again. Lucy and Betty grabbed an arm each and pulled one apart like a wishbone. I don't know if they made a wish. Alex slammed one to the floor, and I hit it with a table.

We kicked the bodies back and forth across the floor, laughing breathlessly. It felt good for all of us, to have something to take out our various frustrations on. We carved them up and trampled the pieces underfoot, and it felt good, so good. I'd never beaten them before. Never.

It wasn't until later that I figured out all the implications. My enemies knew Strangefellows was protected by Merlin's magic. That's why they'd never sent the Harrowing here after me before, even though they had to know I was a regular visitor. Something had made them desperate enough to try anyway; and it wasn't difficult to guess what.

In the end, we all leaned back against the bar, breathing hard, looking contentedly at the horrid mess we'd made. Twelve of the most dangerous and feared creatures in the Nightside now lay scattered across the floor of the bar in so many small, quivering body parts. We grinned at each other. I was feeling ecstatic. I'd defeated my oldest nightmares. The scattered pieces were suddenly still, then they vanished silently away, back to whatever hell produced them. We all whooped loudly, even Sinner.

"Where do these things come from?" he said.

"I don't know," I said. "I've never known."

"Who sends them? Who are these enemies of yours?"

"I've never known who they are, either. No-one knows."

"Powers from the Nightside? From Outside, perhaps? Maybe even from other dimensions..."

"I don't know!"

"Then why," said Sinner, calmly and reasonably, "don't you use your gift to track them down and identify them?"

I gaped at him blankly. The idea had honestly never occurred to me before. Unless I had considered it, but suppressed it, because it scared me so much. But now I'd seen the Harrowing defeated, now I was safe in Strangefellows, surrounded by good and powerful allies... I nodded, slowly, and opened my third eye.

This time, it was different. My gift granted me a Vision. I seemed to be a disembodied spirit, without face or form, wandering in a strange place. I drifted across a dark and devastated landscape, a place of ruins and rubble. It didn't take me long to recognise where and when I was. I had come again to a possible future for the Nightside, a silent and empty place I had experienced once before when I stumbled into a Timeslip. My Vision had brought me to the end of all things, the end of the Nightside and all civilisation.

An event I helped to bring about, or so an old dying friend had told me.

Everywhere I looked, the Nightside had been destroyed. The proud buildings had collapsed or been torn down, nothing left but cracked and broken walls, and piles of rubble. Smashed and abandoned vehicles choked the still streets. Nothing moved anywhere. The Nightside was a dead place. The light had a dark purple texture, as though bruised by what it saw and showed. In the far distance, broken buildings made stark silhouettes against the horizon. And up in the dark, dark sky there was no moon, and only a few dozen stars in all the night.

Everything looked as though it had been dead for centuries, but I knew better. The last time I was here, in the Timeslip, this future's Razor Eddie had told me I had brought down the Nightside, and the world, in just eighty-two years. Wiped out civilization and Humanity. And all because I'd insisted on finding out who my mother was. I'd sworn an oath to that Eddie, before I killed him as a mercy, that I would never let this future happen.

My Vision leapt suddenly forward, as though my gift had finally caught the scent of what it sought. I swooped across the broken landscape, shooting between the wrecked stumps of buildings, focussing in on one particular location. My final destination was a cracked crumbling house, nothing obviously different about it, but I knew that was where I had to be. It was where I would find my enemies. There was no light showing at any of the shuttered windows, but I could tell there was light and life inside. Hidden, barricaded against the dark. As I drifted towards the house, another piece of knowledge came to me. My Vision had brought me into a time some years previous to my appearance in the Timeslip. Humanity was not all dead here. Not yet. I drifted through the crumbling walls and on into a small, desperately defended inner room, lit only by flickering stumps of candles. And then, finally, I saw my enemies.

And I knew them.

My enemies were the last remaining major players of this future time, the last defenders of the Nightside, pooling their remaining power and working frantically together to try and destroy me in the Past, before I could do... whatever terrible thing it was that I had done. My Vision could only tell me so much. My enemies were trying to kill me in order to save the Nightside, and the world.

They sat together around a simple iron brazier, huddling around the heat, binding the last remnants of their power together with unsteady words and shaking hands, while from outside the house came horrible, threatening sounds. They paused briefly, listening. I could hear what they heard. Something large and heavy was moving, out in the dark purple night, drawing slowly closer. And from the awful sounds it made, I was glad I couldn't see it. The handful of ragged figures in the room froze where they were, fear written clearly in their malnourished faces, not daring to speak or even move for fear of being detected; but eventually the awful thing outside moved on. Their defences still shielded them, for now.

Whatever it was that had brought the Nightside down, it wasn't over yet. Though just as clearly, Life was losing. I hung above my enemies, unseen and unsuspected, and listened while they spoke of the monsters from Outside, abroad in the night, everywhere. Apparently there were still other small enclaves of resistance, scattered among the ruins, but they were failing, one by one. Nothing had been heard from them, for months. This small group, in this small room, was quite possibly the last hope of Humanity. If they failed and died, there would be nothing left living in the Nightside but the insects, which were already changing and mutating under the terrible forces released by the War.

It was hard to look upon the handful of pitiful forms that had once been the major players of my day. Jessica Sorrow, no longer the terrible Unbeliever, looked almost human here, though still painfully skinny. She wore a battered black leather jacket and leggings, and hugged an ancient battered teddy bear in her arms. I'd found the bear for her, to help restore her lost humanity. And now she used it as a focus to help the group locate me in the Past. Next to her was Larry Oblivion, the dead detective, wrapped in the tattered remains of what had once been a very smart suit. He said quietly that he wished he could have died fully, like his brother Tommy, rather than witness what the Nightside had come to. Jessica put an arm across his shoulders and hugged him listlessly.

Count Video warmed his wrinkled hands at the brazier. He'd had his skin stitched back on, after the Angel War, the sutures making grotesque designs around the familiar neurotech, silicon nodes, and circuitry patches soldered to his flesh. Strange energies formed a shifting halo around his head. He wore nothing but a series of leather straps, criss-crossing his skinny body, tightly buckled. Perhaps they held him together.

King of Skin was just a man now, stripped of his terrible glamour. Objects of power hung about him on silver chains, half-hidden in the thick pelt of his fur coat. He had a crystal ball in his hands, but it was a poor thing, disfigured with cracks and scorings. He twitched and shuddered at every sudden sound, his eyes rolling pitifully in his head.

Annie Abattoir wore the remains of a wine-dark evening dress, the cutaway back showing the mystic sigils carved into the flesh between her shoulder blades. I wasn't surprised to see her here. Annie had always been very hard to kill, though many had tried. Six-foot-two, and mostly muscle, even now, she still looked somehow... diminished. The War had worn her down. She kept a bowl of blood beside her and used it to refresh the lines of the pentacle around the brazier. She refilled the bowl from a vein she'd opened in her arm.

I listened to them speak, their voices just whispers, drifting to me from far away.

"The Sending has failed," said Jessica. "Our agents have been destroyed."

"All twelve?" said Count Video. "That's never happened before. He must have gathered new allies. Powerful companions."

"Perhaps he grows stronger," said Larry Oblivion. "As his time approaches. Should we try again?"

"No," said Annie Abattoir. "It's too soon. We're too weak. Wait, and gather strength. There is still time."

"We always knew forcing our way past Merlin's spells was a risk," said Jessica.

"I miss him," said King of Skin, his mouth trembling. "He gave us hope. He fought so bravely. When they finally dragged Merlin down, and ate his heart right in front of him, a part of me died with him. He was the best of us, at the end."

"He always believed Arthur would return, to save us," said Jessica.

"Well if he is coming back, he'd better get a move on," said Count Video, and they all managed some kind of smile.

Who could they be fighting? I thought. *Who could this War be against, that could destroy a mighty Power like Merlin Satanspawn? What's out there, in the night?*

"We must make more Harrowing," said Annie. "We must be ready for another Sending, when the opportunity presents itself."

"We already have one body," said King of Skin.

"We can't use him!" Jessica said immediately. "You can't! He was one of us."

"He's just a body now," said Annie. "It's what he would have wanted. You know that. You know how dangerous it is for any of us to go out into the night to dig bodies out of the rubble. Can't make homunculi without bodies."

"But not Julien Advent," said Jessica.

"He was always ready to serve," said Larry. "To be the hero. This is his last chance. You don't have to work on the body if you don't want to."

I missed what they said after that. I was in shock. Julien Advent, the legendary Victorian Adventurer, one of my enemies? He might have disapproved of me from time to time, but we had always been friends and allies. Fought the good fight side by side... How could he have become a part of this? He would never have sided with murder or betrayal... unless the stakes were so high his conscience gave him no choice. Unless all the other alternatives were so much worse. And if Julien were to become a Harrowing... I had to face the possibility that maybe other Harrowing I'd encountered in the past had been made out of the bodies of friends of mine.

I remembered when I first discovered the name of the creatures that had been hunting me on and off since I was a child. The oracle in the mall's wishing well had given me the name, in return for a price I still regretted paying. And years later, Julien had been the one who explained what the name meant. Harrow had been an old Victorian word, meaning to harass, to harry, to chase down. Had Julien Advent been the first to give them that name, here in the future?

"I still say we should just kill John," said Annie Abattoir, dripping blood from her arm into her bowl. "He's too dangerous to take chances with."

"No," Jessica said immediately. "He's too close to becoming now. We have to bring him back here alive, and question him. We have to understand why he did... what he did. Drugged and helpless, he will tell, eventually. And maybe then we'll be able to figure out a way to stop all this happening."

"And afterwards, we'll kill him," said King of Skin.

"Yes," said Count Video. "For all his sins. For the death of the world. For being his mother's son."

And with that the Vision broke, and I was suddenly back in Strangefellows again. I was standing in the middle of the room, shaking and shuddering, cold sweat dripping off my face. Sinner had an arm around me, holding me up. Alex was offering me a new glass of brandy. I took it gratefully, gulping it down, the glass chattering against my teeth. I was in shock—too many truths, too fast.

I told them some of what I'd Seen and heard, but not all. There were things they didn't need to know. Things... I couldn't trust them with. They were almost as shocked as I was, and they all looked at me in a new way, even Madman. The man who would destroy the Nightside. I couldn't blame them. Could my enemies actually be the good guys, after all? Desperately trying to prevent a catastrophe, in the only way left to them?

I had given that future's Razor Eddie my word that I would die before I allowed that terrible future to happen; but could I have already set things in motion by taking on this case? If discovering the origins of the Nightside was tied in with the mystery of my mother's identity, could pursuing this case be the first domino that sent all the others toppling?

"Timeslips are only potential futures," said Alex. "Everyone knows that."

"They're just possibilities," said Sinner. "Time has more branches than a tree."

I shook my head. "The fact that my lifelong enemies are rooted in this particular future means it has to be more probable than most."

"So what are you going to do?" said Alex.

"It's up to you," said Sinner. "Whether you wish to continue with this case. You don't have to. You can turn aside. But if you're determined to go on, Pretty Poison and I will accompany you. If only because I'm fascinated to see what will happen next."

"Hear, hear," said Madman.

"We go on," I said. "I have a case, and I've never let a client down yet. The truth always comes first. No matter who it ends up hurting."

SIX

THE HUNTER RUN TO GROUND

I left Strangefellows through the front door, thinking hard. I'd always known the Nightside was old, had to be really old, but if Merlin was to be believed, the Nightside had been old back when he was still young. Just how far back did the Nightside go? And if it was created for a specific purpose, who created it? I had a horrible suspicion I already knew the answer.

My missing mother.

I led the way up the damp, gloomy alley that led back into the bright neon and hue and cry of the main drag, my companions lagging behind as always. Sinner and Pretty Poison were strolling along arm in arm, murmuring and giggling together, close as any lovey-dovey teenagers. It might have been charming if I hadn't known one of them was a demon from Hell, with centuries of treachery and moral corruption behind her. And Madman was ambling along in the rear, his eyes far away, for which I was grateful. It was when he started taking notice of the world that things started getting dangerous. It occurred to me, not for the first time on this case, that I might have chosen my companions more carefully.

We finally emerged onto the main streets, and I immediately spotted that we were under observation. Walker hadn't wasted any time in putting his people on my tail. At least there was no sign of Bad Penny yet, but then there probably wouldn't be until she was ready to do something appallingly nasty. I couldn't say I was surprised at Walker's people picking me up so quickly. He knew the odds were I'd drop into Strangefellows at some point, so staking it out had to be a safe bet. To be fair, his people didn't exactly stand out in the crowd. He trained them better than that. But Walker had been having me watched and followed for so long now that many of them had actually become familiar faces. In fact, if I was getting nowhere on a case, I quite often took them off somewhere for a drink and tried out my various theories on them. On the grounds that neither of us was going anywhere for a while, so we might as well be comfortable. Most of them went along with it. In the Nightside, today's enemy can be tomorrow's friend, or at least ally. And vice versa, of course. None of us ever mentioned this arrangement to Walker, of course. He wouldn't have understood. Probably have his people hauled up on charges of fraternising with the enemy.

I looked openly about me, counting off the agents. I spotted twenty, half of whom were new faces making a valiant effort to appear inconspicuous. Twenty. I was impressed. A hell of lot more than he usually sent after me. It only went to show how seriously he was taking this case. My companions, naturally, failed to spot any of the watchers, and I had to identify each and every one.

"Don't point at them," I said kindly. "It would only embarrass them."

So we waved at them instead. One was so taken aback he walked right into a lamp-post.

"I don't like being spied on," said Pretty Poison, her schoolgirl face disfigured by a menacing scowl.

Sinner patted her comfortingly on the arm. "It's only because they don't know you like I do, dear."

"I'm pretty sure these are only decoys," I said. "Distractions, to take our attention away from the real observers, hidden behind cloaking spells and invisibility cloaks. I think Walker is seriously concerned about our progress on this case."

"I'd be hard-pressed to name anyone who mattered in the Nightside who isn't," said Sinner. "Whatever we discover, it's bound to affect everyone here. Maybe we should invite some of these watchers along, as backup, for when things get... difficult."

"No," I said immediately. "Walker represents the Authorities; and all they care about is maintaining the status quo. If we do get close to some real answers, I wouldn't put it past them to order us all killed. Just in case."

Sinner looked at me. "You don't seem unduly worried at the prospect."

I shrugged. "There's always been someone who wants me dead. The Authorities can just get in the queue. Besides, we've danced this dance before, Walker and I. As long as I'm leading, and he's following, I have the advantage."

"I don't like being watched," Madman said abruptly. "But then, I know who's watching us. We're not alone here. We're never alone. They watch from the other side of our mirrors, and they hate us for being real. Always turn your mirrors to the wall when you sleep, so they can't come through."

"Well," I said, after a pause. "Thank you for that insight..."

"I'm not mad," Madman said sadly. "It would be so much easier, for me and for everyone else, if I was, but... if you could see what I have Seen... the world isn't what we think it is, and never has been. Where are we going next?"

I blinked a few times, then decided to just answer the question. "We need to get to the restaurant area, in Uptown. I can find Herne from there. But it's a question of distance. You can bet Walker will be able to track us on any of the usual forms of mass transport, and I hate to make things easy for him."

"Why don't you get a car?" said Sinner.

I actually shuddered. "Are you serious? You see the traffic on that road? That's not commuting, that's evolution in action! Half the things that charge back and forth only look like cars, and the other half run on magics so upsetting they'd give Pretty Poison palpitations. And don't even think about sticking your thumb out; someone would steal it."

"I know a way we can get to Uptown," Pretty Poison said unexpectedly. "I can take us straight there. If that's what you want, Sidney."

"Well, of course," said Sinner. "But I didn't know you could..."

A halo of flies sprang up around Pretty Poison's head, buzzing loudly. Vicious claws thrust out of her elegant fingers as she traced fiery sigils on the air. Her face disappeared into shadow, in which two sullen red glows burned. I actually fell back a step. Madman just looked at her sadly. Pretty Poison said something that hurt our ears to hear it, and a circle of hell-fire sprang up around all of us. Sulphur yellow flames that stank of brimstone, though the heat couldn't reach us. The flames leapt high, then died down again, and as quickly as that we were Uptown. The flames snapped off, and Pretty Poison looked like a woman again. I shook my head, disoriented. Just then, in the moment of transition, it seemed to me that I had heard uncountable voices, crying out in torment... I looked at Pretty Poison, who smiled back demurely.

"I didn't know you could do that," said Sinner, framing his words with what I thought was considerable calm, under the circumstances.

"Just a quick side-step through the Infernal Realms," said Pretty Poison. "After all, I am a demon succubus, Sidney darling. We have to be able to get absolutely anywhere; it's in the job description."

"I saw you," said Sinner. "Just for a moment there, I saw you the way you really are."

She looked at the ground. "A girl can't help her background, Sidney."

"It's all right," he said. "It doesn't matter. I've seen your true form before. It was the first thing they showed me when I arrived in Hell. It doesn't change how I feel. I love you for who you are, not what you are."

"I've never understood that," said Pretty Poison.

"Of course not," Sinner said kindly. "You're a demon from Hell."

They laughed quietly together. I looked around me. The crowds bustling up and down the busy street had just seen four people arrive out of nowhere in a circle of hell-fire, but no-one seemed particularly interested. This was the Nightside, after all. People (and others) minded their own business here, and expected the same courtesy from everyone else. Though they did give us a little more room than most. I started off up the street, and my companions followed. I knew where we were, and I knew where to find Herne. I'd been here before. Uptown has all the best clubs and restaurants, the fashionable places where fashionable people meet, but even the gaudiest light casts a shadow, and that was where we'd find Herne.

I passed by an especially renowned bistro, the kind of place where even the finger food costs an arm and a leg, and then took a sudden turn into a dimly lit side street. The contrast between the bistro's brightly coloured come-on and the alley-way that led to its rear couldn't have been greater. The side street was cold and wet and grimy, and it only took half a dozen steps before you knew you were in a whole different world. The street gave out onto a gloomy back square, part of the squalid maze of back alleys, garbage-strewn squares, and cul-de-sacs that gave access to the restaurants' back entrances. The side of fashionable eating that the customers never saw. The tradesmen's entrance, the staff's entrance, and the dumping grounds for all the food the restaurants no longer wanted. Which was why the homeless and the street people and the bums of the Nightside came here, to cluster together away from the indifferent everyday world.

I looked around Rats' Alley. It hadn't changed.

It was darker here than anywhere else in the Nightside, and it had nothing to do with the lack of street lighting. This was a darkness of the heart and of the soul, which touched everything at the bottom of the heap. The bright flaring neon from the main streets didn't penetrate, and even the blue-white glow from the overly large moon above seemed somehow muted. The smell was appalling, a thick organic stench of rot and filth and accumulated despair. The cobbled street was sticky underfoot. People lived here, in the shadows, a small community of the lost and the destitute. Not so much forgotten as wilfully overlooked. Sinner moved in beside me as I paused at the entrance to the square.

"*This* is where Herne the Hunter lives? The old god of the forests?"

"It's a long way down from the top," I said. "But you're never so far up you can't fall. At least in Rats' Alley he has company. A lot of the homeless and destitute end up here, because this is where restaurant staff dump unwanted food at the end of their shifts. Everything from scraps to whole meals. It's cheaper to feed it to the bums than pay to have it carted away."

"Why is it called Rats' Alley?" said Pretty Poison.

"Why do you think?" I said. "And watch where you step."

"I never realised there were so many homeless in the Nightside," said Sinner. "It's like a whole community here. A shanty town for the lost."

"I think we're supposed to call them street people these days," I said. "Because if we call them homeless, it begs the question of why we're not finding homes for them. And they've always been here. The Nightside's finances are based on scamming losers, and it's never been kind to failures."

Rats' Alley was what everyone called the square and its tributaries, packed full of cardboard boxes, lean-to shelters, plastic tenting, and clusters of people huddled shapelessly together under blankets. Men and women of all ages and sizes, thrown together like shipwreck victims, refugees from the overthrown countries of their lives. Bright eyes showed here and there in the shadows, and glimmers of light on what might have been weapons. They might be down and out, but they didn't care for being stared at.

"Do they have dogs?" said Madman. "I thought all homeless people had dogs."

"Not around here," I said. "These people would eat a dog if it showed up. Or the rats would. They have serious rats around here. That's why the street people stick together. So the rats won't drag them off in the night."

Sinner looked at me. "You seem to know this place very well, John."

"I used to live here," I said. "Years ago, when things had got really bad. This is probably the only place in the Nightside where my name and history mean nothing. They'll take anyone here. And this was a great place to hide from everyone, even myself. Having to concentrate on keeping warm and dry, and where the hell your next meal is coming from, is very useful when you don't want to think about other things."

"How long were you here?" said Pretty Poison.

"I don't know. Long enough. This is where I first met Razor Eddie. He still sleeps here, sometimes." I stepped cautiously forward into the square, looking around me for familiar faces as my eyes adjusted to the gloom. "That's Sister Morphine over there, in what's left of her habit. A Carmelite nun who chose to come here and live among the street people, to preach and to console them. Her veins manufacture all kinds of drugs for the needy, expressed through her tears. And there's never any shortage of reasons for tears in Rats' Alley. Her tears are shed for the suffering around her, and no-one is ever turned away. Some time ago, a bunch of thugs decided to kidnap and make use of her, as an endless supply of drugs for them to peddle. They turned up here mob-handed to drag her away, all confident and cocky... and the street people ganged up on them and beat them all to death. Afterwards, they ate the bodies."

Sister Morphine came forward to meet me, holding the dark rags of her habit around her with tired dignity. She looked a lot older than I remembered, but then living out in the open will do that to you. Her robes were spattered with filth, her smile weary but kind.

"John Taylor. I always knew you'd be back."

"I'm just visiting, Sister."

"That's what they all say."

"I'm looking for Herne the Hunter, Sister. We need to talk to him."

"But does he want to talk to you?" Sister Morphine glared at Pretty Poison. "This one has the stink of the Pit about her."

"We're not here to make trouble," I said carefully.

"You are trouble, John," said Sister Morphine. And she turned her back on me and walked away.

I looked around for someone who might be more helpful. For cash in hand, or even the promise of a drink. The Bone Horror peered at me dully, curled up under a propped-up blanket. He'd lost everything at the gambling tables, even his flesh. All he had left was his bones, but still he wouldn't, perhaps couldn't, die. Some of his bones had clearly been gnawed on, and I could only hope it was just by rats. I saw other names, other faces, but none of them looked friendly. There were creatures as well as people, and even a few broken-down machines, hoarding the last sparks of energy in their positronic brains. Even the underside of the Nightside is still a cosmopolitan place. There was even a Grey alien, dressed in the tattered remains of an atmosphere suit. Left behind, presumably. Damn things get everywhere. His badly handwritten cardboard sign said *Will probe for food.* I seriously considered kicking the crap out of the abducting little bastard on general principles, but I made myself rise above the temptation. All are welcome in Rats' Alley, no matter what their past. That's the point. They even took me in.

"Does no-one do anything to help these people?" said Sinner. "Doesn't anybody care?"

"Remember where you are," I said. "The Nightside is famous for not caring about anything. That's what brings people in. There are still a few who give a damn, like Sister Morphine. And Pew still does the rounds of places like this, dispensing hot soup and fire-and-brimstone sermons. Julien Advent raises money for various charities through the *Night Times*. But mostly the Nightside prefers to pretend that places and people like these don't exist. They don't want to be reminded of the price of failure in the Nightside."

My companions and I were beginning to attract attention. Our faces and our stories were known, even here. The street people were getting interested. I kept a watchful eye on the shadowy forms nearest us. Street people have a tendency to gang up on those they consider intruders into their territory. All outsiders, often including do-gooders, are seen as targets of opportunity. I'd been here. I could remember searching quickly through the pockets of unconscious bleeding bodies. The street people weren't afraid of us, or our histories. Fall this far, and you weren't afraid of anything any more. They started lurching to their feet, pulling their blankets around them, rising on every side. A quick look behind showed our retreat was still clear, if necessary. I didn't want to hurt anyone. Sinner and Pretty Poison moved in protectively on either side of me as the ragged forms stumbled forward. They all seemed to be orientating on me, ignoring the others. Surely they couldn't all remember me.

And then they knelt before me, and bowed their heads to me, and murmured my name like a benediction. Some of them wanted to rub their grubby faces against my hands. Some touched my white trench coat wonderingly, as though just the touch might heal them. I looked around for Sister Morphine, but she still had her back to us. The homeless knelt before me like a congregation, their grimy faces full of adoration.

"Well," said Sinner. "This is... unexpected. And just a little worrying."

"Trust me," I said, holding my hands carefully back out of everyone's reach. "If there's one thing I think we can all be sure of, it's that I am not the Second Coming."

"Definitely not," said Pretty Poison.

There was something in the way she said that. Sinner and I both looked at her. "Do you know something you're not telling?" I said.

"More than you could possibly imagine," said Pretty Poison.

When it became clear I wasn't going to perform any miracles, the street people quickly lost interest and drifted away again. Madman went wandering off among them, and they accepted him as one of their own. They could tell he was just as damaged, just as divorced from the world as the rest of them.

"Poor Tom's a-cold," he said, somewhat predictably.

I felt like saying *Get thee to a nunnery,* but rose above it. I was here on business. I made my way carefully through the maze of cardboard boxes and improvised tents and finally found Herne the Hunter just where my gift had told me he'd be. He was still squatting inside his soggy, half-collapsed box, wrapped in something dark and soiled. He saw me and Sinner and Pretty Poison gathered in front of his box, and retreated even further back inside. We all tried coaxing him out, but he wouldn't budge until I used my name. Then he came out slowly, a bit at a time, like an uncertain animal that might bolt at any moment, until finally he stood crouching before us. He could have been just another bum, engulfed in the filthy remains of an old greatcoat, except for the stag's antlers protruding from his bulging forehead. He was smaller than I'd expected, barely five feet tall, broad and squat and almost Neanderthal. His skin was cracked and leathery, his face heavy and broad and ugly. His eyes were deeply sunken, and his almost lipless mouth trembled. He smelled really bad, which in Rats' Alley took some doing. It was a rank, animal smell, thick with musk. In one over-large hand he held firmly onto a begging bowl fashioned from a hollowed-out human skull.

"Not much of a god, yes?" he said, in a deep, growling voice thickened by an accent I'd never heard before. "Should have gone on long ago. But, still a few worshippers left. Mostly New Age hippie types. Bah! But, take what you can get, these days. Belief is still power. Herne the Hunter just a tale for children now. I know, I know. No-one wants to worship at the blood altars any more. Don't blame them. No. Never was a comfortable god to have around, me. Herne embodied the chase and the hunt and the kill, nature red in tooth and claw." His speech improved as he talked, as though he was remembering how. "You sacrificed to me for luck in the hunt, for good weather and the death of your enemies, and to keep me away. I was a dangerous and capricious god, and I loved tricks. Yes... Herne rode high, lived off the best, trampled men and women under my hooves, and the Wild Magic was strong in me. But if you were under my protection, no-one dared touch you! No! No... A long time ago... I have fallen far. What you want with me anyway? Better gods on Street of the Gods, very reasonable prices. I have no powers, no secrets, no wisdom."

"We're looking for information," I said. "The answers to some questions."

Herne shook all over, like a dog. "Don't know anything, any more. World has moved on, oh yes. The forests are gone. All cities now. Steel and stone and brick, and the magic in them does not know me. Hate cities. Hate the Nightside. Hate being old. Live long enough, and you get to see everything you ever cared for rot and fail and fall." He looked at me sharply. "I know you, John Taylor. Know you well enough not to worship at your feet. What you want? What questions?"

"Tell me about the old days," I said. "When England was young, and so were you."

He grinned widely, showing great gaps in his teeth. "Still remember my glory days, leading the Wild Hunt on my moon stallion. All men and women were my prey on that night. Long, long ago... Once I preyed on humans, now I live off their leavings. Anyone could end up like me, oh yes. One bad day... and then you fall off the edge and can't get back. Men become farmers, not hunters. Towns grow into cities. The forests grew smaller, and so did I. Men grew more powerful, and I grew less. Cities... the Nightside was one of the first, the beginnings of the rot."

"Not *the* first?" said Sinner.

Herne grinned again. "Opinion is divided. Before my time. Ask the Old Ones. It was there in the earliest of days, and it is still here. More savage and merciless than I ever was."

"I have heard it said," I said carefully, "that my mother is tied in with the creation of the Nightside. What do you know of that?"

Herne shrugged easily. "Don't know for sure. Don't think anyone does. I have an opinion. Opinions are like arseholes; everyone's got one. You ask me, I think your mother was Queen Mab, first Queen of the Faerie; before Titania. Pretty pretty Titania. I remember Mab. Beautiful as the dawn, more powerful than the seasons. She walked in lightning, danced on the moonbeams, entranced you with a look, and forgot you with a shrug. Queen Mab, the magnificent and feared. The Faerie don't talk much about Mab any more, but still they fear her, should she ever return. She's been written out of most of the stories and the secret histories, in favour of sweet little Titania; but some of us have never forgotten Queen Mab."

"What happened?" I said.

He chuckled briefly. A low, nasty sound. "Ask Tam O'Shanter, dancing on his own grave. Brandishing the broken bones of a rival, and gnawing on the heart he tore from the rival's breast. We took our love affairs seriously in those days. Our passions were larger, our tragedies more terrible. Death had little dominion over such as us. Our stories had the power of fate, and destiny." Herne cocked his ugly head on one side, as though listening to voices or perhaps songs only he could hear. "I remember the Faerie leaving the worlds of men, once it was clear to them that cities and civilization and cold steel would inevitably triumph. They walked sideways from the sun, all of them, retreating to their own secret, hidden world. Yes. I should have gone with them when I had the chance. They did offer. They did! Herne always had more in common with the Fae than with earth-grubbing Humanity. But they were in it for the long term, and we never were. Should have gone with them, yes; but no, stayed to fight and lose and see the world become something I no longer recognise, or have a place in.

"So, here is Herne the Hunter. Among the fallen and the hopeless. Doing penance."

"What for?" said Pretty Poison.

He crawled back into his cardboard box, holding my gaze all the while. "Ask the Lord of Thorns. Now go away. All of you. Or I'll kill you."

We left him crying in his cardboard box.

I looked around for Madman. It was time we were moving on. "Where to next?" I said. "I'm open to suggestions."

"How about the Lord of Thorns?" suggested Sinner.

I winced, and so, I noticed, did Pretty Poison. I looked severely at Sinner. "Only when we've tried absolutely everyone else in the Nightside, and I mean *everybody*. That guy even scares Walker, and with good reason. Why bring him up?"

"Because Herne mentioned him."

"So he did. Next?"

"All right," said Sinner. "How about the Lamentation?"

I actually shuddered that time. "Why on earth would we want to go and see that crazy piece of shit?"

"Because Herne said we needed to talk to the Old Ones," Sinner said calmly. "And the Lamentation is the oldest Being I know of."

"There is that," I said, reluctantly. "There's no doubt it knows all kinds of things; if you can persuade it to talk. But you don't get to be an old Power in the Nightside by being friendly and approachable. No-one's even sure what the Lamentation is any more; except it's supersaturated with death magic and crazy with it. I don't even like saying the name aloud, in case it's listening. It could be a demon or a Transient Being or even a human who took a *really* wrong turn. No-one knows. They say it eats souls..."

"But it's definitely older than Herne," Sinner said stubbornly. "If anyone knows how far back the Nightside goes, I'd put good money on the Lamentation."

"So you think we should just barge in and ask it questions?" I said.

"You can hide behind me if you like," said Sinner. "It's up to you, John. How badly do you want to get to the bottom of this case? Bad enough to beard a Power and a Domination in its lair?"

"Oh, hell," I said. "It wouldn't be the first time."

"Boys..." said Pretty Poison. "I think we have a problem with Madman."

I looked round quickly. And there was Madman, dancing and pirouetting through the boxes and tents of Rats' Alley while flowers blossomed brightly in his wake, springing right out of the cobbled ground and through cracks in the grimy brickwork. He ended his dance with a flourish, and a spring bubbled up at his feet. One of the homeless dipped his metal cup in the stream, tried it, and cried out excitedly that it was pure whiskey. The homeless looked on Madman with new eyes.

They surged forward to crowd around him, demanding he conjure up for them food and drink, heat and light and palaces to live in. They pawed and clawed at him, their voices growing loud and insistent and threatening. Madman tried to back away, but there was nowhere for him to go. I tried to get to him, but there were too many people in the way. I yelled at the street people, using the authority of my name, but they were beyond listening. And then my skin prickled and my heart missed a beat, and I stopped trying to press forward. Something bad was coming. I could feel it.

The brickwork nearest to Madman began to bubble and melt and run away. The ground shook, as though something was heaving up beneath it, trying to break through. The light in Rats' Alley kept changing colour, and there were too many shadows in the square with nothing to cast them. All around there was a growing feeling of... uncertainty. That nothing could be relied on any more. That the curtains of the world might part at any moment to reveal what was really going on behind the scenes. Madman was losing his self-control.

The street people fell back from him, crying out in shock and alarm and growing horror. The world was coming undone all around Madman. I grabbed Sinner by the arm. I couldn't get my breath, and it seemed to me that at any moment I might fall upwards, sailing off into the night sky forever. Everywhere I looked, the details on everything were changing, in utterly arbitrary ways. One of the homeless grabbed at Madman, to make him stop the changes, only to shriek in terror as Madman looked at him, and *changed* him, till he looked like a modern art painting, all angles and dimensions and clashing perspectives. Parts of him were missing. Horribly, he was still alive. Madman looked upon his work, and his face showed nothing, nothing at all.

Sister Morphine pulled the changed man away from Madman and cradled him in her comforting arms. She glared at me. "This is all your fault! You brought him here! Do something!"

I grabbed a few useful items from my coat, braced myself, and was about to start forward again when Sinner pushed past me. He strode forward and locked eyes with Madman. The two men stood silently together, lost in each other's eyes, while the whole world seemed to hold its breath. Madman let out his breath in a long, slow sigh, and looked away, and the world grew calm and steady around him again. Sinner's singular nature had given Madman an anchor, and stabilised him.

Rats' Alley was still and sane again. Many of the homeless were weeping and shaking. Sinner took Madman by the arm and led him out of the square, and Madman went with him as docile as a child.

"Can't take you anywhere," I said.

SEVEN

WHY DON'T THE DEAD LIE STILL

We left the darkness of Rats' Alley behind us and made our way back out into the bright city lights of Uptown. The night was too dark, the neon too bright, but it still felt like home. In many ways, leaving Rats' Alley was like being born again. Like declaring you're ready to take on the world again, and the world had better look out. I'd felt the same the last time I did so, all those years ago. Because no-one ever really lives in Rats' Alley; they're all just existing. I took a deep breath and looked around me. The usual crowds came and went, pounding the pavements, intent on their own very private business, and Walker's watchers were still observing from what they hoped was a safe distance. (Walker didn't pay them enough to go into Rats' Alley after us.) It seemed to me that there were rather more of them than there had been the last time I looked, and I stopped where I was, to check out the situation. My companions waited patiently as I glared openly about me. Some of the watchers stepped back into doorways and the shadows of alley mouths, but the newcomers just stared calmly back. Like vultures scenting dead bodies in the near future. I pointed these people out to Sinner and Pretty Poison. (Madman was already off with the faeries again.)

"We've picked up some new friends," I said. "Not your ordinary, everyday watchers. See those seven Oriental gentlemen, with the ideograms tattooed above their left eyebrows? Combat magicians. Hooded Claw Clan. Just goes to show; everyone answers to Walker."

"Dangerous people?" said Sinner.

"Very," I said.

"That's all right," said Pretty Poison. "We're dangerous people, too."

"Still," said Sinner. "Combat magicians? Walker is taking this case seriously, isn't he... What about those two gentlemen there, with the wolf pelts and claw necklaces?"

"Supernatural trackers. *Lupus extremis*. They could follow our scent through a skunk factory. And teleporting wouldn't throw them off either; they'd just jump right after us, piggy-backing our magics."

"Is there any way to shake them off?" said Sinner.

I grinned. "Sure. Go places they won't dare follow us."

"I don't like the look of those three," Pretty Poison said mildly. "They have the stink of sanctity about them."

I looked where she was pointing, then cursed under my breath. "Now they are serious trouble. The Holy Trio. A man, a woman, and a recently departed spirit; all of them Jesuit demonologists and fully paid-up members of the Fun Is Evil Club. The flip side of tantric magic; they used the tensions caused by a lifetime of celibacy to power their spells. Result—energy to burn, and a really spiteful attitude to the world in general and the Nightside in particular. The Authorities don't normally let them in. Damn! Walker must be really serious about this. We can forget about any more hell-fire teleports; the Trio could stamp the flames out just by glaring at us."

"I could kill them," said Pretty Poison.

"No, you couldn't," said Sinner. "Not if you want to stay with me."

"Well of course, Sidney darling. But you're going to have to explain this whole restraint concept to me again later."

Sinner looked at me suddenly, his usual mild gaze thoughtful and appraising. "I thought you were supposed to be the Vatican's blue-eyed boy, after you got the Unholy Grail back for them?"

"That was a special assignment for the Pope," I said. "Not the Vatican. And Walker has always been able to call on the Church, as well as the State and the Army, to back him up. But I haven't seen a gathering like this for years... and never just for me."

"So what do we do?" said Madman, catching us all by surprise. It was easy to forget he was listening. It was easy to forget he was still there.

"I think... we'll just let them follow us," I said. "It's not a long walk from here to the lair of the Lamentation. An awful lot of them will drop out, once they realise where we're going. I don't blame them. I wouldn't go there myself if I didn't have to. In fact, I do have to, and I'm still trying to think of a way out of it."

"The trouble with shadows," said Madman, "is they watch you all the time, but you can't see their eyes."

We all considered that for a while. "Congratulations," said Sinner. "That actually bordered on pertinent, not to mention lucid."

"No-one listens when I tell them things," Madman said sadly.

Sinner turned back to me in a determined sort of way. "I just had a thought," he said firmly. "Sandra Chance is supposed to have a relationship with the Lamentation these days; even if no-one is sure what it might be. Could we perhaps contact her and ask her for an introduction? Maybe even get her to act as an intermediary?"

"I doubt it," I said. "First, it's just gossip. And second, she's not too keen on me at the moment. Not since I let the butterfly get away."

Sinner waited until he realised I wasn't going to say any more, then sighed. "You have a history with practically everyone, don't you?"

"Not all of it bad," I said defensively. "There must be someone in the Nightside who hasn't wanted to kill me at some time or other."

"I wouldn't put money on it," said Pretty Poison.

We walked out of Uptown, trailing our pack of observers behind us, and made our way through a series of increasingly seedy areas, where even the neon seemed grimy. The buildings huddled together, though the strangers on the streets kept resolutely to themselves. The windows were all shuttered or covered with metal grilles, and the doors were locked to everyone except those who knew the right things to say or ask for. We were in Freak Fair now, where all the fetishists, obsessives, and the more extreme enthusiasts came in search of things that most people wouldn't even recognise as pleasure. Not a place for tourists. The Freak Fair makes even the everyday residents of the Nightside feel dirty. I'd been here once before, on a case, and afterwards I had to burn my shoes.

The people we passed kept their eyes determinedly downcast and made a point of giving each other plenty of room. It was all very quiet and polite, though the stamp of perversion and morbidity hung heavily on the air. The people tracking us began to fall back in ones and twos, then in something of a rush, once it was clear where we were going, clearly deciding that there were very definite limits to their duty. Everyone draws the line somewhere, even in the Nightside. But the hardier souls stuck with us, shouldering people out of their way to maintain their line of sight. I could feel my shoulders hunching as we continued through the narrow streets, as though anticipating an attack. Freak Fair is not a comfortable place to be. Pretty Poison, on the other hand, actually blossomed, striding happily along with a smile for everyone. Sinner didn't seem to be affected at all, but then, he was in love with a demon succubus. Madman hummed cheerfully along with his sound track, which was currently Madonna's *Erotica*. Takes all sorts...

We finally arrived at the deconsecrated funeral parlour that currently housed that old and awful Being called the Lamentation. It changed its location regularly, partly because there were a hell of a lot of people (and others) who wanted it dead and gone, and also because its presence alone was enough to suck all the life out of any environment it inhabited. The Lamentation—also known as the God of Suicides, the Saint of Suffering, the Tyrant of Tears. It had many names but only one nature, and nobody worshipped it. You only turned to the Lamentation when you'd run out of belief, hope, and any kind of faith.

We stood together before the flimsy-looking front door, hanging just a little open between stained stone walls. There were no windows. Above the door was a tarnished brass plaque, giving the name of the place in Gothic Victorian script—the Maxwell Mausoleum. The funeral parlour had been around for almost two centuries, before it was shut down amid general outrage. (This was long before the Necropolis became the only supplier for funeral ceremonies in the Nightside.)

They still tell stories about what happened in the Maxwell Mausoleum all those years ago. Bad stories, even for the Nightside. Of what was done to the dead and the living, in dark and silenced rooms, where the Maxwell family worshipped the insides of bodies, and practised rites so revolting there aren't even words to describe them. The Maxwells were finally discovered, then dragged out and hanged from the nearest street-lamps, their bodies set alight while they were still kicking. Their remains were buried in the same coffin, after certain precautions, and for weeks afterwards people lined up to piss on the grave.

It was because of the terrible things that happened here that the Authorities decided to forget all about free enterprise, and determined that in the future all funeral practices would be supplied by the Necropolis, which they would watch over and control. The Maxwell Mausoleum had been abandoned for years before the Lamentation moved in but you could still feel the evil oozing out of the filthy old stones. The Lamentation presumably felt right at home.

It suddenly seemed a lot quieter than it had a few moments ago, and it took me a while to work out why. Madman's music had stopped. He stood right in front of the door, studying it closely while being careful not to touch it, and frowning, as though listening to a voice only he could hear. "Why don't the dead lie still?" he said, then turned away, without waiting for an answer.

I looked at Sinner. "Is it just me, or is he starting to make more sense?"

"It's probably just you," said Sinner. "So, what do we do? Knock loudly and announce our presence?"

"Oh, I think it knows we're here," I said. " The Lamentation is a Power and a Domination. Beings like that don't believe in being surprised."

I reached cautiously forward and gave the door a gentle push. It swung slowly inwards, the hinges squealing loudly. Like most of the older Beings, the

Lamentation was a traditionalist and a bit of a drama queen. Beyond the doors was a dull red glow, a tense silence, and nothing else. Like opening a gate to Hell. We waited a while, but no-one came to greet us.

"I'm a bit surprised the door wasn't locked," said Sinner. "I mean, this is the Nightside, after all, where communal property tends to be defined as anything that isn't actually nailed down and guarded by trolls."

"Anyone stupid enough to invade the Lamentation's lair deserves every nasty thing that happens to them," I said. "And no-one inside ever leaves, except by the Lamentation's will."

"Excuse me," said Pretty Poison, "but are we ever going in, or is the plan to stand about on the doorstep discussing strategy until the Lamentation gets so bored it comes out to see us?"

I looked at Sinner. "Pushy girl-friend."

"You have no idea," said Sinner.

I led the way in, Sinner and Pretty Poison in flanking position, and Madman bumbling along in the rear. Behind us, the door slammed shut without anyone touching it, and none of us were in the least surprised. Drama queens, the lot of them. The interior of the Mausoleum turned out to be much bigger than its modest exterior indicated. The rooms of the original small business had been replaced by a vast, echoing hall, half-full of curling, blood-tinted mists. We couldn't see the end of the hall from where we were, but the high, vaulted ceiling suggested it was some way off in the distance. We were in a big, big place, and the small sounds of our feet on the uneven flagstones seemed to echo on and on before they reached the distant stone walls. There are those who say space expands to contain all the evil present. And this was the lair of the Lamentation. We had come to a bad place, one of the worst in the world, and all of us could feel it, in our water and in our bones and in our souls.

"I like it here," said Pretty Poison. "It feels like home."

The air was bitterly cold, but quite still. The bloodred mists moved of their own accord, gusting and billowing, thickening and thinning apparently at random. The flagstones beneath our feet were covered in grave dirt. One wall let in shafts of light, falling through old-fashioned stained-glass windows, each depicting the awful deaths of saints and martyrs, the vivid colours glowing through the mists. A dull red glow from the far end of the great hall coloured the mists, pulsing slowly, so that as we moved cautiously forward, it was like walking through the bloodstream of a dying god. The mists smelled of blood and meat and recent death.

"Have we come at last to Hell?" said Madman.

"This isn't Hell," said Pretty Poison. "But you can see Hell from here."

We kept walking. The end of the hall seemed impossibly far away. I had no idea how long we'd been inside the Mausoleum. We were all shivering now, even Madman. The cold was leaching the living warmth right out of us. We stuck close together. And from out of the bloodred mists, the dead came walking to meet us, to welcome their new guests. There were hundreds of them, men and women and even some children, and there was no mistaking the fact that they were all corpses. They still wore the wounds that killed them, the self-inflicted cuts and rope burns they'd used to end their lives. They showed off their gaping wounds and dried blood, their stretched and broken necks, with simple indifference. Their skins were colourless, even the insides of their injuries only pale, muted colours, and their faces were blank. Until you looked into their unblinking eyes and saw a suffering there that would never end.

An army of the dead, shuffling forward on unfeeling feet, the rags of their clothes just the tatters of so many scarecrows. They all raised one hand, and beckoned us forward. An aisle opened up through the mass of them, and I led the way into it. The ranks of the dead continued to open silently up before us, then close behind us. We weren't going anywhere they didn't want us to. Some of the dead pawed at me, the way the street people had in Rats' Alley. They looked at me with their dead eyes, and muttered with their pale mouths, in the barest ghosts of voices.

Help us. Free us from the Lamentation. We didn't know. We didn't know it would be like this. We want to lie down, and rest. Help us. Free us. Destroy us.

And all I could do was keep on walking.

The Lamentation was an old, old Being. Older than most of what passes for history in the Nightside. Served and powered by suicides, it fed on suffering and despair and death. The dead bodies pressed close around us, showing off the deep noose marks on their crooked necks, or the ragged exit wounds in the backs of their heads where they'd shot themselves in the mouth, or in the eye. There were faces thick and puffy from the gasses they'd breathed, or the pills they'd swallowed. Pale red mouths at wrists and throats. The heavy marks of falls and vehicle collisions. They wore their deaths like open books, not as a warning but as proof of their damnation.

And finally, signs began to appear that we were nearing the Lamentation itself. Hanging nooses dropped from the high ceiling like jungle lianas, and we had to push our way through them. There were great sculptures made entirely out of razor blades, and we edged carefully between them. It was just the Lamentation, making itself at home. The blood-tinged mists were thinning out now, taking on the smells and tastes of all kinds of poisonous gasses.

That last development almost took me by surprise. The others weren't affected by the increasingly deadly mists, for their own various reasons, but the first I knew of the danger was when my head began to go all swimmy, and I couldn't seem to get my breath. My thoughts stuttered and repeated themselves, feeling increasingly far away, and then the voice of the unicorn's horn pin sounded loudly in my head.

Poison! Poison gasses, you idiot! Defend yourself! Eat the celery!

I thrust a numbing hand into an inside coat pocket, pulled out the piece of celery, and chewed on it. I always keep a piece handy, pre-prepared with all kinds of useful substances, for just such occasions as this. It tasted bitter as I chewed, but it cleared my head rapidly. It's an old trick but a good one, taught me long ago by a Travelling Doctor I met at the Hawk's Wind Bar & Grill.

Guns and bullets lay scattered in spirals across the dirty flagstones, and we kicked them out of our way. A rainbow of discarded pills crunched under our feet. The dead closed in around us. I kept staring straight ahead.

The corpses were all around us now, filling the vast hall, the furthest of them only dim shadows in the churning mists. For the first time, I was sure I'd chosen the right companions for this case. Anyone else would already have run screaming, and I wasn't far from it myself. The living were never meant to come this close to death and all its horrors. The Lamentation was served by everyone who ever took their own life in the Nightside, and so had acquired the second biggest standing army in the Nightside, behind the Authorities. They allowed this to continue only because the Lamentation had never been much interested in how the Nightside was run. There was never any shortage of suffering and suicides in a place where it's always three o'clock in the morning, and the comfort of the dawn never comes.

The blood-tinted mists suddenly blew apart like curtains, revealing the Lamentation hanging supported in its cage. The great and terrible Being was held securely inside an intricate construction of rusting black metal, a massive cube thirty feet on a side. Black iron bars criss-crossed in elaborate patterns to make up the sides, and then thrust back and forth across the interior, piercing and transfixing the inhumanly stretched and distorted body inside the cage. It was hard to tell just how big the

Being really was, bent over and twisted back upon itself, again and again. Its flesh was stretched taut by the strain of its contortions, and its skin was colourless and sweaty, though whether from pain or pleasure... There was something about it that suggested it might have started out as human, long and long ago...

Whether the cage had been built around the Lamentation, or it had grown inside the cage, wasn't clear. There was no sign of a door or entrance in any of the six sides. The inhumanly long arms and legs stretched out from the crooked torso, twisted back upon themselves again and again, in defiance of all the rules of anatomy, held irrevocably in place by the rusting metal bars transfixing them. There was no trace of blood at any of the many puncture points. More iron bars punched in and out of the torso, which showed no signs of breathing or heartbeat, though the thick body hair swirled slowly, making patterns that sucked in the eye. The face thrust up against the bars of the cage, looking out at its new visitors; stretched impossibly wide, the skin was taut to the point of tearing, and a rusty black spike thrust up out of one eye-socket. The nose had rotted away, or perhaps been bitten off, and the ears were gone, too. The mouth was a wide, suppurating wound, full of metal teeth. Cracked and crumbling goat's horns curled up from the wide, distorted brow.

It hurt to look at the Lamentation for any length of time. It was just too big, too... other.

It stank of desperate emotions, of hate and despair and thwarted needs, and the sorrow that can only see one way out, and all of it was thick and overpowering with the headiness of musk. None of this was natural, of course. The Lamentation radiated all the horrors of sudden death, of unnecessary death, of suicides and lives wasted, of potential unrealised and families blighted. For suffering was food and drink for the Lamentation.

"Whose stupid idea was it to come here?" Sinner said quietly. There was something about the place that imposed quiet, like an anti-church.

"Yours," I said.

"Why do you listen to me?" said Sinner.

A clump of mists beside the cage suddenly dispersed, blown away by some unfelt breeze, revealing the dead remains of the Brittle Sisters of the Hive. Their bodies had been piled up to a great height, carelessly dumped there like so much rubbish. There had to be hundreds of them, maybe even thousands; enough to boggle the mind. Shimmering shells of insect husks, spindly limbs already rotting where they stuck out of the pile. Their devil's faces were cold and uninhabited, their compound eyes and complex mouth parts seeming somehow resigned. The Brittle Sisters of the Hive—genetic terrorists, insect saviours, ravagers of the subconscious mind. Hated by pretty much everyone. And yet still it didn't please me to see them lying broken and shattered, like offerings to the Lamentation.

When it spoke, the Lamentation's voice sounded like someone who pretends to be your friend, then whispers lies and distortions in your ear when you're at your most vulnerable.

"This is all of them," it said, its quiet rasping voice the only sound in the great hall. "There are no more. They came here earlier, looking for you, John Taylor. They intended to ambush you and bear you away to the dissecting tables, to open you up and dig out all your secrets. To steal your heritage for themselves. They knew you'd be coming here. They bought the knowledge from an oracle. They really should have inquired further. I will not permit anyone to interfere with my guests, or my intentions. So I lured them all in here, with lies they wanted to believe, then watched them all kill each other under my influence, until none were left. They screamed in quite a satisfactory way, for insects. And now they're all gone. The Hives stand empty, now and forever. My gift to you, John Taylor."

"Thank you," I said. "That was... kind of you."

"Not really," said the Lamentation. "I don't do kind. Why have you come here, John Taylor?"

"I'm investigating the origins of the Nightside," I said. "On behalf of the Transient Being known as Lady Luck. My companions are Madman and Sinner and the demon Pretty Poison. I have already consulted with Merlin Satanspawn and Herne the Hunter." I tried to think of some more names I could drop, but it was taking everything I had just to keep my act together, in the relentless presence of the Lamentation, so I kept it simple and direct. "What can you tell me about the beginnings of the Nightside, of its creation and true purpose?"

"The Nightside is much older than I," said the Lamentation, its voice a sly and insinuating murmur. "Older than anyone I know. The only one who could give you the answers you seek... is your mother. Wherever she may be."

"What do you know about my mother?" I said.

"She was gone, but now is returned to us. Lucky old us. Babalon, Babalon. It took an army of the Light and the Dark to rid us of her, all those centuries ago, but only three foolish mortal men to bring her back."

"Three men," I said, my mind racing. "My father, of course, and the Collector, and... *Walker*?"

"Of course. Who else? Those three good and true friends, who had such great dreams and meant so well..."

It stopped talking, thick pus dribbling from one corner of its distorted mouth. It looked at me expectantly with its single unblinking eye. I thought hard. This wasn't going where I'd expected, but then my whole day had been like that.

"I met the Primal once," I said finally. "Ancient demons, from the very dawn of Creation, when they possessed some bodies at the Necropolis. They spoke of my mother. They said, *She who was first, and will be again, in this worst of all possible worlds.* Do you know what they meant by that?"

"She is back," said the Lamentation. "And the Nightside will never be the same again. I remember the early days of the Nightside, back before there were Authorities to curb the appetites and ambitions of those who would play here. We all ran free in those days, the Light and the Dark, and those who couldn't or wouldn't choose. That was the point. It was a time of miracles and monstrosities, dreams and damnations built with pride, where anything and everything seemed possible.

None of us now are what was intended then. The Nightside was young when the world was young, and all the kingdoms this world has ever known have never produced anything as wild or as free or as glorious as the Nightside was then."

"What happened... to that place?" I said.

"We drove your mother out, for we wished to be free even from her intentions, but without her, we lost our way. The Nightside's potential collapsed under the weight of our... limitations, and became a shadow of the dream that was. All we have now is a place of small ambitions and furtive pleasures, where all that matters about a thing is the price it will bring."

"You knew my mother?" I said.

"Perhaps. It was all such a long time ago. I no longer remember things clearly. Not even my own past, never mind another's. But I do know that the Nightside was already old when I was a young thing and newly formed."

"And human?" suggested Sinner. I jumped. I'd honestly forgotten anyone else was there.

"Human?" said the Lamentation, not bothering to hide the scorn in its voice. "Such a little thing to be. I am large and glorious. I have always been here, and always will be."

"Nonsense," Pretty Poison said briskly. She stepped forward to stare closely at the twisted thing in its cage. "You're not one of my kind. You were made, not created, this way. The world, or your own desires, made you what you are. There is nothing of the eternal in you, nothing of the Infernal or the Elect. You're just meat, with meat's needs and delusions."

The whole cage shook as the Lamentation howled, an awful, disturbing sound, black flecks of rusting iron falling from the metal bars as the distorted body shook with rage, and perhaps shock. It must have been a long time since anyone had dared speak to it in such a fashion. I felt like applauding. The black iron bars rattled, but the cage held. The Lamentation's skin stretched and tore, but still no blood flowed. The dead bodies in the hall stirred restlessly, and the blood-tinted mists churned and roiled. There was a power pulsing on the air, and we could all feel it. Pretty Poison watched it all calmly. Sinner and Madman were hiding behind me, and I wished I could hide, too. There was no easy way out of the Mausoleum, no obvious exit, and the rage of a Power and a Domination can be a terrible thing. Just ask the Brittle Sisters of the Hive. Eventually the Lamentation settled down again, fixing me with its one awful eye.

"You want to know who your mother was?" it said, and its voice was cold, cold. "If I ever knew for sure I have forgotten, or was made to forget, but they could not keep me from thinking and deducing all these years. It is my belief that she was that old and terrible one sometimes called Morrigan, of the Badhbh; the Celtic war goddess, who also manifested as a wolf and a crow and a raven. That old goddess of battlefields and of slaughter, who dressed in the entrails of her worshippers and whose laughter was the gathering storms of war. To whom every dead soldier was a sacrifice, and every massacre a delight. The secret goddess and guiding spirit of the twentieth century, some say.

And you are her only son, already spreading death and destruction. You almost brought down the Nightside with your Angel War. Whatever will you do next, John Taylor?"

"You don't really know a damned thing about her," I said, with the certainty of sudden insight. "It's all just guesses and wishful thinking. You gave up or lost your memories, in order to live entirely in the present. To better savour the suffering you steal. How would you know who my mother really was? You can't even remember your own beginnings, never mind the Nightside's."

"It doesn't matter," said the Lamentation, its dry, whispering voice suddenly calm again. "Your quest stops here. Let the past remain the past; I care only for the way things are. It may be that the old days were not as free and fine as I choose to remember, but I won't let you threaten what I have now. All the sweet suffering, the despair and damnations... you would take it all away. I don't think so. I won't have you digging up old secrets that might overturn the source of my power, and my delight."

"You're scared of my mother," I said.

"I'm not scared of you, John Taylor. When I kill you here, and make you one of my army, I close the only doorway through which your mother might return to rule the Nightside and spoil all our fun. We shall be safe again."

I glanced round at my companions, just to make sure they were still there, then lifted my chin and gave the Lamentation my best confident look. If you're going to bluff, bluff big. "You really think you can take the four of us? You do know who and what we are?"

"It doesn't matter," said the Lamentation, its voice slowly fading away, as though it was losing interest. "You are in my place, and in my power. I will show you things, awful things, until you kill yourselves rather than have to see them. And then you will rise again, trapped in your dead bodies, to serve me forever, with no will in you but mine. And your suffering will sustain me for centuries."

There was a pause, then Madman laughed cheerfully, and the mood was broken. Sinner was shaking his head, too.

"What can you show us, you caged freak? I am Sinner, and I have known the secrets of the Pit."

"I am Pretty Poison, a demon of the Inferno."

"I'm Madman, and I have seen the Truth."

"And I," I said, "am John Taylor; and you wouldn't believe the shit I've seen. So bring it on, Lamentation. Bring it all on."

The Lamentation shook and rattled its cage again, and now its voice was a shrill inhuman scream. "*Kill them! Kill them all!*"

The dead came surging forward out of the bloodred mists, moving quickly but without grace, cold bodies forced on by an inhuman will. They had no weapons, only the endless implacable strength of the dead and the overwhelming numbers to drag us down. They came from every direction at once, reaching out with pale, clawed hands. But they couldn't seem to find Madman. They stumbled all around him, striking out at anyone but him, while he looked sadly back at them, unmoving. Pretty Poison was already tearing a path through the dead, flashing back and forth impossibly quick, laughing loudly as she tore the dead bodies limb from limb and trampled the twitching pieces under her feet. Chunks of unliving flesh flew through the air, tossed about with glee, and the overwhelming numbers meant nothing to her. Pretty Poison was enjoying herself. Sinner watched her, frowning, but did nothing to try to stop her. The dead surrounded him, their hands bumping uselessly against him, unable to harm a man that Heaven and Hell had already forsworn.

I took a bag of salt from an inside pocket and sprinkled a wide circle around me. The dead couldn't cross the salt, so they circled round and round me, clawing clumsily with their empty hands, driven forward even as the salt forced them back. My heart pounded painfully fast as I turned around and around, constantly checking that the salt circle remained unbroken. I was breathing so fast I was practically hyperventilating. I really didn't like this. None of my tricks or magics were strong enough to hold back a whole army of the living dead. I called out to the others, but they were too far away to help. And then I looked into the unblinking eyes of the dead faces lunging at me from every side, and all I saw in them was suffering. None of this was their idea. They only ever moved in obedience to the will of their master; slaves to the Lamentation. They had killed themselves with the last little bit of their courage, hoping to be free from the pains and obligations of their unbearable lives, only to find themselves eternally bound to something far worse. No peace for the dead here, no rest for those who had been, briefly, wicked.

And the more I thought about that, the angrier I got. I've known what it feels like, when your whole life hurts so much that you're ready to die, just for the pain to stop. A little less stubbornness, a little more resolve at certain moments, and I might have been one of these poor trapped souls... What kind of a place had we made of the Nightside, where even the dead weren't allowed to rest in peace? My anger burned through me like a cold flame, clearing my head and calming my racing heart. I fired up my gift, and my third eye, my private eye, opened deep in my mind, allowing me to find and identify the link between the dead and their master. My eyesight lurched, and suddenly I could See a tracework of glimmering silver lines, rising from the tops of the corpses' heads and trailing away back to the Lamentation in its cage; the strings by which it manipulated its puppets. And powered by my anger and outrage, it was the easiest thing in the world for me to reach out with my mind and sever all those silver cords in a single moment.

The dead froze where they stood, stopped in mid-movement and even mid-lunge. There was a new feeling in the Mausoleum, as though an endless tension had finally snapped. The Lamentation screamed, a horrible inhuman sound that rasped through the great hall like a saw through flesh. And one by one the dead bodies dropped to the floor and lay still, as their souls burst up out of them like incandescent stars, blasting out of their rotten husks, rising up and up, free at last. They blazed brightly in that dark place, then were gone, to wherever they should have gone long ago.

I've never believed all suicides go to Hell. God has more mercy than that.

The last of the souls departed, and my Sight returned to normal. I looked about me. The blood-tinged mists were gone. Sinner and Pretty Poison and even Madman were staring around in a puzzled way. The dead were piled up all around us, and none of them so much as twitched. The oppressive atmosphere of despair and horror that had permeated the great hall was already fading away like a bad dream, because there was no longer anything here to be scared of. We looked down the empty hall at where the Lamentation had been. The black iron cage was already falling apart, the metal bars cracking and dissolving in showers of black rust. And lying at the bottom of the cage, under the criss-crossed bars, stripped of all power, a naked man and woman clutched each other desperately, weeping angry tears of shock and loss. No longer joined, no longer a Power, no longer that vicious old Being called the Lamentation. Whatever they had done to themselves, or caused to be done, it was over now. Must have been hard on them, to be just human again, after so long. I did think about killing them, but I had no reason to be merciful. I turned my back on them and nodded to my companions.

"Time we were going," I said. "I think we've learned all we're going to here."

"What about... them?" said Sinner.

"Wait till the word gets out," I said. "That they are human again, and defenceless. Then they'll learn what suffering really is. Lot of people in the

Nightside have old unfinished business, for loved ones lost and enslaved."

"You can't just leave us here like this!" howled a voice from the dissolving cage. It could have been the man or the woman. "You're supposed to be the great hero of the Nightside! You can't just abandon us!"

"Watch me," I said.

I led the way out of the great hall, and my companions followed me without comment. The hall was already breaking down, disappearing in bits and pieces as the magic that sustained it leaked away. Soon enough the old rooms would return, with all the old memories of what was done there by the Maxwell family. And then maybe, in that old atmosphere of torture and despair and death, the man and woman who had once been the Lamentation might see no other way out than to take their own lives. I smiled at the thought. I could live with that.

Why don't the dead lie still? Because in the Nightside there are always Powers and Dominations ready to make use of them.

We stepped out of the Maxwell Mausoleum, and the perverse atmosphere of Freak Fair was like a breath of fresh air. Until I noticed that all of Walker's watchers seemed to have disappeared, along with everyone else. The street was deserted. All the doors around us were firmly shut, and there wasn't a light showing at a window anywhere.

"Why are you scowling?" said Sinner. "It's always a really bad sign when you start scowling. And Madman's sound track has gone all tense again."

"It looks like Walker has withdrawn his people and closed off the area," I said. "And he wouldn't do that unless he had something really nasty planned and didn't want any witnesses. And given the kinds of horrible things I've known him do in front of whole crowds of people, this new caution does not bode well for us."

We all huddled together for protection, even Madman, and did our best to look in every direction at once. I could have used a break after taking down the Lamentation, but that's Walker for you—always strike when your enemy is weakest. The street remained empty, the busy sounds of city life sounding very far away. Could Walker really know already that I'd destroyed the Lamentation? Had that been the final straw that made him decide I was too dangerous to be allowed to live? Was he finally ready to have me killed, after all these years?

Did he know that I knew about his part in my mother's return?

It could be that the Authorities had given him no choice in this. Had ordered him to stop me getting any closer to answers that might upset their precious status quo. He had tried to warn me of that possibility, back at the Londinium Club. And as I thought that, I knew who was out there, watching and waiting for just the right moment to make her entrance. Who it had to be.

From out of the shadows that cloaked the end of the street came the sudden sound of expensive shoes click-clacking on the pavement. We all turned to look, and from out of the dark Bad Penny came swaying down the street towards us.

Bold and brassy, that sweet sensation, death on high heels and loving it, the sexiest, most voluptuous assassin of them all. She was still wearing the classic little black dress she'd somehow crammed herself into at the Londinium Club, but now there were splashes of blood across the front of it, and more standing out starkly against the shimmering white of her elbow-length evening gloves. She came to a halt a sensible distance away from us and favoured us all with a dazzling smile. Down by one thrusting hip she carried a set of blood-flecked antlers in her hand.

"Hello, John," she said, in a voice that promised absolutely everything that's bad for you. "Journeys end in lovers' meetings. And your journey ends right here."

"We were never lovers," I said firmly. "I'm not entirely sure what we were, but *lovers* is definitely not the word. So Walker's finally given you the go-ahead, has he?"

She raised one perfect eyebrow. "You already know I'm working for Walker? Of course you do. I was forgetting; you're John Taylor. You know everything."

"Not necessarily," I said. "Where did you get those antlers, Penny?"

"From Herne the Hunter, after I killed him," Bad Penny said lightly. "Walker wanted Herne made an example of, to anyone else who might be considering answering any of your questions. Oh, don't look so sad, darling! He was a very old god, and his time was over. I can't abide people who outstay their welcome. And there's no greater sin than insisting on being unfashionable."

She dropped the antlers carelessly to the ground, and they made only the briefest of sounds in the quiet. Not much of an end for a once powerful god.

"I bear a message from Walker," said Bad Penny, falling naturally into a provocative pose. "The Authorities really are frightfully keen that you abandon this case, right here. Turn back now, go no further, do not collect two hundred pounds. Or else."

"Am I to presume that you're the *or else*?" I said.

"Got it in one! I do hope you're going to do the sensible thing for once in your life, sweetie. What's so wrong with wanting things to stay the way they are? I've always been a great supporter of the status quo, if only because it continues to supply me with so many good business opportunities. There's always money to be made out of murder, and a girl has to eat."

"And if I refuse?" I said.

"Like I said, darling—there's always money to be made out of murder."

"You'd kill me, after what we had between us?"

"Because of what we had between us! No-one walks out on me, honey."

"Would I be right in thinking there's a history between you two?" said Sinner. "You do get around, don't you, Jack?"

"Shut up," I said.

"Aren't you going to introduce me to your new friends, John?" said Bad Penny, spreading her smile generously around her.

I raised an eyebrow. "Walker didn't brief you? Or haven't you reported in recently? You always were slack when it came to doing the research on a case. Well, this is Sinner, and his girl-fiend Pretty Poison, and that is Madman. We've just destroyed the Lamentation."

"Oh, dear," said Bad Penny. "How sad. Fallen in with bad company again, I see. What am I going to do with you, John? I know! I'll kill you right here and now. And just to keep everything neat and tidy, your friends can die with you." She turned her powerful smile on Sinner. "You disapprove of John, don't you? How sweet. Perhaps you'd like to break his neck for me? I'd really like that. In fact, I'd like it if you all beat each other to death, right in front of me."

And just like that, she was suddenly the most attractive woman in the world. Her sexuality blazed like someone had just opened a furnace door. Her presence filled the street, impossible to look away from, impossible to resist. To see her was to want her, to need her, more than life itself. I had my gift, and Bad Penny had hers. She had become the woman you'd do anything for, including murder. Her greatest weapon had always been herself. No-one could resist her body, once she'd turned it up to eleven. Except... for all our special abilities, Sinner and Madman and I were just men, while Pretty Poison was a demon succubus from Hell.

"Amateur," she said.

And just like that, the spell was broken. Bad Penny's glamour snapped off, and she was just another really good-looking woman with a bit of a weight problem. She looked at us, open-mouthed, absolutely dumbfounded. I don't think anyone had ever broken her spell that easily, that casually, before. I smiled at her.

"Nice try, Penny. But I have been there, and done that, and, to be honest, I've known better."

She stamped one high-heeled foot, said a few baby swear words, and suddenly she had two really big guns in her white-gloved hands. She opened fire at point-blank range, the explosions deafeningly loud, but I was already moving. I knew how she operated. And yet even as I dodged and ducked, it was clear she wasn't just targeting me. We all had to die, so no-one would ever be told about the failure of her glamour. And that... was a mistake. If she'd concentrated on me, she might have got somewhere. I'm fast, and I'm tricky, but I'm not bullet-proof.

The bullets couldn't even find Madman. He just stood there, blinking owlishly, his mind on other things, while bullets ricocheted from the wall behind him. I wasn't sure what damage bullets could do to a demon succubus, but Sinner didn't wait to find out. He stepped quickly forward, to stand between his love and Bad Penny, and the bullets thudded into his chest over and over again, to no obvious effect. Bad Penny blinked a few times, then shot him in the head. That didn't help, so she kicked his feet out from under him. He crashed onto his back, and Bad Penny targeted Pretty Poison. I grabbed Bad Penny from behind, pinioning her arms, and she bent sharply forward at the waist and threw me right over her head. I hit the ground hard, but kept rolling. Bullets smashed into the ground where I'd been. Sinner was back on his feet and advancing on Bad Penny. She emptied her guns into him, going for all the most vulnerable points, but he didn't even flinch as the bullets punched into him. No blood flowed. Like Cain before him, he bore the mark of his offence on his brow, and nothing of this world could ever really harm him again. He stopped right in front of Bad Penny, and she put her last bullet right through his left eye.

"Ouch," Sinner said dryly. There was only the slightest of pauses before his eyeball rebuilt itself, then he gargled and spat the bullet out into his palm. He offered it to Bad Penny. "Yours, I believe."

She snarled prettily, made her guns disappear, and snatched two silver knives out of nowhere. She buried them both up to the hilt in his chest. They were magical weapons, scored with ancient runes, one cursed and one blessed. I'd known gods who would have died from an attack like that. Sinner just stood there and took it. I felt like applauding. Bad Penny folded her arms over her impressive chest and pouted.

"Now that's just not fair, darling."

"Step aside, Sidney," said Pretty Poison, at Sinner's shoulder. "I have business with this woman. Very nasty business."

"No," said Sinner.

"She tried to kill you, my darling! I can't allow that to go unpunished. It's not in my nature."

"You came up out of Hell to be with me, in order to change your nature. Remember?"

"Yes, but..."

"Hush," said Sinner, and the demon succubus hushed, for the moment.

Bad Penny poked out her tongue at Pretty Poison, then smiled hopefully at Sinner. "If you're not actually going to kill me, darling, could I please have my knives back? They are family heirlooms, and Daddy would be furious if I lost them."

Sinner tugged the blades out of his chest with some effort and handed them back in a gentlemanly way. Bad Penny accepted the knives, glanced briefly in my direction to see if she still had a chance of picking me off, decided she hadn't, and made the knives disappear. I came forward to join her.

"What are we going to do with you, Penny?" I said. "We can't just let you go. You'd only carry on following us, looking for another good place to ambush us, with better weapons. You're like me; you never give up on a case."

"I am nothing like you, John Taylor! I have style."

Faster than any of us could react, Pretty Poison surged forward, grabbed Bad Penny by the throat and bent her over backwards. Penny squealed and struggled furiously, but couldn't break the succubus's hold. Pretty Poison's fingers now ended in claws, and her widely smiling mouth was packed full of pointed teeth. The red lips were very close to Penny's neck, and she didn't look like an English public school girl any more. She looked like what she was, a demon spat up from Hell.

"Don't!" said Sinner. He started forward, then stopped abruptly as Pretty Poison set her sharp teeth directly against Penny's throat, the points just dimpling the skin. Sinner raised his hands calmingly. "Please. Don't kill her."

"She has to die," Pretty Poison said reasonably, her lips brushing Penny's throat. "You heard her, Sidney; she's under orders to kill anyone who might talk to us. Either I rip her throat out, or the case stops here."

"No case of mine has ever been worth the sacrifice of an innocent life," I said.

Pretty Poison raised an eyebrow. "You think this is an innocent?"

"Maybe not technically, but yes. Kill her, and you're my enemy. Forever."

Pretty Poison grinned. "Never threaten a demon, John Taylor. We have long memories." She looked at Sinner. "Besides, you wouldn't let him hurt me, would you, Sidney?"

"You're trying to confuse the issue," said Sinner. "All that matters is that you can't kill this woman now that she's helpless. It may be that she deserves it, but we are not like her. We have to be better than that. So let her go. For me."

Pretty Poison considered this for a long moment, while Bad Penny barely dared breathe, then the demon succubus abruptly dropped her victim to the ground and strolled unhurriedly back to Sinner. Bad Penny rose to her feet, brushed herself down, and gave me a smile that was only just a little shaky.

"I knew you wouldn't let her kill me, John. You always were a soppy, sentimental sort. But I will find you again. And I will kill you."

"Not on the best day you ever had," I said calmly. "I'm getting very close to my mother now, Penny. Get in the way of that, and someone will quite definitely kill you."

Bad Penny looked startled, then turned and walked quickly away, moving quite rapidly for someone in a clinging dress and high heels, and soon she was lost in the shadows at the end of the street. I watched her go and allowed myself a small smile. I couldn't kill her in cold blood, but I wasn't above putting a good scare into her. Sentiment only goes so far. And I wasn't too worried about her following us. It felt like we were getting near the end of the quest. I knew where we had to go next.

"Where are we going next?" said Madman, joining us in spirit at least. "Anywhere fun?"

"Not really," I said. "I'm pretty sure we need to go and see the Lord of Thorns."

Sinner gave me a hard look. "Correct me if I'm wrong, John, but I thought we'd agreed that was a really bad idea? I mean, ten out of ten for ambition, courage, and lateral thinking, but minus several thousand for self-preservation. The Lord of Thorns... Possibly the oldest Being in the Nightside who still inhabits this level of reality, and the most powerful. I only mentioned him in Rats' Alley because Herne brought him up. I didn't really expect to be taken seriously."

"The Lord of Thorns," said Pretty Poison. "We know of him in Hell. They say he knew the Christ. They say angels and demons are forced to kneel in his presence."

"And if anyone should know the beginnings of the Nightside, it will be him," I said. "He was here before the Romans made Londinium into a city. And just maybe, Walker had Penny kill Herne for a reason; so he wouldn't point us in the direction of the Lord of Thorns."

"This is a really bad idea," said Madman, and we all looked at him sharply, but he had nothing more to say.

EIGHT

I AM THE STONE THAT BREAKS ALL HEARTS

I had a lot on my mind as I led my companions back through Freak Fair, not least trying to remember whether I'd updated my will recently. I'd always meant for Cathy to inherit my business if, or more likely when, something happened to me, but I'd never actually got around to putting it in writing. Changing your will is one of those things you always put off because you don't like to be reminded of your own mortality. You always think there's plenty of time... until you find yourself on your way to a meeting with the Lord of Thorns. Part of me wanted to phone Cathy, talk to her one last time, but the sensible part of me overruled it. What could I say, except *Good-bye*?

My companions didn't seem too worried. Sinner and Pretty Poison were strolling along hand in hand, giggling like teenagers again, and Madman was off in his own private world. I had tried to explain to them just how dangerous this was going to be, and they'd smiled and nodded and said they quite understood, but they didn't. Not really. Or they would never have agreed to accompany me to the World Beneath. Part of me wanted to forbid them to come, for their own protection, but another more practical part over-ruled it. I was going to need their help if I was to survive this last part of my journey. Was I really prepared to sacrifice them, to learn the truth about the Nightside, and my mother?

Maybe. It wasn't like they were my friends or anything. Perhaps that's why I'd chosen them for this case—because it wouldn't matter to me so much if I had to throw them to the wolves.

The cold-bloodedness of that thought shocked even me, and I looked around for something to distract me. And that was when I finally noticed that all of Walker's watchers had reappeared, gathered together at the far end of the street and staring at us openly, not even trying to conceal themselves. They huddled together for comfort as I and my companions approached, but looked ready to defend themselves at a moment's notice. The combat magicians actually traced protective sigils on the air between them and us. They blazed brightly, sparking and dripping eldritch fires. I came to a halt a respectful distance away and considered the watchers thoughtfully.

"Told you we should have killed her," said Pretty Poison. "Bad Penny always was a tattle-tale. She's told them where we're going."

"They're upset, scared, and demoralised," I said. "Just how I like Walker's people. Now watch, and learn." I took another step forward, and they all flinched visibly. I gave them my best enigmatic smile. "Hi, guys, I've got some good news and some bad news. The bad news is yes, we did just kick Bad Penny's arse and send her home crying; and yes, we did just destroy the Lamentation; and yes, we are off to see the Lord of Thorns. The really bad news is that I lied about there being any good news. Any questions?"

Pretty much as one, the watchers decided that they really needed to return to Walker to ask for fresh instructions, and within moments they were all gone. The Jesuit demonologists actually departed running.

"Now that is worrying," said Sinner.

To meet with the Lord of Thorns, you have to go underground. There's a whole system of extensive catacombs, tunnels, canals, and sewers deep under the streets of the Nightside, usually referred to as the World Beneath. It is inhabited by people, and others, who can only exist and move in darkness, away from the open skies and hot neon of the streets above. You can be born, live your whole life, and die in the World Beneath, and countless have down the centuries. The dark tunnels and canals also provide a means of getting back and forth in the Nightside without being observed. They're not much used for general travel, because those who live in the

World Beneath tend to discourage it, by killing and often eating those who annoy them. And they're easily annoyed.

But, it was the only way to reach the Lord of Thorns' domain. I'd never been there myself. Didn't even know anyone who'd been crazy enough to try. But sometimes I make it a point to be paid in secrets as well as hard currency, because you never know when even the most obscure piece of information will come in handy while working a case. The man who told me about the Lord of Thorns, and the World Beneath, no longer had any eyes. They'd been bitten out. He told me in a harsh whispering voice of a darkness deeper than the night, of tunnels that went on forever, and silent folk who passed through arching catacombs like worms in the earth.

There are no advertised entrances to the World Beneath. Either you know where to find them, or you don't need to know. I led my people through a series of increasingly narrow and ill-lit streets, where people scuttled away to hide in the shadows when they saw us coming, to the nearest entrance I knew of—a small private garden, held inviolate behind heavy stone walls accessed only by a securely locked gate. I studied the garden through the spiked iron bars; it seemed a pretty enough place, lit by flaring gas jets. Like finding a single perfect lily floating on a cesspit. There were trees and flowering shrubs and rich blooms laid out in attractive displays. A thick, heady perfume drifted through the gate to me. Pretty Poison snuggled in close beside me.

"What's a pretty place like this doing in an area like this? And why is this gate absolutely crawling with protective spells?"

"The Nightside is full of surprises," I said. "And mysteries are our food and drink."

"You mean you don't know," said Sinner.

"Got it in one," I said. "But I do have a key. Part payment from an old case."

"Which you're not going to tell us about," said Pretty Poison.

"The world is not ready to know," I said solemnly.

"You are so full of it," said Madman. We all turned sharply to look at him, but he had nothing more to say.

I took the key off my key-ring, and turned it in the gate's lock. It didn't want to turn, and I had to put some muscle into it, but finally it lurched into place, and I pushed the gate open. I could feel the protective spells deactivating, like a sudden release of tension on the air. I stepped aside to let the others go in first. Not entirely out of courtesy; I didn't trust the garden. When nothing immediately awful happened, I followed them in and shut and locked the gate behind me.

Blue-white light from the impossibly huge moon overhead gave the garden an unreal, ghostly look. The trees were tall and spindly, stark silhouettes against the butter-yellow glow of the old-fashioned gas jets set high on the walls. A single narrow path of beaten earth curved back and forth through the garden, between hulking bushes and shrubs and past intricate displays of night-blooming flowers. Everything in the garden was moving slowly, though there wasn't a breath of breeze. Even the petals of the flowers opened and closed, like pursing mouths. The flowers were mostly white and red, and something about them made me think *White for bone, red for meat*. I once heard a rose sing, and it was the most evil thing I've ever heard.

"Nice place," said Sinner, stooping to sniff a flower. He then pulled his head back quickly, wrinkling his nose.

"No," said Pretty Poison. "I don't think so."

"Top marks for insight to the demon from Hell," I said. "Everything here has really deep roots. You don't want to know from what they draw their nourishment. Now let's all head for the statue in the middle of the garden; and *don't touch anything.*"

The narrow path wound back and forth, to make sure everything in the garden got a good look at us, but finally it brought us to the statue of an angel, kneeling and weeping over its torn-off wings. The features on its face had been eroded away, by wind and rain and time, or perhaps just by tears. Behind the angel was a moon-dial, showing the exact right time. I took hold of its pointing gnomon with a firm hand and turned it slowly through one hundred and eighty degrees. The whole moon-dial shuddered violently, then slid jerkily to one side to reveal a dark shaft, just big enough to take a man, falling away deep into the earth. A black metal ladder clung to one side of the shaft. We all took it in turns to stare dubiously down into the darkness, then Pretty Poison summoned up a handful of hell-fire. She held the leaping flames out over the shaft, but the light didn't penetrate far. In the end, we made her go down first, so she could carry the light ahead of us. None of us liked the idea of descending blindly into that dark.

So she went first, then Sinner because he wouldn't be parted from her, then Madman, and finally me to keep Madman moving. The heavy rungs of the metal ladder were hot and sweaty under my hands, and the narrow circle of light above soon disappeared into the distance. The light below, now dancing at Pretty Poison's shoulder, was barely enough to let us see each other. I didn't like the colour or the texture of the hell-fire; it made me feel... uneasy. I made myself concentrate on the ladder. The rungs had been set uncomfortably far apart, as though not designed or intended for human use. My shoulders bumped against the sides of the shaft as I descended, and the ladder seemed to fall away forever. Down and down we climbed, until my arms and legs ached from the strain, and still there was no sign of any bottom to the shaft. I would have liked to change my mind and go back up, but I didn't think I had the strength to climb up that far, so all that was left was to keep going down. We were all breathing hard, the harsh sounds loud on the quiet.

When Pretty Poison suddenly announced that her feet had hit bottom, we all cried out in relief, even Madman. He seemed more *with us*, of late. Perhaps he just needed shared company and events to ground him; or perhaps he sensed some danger coming, so great he needed to be more focussed to deal with it. I wasn't about to ask. I just knew he would say something that would make my head hurt. One by one we climbed down out of the end of the shaft and emerged onto a bare path beside a canal; dark waters in a dark place. The stone wall on the other side of the canal showed huge claw marks, gouged deep into the stone by something monstrously large. There was no sign of anyone or anything for as far as Pretty Poison's leaping flame could carry, except for a small silver bell hanging from a tall support. The four of us stood together on the narrow bank, huddled close for comfort. We could all tell we'd come to a really bad place. The air was hot and sweaty, like a fever room, and it smelled bad. Spoiled.

"Now what?" said Sinner. His voice didn't echo, or carry.

"I suppose we ring the bell," I said. "This is as far as my knowledge takes us. From now on, it's all unknown territory."

"Ring the bell?" said Sinner. "How do we know it doesn't just announce to the local nasties that lunch has arrived?"

"We don't," I said. "Feel free to chime in with any other ideas you may have. Besides, what have you got to be worried about? You're supposed to be invulnerable."

"Not exactly. Just very resistant to punishment. I'm not sure even I could survive being eaten, digested, and excreted by something sufficiently large and determined. I am a unique case, but even I have my limits."

"Now he tells me," I said.

"Boys, boys," said Pretty Poison. She was kneeling at the edge of the canal, holding her flame-covered hand out over the dark waters. "I'm pretty sure I saw something move in here... Do you suppose they have alligators down here? You hear stories, about pets being flushed away..."

"I have a strong feeling that whatever lives in these waters would probably consider alligators an appetiser," I said firmly. "I'd back away if I were you. Slowly and very carefully. This is where all the things too nasty for the Nightside end up."

"Ring the bell," said Sinner.

I gave it a good hard ring, and the sharp, almost painfully intense sound travelled up and down the canal, without any trace of echo or distortion. We all braced ourselves, ready for whatever attack might lurch forth out of the darkness, but nothing happened. The sound died away, and all was still and quiet. We all slowly relaxed again. I realised that Madman's personal sound track had shut itself down sometime back. Presumably because it couldn't come up with anything appropriate. And then, from out of the darkness to our right, further down the canal, came the sound of something moving. The slow steady sound of some craft ploughing through the dark waters. We all stared, straining our eyes against the gloom, until finally a low-bottomed barge appeared, in a warm golden glow that surrounded it from stem to stern. It headed unhurriedly towards us, a single human figure standing amidships, poling the barge along with a solid silver staff. The barge was a good twenty feet long, painted a cheerful pastel blue, with big black eyes delineated on either side of the pointed prow. The human figure propelling the barge with his efforts wore a concealing scarlet cloak and a featureless pale cream mask that covered all his face. Disturbingly, the mask only had one eyehole, the left. The barge slid to a halt before us, and the cloaked figure gave us a deep, formal bow.

"Welcome to the World Beneath, you poor damned fools," he said, in a deep resonant voice with more than a hint of a French accent. "Where do you wish me to take you? Not that there is a lot of choice, I'll admit. Upstream is bad, downstream is worse, though at least the Eaters of the Dead have been quiet lately. Someone tried putting poison down a while back, but the rotten buggers positively thrived on it. I hope you've got a specific destination in mind, because I don't do tours. I'd go back up, if I were you. It doesn't get any better, the deeper in you go."

"Pretty much the kind of welcome I'd expected," I said, when I could finally get a word in edgeways. "Can you take us to the Lord of Thorns?"

"Is life really that bad?" said the bargeman. "There are easier ways to kill yourself, and most of them are a lot less painful."

"The Lord of Thorns," I said firmly. "Yes or no?"

"Very well, my friends. Climb aboard. Don't fall in the water. The natives are restless, and very hungry."

We all boarded his barge very carefully, and it hardly rocked at all under our weight. The bargeman pushed his silver pole into the water and started us on our way with one long, effortless movement. There was more to him than there seemed, but then, there would have to be. Surrounded by the golden glow of the barge, Pretty Poison doused her hell-fire, and we all relaxed a little. The barge moved silently and easily on into the enveloping dark. The bargeman stared straight ahead, but whatever he saw with his single eye, he kept to himself.

"Don't get many tourists down here these days," he said, his voice quite distinct behind the pale mask. "Not that we ever did have many visitors, and for the most part we like it that way. Peace and quiet's a wonderful thing, you know? Are any of you famous? I don't keep up on the gossip like I used to."

"This is Sinner," I said. "This is Pretty Poison, and that is Madman. I am John Taylor."

The bargeman shook his head. "No. Sorry. Means nothing to me. I had that Julien Advent in my barge once. A real gentleman, he was."

"How long have you been down here?" I asked.

"I have no idea. And don't tell me, because I don't want to know. It was the beginning of the Twentieth Century when I first came to the Nightside, boarding the newly opened subway from Paris with a howling mob hot on my heels. I soon found my way down here. I'd had enough of the hurly-burly of city life, and wished only solitude. I do miss the opera, though... Still! I provide a service here, to keep myself occupied, and as a small act of penance for the days of my hot-headed youth."

"What can you tell us about the World Beneath?" said Sinner.

"Parts of it are as old as any other part of the Nightside, and as dangerous. It started out as a collection of sewers, canals, and offshoots of the Thames, covered over by the growing city, running through and around a huge system of catacombs built by the Romans, so they could do things down here that the world above wouldn't approve of. Very practical people, the Romans. They believed that if the gods couldn't see what you were doing, it didn't count. Lot of people in the World Beneath still think that way, though of course I use the term *people* very loosely. We have quite a population down here, these days. Solitudes, of course; religious types sitting in dark stone cells for the good of their souls. Then there's the odd type who just can't get on with anyone, even in the Nightside. And those on the run, like my good self. The Subterraneans have been down here for centuries, making their own little city out of the catacombs. Don't bother them, and they won't sacrifice you to their gods. Then there's vampires and ghouls and various offshoots of the Elder Spawn... We get all sorts down here. But don't you worry yourself about them, my friends. My barge and I are protected, by old custom. You sit tight, and I'll bring you right to the Gate of the Lord of Thorns' domain. And after that—may God have mercy on your souls, because it's a safe bet the Lord of Thorns won't."

"Have you ever met him?" said Sinner.

The bargeman snorted loudly behind his mask. "No. And the odds are you won't get to, either. He is very well guarded."

He poled us along the canal for some time, singing snatches of grand opera and saucy French drinking songs in a fine baritone voice. Madman's sound track joined in, producing perfect harmonies and descants. Things came and went in the dark waters, occasionally bumping against the sides of the barge, but never breaking the surface of the water. The golden glow surrounding the boat was just bright enough for me to make out the strange astronomical symbols carved into the curving stone ceiling above us. Star systems never seen from earth, in this or any other time. Pretty Poison snuggled in close beside Sinner, ignoring the surroundings to murmur in his ear. He didn't respond, except to sometimes shake his head.

The barge finally slowed to a halt beside a section of the canal bank that at first glimpse seemed no different from any other. The masked bargeman leaned on his pole, and looked thoughtfully about him.

"This is as far as I can take you. A bad place, my friends. I would say au revoir; but I doubt we'll meet again."

They disembarked, and he pushed the barge away from the bank and set off back the way we'd come. He wasn't singing any more. The golden glow departed with the barge, replaced by a sullen red glare emanating from a high archway set into the dark stone wall. Ancient Greek characters had been etched into the cracked and pitted stone slabs that made up the arch. We all looked at each other for a while, then Pretty Poison tutted loudly.

"No-one studies the classics any more. Allow me. Translating very freely, it says, *Meat is Murder.*"

"Wonderful," said Sinner. "We have fallen among vegetarians."

"Somehow I rather doubt it," said Pretty Poison. "I can smell rot and decay and the corruption of living things. And the smell is wafting out of this archway."

I could smell it, too. A heavy, noxious smell that left a bad taste in the mouth. Like a charnel-house left to simmer in a hot sun. It was definitely drifting out of the open archway, even though there was no trace of movement in the air. A warning, perhaps... or a threat. It didn't make any difference. There was nowhere else for us to go, except back. I led the way in, and the others followed reluctantly after me.

A short tunnel, its curving stone walls beaded with sweat, soon gave way to a fair-sized cavern hollowed out of the living rock. Big enough to hold a fair-sized congregation, but not of any church you'd choose to visit. Butcher's tools hung down from the ceiling on wires, saws and knives and skewers, all of them stained with old, dried blood. At the far end of the cavern was a crude throne, made up of slabs of meat, some of it fresh, most clearly spoiled, all of it surrounded by a great cloud of buzzing flies. And all the walls of the cavern were covered in people's names, drawn spikily in blood, from a wide variety of languages and cultures.

"The names of those who came before us?" wondered Sinner.

"I don't know if anyone else has noticed," said Pretty Poison. "But there doesn't seem to be any other way out of here."

"I'd noticed," I said.

"This isn't at all how I'd pictured the Lord of Thorns' domain," said Sinner. "I think there is a strong possibility that we've been had, people."

"I don't think so," Pretty Poison said slowly. "We're not alone here."

The cloud of flies rose up suddenly from the meat throne, buzzing angrily. They swirled around the cavern horribly quickly, while we ducked our heads and swatted at them with flailing hands, then the cloud returned to the meat throne, swelled in size and took on a roughly human shape. It stood on stocky legs, a dark blocky shape towering over us, its unfinished head brushing against the cavern ceiling. And then it sat down abruptly on the meat throne, and the heavy buzzing gradually resolved itself into something like human speech. It sounded foul and hostile, a mockery of language.

"Welcome, dear travellers," said the flies. "You have found your way to the entrance to the domain of the Lord of Thorns. And this is as far as you go. He does not wish to be disturbed. And so he has set me here, a demon summoned up out of Hell and bound to this place, just to ensure he gets his rest. A Prince of the Pit, damned to obey a servant of Heaven, until the Nightside is destroyed or Time itself runs out. Sometimes I think the whole universe runs on irony. Still, the eating's good. Hello, Pretty Poison. It's been a while. How do you like my place? It's not much, but it has some of the comforts of home."

"Hello, Bub," said Pretty Poison. "How is it that thou art bound here, to a mortal's purpose?"

"Because he is the Lord of Thorns and knows much that is forbidden. Is that your Sinner with you? The only soul that still loved in Hell?"

"Yes," said Pretty Poison. "This is my dear Sidney."

"Pervert," the demon said to Sinner. "And fool, to still believe in Hell's lies. She will corrupt you and drag you back down into the Pit. It's what she does. And she has always been very good at her job."

"Given enough time, and sufficient motivation," said Sinner, "I could probably swat you to death."

I decided to intervene, before the conversation could deteriorate any further.

"Hi. I'm John Taylor. No doubt you know the name. I'm here to speak with the Lord of Thorns. So step aside, or I'll think of something amusing to do to you."

"John Taylor?" The writhing shape leaned forward on its meat throne to get a better look at me. "I'm impressed. Really. Though I'd always thought you'd be taller. But it's more than my job's worth to let you pass. Pride in my position is pretty much all I have left here. And whatever you might do to me would be nothing compared to the torments the Lord of Thorns would visit on me. I am bound to this place, and to his will. Besides, it's been a long time since my last visitor, and I'm *hungry*."

The dark shape stood up abruptly, and huffed and puffed itself up into a great hulking figure, taking up half the cavern, buzzing almost painfully loudly. It tried to pick up Madman with one huge black hand, but the flies just slipped harmlessly past him. The demon hesitated a moment and thrust a hand in my direction. The fingers extended, becoming shafts of flies rushing towards my face. They swept over me, trying to force their way into my mouth, nose, ears, and eyes. I panicked, flapping my hands wildly about my head while pressing my lips and eyelids firmly together, as the flies crawled over my face. And then to my astonishment they all leapt off me and retreated, apparently repulsed. The demon froze where it was, seemingly just as astonished as I was, and I seized the moment to summon up my gift. My inner eye snapped open, and it only took a moment for me to find and identify the Words of Power that bound the demon to this place.

(And yet even as I used my gift, some instinct made me slam my inner eye shut again, the moment it was no longer needed. While my mind was open and vulnerable, I sensed Something awful closing in on me, trying to pin down my location so it could manifest. My enemies had found something worse than the Harrowing to send after me, and all my instincts screamed that if I were to use my gift one instant longer than necessary, this new horror would find me and carry out its makers' terrible intent.)

I said the Words of Power. They arose from no human tongue, or even human sounds, and just to hear them said aloud would reduce most men to madness. I said the Words, slowly but distinctly, forcing them out syllable by syllable, and the terrible sound of them reverberated in my skull until I thought they'd blow my head apart. The demon screamed in thwarted rage, then was gone, taking with him his meat throne and his butcher's tools. All that remained was the sullen red glare, and the names of his victims traced on the cavern walls in their own blood.

Pretty Poison looked at me, taken aback. "How is it that you were able to speak those Words? The sheer power involved should have blasted the soul right out of your body."

"I have hidden depths," I said. My throat hurt. Where the meat throne had stood, there was now an opening in the cavern wall. "And so, it seems, has this place."

We all moved cautiously forward to study the new opening. It was shaped like a door, with smooth sides and top, but that was all there was to it. No warning signs, no welcome mat. Beyond the opening lay a long, descending stairway, carved into the rock face of a vast open space. Hovering lights marked the stairs here and there, but their pale light did little more than show just how far down the steps went. It looked like a hell of a long way. There was no railing, nothing between the open edge of the steps and an impossibly long drop. I started down the steps, one shoulder pressed firmly against the rock face, and after a moment the others followed me. We descended into the dark abyss, step by step, for a very long time.

"Are we there yet?" said Madman.

"Shut up," I said.

"Are we even still under the Nightside?" said Sinner. "We do seem to have travelled rather a long way."

"We haven't left the Nightside, sweetie," Pretty Poison assured him. "I'd know."

"We are in the dark places of the earth," said Madman. "Where all the ancient and most dangerous secrets are kept. There are Old Things down here, sleeping all around us, in the earth and in the living rock, and in the spaces between spaces. Keep your voices down. Some of these old creatures sleep but lightly, and even their dreams can have force and substance in our limited world. We have come among forgotten gods and sleeping devils, from the days before the world settled down and declared itself sane."

"I think I liked it better when you made no sense at all," said Sinner.

The hovering lights turned out to be paper lanterns, nailed to the rock face at regular intervals. Their tightly stretched sides were made up of silently screaming faces. The eyes in the agonised faces turned to watch us as we passed.

"Are they still alive?" I said. "Still suffering?"

"Oh yes," said Pretty Poison, her voice heavy with a certain satisfaction.

"Hush," said Sinner.

"But what are they?" I said. "Who were they?"

"Uninvited guests," said Madman, and after that no-one felt like talking for a while.

We descended further and further into the earth. The stairs wound around the curving wall of the vast abyss. The dark rock of the wall showed clear signs of having been worked on long ago, at first by tools but later by what seemed to be bare hands. Someone had fashioned this great gulf under the Nightside for a purpose, but who and why and when remained a mystery. Could men have done this, alone or with help? Why would they have wanted to? Was the Lord of Thorns really so dangerous that they had to bury him this deep in the earth? The deeper I went, the more scared I became. My hands were trembling, and my mouth was dry. This was all getting too big, too important for me. I wanted to go back to being just another private investigator, dazzling the natives with tricks and mind games, trading on a reputation I'd never really earned. But I had to go on. I'd come this far for the truth, and though I'd run out of courage and good sense, stubbornness kept me going.

The wall at my shoulder became increasingly pitted and corroded, and thin streams of liquid trickled down the dark stone. I stopped and studied the wet surface closely.

"Don't touch it," said Sinner.

"I wasn't going to. What do you suppose this is? Acid rain, or the underground equivalent?"

"No," said Pretty Poison. "Tears."

Sinner looked at her dubiously. "You know this place?"

"Of it. All demons and angels are warned about this place. We are almost at the domain of the Lord of Thorns, the Overseer of the Nightside."

"The Overseer?" I said. "Does that mean he's the one behind the Authorities?"

"No," said Pretty Poison. "He's much more powerful than that. He sits in judgement, and mercy and compassion are not allowed to him."

"I want to go home," said Madman.

"Most sensible thing you've said all day," said Sinner.

The stairs finally curved around a corner and came to an end, facing a great and elegant chamber carved out of crystal. A pleasant, comfortable light appeared suddenly overhead, bursting out of one crystal facet after another, until the whole chamber was bright as day, like standing in the heart of a huge diamond. In the centre of the crystal cave was a single raised slab of polished stone, and on that slab, sleeping peacefully, a man. He didn't look particularly dangerous, with his grey hair and grey robes, and a calm face apparently untroubled by care. We all filed into the shining chamber, looking uncertainly about us. I think we'd all been expecting more guardians, more defences, but everything was still and quiet. Like the eye of the storm.

Etched into every crystal facet were characters from the language known as Enochian, a tongue created for men to speak to angels. I recognised it, but I couldn't read it. Not many can. It is corrosive to rational thinking. Pretty Poison moved along one wall, tracing the characters with a fingertip.

"These are names," she said softly. "Names beyond number, of angels from Above and Below, from all ranks and stations... Even my name is here. My true name, from before the Fall. No mortal should have access to this knowledge..."

"But... why write them here?" said Sinner.

"Because to know the true name of a thing is to have power over it," said Pretty Poison. "To command and to control. Whoever put the Lord of Thorns here, and made him Overseer of the Nightside, has given him power over all the agents of Heaven and Hell."

"No wonder he was ripping the wings off angels during the Angel War," said Sinner. "But who could give him that kind of power?"

"Two possibilities come to mind," said Madman.

"Shut up," said Pretty Poison.

She sounded shocked, upset. I was concentrating on the man on the slab. He hadn't moved at all since we entered his domain. But I didn't think he was sleeping. Sleeping people usually breathe now and again. And then my heart missed a beat as he sat up abruptly, swinging his legs over the side of the slab, and sat facing us. We all froze where we were, caught in the gleam of his gaze, like burglars picked out by torchlight in a place they should never have entered. With his long grey robes, hair, and beard, the Lord of Thorns looked like nothing so much as an Old Testament prophet. The kind that told you the Flood was coming, and you'd left it far too late to book seats on the Ark. His face looked older than any man's should, and his eyes were fierce and wild and touched with a divine madness. His presence filled the crystal cave, and under his gaze we all flinched and felt unworthy.

Except, of course, for Madman, who shouted *Daddy!* and tried to climb into the Lord of Thorns' lap. We all grabbed him, and dragged him away by brute force. And then one by one, we knelt before the Lord of Thorns. His presence demanded it. Madman shrugged, and knelt with us. I kept my head down and tried to look penitent. This was a place of judgement. I could feel it. And judgement without mercy or compassion is always to be feared.

The Lord of Thorns stood up slowly, his joints cracking loudly, and I risked a quick look. He was leaning on a simple wooden staff, and I felt something inside me shudder at the sight of it. Word was the wood of that staff had been taken from a tree grown from a sliver of the original Tree of Life, brought to England in Roman times by Joseph of Arimathea. There were those who said the Lord of Thorns *was* Joseph of Arimathea. He looked old enough. When he finally spoke, his words sounded like rocks grinding together.

"I am the stone that breaks all hearts. I am the nails that bound the Christ to his cross. I am the arrow that pierced a king's eye. I am the necessary suffering that makes us all stronger. The cold, clear heart of the Nightside. It was given to me to have dominion over all who exist here, to protect the Nightside from itself. I maintain the Great Experiment, watching over it, and sitting in judgement on all who might seek to disrupt or tamper with its essential nature. I am the scalpel that cuts out infection, and the heartbreak that makes men wiser. I am the Lord of Thorns, and I know you all. Sinner, Pretty Poison, Madman, and John Taylor. Stand up. I've been waiting for you."

We rose to our feet again, glancing uncertainly at each other like children brought unexpectedly before the headmaster. I made myself speak up. Because if there's one thing I've learned from dealing with the Nightside's major players, it's that it doesn't matter how frightened you are, you can't let them know it, or they'll walk right over you.

"So," I said. "Are we here for judgement?"

"No," said the Lord of Thorns. "You are welcome in this place, John Taylor."

I felt a great rush of tension flow out of me, but I didn't let him see that either. I looked at him narrowly. "Lot of people think I'm a threat to the existence of the Nightside. Are you saying they're wrong?"

"No. Just that you're a special case." And then he smiled, just a little. "And no; I don't know why. You're as much a mystery to me as you are to everyone else. And if you find that infuriating, think how it makes me feel."

He smiled round at all of us, and just like that the pressure of his presence disappeared. The Lord of Thorns wasn't one bit less impressive, but at least no-one felt like they might be destroyed at any moment. The Lord of Thorns stretched his back, like a cat that's been sleeping in the sun too long.

"You've come a long way for answers," he said. "I wish I could be of more help. But truth be told, I'm just a functionary, a servant of the Nightside. Powerful beyond hope or reason, yes, because I need that power to enforce my will. But still in the end just an old, old man, unable to put down a burden he has carried for far too long. I am the heart that beats in every action and decision that makes up the Nightside, and I'm getting bloody tired of it. So ask your questions, John Taylor, and I will answer what I can. Perhaps because it's the only form of rebellion still left to me."

"Excuse me," said Sinner, very politely, "but what about the rest of us? Are we also immune to your judgement?"

"You don't matter," the Lord of Thorns said calmly. "Only John Taylor matters. Though you three are unique in the whole of the Nightside, in that it has been given to you, for various reasons, to shape your own destinies. This has been decided where all the things that matter are decided—on the shimmering plains, in the Courts of the Holy. I have no power over you—sinner, demon, madman." He looked at them thoughtfully, then at me. "You chose your companions for this quest wisely. No others could or would have escaped my judgement. Now ask your questions."

"All right," I said. "Tell me all you know about the beginnings of the Nightside, its purpose and true nature."

"The Nightside is old," said the Lord of Thorns. "I think probably only its creator knows exactly how old. Certainly it existed before me. Though at that time it was not so much a place of people, more a gathering place of Beings and Forces, still moulding their identities and intentions. The Romans knew of the Nightside when I first came to this land, back when it was still called the Tin Isles as much as Britannia. The Romans feared and venerated the Nightside, and built their city of Londinium around it, to protect and contain it, and to protect their people and their Empire from its influences. They knew of your mother, too, John, and worshipped her; though no-one now knows under what name. If I ever knew, I have forgotten, or more likely was made to forget. I have had a long time to consider the question, of who and what she might have been... and down the long centuries I have chosen and discarded many names. My best guess, my current belief, is that your mother was the Being called Luna, sister to Gaea."

"Hold everything," I said, holding up a hand. "Gaea... as in the *earth*? That Gaea? You think my mother is *the Moon*?"

"Yes. The living embodiment of the moon that shines so brightly above the Nightside. Why do you think it's so big here? Because she's keeping an eye on her creation. You are a Moonchild, John Taylor, neither truly of the light or the dark, and half-brother to the infamous Nicholas Hob, the Serpent's Son. It is my belief that Luna created the Nightside in order that she might have a stake in the earth, along with her sister, and a say in the development of Humanity."

"But... I have heard," Sinner said deferentially, "that the lady in question is, and has been for some time... quite mad."

"Yes," said the Lord of Thorns.

Sinner looked at me. "It would explain an awful lot."

"Bullshit," I said, and everyone looked at me, startled. I shook my head firmly and glared at the Lord of Thorns. "You're guessing, just like all the others. Everyone I've talked to has had a completely different idea on who my mother is, but none of you really know anything for certain!"

"Can you please not shout at the Overseer of the Nightside?" said Pretty Poison. "Some of us would like to get out of here reasonably intact."

"If I ever knew the truth, it has been taken from me," the Lord of Thorns said calmly. "And, I would guess, from everyone else. Your mother covered her tracks with great care. And I am afraid there is no-one left older than myself for you to ask. Your quest ends here."

"No," I said again, glaring right back into his cold eyes. "I have to go on. I have to *know*. Are you going to try and stop me?"

The Lord of Thorns smiled slightly. "Perhaps I should, but no, I don't think so. You are a dangerous man, John Taylor, but you represent the possibility of my long function here finally coming to an end. I would welcome that."

I tried to think of what it must have been like, condemned to this small cave for thousands of years, his only occasional company those who came before him to be judged. Endlessly watching over the Nightside, seeing generations come and go in a world from which he must have felt increasingly distanced, his only comforts the cold exercise of responsibility and duty. He'd been a man, once. Just a man. He might be the Overseer of the Nightside, but he was really just a prisoner.

"Who put you here?" I said.

"If I ever knew, the knowledge has been taken from me." The Lord of Thorns looked broodingly at nothing for a while. "I suppose it is possible that I volunteered, but I rather doubt it."

"There must be somewhere else I can go," I said. "With all the Beings and Powers and Dominations that swan about the Nightside, there must be someone who still knows something..."

"Use your gift," Pretty Poison said suddenly. "It's a part of your legend that you can use your gift to find anything. Why couldn't it find your mother for you, or at the very least, identify someone who could lead us to your mother?"

"It's not that simple," I said, "Or I'd have done it long ago. The more hidden a thing is, the harder and longer I have to look to find it. And the longer I spend with my mind open and vulnerable, the easier it is for my enemies to locate me and send something after me. The last time I used my gift, to banish the demon at the Gate, I felt Something closing in on me, trying to manifest. Something much nastier than the Harrowing. If I open up again, it will find me, even here. And I don't think even the Lord of Thorns could stop this new awful thing my enemies have unleashed. From now on, my gift can only be used as a very last resort."

"There's always the Tower of Time," said Sinner.

I winced. "I'd really rather not. Time travel is what you turn to after you've tried everything else, including closing your eyes and praying the problem will just go away. Time travel tends to cause more problems than it solves."

And since I now knew my enemies were operating out of a possible future, and sending their agents back through time, there was always the chance travelling in time might give them direct access to me.

Pretty Poison wasn't convinced. "But we could use time travel to go right back to the beginning of the Nightside and witness its creation for ourselves! All the answers and no more mysteries!"

"Not a good idea," said Madman. "There were Beings and Forces abroad at that time that could destroy us all. I have Seen them. The Past is not what we think it is."

We all looked at him, but that was all he had to say. He was definitely getting more lucid, but not any easier to have around.

The Lord of Thorns raised his head sharply. "The Authorities have sent people down into the World Beneath, against all truces and agreements. Apparently your banishing of the demon at my Gate set off some kind of alarm. They have blocked off the Gate and are working to seal off all the other entrances they know about." He looked at me. "I could kill them, if you wish. There are only a few thousand of them."

I had no doubt he could do it. I shook my head quickly, thinking of angels with their wings ripped off and all of Walker's watchers I'd spent good times with in the past.

"Sometimes death can be the tidiest of solutions," said the Lord of Thorns. "But as you wish. I can offer you another way out. No-one knows all the entrances and exits to my domain these days."

"You mean you keep secrets from the Authorities?" said Sinner. "I am shocked, I tell you, shocked."

The Lord of Thorns sniffed. "We haven't talked for centuries. They are in charge of the Nightside's politics. I am in charge of its soul."

"But we're still going to need Walker's people off our back, while I work out where to go and whom to see next," I said. "If the Authorities have ordered him to declare open season on me..."

"I may be able to help," Pretty Poison said slowly. "I have a... history, with Walker."

Sinner gave her a hard look. "You've kept very quiet about that."

"I have known many men," said Pretty Poison, just as sharply. "Countless men, over countless years. I was given to Walker once, as a present, by the Authorities. I could revisit him, using our old connection, and... talk with him. Try and use our shared past to get him to call off his dogs for a while. Maybe even get some answers out of him. Of course, if he won't be reasonable..."

"You are not to kill him," said Sinner.

"Of course not, sweetie. I need him alive to answer questions and call off his people."

"Alive and intact," Sinner said sternly.

"You're such a spoil-sport, sometimes. Very well, I'll do it the hard way, then. I'll set up a spell so you can all observe our meeting." She reached out and took Sinner's face in her hands. "You have to learn to trust me, dear Sidney. I need to do this, to prove myself to you." She smiled suddenly. "I promise you this; Walker isn't going to know what's hit him."

NINE

MEMORIES OF
THE WAY WE
USED TO BE

Pretty Poison stepped delicately through a halo of
hell-fire and materialised smiling before an astonished Walker. I could tell he was astonished
because he actually raised both eyebrows at once.
He was sitting at a table covered with a pretty pat-
terned cloth, and a cup of tea raised half way to his
mouth. Pretty Poison looked unhurriedly about
her, and the vision she was sending the rest of us
pulled back to show an old-fashioned tea room,
complete with live classical musicians and maids in
traditional black-and-white uniforms. The musicians had stopped playing, staring open-mouthed
at the new arrival, and the maids were falling back

in pretty disarray. Pretty Poison smiled widely at Walker.

"The Willow Tree tea house! One of our special places. How sweet that we should meet here again, after all these years."

Walker sighed and put down his cup. It was delicate bone china, with a willow tree pattern. Armed men and women came running forward from every direction to surround the table, their guns trained unwaveringly on Pretty Poison. Some of them brandished amulets and crucifixes, and at least one had an aboriginal pointing bone. Pretty Poison just looked at Walker and raised an eyebrow. Walker gestured tiredly to the armed men and women.

"Everyone stand down. It's all right. This person is known to me. Resume your positions. Good reaction times, everyone. Except you, Lovett. See me later."

The security people reluctantly lowered their weapons and retreated. People sitting at nearby tables began to relax again. Walker looked at the musicians, who consulted hastily among themselves, and began a piece by Bach. Walker looked at Pretty Poison. He wasn't smiling.

"Hello, Sophia."

"Hello, Henry. It's been a while, hasn't it?"

"May I ask how you got in here, past all the Willow Tree's defences and my own personal protections?"

"Because of our past history, darling. We're linked together, now and forever."

"The past haunts us all," Walker said dryly. "Especially in the Nightside. I won't say it's a pleasure to see you again, because it isn't."

Pretty Poison pouted fetchingly. "How very ungallant. Aren't you at least going to ask me to sit down?"

Walker sighed again and indicated the empty chair opposite him with a non-committal hand. His face was calm and composed as always, but I knew that behind his usual world-weary façade he had to be thinking furiously. Walker was never caught off guard for long. Pretty Poison sat down gracefully, put her hands on the table so Walker could keep an eye on them, and beamed at him.

"I'd absolutely adore a cup of tea, darling."

Walker checked the ornate china teapot before him, found it was practically empty, and gestured for a waitress. The waitresses looked at each other, there was a brief but silent communication of raised eyebrows and shaken heads, then the most recently employed was forced forward by peer pressure. She tottered up to the table, smiling gamely, and Walker ordered a fresh pot of tea and another cup.

"Anything else?" quavered the waitress. "Fairy cakes? Fresh cream? Can I take your coat?"

"Go away," said Pretty Poison. "Or I'll burn you alive from the inside out."

The waitress departed, running, to have hysterics at a safe distance. Walker looked reproachfully at Pretty Poison.

"You haven't changed a bit, Sophia. It'll take more than a generous gratuity to smooth that over. I'll be lucky if I'm not banned."

"But I thought you ran things in the Nightside these days, Henry."

"There are limits. Do try and behave in a civilised manner. I have my reputation to consider."

A different waitress arrived and set out a new tea service. She pushed the second cup in Pretty Poison's general direction, without looking at her, then fled. Walker poured Pretty Poison a cup of hot, steaming tea, adding a dash of milk and one sugar without having to be asked. Pretty Poison clapped her hands together delightedly.

"You remembered! You always were good about the little things, Henry." She looked at him critically. "You look older, dear. Distinguished."

"You look just like I remember you," said Walker. "But then you would, wouldn't you? Being what you are."

"What do you see, when you look at me?" said Pretty Poison, sipping carefully at her tea with her little finger carefully extended. "I look different to everyone, so I never know."

"Let's just say I was perhaps a little too fond of Marianne Faithful in my younger days, and leave it at that." Walker gave her a hard look. "What did you mean, when you said we were still linked? Our... arrangement was over years ago. And I'm supposed to be protected from... unexpected visitors."

Pretty Poison shrugged. "When I was given to you, all those years ago, it created a connection between us, so that you could summon me at will. That connection cannot be broken by anything except your death or my destruction. That's the rule. A succubus isn't just for Christmas, she's for life. Dallying with such as me is a mortal sin, after all. Still, it is nice to see you again, Henry. I must say you're taking this very well. I half expected you to shout and throw things. Or call for an exorcist."

"I don't get excited any more," said Walker. "It's bad for the image. What are you doing here, Sophia?"

She looked away from him, leaning back in her chair to contemplate the tea room. The musicians played, the waitresses came and went, and people at other tables enjoyed their tea and exchanged polite conversation. Absolutely no-one was showing any interest in Walker's table. Pretty Poison looked back at Walker, nodding happily.

"I always liked this place. So calm and civilised, and everyone minding their own business. I'm glad it's still here. It hasn't changed at all, but then I suppose the charm of such places is that they don't. And the tea is very good. Maybe I should have asked for some fairy cakes after all."

"The Willow Tree has never really been fashionable," said Walker. "But I like it."

"Because it used to be one of our special places?"

"In spite of that."

Pretty Poison gave him a hard look. "Now don't spoil it, Henry. We're having a perfectly nice conversation. I shall change the subject." She indicated the crystal ball sitting on the table at Walker's left hand. Mists curled inside it. "Keeping touch with all your people in the field, I see. I didn't know people still used those any more; but then, you always were a traditionalist."

"I do tend to prefer things that have stood the test of time," said Walker. "The new is never to be trusted, until it has proven itself."

"You weren't always so stuffy," said Pretty Poison. "Remember our other special place?"

"Oh please," said Walker. "Not that opium den..."

"The Purple Haze," Pretty Poison said gleefully. "The in place for way out people, back in the Sixties. Best dope in the Nightside, with free scatter cushions and psychedelic light shows thrown in. The very best place to listen to the latest sounds and get stoned on imaginary drugs like taduki and tanna leaves. Oh, we spent many a lost weekend there, didn't we darling; spiralling out into the infinite... You really were a lot looser in those days, Henry. Is the Purple Haze still around?"

"Fortunately, no. It's currently a health spa and gymnasium, called Health Freaks. The sort of place where corporate young men go to crunch their abs on their lunch-hour, going for the burn and flexing their way towards their first heart attack."

"Such a pity," said Pretty Poison. "I wonder if a trace of the old place still lingers in the air-ducts? In the old days you could get a contact high just from saying the name of the place aloud."

"I haven't thought about the Purple Haze in years," said Walker. "But then, there's a lot of things in my past I prefer not to remember."

"Don't look at me like that, Henry. Aren't you glad to see me again?"

"No."

"But we had such good times together!"

"You were a succubus. Can you honestly say it meant anything to you? I look at you now, and I have... conflicting emotions."

"I made you happy."

"You were given to me, as a bribe."

"As a gift," said Pretty Poison. "A succubus, to indulge your every pleasure, your every fantasy. A reward from the Authorities, for work well-done on their behalf. I made you laugh, and cry out in the night, and you never slept as peacefully as you did in my arms."

"Beware the Authorities, bearing gifts," said Walker. His face was still calm, but there was a sharpness in his voice. "You were bait, to draw me in and tie me closer to them. Their usual practice— to ensure their people became used to, even addicted to, the kinds of extreme pleasures only the Authorities and the Nightside could provide. I should have known, even then, that such attractive bait was bound to have a hook concealed in it somewhere."

"If I seemed to adore you, in our time together, then I was just doing my job," said Pretty Poison. "It wasn't supposed to be real, or taken for real; any more than any other transaction with a sex professional. I thought you understood that. I was yours, to do whatever you wished with, yes; but only for the duration of the contract. You can't say I wasn't entirely truthful, when I was first present-ed to you."

"I know," said Walker. "But I was still devastat-ed when you left. I thought I'd come to matter to you, but you walked out on me without a single backward glance."

"Well of course, darling. That was my job. Corrupting mortals and tempting them into sin. I couldn't take your soul, that was forbidden me by the Authorities: but I was supposed to reduce you to such a state that you'd do anything to have me back again."

"I did everything to try and persuade you to stay. I would have done anything for you."

"That's all very flattering, but I had another contract. I was only ever there for sex. You were the one who insisted on bringing love into it."

"I was young," said Walker. "It's a common misunderstanding, at that age. But I shouldn't have threatened you."

"No, dear, you shouldn't. I was forced to show you something of my true nature. What I really am."

Walker nodded slowly. "Just the glimpse of what I saw gave me nightmares for months. That I had been intimate with such a thing... I scrubbed my skin raw, till it bled... And you cut me a good one with a claw, before you left. I still have the scar."

Pretty Poison grinned suddenly. "Want me to kiss it better?"

"I'd rather you didn't." Walker leaned back in his chair and studied her thoughtfully. "I was shocked, horrified, at what I'd actually been sleeping with. I let you go, and did my best never to think about you again. I suppose... you were what first turned me against the attractions and seductions of the Nightside. The bright neon lies and the dirty little secret pleasures. You opened my eyes to what a moral cesspit this place is, and the duplicity of those in charge. The Authorities don't care about anything except the money, power, and influence the Nightside provides them. And to hell with the poor bastards that get ground underfoot here every day. I decided I had to be... better than that."

"And now you run things here?"

"Only to keep anyone else from doing it. I can't trust anyone else not to be seduced by the temptations on offer. Someone has to keep a clear head and see this place for what it really is. Someone has to keep the animals in their cages. You made me understand just how... corrupting the Nightside is."

"And that's why you, and the others, performed the Babalon Working?"

"Yes." Walker sipped at his tea, taking his time to make it clear he was changing the subject. "Once again—what are you doing here, Sophia? I wasn't aware demons from Hell got nostalgic over their old victims. Or have the Authorities given you to someone else, someone I should know about?"

"No," said Pretty Poison. "I'm with Sinner now."

Walker put down his cup and raised an eyebrow. "You're *that* succubus? Well... I'm impressed. Really. So you're the demon currently working with John Taylor. You do have a taste for powerful men, don't you?"

"I'm with Sinner now," Pretty Poison said patiently. "And only Sinner. Officially, I was sent up out of Hell to corrupt him, break his heart, and blacken his soul, so that the Pit can claim him again. Actually, I volunteered for this mission, to try and understand a love that could survive even in Hell. How anyone could honestly love a Fallen thing like me."

"You expect me to believe that?" said Walker. "I know better than anyone that love means nothing to you."

"That was then," said Pretty Poison. "Much has changed since then. After all this time with my Sidney, I'm still just starting to understand how he feels about me. And just possibly, I'm starting to understand what you felt for me, back then. And how badly I hurt you."

"I'm married," said Walker. "Very happily married. Almost twenty-three years now."

"I'm glad. What's her name?"

"Sheila. We have two boys. Keith is at Oxford, Robert is in the military. Good boys, both of them. I had them raised outside the Nightside. They know nothing about what I really do for a living."

"I'm glad, Henry. Really."

"So, this Sinner." Walker's voice was entirely casual. It would have fooled anyone else. "He really loves you?"

"Yes. A legendary love, even in Hell."

"I loved you."

"He loved me even after he saw my true nature. What I really am. My dear Sidney... I'm sorry I hurt you, Henry."

Walker drank his tea. "Demons lie. That's their true nature."

"Even demons can change."

Walker looked at her coldly. "You expect me to believe that?"

"I believe it," said Pretty Poison. "I have to."

They sat together for a while, drinking their tea, saying nothing, surrounded by civilised sounds.

"I know you've got people blocking the Gate to the Lord of Thorns' domain," Pretty Poison said abruptly. "And more people blocking other entrances. Under orders from the Authorities, I take it?"

"Of course," said Walker. "But if you can get out to visit me here, I have to assume the others can, too. I'd better talk to my security people, arrange to have the containing wards strengthened. Maybe call in some more specialists. Is that why you've come here to see me? To beg for my help?"

"All the wards and specialists in the Nightside won't stop us, darling," Pretty Poison said calmly. "The Lord of Thorns is on our side."

Walker actually blinked a few times. "How the hell did you manage that? I didn't think anyone escaped his judgement."

"He believes in us," said Pretty Poison. "And most especially, he believes in John Taylor. Talk to me about the Authorities, Henry."

"Why?"

"Because. Indulge me."

Walker shrugged. "If it'll get you out of here any quicker... There's no big mystery about the Authorities, really. They're just who everyone thinks they are; the city Names, the old, established business families who've gained so much wealth, power, and influence from centuries of investment in the Nightside. The people in and behind the Londinium Club, who avoid celebrity and open displays of wealth and power, but pull the strings of those who do. The men behind the scenes, who will do or authorise anything at all, to maintain the status quo that has always benefited them. And I work for them because all the other alternatives are worse. I have investigated other options, down the years, but most people just didn't want to know. The thought of so much responsibility scared the shit out of them. And the few who were interested turned out to want it for all the wrong reasons. So I turned them in to the Authorities. I'm in charge, inasmuch as anyone is, because I alone have no interest in the temptations and seductions of the Nightside. I know better. I know this place for what it really is."

"And what is that?" said Pretty Poison.

"A freak show. A city of ill repute. All of Humanity's bad ideas in one place. Which is why the Authorities are the best people to run it. Because they only care about the money it brings them. They might play here, on occasion, indulge passions that would not be allowed in the world outside, but at the end of the day they all go home and leave the Nightside behind them. Just like me."

"And you don't play at all. The only honest man in the Nightside. Or at least, the only moral man. And... perhaps the most scared. Why are you so afraid of the Nightside, Henry?"

Walker did her the courtesy of considering the question for a moment. "Because... there's always the chance that someday all the evils and temptations and corruption will break through the Nightside's boundaries and rush out to seduce the whole world."

"Would that really be such a bad thing?" said Pretty Poison. "If everyone knew the truth about how things really operate? If they could all finally see the big picture? If they could see and talk with Powers and Dominations, the Beings and Forces that move behind the scenes of the world... if they knew the score, it might change things for the better."

"No," said Walker. "Things are bad enough in the seemingly sane, cause-and-effect world. If all the fanatics and terrorists, or even the simply ambitious and well-meaning, knew what their options really were, they'd tear the world apart fighting over it."

"You weren't always like this," said Pretty Poison. "So... cynical."

And as she and Walker continued to talk in the Willow Tree tea room, she worked a change in the vision the rest of us were watching, to show us the Past.

Information came subtly to us, along with the new sights, seeping painlessly into our thoughts. We all knew at once that the year was 1967, and that the three young men walking down the Nightside street together, talking and laughing and shoving at each other in sheer good spirits, were Henry Walker and Charles Taylor and Mark Robinson. I recognised Walker first, because his face hadn't changed that much, but his clothes actually startled me. It seemed that back in his younger days, Henry Walker had been a hell of a dandy and a dedicated follower of fashion. He strode along like a slender peacock, outfitted in dazzlingly bright colours, the best the King's Road

had to offer, complete with narrow oblong sun-
glasses and a great mane of wavy dark hair. He
looked like a young god, too perfect for this material world.

Mark Robinson, who would one day know both
fame and infamy as the Collector, was also easy to
spot, if only because he was clearly an Elvis fanat-
ic even then. He had that whole young Elvis thing
down pat, even to the greasy black quiff and the
practised curl of the upper lip. His black leather
jacket had far too many zips and chains, and rattled loudly as he walked. He was never still,
packed full of nervous energy, and was always that
little bit ahead or behind the other two, talking
sixteen to the dozen and bouncing up and down
on his feet. His laughter came free and easy, from
sheer joi de vivre. He had plans and ambitions,
and thought he had his whole future mapped out.

It took me rather longer to recognise Charles
Taylor. My father. I had no photos of him. He
threw everything out, or burned it, after my mother left. In the vision, he was younger than I was,
and he didn't look much like me. He didn't look at
all like I expected. Unlike his colourful friends, he
wore a smart dark three-piece suit and a tie, short-
haired and clean-shaven. He could have been just
another anonymous executive, toiling in the big
city. But what surprised me most of all was how
free and easy he looked, how happy in the company of his friends. That was why I had so much
trouble recognising him. Because I'd never seen my
father happy before.

It was 1967, a time of change in the Nightside,
just like everywhere else. They were three young

men on the way up, men with great futures before them. They were going to change the world.

They finally entered that most fashionable meeting place, the Hawk's Wind Bar & Grill. I'd never seen the original place. It burned down (some said self-immolation) in 1970, and now existed as a ghost of itself. A haunted building, with real people as its customers. In the vision it looked much the same, though. A glorious monument to the psychedelic glories of the Sixties, complete with rococo dayglo neon and Pop-Art posters with colours so bright they practically mugged the eyeballs. Even at a distance, I thought I could still smell the usual aroma of coffee, joss sticks, dodgy cigarettes, and patchouli oil. The Go-Go checked jukebox played all the latest sounds, and the Formica-covered tables were surrounded by all the familiar faces of the period, from the enigmatic Orlando to the Travelling Doctor and his latest companions. Walker and Robinson and Taylor smiled and waved easily to one and all as they entered, but no-one paid them much attention. They weren't important people, then, these three. The man who would run the Nightside, the man who would collect it, and the man who would damn it.

Henry, Mark, and Charles commandeered the last remaining table in the far corner, ordered various kinds of coffee from the gum-chewing, white-plastic-clad waitress, then poured over the latest issue of *OZ* magazine, the special Nightside issue. Charles had just picked up his copy, and Mark grabbed it from him, to check if they'd printed his letter about Elvis being the real shooter of JFK. Walker had already read the issue, of course. He was always the first at everything.

We all listened as the three young men talked. It seemed they were impatient, for all their good humour. Their inevitable bright future seemed unfairly far off. They were being held back, by entrenched interests and people who weren't interested in trying anything new—anything that hadn't been around for decades, and preferably centuries. Fashion was one thing, sin always thrived on the very latest fashions; but no-one at the top wanted to know about institutional change. These three young men were determined to seize power and influence, if necessary, so that they could force through necessary changes. For the greater good of all, of course. They wanted to usher in the Age of Aquarius, and the mind's true liberation. Everyone young was a dreamer and an idealist in 1967.

When they'd finished with the magazine, it was time for show-and-tell. Mark was a collector even back then, and had got his hands on something special. He took it out of his shoulder bag, looking quickly about to make sure no-one was watching, then laid his find reverentially on the table before them. Henry and Charles looked dubiously at the cardboard box full of tatty, handwritten pages.

"All right," said Walker. "What is it this time? And it had better not be about Roswell again. I am sick to death of Roswell. If anything had really happened there, we'd know about it by now."

"You just wait," Mark said darkly. "I'll get you proof yet. I know someone who knows someone who claims one guy actually filmed the autopsy on the aliens... Of course, this is the same man who claims we'll be landing men on the moon in two years, so..."

"What have you found, Mark?" Charles said patiently. "And what good does it do us?"

"Is it something we can blackmail people with?" Walker said wistfully. "I've always wanted to be able to blackmail someone."

Mark grinned wolfishly, one hand pressed possessively on the pile of papers, as though afraid someone might sneak up and steal them. "This, my friends, is the real thing. The mother lode. An unpublished manuscript by the one and only Aleister Crowley—the Magus, the Great Beast, the Most Evil Man in the World. If you believe the newspapers, which mostly I don't. But Crowley was the real thing, for a time at least, and there have always been those who said his best, or more properly his worst, stuff was never published. This manuscript was apparently put on the market some years back, when Crowley was desperately short of money, but no-one was interested. He was out of favour among the conjuring classes, and the papers were bored with him. Eventually a copy of this manuscript turned up at the *International Times*, and a sub-editor there passed it on to me, in return for a complete set of *Mars Attacks!* cards. Unlike most of the fools whose hands the manuscript passed through, I actually read it from end to end, and I am here to tell you, my friends... this is the answer to all our prayers. A direct means to our much desired end."

"God, you love the sound of your own voice," said Henry. "*What is it*, Mark? Not just another grimoire, I hope."

Mark was still grinning widely. "One chapter in this manuscript describes a particularly powerful spell, or Working, that Crowley began but never dared finish. And let us not forget, Crowley dared a lot. He started the Working, to summon and bind to his will a most powerful Being, but abandoned the ritual after catching a glimpse of just what it was he was attempting to summon. *Beautiful, terrible,* he wrote... and that was all. He ran away from his splendid home on the bank of a Scottish loch, and never returned."

"Hold everything," said Charles. "We're supposed to attempt something that was too scary and too dangerous for *Aleister Crowley*? Called by many, not least himself, the Most Evil Man in the World?"

"Ah," Mark said smugly, "but we will succeed where he failed, because I have knowledge that Crowley lacked. I recently acquired a sheaf of letters from an ex-friend of Kenneth Anger, in which the writer positively identifies which spirit Crowley was trying to summon, and the means whereby it can be safely controlled. My friends, we have the means to summon up and bind to our will the Transient Being known as Babalon; a physical incarnation of an abstract ideal."

"Which ideal?" said Henry.

"All right, I'm still working on that," Mark admitted. "Depending on how you translate certain parts of the letters, the Being is either the personification of love, or lust, or obsession. Or perhaps even some combination of the three. Look, does it really matter? We've been searching for a power source, something we could use as a weapon to bring about change, and this is it!"

"What if it backfires?" said Charles. "This doesn't sound like the kind of magic you can afford to make mistakes with."

"What if we get found out?" said Henry. "Ambition is all very well, but we do have our careers to think of."

Mark glared at them both. "It's not enough to talk the talk; you have to be prepared to walk the walk! Anything worth having entails risks. We're not going to overthrow the Authorities with just good intentions!"

Henry sniffed, unconvinced. "Are you sure about the provenance of the letters, Mark? Are you sure they contain everything we're going to need?"

"Yes and yes," said Mark. "Now are you in, or out?"

"We'll need somewhere secure for the Working," Henry said thoughtfully. "I may know somewhere... leave it with me. Charles?"

"I want to study the manuscript, and the letters, first," said Charles. "And I want enough time to do some research of my own. Make sure of what it is we're getting ourselves into... But if it all checks out... Yes. We have to do this. We'd be fools not to seize an opportunity like this."

The vision changed abruptly, now showing the three young men looking around what seemed to be an empty warehouse. Shafts of gaudy neon light streaming through boarded-up windows revealed a large open space, with bare floorboards and walls plastered over with peeling posters for long-forgotten rock groups and political organisations. DAGON SHALL RISE AGAIN! declared a particularly faded example. The walls also featured large crude paintings of flowers and rainbows and the occasional exaggerated male and female genitalia. There were waxy candle stubs and scuffed-out chalk-markings all over the floor. Henry looked around the place with a certain pride. Mark stalked back and forth, pointing out things of interest, burning with nervous energy. Charles was leaning his back against the securely closed door, jotting things down in a thick notebook, scowling heavily.

"It's damp, it smells, and I can hear what I really hope are just rats in the walls," he said heavily, without looking up from his notebook. "And I have a horrible suspicion I'm standing on a used condom, but I'm afraid to raise my foot and look. Honestly, Henry, is this the best you could do? How much are we paying for this dump?"

"Practically nothing," Henry said smoothly. "The owner owes me a favour. It's not that bad... All right, it is that bad, but then we're not planning to live here, are we?"

"What's the history?" said Mark. "Anything that might interfere with what we're planning?"

"The history is dubious, bordering on squalid, but nothing that need concern us," said Henry. "I came here a few years ago, with a girl I knew then. Jessica something. The owner rents this place out for new groups to show off their stuff, and the occasional hippie happening. Whole room is probably permeated with drug residues. Try not to breathe too heavily, and don't lick the walls."

"I can honestly say the thought had never occurred to me," said Charles. "Though I'm now having a hard time forcing it out of my mind. How long have we got the room for?"

"We'll have the whole building for ten days," said Henry. "More than sufficient."

"And in a dodgy neighbourhood like this, no-one is going to stick their nose in and ask questions," said Mark, rubbing his hands together briskly. "Perfect!"

Henry looked at Charles. "Are you happy about this? You've hardly left the Michael Scott Library for the past week. Did you turn up anything we ought to know about?"

Charles scowled. "Not really. The Babalon Working is nothing new. It's been around for ages, in one form or another. There's quite a bit about it in Dr. Dee's *The Sigillum Aemeth*, and of course Babalon is mentioned in the Book of Revelations, and not in a good way. The only thing everyone seems to agree on is that it's a very dangerous undertaking. I can't find a single report of anyone completing the ritual successfully."

"That's because they didn't have the information in my letters!" said Mark. "Come on, we have to do this! We can't turn back now! Not when we're so close to everything we ever dreamed of!"

"It's up to you, Charles," said Henry, ignoring Mark. "You're the brains. Do we go ahead, or not?"

Charles thought for a long moment, then shrugged. "Oh hell. Let's do it."

They were all very young then. It's important to remember that.

The vision changed again, to show us the Babalon Working. Only edited highlights, of course, but it was still pretty impressive. The lengthy ritual was designed to summon, hold, and physically incarnate one of the Transient Beings; not just a demon or spirit, but one of the real Powers and Dominations. The living embodiment of an abstract concept, in this case love or lust or sexual obsession. (Babalon was an old, old name, and no two sources could agree on exactly what it represented.) The three young men saw it only as a weapon they could use against those they perceived as the villains of the day, and those in the Authorities who might try to obstruct the forthcoming changes. The three young men were determined not to be stopped. They would bring about freedom by force, if necessary. Like most fanatics, they were blind to irony, and even if they had seen it, they probably wouldn't have cared. They were doing this for the greater good, after all.

The Babalon Working involved days of fasting for all three men, and almost continual chanting, drawing circles and pentagrams on the floor, and protective sigils and wards on the walls, along with the regular ingestion of sacred herbs and drugs. They guzzled thirstily at bottled water and sweated it all out again as they stamped their way through ritual dances. They weren't allowed to sleep, or even rest. By the end of the sixth day they were all looking pretty ragged round the edges. They worked naked now, stinking from dried sweat and the human wastes that piled up in the room's corners. Their eyes were red and staring, their voices hoarse and pained from the endless chants, and their hands shook so badly the sigils they drew had to be traced over and over again to get them right. They were beyond hunger, beyond thirst, chemicals roaring through their veins, expanded thoughts clamouring in their minds. They staggered in spiral patterns across a floor covered in chalk-marks of all shapes and colours, timing the rhythm of their ragged voices to the pounding of their bare feet on the bare boards. They were half out of their minds, half out of the world, pushing their thoughts by brute force into another level of reality, until finally they found what they were looking for.

Or it found them. It was much bigger than they'd thought, bigger than they could bear, but they held their nerve. They retreated to the physical plane of existence, calling it after them, and it followed them home. That ancient Force, that terrible female principle known as Babalon. The three men could feel it drawing closer, and a new strength pounded through their racked bodies and raw voices. Their minds snapped into sharp focus as their intent crystallised, and Babalon grew clearer in their linked thoughts. She was indeed beautiful and terrible, and intoxicating in her power.

And that was when it all went wrong. Horribly wrong. An inhuman howl filled the warehouse, resonating in every physical surface, as the entity known as Babalon was suddenly thrust aside by something else; something far more powerful. Somehow it had detected the opening between the planes of existence and seized the opportunity to manifest in Babalon's place. The Transient Being was forced back, for all its power, and this new thing came forward in its place. The whole warehouse shook, the walls bending and twisting. The three men were thrown around like rag dolls, until they were left clinging to the shuddering floor like mariners on a raft, all their carefully traced circles and pentagrams and wards nothing more than chalk-dust, meaningless in the face of the unknown Force that was incarnating. Something impossibly old and powerful, terrifying, bewildering, something that had been banned from the material world since time out of time, but was now forcing its way back into reality. There was a blast of unbearable light, the sound of all the birds in the world singing at once, as Something impossibly vast and complicated compressed itself into physical existence. The three men clung together, helpless in the face of what they had allowed back into the world. They caught a glimpse of something that was denied to those of us watching the vision, and they all cried out miserably in shock and horror, like children discovering that there are monsters in the dark, after all. And then the Power they had let in erupted out of the warehouse, smashing contemptuously through the walls and the wards marked on them, out and loose in the Nightside.

The whole warehouse was blown apart, and all the buildings surrounding it for a three-block radius. Massive fires raged among the ruins, reducing everyone who lived there to little more than bone and ash. Hundreds died. Nobody could be sure exactly how many. The only survivors were Henry Walker, Mark Robinson, and Charles

Taylor, who staggered dazed but unhurt from the smouldering remains of the warehouse. They had been spared, though they didn't know why. They were in shock, most of their memories gone. No-one ever suspected what they'd tried to do, and what they'd actually done. They themselves only remembered after some time had passed. Bits and pieces came back to them, but by then it was far too late to say or do anything. Whatever they had unleashed had gone to ground in the Nightside, and all the people whose deaths they had caused would not be brought back by explanations or apologies. So in the end, they said nothing.

They waited fearfully for a long time, for some sign of whatever they'd let loose, but all went on as it had before, and as the months passed with no unusual reports or warnings, the three young men came to believe that just maybe they had dodged the bullet after all. That the incarnation hadn't taken, and the Power hadn't been able to maintain its presence in the physical world. Henry and Mark congratulated themselves on their lucky escape, but Charles wasn't so sure. He haunted library after library, digging through their deepest stacks in search of old knowledge, trying to make sense of what had happened. And when he couldn't, he went to the others and told them they had to speak out. To warn the Authorities about what might still be out there, somewhere.

Henry and Mark couldn't have that. They decided they had no choice but to discredit Charles, to save themselves. So they started a whispering campaign, the gist of which was that Charles had caused the warehouse area disaster through following his own private, unsanctioned researches. There was no proof, of course, and no charges were ever brought, but Charles's career in the Authorities was finished. He resigned just ahead of being fired and went into private research. He took every paying job going, using the money to continue his own ongoing research, to discover just what he'd been a part of. He became very successful, as the years passed, and kept his obsession strictly private.

The three ex-friends went their own separate ways, each blaming the others for the Working's failure. Walker's position was that the ritual was just too dangerous and should never have been attempted. He stayed on in the Authorities, working for reform from within. He became obsessed with Getting On, rising higher and higher in the ranks. Mark left the Authorities and became the Collector, as obsessed in his own way as the others. And so the years passed, and three no-longer-young men made new lives for themselves.

The vision returned to Henry Walker and Pretty Poison drinking their tea in the Willow Tree. And after such an intense ride, I think all of us were glad of the break. We watched as Walker freshened Pretty Poison's cup. He always was a gentleman.

"That was all a long time ago," Walker said, in answer to some unheard comment. "We were all different people then."

"Did you ever find out exactly what it was that crashed your Working?" said Pretty Poison, sipping her tea with style and grace.

"No more questions," said Walker. "I've already told you far more than I should. Why are you here, Sophia?"

She smiled at him over her cup. "There are those who say John's mother is coming back."

"Then God help us all."

"Why would she be coming back now, Henry? What is her connection with John's current case?"

For a moment I thought Walker would just order her to leave, or even summon his people and have her dragged away, but the strength seemed to seep right out of him, as though he'd been carrying the burden for far too long and just didn't care any more. He sat back in his chair, looking suddenly old as well as tired, and his eyes were lost in yesterday.

"Mark set it all in motion," he said finally, his voice flat, almost empty. "Back when he introduced Charles to his wife-to-be. I prefer, however, to believe he didn't really know what he was doing. That he was being... used. By then, he was the Collector. Revered, or despised, depending on whom you talked to. Charles was a research specialist, almost a hermit. He called Mark, in his capacity as the Collector, looking for a research assistant to help him in his very narrow field. (Was that Charles's idea, I wonder, or did some Voice whisper in his ear?) By that time, Charles was investigating the beginnings of the Nightside, using all the money he'd made to fund his new obsession. Mark consulted with various experts, for an exorbitant fee, and finally presented Charles with a young lady called Fennella Davis. An up-and-coming young scholar with an excellent reputation, pretty and bright and articulate, and also very interested in the origins of the Nightside. Soon enough, she and Charles were in love, then they were married."

Walker frowned into his empty cup but made no move to refill it. "Poor Charles. He didn't understand that he was just a means to an end. Charles wasn't the point. John was the point."

"How do you mean?" said Pretty Poison, leaning forward. "What is it that makes John so important?"

"I remember when he was born," said Walker, not looking at her. "I'd never seen Charles so happy. He spent less and less time on his private work and more and more time with his new family. He stopped being a hermit and embraced life. He accepted new research commissions and rebuilt his reputation as a scholar all over again, with Fennella's help. He and I and Mark became reconciled again, friends again, after so many years. We were older, and perhaps a little wiser, and we were... happy again.

"We all liked Fennella. She was such good company.

"And then Charles finally discovered who and what his lovely wife really was. I don't know if there was ever a confrontation, but suddenly she was gone. She disappeared into the Nightside, and none of us ever saw her again, though we all searched for her in our various ways... Charles retreated into his old obsession about the true beginnings of the Nightside and drank himself to death, despite everything Mark and I could do to help. We did try. I'm sure we did. But he shut us out; and all the time he watched his young son as though John was something that might turn on him. Mark and I kept an eye on John, from a distance, looking out for him when we could. We intercepted quite a few attacks from the Harrowing, until John was old enough to fend for himself."

"Does John know that?"

"I never asked him."

"But... what's bringing his mother back now?"

"No-one knows for sure. If we did, we'd do... something..."

"To stop her?"

"I'm not sure she can be stopped. Sophia, why are you so interested in all this?"

"Because I'm working with John to uncover the true origins of the Nightside. And the closer we get to the truth, the more it seems tied in to the identity of John's missing mother. Though everyone we meet has very different ideas on who she was, or is."

"If I cared about you," said Walker, "I'd tell you to get the hell away from John Taylor. For your own sake."

"You should stay away from us," said Pretty Poison. "I'd hate for you to get hurt, Henry."

Walker raised an eyebrow. "Would you? Really?"

"Perhaps. I'm still working on this whole love thing. Call off your people, Henry. For old times' sake."

"I can't. John's gone too far. Made himself too dangerous to the status quo. He must be stopped."

"You mean killed?"

"I'll take him alive if I can. For old times' sake."

"Oh, Henry... what is it that makes him so dangerous? Who could his mother be, to terrify so many powerful people?"

"Haven't you been listening?" said Walker, almost angrily. "Whatever we called up and let loose, through the Babalon Working—that was John's mother!" He turned his head abruptly to look right at me. "I know you're there, John, watching and listening. I should have told you all this long ago, but I still hoped to spare you the consequences of our sins. I'm sorry for how things turned out. But either you step back from the edge now, and give yourself up, or I'll have no choice but to have you killed. Just in case you are... your mother's son."

TEN

THE WIFE

After all that, I felt I deserved a very large drink. In fact, I felt I deserved several very large drinks, followed by an extremely large drink, as a chaser. And then maybe I'd go and sit in a dark corner and twitch quietly for a while.

Pretty Poison did her hell-fire trick, and teleported herself out of the Willow Tree and back into the Lord of Thorns' crystal cave with the rest of us. She took time out to give her Sinner a good hug, just to show she was definitely over Walker, and they exchanged gooey endearments for a while. And then she turned an accusing gaze on me.

"Just how is it that Walker was able to see you through the vision I set up? That isn't supposed to be possible."

I shrugged. "Hey, this is Walker we're talking about. He can do anything. I think that's actually part of his job description. What matters now is that we have to get the hell out of here, before Walker's people discover and nail down all the other exits to this place that you just happened to mention to him—Sophia."

"You don't get to call me that," the demon succubus said sniffily. "Only Henry gets to call me that."

I looked at Sinner. "And what do you call her, when you're at home?"

"Darling," Sinner said solemnly. "And no; you don't get to call her that, either."

"Dearest Sidney," said Pretty Poison, giving him another hug.

"It's time for you all to go," said the Lord of Thorns. "I'll see if I can buy you some time by keeping Walker's people occupied. I could use the exercise."

Sinner looked unconvinced. "How can even you hope to stand against all the armies Walker will send against you?"

"Because I am the Lord of Thorns. I was given dominion over all who live or otherwise exist in the Nightside."

"Try not to hurt them too much," I said. "A lot of them are just working stiffs, doing their jobs."

"I will be the judge of that," said the Lord of Thorns. "And I make no promises. I trim the fat. That's in my job description."

I gave him my best thoughtful look. "Why are you so ready to help us?"

The old man shrugged and lay down on his stone slab again, arranging himself comfortably. "I told you. Because I seem to sense that things are reaching an ending, because of you, and I welcome the chance to put down my ancient burden. Don't slam the door on your way out, or I'll turn you into something."

He closed his eyes, and I scowled so hard my forehead hurt. I didn't like the way people seemed to be lining up to inform me that The End really was bloody nigh. All I had to do was close my eyes to see the devastated future Nightside I'd encountered in the Timeslip, in all its terrible detail. The ruined buildings, the dead night, the scuttling insects. And Razor Eddie dying in my arms, as I gave him my word that I would die before I would let such a future happen.

"So, where do we go next?" said Pretty Poison, adjusting the straw bonnet on the back of her elegant head.

"Where is there left to go?" asked Sinner.

"Back to Strangefellows," I said, reluctantly. Alex was not going to be a happy bunny about this. I took out my Membership Card. "If I have to go head to head with Walker, and it's looking increasingly like I don't have any choice in the matter, I'd much rather it was on familiar ground."

No-one else had any ideas, so I activated the Card and we stepped through into the bar, surprising Alex Morrisey, who was just getting ready to go to bed. He'd shut down most of the lights, put the chairs on the tables, and was standing by the bar wearing only a long white nightie and matching floppy night-cap with a tassel on the end. He stared us all down with great dignity, then moved behind the bar to conceal his knees from prying eyes. If I'd had knees like those, I'd have wanted them concealed as well. He really should have invested in a longer nightie.

Alex had his own private apartment, up above the bar. I'd crashed there a few times in the old days, on his extremely uncomfortable couch. Awful place. He collected tacky little pornographic porcelain figures, which cluttered every available surface. His furniture looked like the city dump would reject it, and he only ever washed up when the dirty dishes actually overflowed the sink. His ex-wife used to keep the place spotless. There's probably a moral in there somewhere, except Alex wouldn't know a moral if you clubbed him over the head with it, and said, *Look. This is a moral.*

"We are closed," he said icily. "Closed as in Not At All Open, and Get the Hell Out of Here Haven't You Got Homes to Go To?"

"Well, open up again," I said ruthlessly. "You have some seriously thirsty people here, and you wouldn't believe the kind of day we've had."

Alex sighed. "I hear that a lot. All right; one drink each, at my very special Extra Expensive After Hours prices. And no, I'm not warming up any food for you. What do you think I am, your mother? And give me back that bloody Membership Card, Taylor! If I wanted people dropping in unexpectedly at all hours, I'd advertise for a stalker. Would I be right in supposing that the bad guys are once again hot on your trail and that I can expect armed invasions, mayhem, and bad language at any moment?"

"Got it in one," I said.

"You're a jinx, Taylor, you know that? I know people who sexually molest albatrosses for a living who have better luck than you."

I looked around. "Where are the Coltranes? I could use a little extra muscle."

"I already sent them home," said Alex, reluctantly fixing our drinks. I had a large wormwood brandy, Sinner had a Malvern water, Pretty Poison insisted on a Manhattan, complete with little umbrella, and Madman wanted a pile-driver—which turned out to be vodka with prune juice. Alex actually winced as he served it, and we all winced as Madman drank it. I nursed my drink and considered the bar thoughtfully. Strangefellows at least had the advantage that it was terribly difficult to get into unnoticed. The bar was surrounded by all kinds of protective wards, on more than one level of reality, powered directly by Merlin Satanspawn's magic. If nothing else, we should get plenty of warning of any attack.

"So," Alex said heavily. "What exactly is it that brings you scurrying back here so soon?"

"Walker is almost definitely on his way here," I said. "Once he figures out that we're not where he thought we were, it won't take him long to fix on this place as my most likely bolt-hole. And when he gets here, he is not going to be at all pleased with me. In fact, he may well have his people shoot first and ask questions through a medium afterwards."

"I could call the Coltranes back," said Alex. "Or do you want I should try and get word to Shotgun Suzie?"

"She's already working a case," I said. "By the time we could track her down, the odds are it would all be over anyway. One way or another. Besides, we have Sinner and Pretty Poison to protect us."

"And me!" Madman said cheerfully.

"Well, yes," I said tactfully. "But you're not always here, are you?"

"True," said Madman, and tried to eat his empty glass.

Alex was looking hard at Pretty Poison. "Why does she look so much like my ex-wife, only with much bigger breasts?"

"Let us discuss what we're going to do next," I said, in a loud and determined I Am Changing the Subject kind of voice, on the grounds that you just know some conversations aren't going to go anywhere useful. "The case we're working seems to have reached an abrupt end. There's no-one left we can talk to, old enough or important enough, to be able to tell us about the Nightside's true beginnings. Well, there are others, like the Awful Folk, or the Giants in the Earth, but you don't disturb Beings and Forces like those unless you've already picked out your coffin and favourite hymns in advance. And there's no guarantee they'd talk to us anyway. I can bluff and stare down most people, plus a whole bunch of things that aren't at all people; but even I have my limits."

"I'm relieved to hear you say that," said Alex. "You've changed since you returned to the Nightside, John. You've been using your reputation more and more like a weapon, like you're starting to believe you really are a king-in-waiting."

"Maybe I am," I said, finishing off my drink. "But then, there's never been any shortage of those in the Nightside. Right now I'm just a private investigator who's run out of leads."

"You still have your gift," said Pretty Poison, fluttering her heavy eyelashes at me over the rim of her cocktail glass. "Why not use it to track down someone else who can tell you what you need to know?"

"Because I don't dare," I said. "My enemies would be bound to find me... and they have a new weapon to send against me. Something even worse than the Harrowing. I don't know what it is yet, but I can feel it hovering, waiting for its chance to manifest and take my enemies' revenge for the terrible thing I've done..."

I realised everyone was looking at me, and shut my mouth firmly. There were things they didn't need to know. Luckily, at that point we were all distracted by the sound of heavy, measured footsteps descending the metal stairway into the bar. We all turned sharply to look at the stairs. Even Madman seemed momentarily focussed on the matter at hand. I could feel my breath coming short and fast as I rummaged in my coat pockets with both hands, searching for something I could use to slow down the inevitable. It couldn't be Walker already... it just couldn't. And then Lady Luck stepped daintily down the last few metal steps into the bar, and we all breathed a little more easily again. Even a Transient Being had to be easier to deal with than Walker in a bad mood. Lady Luck looked just as she had before, a small and delicate Oriental in a long, shimmering silver evening gown. Her rosebud mouth was red as a plum, and her eyes shone like stars. She stood before us, proudly poised and smiling, the living incarnation of all chance, good and bad. The lottery win and the heart attack, the sudden cancer and the perfect moment, and everything in between. I think we were all impressed; except, of course, for Alex, who sniffed loudly behind his bar.

"Doesn't anyone take *Closed* for an answer any more? I can remember a time when locking my door actually made a difference. I've got to get those protective wards upgraded. What do you want, Lady?"

"Hello, John," said Lady Luck, ignoring everyone else to fix her attention on me. It felt like suddenly being hit by a spotlight. "I thought I'd just look in on you, see how you were getting on. Do you have any answers for me yet?"

"Well," I said. "There have been some interesting developments..."

"That isn't what I asked you, John."

"So you're an actual Transient Being," said Sinner. "Wow. I'm impressed. Really. It's not often we get to see one of your station in the flesh these days. In fact, I was under the impression that you only appeared once in a Blue Moon."

"I'm here for a reason," said Lady Luck, still looking only at me.

"Yes," Madman said abruptly. "You are. But you're not Lady Luck. You're not even a Transient Being." We all looked at him. His face was white and strained, with blotchy patches of colour, but he seemed entirely rational. "I know you, Lady. I have Seen you before."

"So you have," said the woman who wasn't Lady Luck. "Poor thing." She smiled graciously at him, and he winced, raising his hands as though to protect himself. Her voice was calm, perhaps a little regretful, as she turned her gaze and her smile on me again. "I'm sorry to have deceived you, John, but if you'd known who you were really working for, you wouldn't have taken the case."

She dropped the glamour that surrounded her, and the sweet and delicate Oriental disappeared, replaced by a new vision. Madman shrank back against the bar, horror stamped on his face. Even in his confused state, he still Saw more deeply than the rest of us. He looked away, squeezing his eyes shut and whimpering. By now the woman looked entirely different. She was tall and thin, with colourless skin and jet-black hair, eyes, and lips, like a black-and-white photograph. Her face was sharp and pointed, with a prominent bone structure and a hawk nose. Her mouth was thin-lipped and somehow subtly too wide, and her dark eyes were full of a fire that could burn through anything. She was still wearing the shimmering silver dress, but on this new her it looked more sinister than stylish.

"Hello, John," she said, in a deep, smooth voice like bitter honey. "I'm your mother."

The words seemed to fill the bar. Everything had gone still and quiet, as though history itself had paused to appreciate such a significant moment. I didn't know what to do or say. I'd thought and planned and dreamed about what it would be like, when I finally came face to face with my mother, but I'd never thought it would be like this. After all the years of searching and wondering, I'd never expected her to just stroll casually back into my life... but I should have known it would always be on her terms, not mine. I'd thought I'd know what I would say. I'd rehearsed it often enough in dark moments, all the accusations and harsh words, but...

I had no memories of her, from before she'd left. I should have, I wasn't that young, but it was as though she'd taken everything of her with her when she left. And yet I'd always thought I'd just... *know*, when I saw her. How could I not know my own mother? But the stark and sinister woman before me was a stranger. I didn't know what I felt about her. It was all just too sudden.

My mother smiled at me. I think it was supposed to be an understanding smile, but on her it just looked intimidating. Like some graceful feline predator assessing its prey.

"Come on, John, pick up the slack. We have so much to discuss, before Walker arrives. Why, for instance, did I disguise myself as Lady Luck? She was just a mask I hid behind, to get your investigations started."

"Why did you want me to take the case?" I said finally. "Why did you send me searching for questions you already know the answers to?"

"Because I wanted you to stir things up. Stir people up. I want everyone to be thinking and talking about the true beginnings of the Nightside, and what it was supposed to be. I wanted everyone talking about how much the Nightside has changed, down the many centuries. And I wanted you to be able to tell them how and why it all began, and who began it, so that they would understand what it meant, that I was coming back." She fixed me with her burning gaze, and her smiled widened. "I am back, John. Aren't you glad to see me again, after all these years?"

"You abandoned me," I said.

She shrugged easily. "It was necessary. I knew you'd survive. You're my son."

"Where have you been all this time?"

"Walking up and down in the Nightside, wearing many faces, learning the shape and condition of the current Nightside. It has changed so very much. It was never meant to be as dark as this. Or as tacky."

"Did you ever love me?" I didn't know I was going to say that, so bluntly, until I said it. The words forced themselves out of me.

"Of course. That's why I left you with your father. So you could be human, and innocent, for a while."

"*Who are you?*" I said.

And she said; "I am Lilith. Adam's first wife, thrown out of Eden for refusing to bow down to Adam's authority. Though, of course, you must understand, that's just a parable. A simple fiction to help you comprehend a far more complicated reality. You don't think I really look like this, do you? I am far greater, and more powerful. This is just another mask, put on for old times' sake. This is the face and body I wore to be your mother, John."

"Fennella Davis," I said. Even as I was still thinking, *Lilith? My mother is a biblical myth?*

"Exactly."

Madman peeked at her, past my shoulder, his voice shocked almost normal. "Lilith is just a projection into our limited reality of something much bigger. This female human body is just something Lilith wears to walk around in, like a glorified glove puppet. She's really..." He stopped, hesitating. "She is really..." But he didn't have the words. Perhaps there were no words, in our simple rational language. Whatever his mathematics had enabled him to See of her, in his brief glimpse of the Reality behind reality, he still couldn't describe it to us. He started to shake and tremble, then to cry, and the bar and all the things and people in it began to shake along with him. It was as though an earthquake had hit the place. Tables and chairs danced and clattered on the juddering floor. The walls bowed in and out, the solid stone flexing unnaturally. Strange colours came and went, and sounds that made no sense. Distance became uncertain and unreliable, and things were both close and far away at the same time. Directions changed without warning. Madman's hold on reality was weakening again, and reality around him weakened as well. Merlin's great oak tree slammed back into the bar again, taking up the middle of the room; and then it was a tower built of stained and discoloured bones; and then it was gone again. Cracks crawled jaggedly across the floor, opening wide to show vast watching eyes. I could hear things scuttling across the outer walls of our perception. Things that wanted *in*.

"That's enough of *that*," Lilith said sharply.

And just like that, everything was still and normal again. Madman's projected unreality was immediately suppressed, the bar snapping back into sharp focus as Lilith's super-presence stabilised the world, and him. He stopped shaking and crying, and a little colour actually seeped back into his cheeks. Lilith looked at him thoughtfully.

"You Saw what mortal man was never supposed to See. Was not designed to cope with. Let me take the knowledge away from you, so that you can be ignorant and happy again."

"No," Madman said firmly, surprising us all. "Even a bitter truth is better than a comfortable lie."

"But the truth is killing you," said Lilith.

"No," said Madman. "I'm adapting."

Somehow, that thought was even more worrying. I cleared my throat loudly, to get everyone's attention.

"So," I said to my mother, trying really hard to keep my voice calm and casual. "You're Lilith. I know some of your story. Pew told me, a long time ago, when he was still my teacher."

"Blind Pew?" said Alex. "The rogue vicar? The Christian terrorist? Is he still around?"

"Yes," I said. "And if you interrupt me again, Alex, I'll have my mother turn you into a tea cosy."

"That's it," said Alex, snatching my empty glass off the bar top. "You're cut off. You get nasty when you've been drinking, John."

I ignored him, concentrating on Lilith. "According to the stories, after you were expelled from Eden you went down into Hell, where you coupled with demons and gave birth to all the monsters that have plagued the world."

"I was young," said Lilith. "You know how it is. We all do things we later regret, when we're being rebellious teenagers. Anyway, I got over that phase, and after travelling extensively through the many levels of reality, seeing the sights and working out my options, I finally ended up in the world of men. Not that men had made much of an impression on the place, in those days. Beings and Forces still walked freely, and a new legend was born every minute. I created the Nightside, a world within a world, in a place the Romans would later name Londinium. Interesting people, the Romans. A very savage form of civilization. Some of them worshipped me, and I let them.

"Now pay attention, John, because this is the important bit. The Nightside was created and designed to be the one place on Earth where Heaven and Hell could not interfere or intimidate. A place set apart from the ordained war between Good and Evil. An alternative way to live. The only truly free place on Earth. It didn't turn out the way I expected, but then, that's life for you.

"Creating the Nightside, on Earth but not of it, stable but entirely separate, seriously weakened me. My power was much diminished, and the rising major players of that time, some human but mostly not, seized the opportunity to band together and thrust me back out of this reality, and into Limbo. So that they could be truly free, even from my intentions. I don't bear them any malice. Not really. I've outlived nearly all of them. And Limbo wasn't the worst place to be exiled to. Limbo is a place, or not-place, where things only exist in potential. Ideas without form."

"Like the Primal?" I said, just to show I was paying attention.

"Oh, please. They're just chalk-drawings, compared to me. But as an idea without shape or form, I was helpless to do anything. I was trapped in Limbo, unable to open a door into any other realm. Until someone here created an opening I could use. They were trying to incarnate a female principle into physical existence, a part of the Babalon Working, and it was easy for me to push the Transient Being aside and imprint myself upon the summoning. Someone in that group hadn't done his homework properly. He'd left all kinds of openings for a determined mind to take advantage of. And once I'd left Limbo behind, they couldn't keep me out. All the Powers and Dominations that ever were couldn't have stopped me then.

"I came through, decanted myself into the idealised body I found waiting in their minds, then disappeared, losing myself in the Nightside. Partly because I wanted to walk incognito to see how much things had changed in my absence, and partly to conceal myself from any of my old enemies who might have survived. I was still vulnerable, then. I needed to rebuild my power in peace. After some time, when I was myself again, I chose one of my unwitting summoners, who seemed to have grasped a little of the truth, and—disguised as the woman Fennella Davis—I made a child with him. The child rooted me in this reality, so that I could never be forced out again. I hadn't planned to stick around afterwards, but you were so fascinating, John... I'd never had a human child before. Flesh of my flesh, spirit of my spirit... I was curious to see how you'd turn out. And I enjoyed playing human. Being mother. Carrying out the role I had originally been intended for...

"And then Charles found out. Somebody told him; I never did discover who. But it meant I had to disappear again, back into the more secret depths of the Nightside, so that no-one would ever guess your true identity, your true nature and purpose. If any of the day's major players had even suspected, they would have been lining up to kill you, for any number of reasons. I knew Charles wouldn't talk. If anyone ever suspected he was responsible for bringing back Lilith, the manner of his death would have been legendary, even in the Nightside. And, of course, he still believed his research would uncover a way to banish me again. He couldn't talk to his old friend Henry, by then so highly placed in the Authorities, and he wouldn't talk to his old friend Mark, who had been the Collector, because Mark had found Fennella Davis in the first place. Charles was alone. He couldn't trust anyone any more. Not even his young son. Poor Charles.

"I never did find out who told him. But whoever it was, they never talked either. Perhaps because they knew what I would do to them, the moment they revealed themselves.

"Now my power is back. The stars have come round again, and all the most dangerous Powers and Forces in the Nightside have been nicely weakened by the Angel War. I knew causing the Unholy Grail to be brought to the Nightside would shake things up. The time is right for me to remake and refashion the Nightside into what I always intended it to be. Something much... purer in concept. A great many people will undoubtedly die in the process, yes, but you can't make an omelette without beating hell out of the eggs."

She smiled around at all of us, inviting comment. And all I could think of was the awful dead landscape I'd walked through in the Timeslip. Was that her idea of a purer concept? Or did it mean that something was going to go horribly wrong with her plans? That the Powers and the Dominations of the Nightside would go to war with her, to preserve their vision of the Nightside, and everyone would lose?

"No," I said, and everyone looked at me. Even I could hear the coldness in my voice. I met Lilith's dark gaze as steadily as I could. "I can't let you do that, Lilith. I've seen the world that's coming, because of you and me, and I'll see us both dead and gone before I'll ever let that happen."

Lilith shook her head. "How sharper than a serpent's tooth..."

"And the fruit never falls far from the tree," said a familiar voice.

We all looked round, startled, as Walker unhurriedly descended the metal stairs into the bar. He still looked every inch the city gent, calm and unruffled. He stopped at the foot of the stairs, smiled at us all, and raised his bowler hat politely to Lilith.

"Doesn't anybody ever bother to knock any more?" Alex said bitterly. "That's it; I'm putting in barbed wire and anti-personnel hexes."

"You didn't really think the Lord of Thorns would fool me for long, did you?" said Walker, looking only at me. "Not when we have such urgent business to discuss."

"You're very brave to come in here alone," I said. "How does it feel, Henry, to be faced with a whole bunch of people you can't control with your famous Voice?"

Walker just smiled. "That's why I brought reinforcements, John."

And that was when a whole army of people came clattering down the metal steps to back up Walker. They fanned out on either side of him, taking up half the bar. I recognised some of the combat magicians, but there were a hell of a lot more of them now, all looking grim and determined and ready for action. These were professional fighters, cold-hearted killers, the kind the Authorities send out when they don't want anything left behind but scorched earth. But it was the last two to enter the bar who really caught my attention.

Bad Penny descended the stairway with her head held high, like a member of the Royal Family visiting an abattoir. She flashed me a brief, vicious smile. And right behind her came Pew, my old enemy Pew, tall and broad-shouldered, a soldier of Christ in his usual battered grey cloak over his vicar's outfit, a mane of long grey hair and a simple grey cloth hiding his blind eyes. Descending confidently and valorously into a world of sin, having already made a deal with the devil called Walker. Pew turned his great blocky head in my direction and nodded slowly, armoured in his cold and brutal faith.

"I apologise for the small turn-out," murmured Walker, brushing an invisible bit of lint from his immaculate sleeve. "But most of my people are currently earning their money for a change, by keeping the Lord of Thorns occupied so he won't interfere here and save your worthless souls. I'm afraid this is the end of the road, Taylor. You can't say I haven't given you every chance, since you returned. But now the Authorities want you and everyone else here dead, for the sin of making a bloody nuisance of yourselves." He paused then, looking at Lilith. "Fennella... my oldest sin, come back to haunt me. I shall enjoy seeing you destroyed."

"Poor Henry," said Lilith. "Always putting your money on the wrong dream."

I ignored them both, looking at Pew. He felt my gaze and stirred uneasily, one hand rising to his white collar. And then he squared his broad shoulders defiantly, his mouth hard and unyielding, and I knew nothing I could say would change his mind. I still had to try.

"Hello, Pew. I thought you didn't set foot in dens of iniquity like this."

"My business is with sinners, so I must go where the sin is," Pew said roughly. "Time to pay the piper, John, and make your peace with God."

"Are you really here to kill me at last, Pew?"

"Yes. I will save your soul, if I can. For old times' sake."

"My mother is here," I said. "Do you know my mother, Pew?"

"Of course. I've always known. I told you I gave up my eyes for wisdom. I was the one who told your father who and what he was married to. I still had faith you could be saved, then."

Cold anger pushed aside the shock of what I was hearing. "*You* told him? You broke up my family! You destroyed my life!"

"You should never have been born, John. Abomination." His voice was almost kindly now. "I should have killed you long ago, and now I pay for the weakness of my resolve with the pain I will feel for killing... such a worthy adversary."

"You will not touch my son, preacher," said Lilith.

Pew's head snapped round in her direction, and he stabbed a finger right at her before launching into a long, angry incantation. I recognised some of it, from old parchments and forbidden books. It was an exorcism, and a very old one, in Aramaic and Latin and corrupt Coptic. The old words hammered on the air, full of significance and power, and Lilith laughed at them. Pew broke off, confused.

"I know that song," said Lilith. "It's the exorcism the Christ used against the possessors called Legion, who ended up in the Gadarene swine. But I am much older than that, and such bindings have no power over me."

"You cannot stand against me!" said Pew, almost spitting out the words. "I speak for God!"

"We never got on," said Lilith.

She gestured almost negligently with one hand, and Pew was thrown the whole width of the bar, hurtling ungainly through the air to smash into the far stone wall with sickening force. We all heard his bones break. Blood flew from his mouth. He slid down the wall and curled up on the floor, twitching spasmodically. Lilith laughed, a brief, happy sound like water splashing in a fountain. I ran over to Pew, knelt beside him, and cradled him in my arms. There is no-one closer than friends or family, except perhaps an enemy you've known all your life. I cradled his noble head on my chest, and blood spilled out of his mouth to stain my white trench coat. His grey blindfold had come loose, revealing dark empty eye sockets. His breathing was harsh and uneven, spraying the air with blood from deep in his lungs.

"John?" he said.

"Hush, Pew. I'm here. I'm here."

"Pride. The sin of pride. I really thought I could take her."

"Hush."

"I should have killed you long ago."

"I know."

"But you were a child, and I thought you could be saved. And later, I saw you trying so hard to be a good man, and I doubted. When you left the Nightside, I thought perhaps it was a sign. I wanted to believe that. And then you came back. Why did you have to come back, John?"

"Hush, Pew."

"Always knew you'd be the death of me. I wish... I could have brought you to see the Light. It really is so... glorious..."

I glared at Lilith. "Do something. Save him! He's a good man, and he doesn't deserve to die like this!"

"You must learn to be strong, John," said Lilith. "To be able to do what's necessary."

I would have shouted at her, begged and threatened and promised her anything, but Pew had stopped breathing. "You didn't have to kill him," I said. "It wasn't necessary."

"I will decide what is necessary," said Lilith. "You must forget these old restrictive ideas of Good and Evil. The only real good is what serves the Nightside, the only real evil that which opposes its best interests. Come with me, my son, and I will teach you many things."

And then Walker's people responded to some unseen signal from him, and launched their attack, focussing their destructive magics on Sinner and Pretty Poison. The combat magicians waved their hands around, shouting their Words of Power, brandishing magic amulets and wands and pointing bones, and powerful energies crackled on the air. Tables and chairs exploded, but Sinner and Pretty Poison stood firm. Alex quickly disappeared behind the bar, head well down, dragging Madman along with him. I could hear him shouting something about Merlin's defences kicking in anytime soon, but I knew better. Walker was the Voice of the Authorities, and Merlin... was just a dead sorcerer. While he was sleeping.

Walker and Lilith looked at each other, ignoring the chaos around them.

I laid Pew's body carefully on the floor and moved the grey cloth back to cover his empty eyes. I raised my head and yelled out to Alex.

"Any chance you could get Merlin to manifest again?"

"And make things even worse?" said Alex, without raising his head above the bar. "I think we should wait until we're really desperate."

"Personally, I think we passed desperate some time back," said Madman.

I could barely hear them above the roar of discharging magics. Sinner was standing in front of Pretty Poison, protecting her with his invulnerable body. At first the magical attacks couldn't seem to find him, exploding everywhere except where he stood, doing great damage to the bar and its furnishings, but not much else. But the sheer amount of power amassed against Sinner overwhelmed even his innate condition, and the attacks began to strike home. Bullets from specially blessed and cursed guns slammed into his chest, and though no blood flowed, the holes in his chest did not heal or close. Curses burned his flesh and cracked his bones. Elemental forces ripped and tore at him, and one eye exploded messily in his head. Sinner made no move to attack those who were trying to kill him. For all his dubious history, he'd never learned to hate anyone. I don't think he had it in him. He just stood his ground, standing firm against everything anyone could throw at him, refusing to go down, refusing to allow Pretty Poison to be hurt.

None of the magics went anywhere near Lilith.

And while I was watching all this and trying to decide what to do for the best, Bad Penny took advantage of my distraction. She used her ability to turn up unexpectedly, appeared out of nowhere behind me, and stuck a knife in my back. Some instinct warned me at the very last moment, and I twisted aside, but the long blade still sank deep into my back, jarring against my spine. I lashed out with one arm, throwing Penny backwards, and then the pain paralysed me, screaming through my lower back. I dropped to my knees, panting for breath, my head reeling. I gritted my teeth and clung grimly onto consciousness, forcing my thoughts to make sense. There didn't seem to be any blood in my mouth, so hopefully Penny had missed the lung. The pain was bad, but it was bearable. I reached slowly round with one hand, crying out at the pain, trying to get hold of the knife hilt, but it was out of reach. So, leave it where it was and worry about it later.

I forced myself up onto my feet again, sweat dripping from my face at the effort, and Penny swore and stamped her foot angrily as she saw she hadn't finished me off after all. She started forward, another knife in her hand, and then our eyes met, and we both hesitated for a moment. I didn't really know her. We'd worked a few cases together, been to bed a few times, but we'd never been close. And right then, I don't think it would have mattered even if we had been. She was ready to kill me. I could see it in her eyes and in her cold, nasty smile. And I was so angry at Pew's death and needed someone to take it out on.

She came at me with the other knife, and I reached deep inside myself, powered up my gift, opened up my third eye, and found within Bad Penny the magic that allowed her always to turn up unexpectedly. And it was the easiest thing in the world for me to shut down that magic and rip it right out of her, taking away her ability to turn up anywhere at all. She looked at me with horror as she lost her grip on the world and faded slowly and silently away, never to return.

I waved good-bye. I don't think I smiled. I don't like to think I might have smiled.

But in using my gift, I had made myself vulnerable to my enemies. They found me almost immediately, and sent their new weapon after me, punching right through the bar's defences. Bright actinic energies flared, sharp and powerful, dazzling as the sun. Everyone cried out and fell back, except for Lilith. All hostilities paused, as the terrible thing that had been haunting me so remorselessly materialised. The terrible light faded away, revealing the awful weapon my enemies had sent to kill me.

It was Shotgun Suzie.

She looked older, hard-used, and horribly disfigured. Her long straggly hair was white, streaked with grey and packed dirt. Inside her torn and battered leathers she was painfully thin, but she burned with a fierce unnatural energy. Her presence crackled on the air, dominating the scene, like Death herself come walking among mortals. Her gaze was cold and implacable. Half her face had been burned away, long ago; the skin was blackened and crisped and twisted around the seared-shut eye. One side of her mouth was twisted up into a permanent caustic smile.

But that wasn't the worst thing. Her right forearm was gone, stopped at the elbow. In its place someone had fitted the Speaking Gun. A weapon originally designed to kill angels. It had been refashioned from the last time I saw it, from a handgun to a shotgun, but it was still the ugliest, vilest weapon I had ever seen. It was made of meat, of flesh and bone, held together with dark-veined gristle and shards of cartilage, bound with long strips of pale skin. The long handle was discoloured bone, plugged clumsily into what was left of her elbow. Thick fleshy cables rose up out of the stock of the Gun and plunged into her upper arm. The red meat of the elongated barrels glistened wetly, and the strands of skin had a hot, sweaty look.

It was the Speaking Gun, that old, old weapon. It was plugged into the continuing echoes of the Sound at the start of Creation, when God said *Let there be light*. The Speaking Gun knew the secret name of everything and everyone, and by Saying it backwards, could uncreate anything. Wipe it out completely, make it never have happened... An unstoppable weapon, that dreamed bloody dreams and lusted to be used.

Suzie Shooter looked slowly round the packed bar, and everyone looked back at her, not daring to move or make any sound that might attract her attention. Finally, her gaze fell on me. I wouldn't let myself flinch, or look away.

"I'd forgotten... you used to look like this," she said, her voice cracked and harsh, as though it pained her to speak.

"Suze?" I said.

"No. Not any more. Not for a long time."

"Oh God, Suze; what have they done to you?"

"Nothing I didn't ask them to. I couldn't hope to survive in the world you made, John, so they remade me. Gave me this Gun, and stitched the two of us together, forever. The Speaking Gun is mad, and now so am I, but I'll last long enough to put you out of everyone else's misery. If there's anything human left in you, John... die now, and save the world. Resist me, and I'll blow this whole bar apart."

One of the combat magicians panicked then and threw a killing spell at her. The others immediately all joined in, and vicious magics flared and spattered all around Shotgun Suzie, but the Gun protected her. She turned on her attackers, and her face contorted, her mouth stretching impossibly wide, as the Gun spoke through her, Saying the Words of Undoing. It was the most terrible sound I'd ever heard. Everyone in the bar cried out, sickened and horrified. Even Lilith turned her face away, as Suzie Shooter spoke the Words and all the combat magicians disappeared in a moment, made unreal, uncreated.

People were falling to their knees and vomiting. Others turned and ran, up the metal stairway and out of the bar, their eyes wild and mad. Walker didn't try and stop them, but he wouldn't leave. Even now, he still had his pride and his duty. Suzie turned slowly back to look at me. I was shaking, my legs hardly strong enough to hold me up; but still I made myself face her, staring right into her cold gaze. I showed her my empty, unsteady hands.

"I won't fight you, Suze," I said. "I can't hurt you. I would never hurt you."

"But you did, John. You did."

Her mouth opened to Say the awful sounds that would uncreate me, unmake me; and then Merlin Satanspawn manifested through his descendant Alex Morrisey, and stopped Time with a gesture. Everything ground to a halt, turned to stone, unmoving, even to the flecks of dust on the air. I couldn't move, but I could sense what was going on. Could feel the Speaking Gun straining against the magic that was holding it back from what it lived to do. And Merlin Satanspawn came walking through the petrified world, dead but not gone, untouched by Time. He walked unhurriedly over to Shotgun Suzie, studied her for a moment, then ripped the Speaking Gun away from her upper arm. Flesh stretched and tore, and bright blood flew on the air. Suzie screamed as the energies that bound her to the Gun were shattered, and the Speaking Gun screamed, too, an awful hateful sound of frustrated rage and spite. Suzie snapped out, gone in a moment, banished back to the dreadful future I'd made for her and everyone else. The Speaking Gun disappeared, too, perhaps to that future, perhaps to somewhere else, where it was needed, or desired.

Time returned in a rush. Merlin and Lilith looked at each other, and everyone else held their breath. The Devil's only begotten son and God's first creation. And in the end Merlin bowed to Lilith, and disappeared, leaving Alex shaking and bewildered behind his bar again.

The remaining combat magicians opened up on Sinner and Pretty Poison again. After what had been done to them they needed to strike back at someone, and they weren't ready to take on Lilith yet. Especially after Merlin Satanspawn had bowed to her. Sinner still stood between them and Pretty Poison, his body soaking up the punishment of spells and cursed bullets. He was taking more and more damage now, being slowly chipped away; but he wouldn't step aside from the demon succubus he protected, and he wouldn't fight back. Everything else had been taken from him, but he still had his love and his determination to do the right thing. Behind him, Pretty Poison looked beseechingly at Walker, but he just looked back at her, his face calm and composed as always. He was here to do a distasteful, necessary thing, and he would see it through.

Sinner stood his ground, even though he knew the magics were destroying him by inches. He couldn't let the attacks get past him, to hurt Pretty Poison. Such potent magics could destroy the succubus's body, leave her without a human form to manifest in; she would be just another damned soul, suffering in Hell. He couldn't allow that. And so he stood, enduring the pain and the horror as his body was slowly whittled away, because she was his love. And nothing else mattered.

Bullets smacked into his side, chipping away at the exposed ribs, and he grunted at the impact, but would not cry out, for fear it would distress his love. Spells burned the flesh from his bones and the skin from his face, tore at him with whips and razors, and every moment there was less and less of him. In the end, he knew he could be left without a body—just an orphaned spirit denied a place in either Heaven or Hell, a ghost slowly dissipating into nothing at all, as though he'd never been. He knew he could still save himself, could still run and abandon Pretty Poison to her fate. But having finally found love, he would rather die than see it destroyed.

Pretty Poison knew all this. Knew that Sinner's stubborn love for her would have him stand there for as long as his will could hold him up, and perhaps beyond. All to protect her. And in that moment, she knew she couldn't allow that. Couldn't allow the man who had suffered so much on her account to sacrifice everything for her. He mattered more than she. And so she stepped out from behind him, and stepped in front of him, to protect him with her body. Finally understanding the meaning of love, and self-sacrifice. Loving him as he loved her.

There was a blast of incandescent light, bright and glorious, as Pretty Poison remembered the angel she had once been, before the Fall. All her old evils were burned away, transfigured by the power of her love, and she became again the angel she had once been, fit to take her place in Heaven. She was too bright to look at, and we all turned our heads away, but we could still hear the slow, heavy beating of mighty wings.

"Come with me, to Paradise," said the angel to the man called Sinner. "For you have been found worthy, as have I."

The light flared up unbearably, then died away, and they were both gone.

It was very quiet in the bar then, as we all looked at each other, staggered by what we'd just witnessed. In the end, Walker recovered first. He gestured to his combat magicians, and they turned their gaze on me. Because if I could be destroyed, my mother would no longer have an anchor in this reality and could perhaps be driven out again. I straightened up as much as the knife in my back would allow and faced them all with a slow, cold smile. When there is nothing left but to die, die well.

And then Madman, perhaps inspired by the revelations he'd witnessed, came strolling out from behind the bar, and everyone turned to look at him. He laughed suddenly, and it was a rich, sane sound.

"When reality becomes unbearable," he said calmly, "change reality."

All his strength and power focussed through his will, and rushed out into the bar, enforcing his vision of reality on everything. All the remaining combat magicians cried out as their magics were stripped from them, leaving them defenceless. Walker staggered back, his Voice silenced. The knife in my back disappeared, along with the damage it had done. Madman turned his uncompromising gaze on Lilith, and she put up a hand as though to defend herself.

Not all of Madman's power, even focussed through his new-found will, could undo Lilith; but it did diminish her. She wavered, uncertain for the first time. Her power clashed with his, as he strove to drive her away, and she struggled to remain. For a long moment the stalemate held; and then I used the last of my power to find the door through which she'd entered Strangefellows, and pushed her back through it.

She disappeared, but her voice whispered a last message in my mind.

I'll see you again, John. My son, in whom I am well pleased. We have such marvellous work ahead of us.

It was very quiet in the bar, after that. Lilith was gone, as were Merlin and Sinner and Pretty Poison. And poor Suzie Shooter, damned to the awful future I had made for her. Most of Walker's people were dead or gone, or stripped of their magics. Madman lay curled up on the floor in front of the bar, sleeping soundly. Walker strolled over to look down at him.

"It's always the ones you overlook who turn out to be the most bother," he said mildly. "I wonder what he'll be like, when he wakes up?"

"Sane, hopefully," I said. "I think that last effort used up all of his power, and his madness. Maybe now he'll be able to forget what he Saw and live in the same reality as the rest of us."

"You always were an optimist, John," said Walker. "I'm not allowed that luxury." He looked at me for a long moment, his eyes very cold. "You no longer have any friends in the Nightside. You are a danger to everyone and to everything here. We are all your enemies now."

"You don't know the half of it," I said.

Walker nodded slowly, then tipped his bowler hat to me, gathered up his remaining people with his eyes, and led them back up the metal stairway and out of the bar. They took Pew's body with them. Alex came out from behind his bar to blow a rude noise after them and look mournfully round at the scattered wreckage of his chairs and tables. He sighed heavily.

"I'll have to call the Coltranes back to clear this mess up. And I hate having to pay after-hours triple time. What are you going to do now, John?"

"I am going to the Tower of Time," I said. "I'm going back in Time, to search through the earlier incarnations of the Nightside, and dig up people or Beings or Forces who can tell me what I need to know. How to stop my mother Lilith. Because I will use any weapon, any knowledge, to prevent the future she intends to bring about."

Alex sniffed, unconvinced. "Do you think what we saw was really Suzie?"

"Some possible future version, perhaps. But I'll never let that happen to her. I won't let her be hurt by anyone. Even me."

"At least now we know who your mother really is," said Alex. "Lilith. Who would have thought it?"

"She's not my mother," I said. "She was never my mother."

Simon R. Green holds a BA in English Literature and Philosophy, Joint Honours, and an MA in Modern English and American Literature from the University of Leicester. His first publication was in 1979 and he has since written many SF and Fantasy novels.

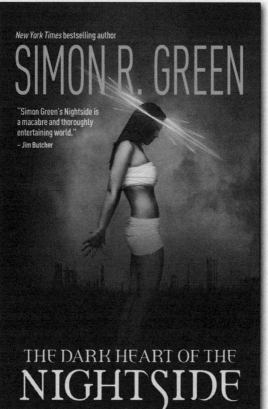

New York Times bestselling author

SIMON R. GREEN

"Simon Green's Nightside is a macabre and thoroughly entertaining world."
– Jim Butcher

THE DARK HEART OF THE
NIGHTSIDE

www.solarisbooks.com   ISBN: 978-1-84416-635-0

It's just another day at the office as John Taylor has to save the Nightside, and all of reality from the greatest threat it's faced since the last one. Himself. The Dark Heart of The Nightside collects *Paths Not Taken* and *Sharper Than A Serpent's Tooth*, the third two volumes in the astounding Nightside series.

◖ **SOLARIS** DARK FANTASY

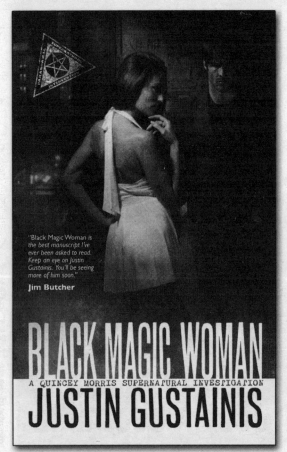

"Black Magic Woman is the best manuscript I've ever been asked to read. Keep an eye on Justin Gustainis. You'll be seeing more of him soon."

Jim Butcher

BLACK MAGIC WOMAN
A QUINCEY MORRIS SUPERNATURAL INVESTIGATION
JUSTIN GUSTAINIS

www.solarisbooks.com   ISBN: 978-1-84416-541-4

Supernatural investigator Quincey Morris and his partner, white witch Libby Chastain, are called in to help free a desperate family from a deadly curse that appears to date back to the Salem Witch Trials. To release the family from danger they must find the root of the curse, a black witch with a terrible grudge that holds the family in her power.

SOLARIS DARK FANTASY

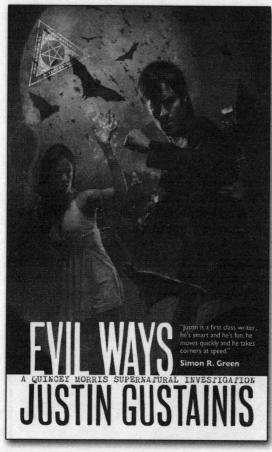

EVIL WAYS

"Justin is a first class writer, he's smart and he's fun, he moves quickly and he takes corners at speed."

Simon R. Green

A QUINCEY MORRIS SUPERNATURAL INVESTIGATION

JUSTIN GUSTAINIS

UK ISBN: 978-1-84416-653-4   US ISBN: 978-1-84416-593-3

www.solarisbooks.com

Eccentric billionaire Walter Grobius is attempting to unleash the Black Wind, a devastating evil that has its roots in ancient religion. He is using a series of murders to bring about a white supremacy across America. More than that, he's in a league with a demon that he thinks is an angel of the lord. Our heroes, Morris and Chastain, are drawn into a deadly case as they investigate a series of witch murders.

⊙ SOLARIS DARK FANTASY

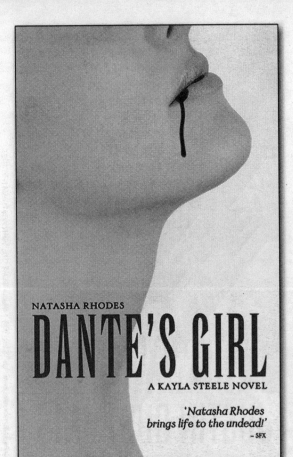

NATASHA RHODES

DANTE'S GIRL

A KAYLA STEELE NOVEL

*'Natasha Rhodes
brings life to the undead!'*
~ SFX

ISBN: 978-1-84416-666-4

www.solarisbooks.com

Kayla Steele is a girl with an unusual problem, she's on a mission to learn
the Dark Arts so that she can avenge the death of her boyfriend and bring
down the cabal of supernatural entities that is stalking the streets of LA.
Then, of course, there's the dead boyfriend himself, Karrel Dante. She's
really got no idea where that relationship is going at the moment...

SOLARIS DARK FANTASY

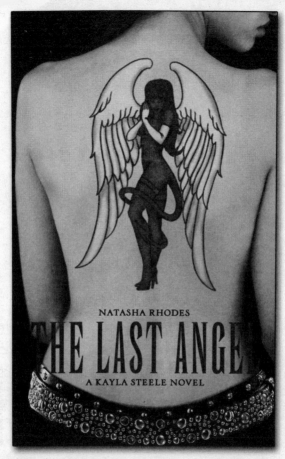

NATASHA RHODES

THE LAST ANGEL

A KAYLA STEELE NOVEL

www.solarisbooks.com   UK ISBN: 978-1-84416-646-6   US ISBN: 978-1-84416-577-3

An angel is found murdered on the streets of Sunset Boulevard. To the media gossip mongers, it's the biggest story ever. To the Hunters, an underground monster-fighting hit-squad, it's just another case of "whodunnit". To Kayla Steele, their newest member, it means a last chance to bring her murdered fiancé back from the dead, and to others with a far darker purpose it is the means to destroy the human race.

Ⓖ SOLARIS DARK FANTASY